There were six w...
The only question w...

Praise for
PAMELA MORSI

"Like LaVyrle Spencer, Pamela Morsi writes
tender books about decent people."

Susan Elizabeth Phillips, author of First Lady

"A sweet love story."

Publishers Weekly on Sweetwood Bride

"Morsi is best known for the sweet charm
of her novels. . . . Awfully good."

Publishers Weekly on Sealed with a Kiss

"I've read all her books and loved every word."

Jude Deveraux

Other Books by
Pamela Morsi

Pamela Morsi

Here Comes The Bride

AVON BOOKS
An Imprint of HarperCollins*Publishers*

This is a work of fiction. Names, characters, places, and incidents are products of the author's imagination or are used fictitiously and are not to be construed as real. Any resemblance to actual events, locales, organizations, or persons, living or dead, is entirely coincidental.

AVON BOOKS
An Imprint of HarperCollins*Publishers*
10 East 53rd Street
New York, New York 10022-5299

Copyright © 2000 by Pamela Morsi
Excerpt from *Here Comes the Bride* copyright © 2000 by Pamela Morsi
Excerpt from *Heaven on Earth* copyright © 2000 by Constance O'Day-Flannery
Excerpt from *His Wicked Promise* copyright © 2000 by Sandra Kleinschmidt
Excerpt from *Rules of Engagement* copyright © 2000 by Christina Dodd
Excerpt from *Just the Way You Are* copyright © 2000 by Barbara Freethy
Excerpt from *The Viscount Who Loved Me* copyright © 2000 by Julie Cotler Pottinger
Inside cover author photo by Jennifer Jennings
ISBN: 0-06-101366-8
www.avonromance.com

First Avon Books paperback printing: July 2000

Avon Trademark Reg. U.S. Pat. Off. and in Other Countries, Marca Registrada, Hecho en U.S.A.
HarperCollins® is a trademark of HarperCollins Publishers Inc.

Printed in the U.S.A.

WCD   10 9 8 7 6 5 4 3 2 1

For Bill

1

THERE COMES A TIME IN EVERY WOMAN'S LIFE WHEN SHE must get herself a man or give up on the idea entirely. Augusta Mudd had reached that moment. Miss Gussie, as she was known to all, was in the spring of her thirty-first year. All through her twenties she had reminded herself that there was still plenty of youth ahead. At thirty itself she had taken comfort in the fact that she was barely out of her twenties. But thirty-one—thirty-one was definitely an accounting that brought realization, or perhaps even resignation.

"Get it done or past contemplation."

That's what her father would have said to her. Papa tended toward sound advice. Gussie always weighed in with what she thought would be his opinion.

Thoughtfully, she carried her account books outside and lay them upon the little makeshift desk on the porch. The cut-glass pitcher of lemonade was already sweating in the warmth of the afternoon, two glasses at the ready. In the matching vase behind the serving tray, she had arranged some of the irises and zinnias grown in the shadows of the white picket fence around her home.

It was her home now. Her home completely. A big, sprawling place with Greek columns and wide verandas that her father had built to impress his friends. Her mother had never been quite comfortable in it. Gussie actually liked the place. She had made it seem small and cozy.

Like a spinster's house.

The thought came to her unexpectedly and she didn't like it one bit. Spinsterhood might be a fine and noble calling. But, Gussie assured herself with stern determination, it did not call her. She would have a perfect wedding, an acceptable husband and children. That was what she wanted, and that's what she would have.

Immediately, of course, her thoughts turned to Amos. Tall, gentlemanly, handsome Amos. Her heart ached with a sad bitterness that was more painful than she would ever have expected. Last evening he sought her out after the Fire Brigade Pie Supper and made his feelings, or rather his lack of them, perfectly clear.

"I do believe, sir," she told him as she stood at the top of her porch, staring straight into his face as he hesitated upon the lower step. "I do believe that, for the sake of my future and my reputation, a declaration of your intentions should be forthcoming."

His reaction was immediate. The dark, handsome eyes, which she so admired, widened behind the round lenses of his spectacles and his jaw dropped in shock. He stepped back from her a good two paces, stuttering and stumbling upon his words.

"Miss Gussie, I . . . I mean, I never, I . . . w-well, what I'm saying is—ah—"

Humiliation welled up inside her at his hesitation. It

had been her fondest hope that he had been actively contemplating a proposal. She'd been so sure. It was shyness, she'd assured herself, that held him back. One glance at his horrified expression swept away that notion completely.

Gussie's face flushed at the memory. There was nothing in the world, she imagined, that was quite as lowering as proclaiming one's ardent devotion and having the recipient of it react with incredulity and near horror.

However, Gussie was not the kind of woman to allow the world to bring her to tears. She was not one who held onto her place in life by clutching a lacy hankie like a lifeline. Under no circumstances would she allow her disappointment to send her into a decline. Other women might find comfort in an all-consuming black morass or a fit of the vapors. But Gussie had no time to waste on such self-indulgence. When she wanted something, she simply set it as a goal. And if she was to wed, this spring was undoubtedly the last chance.

A jangle of harness bells intruded upon her thoughts and she glanced up to see Old Jezzi, a milk-white dray, pulling the familiar bright yellow wagon up the dusty, tree-lined street. The sign on the side was painted in brilliant blue. At the top it read: T.P. MUDD MANUFAC-TURED, and then, in two-foot-high letters trimmed with artistic frosty snowcaps, ICE. Beneath that: FROM PURE DISTILLED WATER.

The driver stopped the wagon directly in front of Gussie's house. He jumped to the ground next to her gate and tipped his hat to her.

"I saved a block for you, Miss Gussie, if you are in need of it," he called out.

Gussie nodded. "Yes, please, Mr. Akers," she replied. "Twenty-five will do me."

He stepped to the back of the wagon and opened the rear door. Using the hook side of his chisel, he wrestled a fifty-pound block of clear, cold ice into position and scored it in half. Placing the flat side of the bar against his mark and pounding it with a mallet, he deftly cut the block in two, sending shards of frozen crystal flying all around him. One-handed, with sturdy metal tongs, he toted the gleaming block. Carrying the entire weight on his right side gave him a slope-shouldered appearance as he came through the gate.

Gussie's thoughts were elsewhere while she watched him walk around the side of the house toward the kitchen door at the back. The icemen in her employ tried to be efficient and unintrusive. Mr. Akers was the perfect example. She didn't even notice.

He came back around the corner of the house very shortly, but did not return to the wagon. He hung his tongs on the rail and rolled down his shirtsleeves, buttoning the cuffs as he climbed the steps to the porch. Politely removing his cap, he stood before her expectantly.

"Did you drip water on my clean floor?" she asked him.

"No, ma'am," he answered, pulling out the damp towel that dangled from his back pocket. "And if I had, I would have mopped it up."

He sounded unoffended, though she spoke to him as if he were a rowdy youth. In fact, Mr. Akers was a few years older than she. He was a burly man, thickly muscled from hard work. His chestnut hair was baby-fine and had a wild, rather unkept look about it. And although his jaw was clean-shaven, he sported a long handlebar mustache that dipped low on either side of his mouth and then curled upward elegantly as if in parody of a smile.

Gussie indicated the other chair. He seated himself and withdrew a small pressboard memorandum tablet from inside his jacket. With the aid of his notes, he began a recitation of the day's business.

"Manufacturing was thirty-two hundred pounds since yesterday," he said. "We had four hundred fifty remained from the previous day undelivered. That makes three thousand six hundred fifty. We delivered only two commercial accounts at a thousand each and one commercial at four hundred pounds. There were three residential deliveries of seventy-five pounds each, two at fifty pounds and eleven, including yours, at twenty-five weight."

Gussie listened to the report and poured lemonade. The ice plant had been her father's business. It had made her family secure and comfortable in Cottonwood. Now it was hers. Many young women would have sat back and allowed a competent employee to manage its operation. But Gussie felt it behooved her to take an active part. More than that, she was genuinely interested. She found that she had a head for business. It intrigued her. It gave her a sense of order and control in the world. Though she was not now, nor would ever be, some mannish bluestocking going down to an office and directing men to do this or do that. Or smoking cigars with the banker and engaging in the wiles of commerce. But she couldn't leave it alone either. So she and Mr. Akers had begun these daily business briefings.

It was no secret that Rome Akers wanted desperately to be a partner in T.P. Mudd Manufactured Ice. When the time came that he could afford to buy into the business, he wanted Gussie to be keen on welcoming him in. In truth, she was quite interested. And the opportunity to stand with her on an equal footing might well be coming sooner than he'd ever anticipated.

His glass of lemonade remained untouched as Mr. Akers went through the accounts receivable. The same people who had trouble paying on time still did. And those who were always up-to-date retained that status.

The plant was the larger of the two ice manufacturers in town. For years now, the people of Cottonwood had become accustomed, even in the driest, hottest part of the long Texas summer, to iced tea, iced lemonade and the convenience and practicality of ice-cooled food storage. Now, with the increasing popularity of soda fountains, demand increased steadily. Enough so that Gussie had little cause for concern about her financial security. She was, by small-town standards, a well-to-do woman. But what mattered most at present was she was unmarried.

A cool breeze fanned across the yard, bringing the delightful scent of the lilacs in the flower garden to the chairs upon the porch. Gussie listened to Mr. Akers with polite attention. He was an exemplary employee. He could also be kind and decent, as well as occasionally annoying and opinionated. But he did run the business well and he was ambitious . . . She was counting on that.

When he finished his report, she nodded appreciatively. It was meticulously thorough and complete. Mr. Akers, it seemed, knew no other way to do things than with painstaking accuracy.

"Is that it, then?" she asked him.

"Yes, ma'am," he said, nodding, and reached at last for the glass of lemonade on the table. Every day when he finished his report, he hastily downed the refreshment and took his leave. Today would be no different, unless . . .

"I have a business proposition for you, Mr. Akers," she said.

The glass of lemonade stopped still, the rim near his mouth, and he gazed at her over it.

"A business proposition, ma'am?"

Gussie's courage almost failed her. Just because a woman was forthright and plainspoken didn't mean she couldn't be crushed by a man's rejection. In her memory she saw the horrified expression on Amos Dewey's face.

She stared now into the clear blue eyes of Rome Akers, a fine employee in his mid-thirties and an ambitious man. Would those attributes be enough to conscript him into her plot?

Deliberately she sat very straight, her back and shoulders two inches removed from any chance of contact with the chair. Her hands were still in her lap; her tone was superior and businesslike.

"Mr. Akers," she began, a little tremor of nervousness barely distinguishable in her voice. "With what I am about to say to you, I expect complete and absolute discretion."

Rome took a big gulp of his lemonade and nodded assuringly.

"Of course, ma'am," he said. "You surely know you can trust me on that. All of our discussions and dealings are within the strictest confidence."

"Yes, very well, then," she replied. "I am prepared to make you a partner in the company."

The silence on the porch was almost total. Only the chirp of birds in the trees and the creak of leather harness as Old Jezzi grew impatient in the street intruded upon the quiet.

"Ma'am, I . . . I don't yet have enough money saved to buy in as a partner," Rome admitted.

"Keep your money, Mr. Akers," Gussie said. "This partnership will not cost you anything. I simply require that you perform a small service for me."

"A service, ma'am?"

"Yes, Mr. Akers. I need you to pretend to be in love with me."

The glass of lemonade slipped through his fingers and broke into a million pieces on the plank-floor porch.

Breaking a piece of fine crystal and splashing lemonade upon your employer was not necessarily the best way to start a discussion on business partnerships. Rome Akers had been taken completely off guard by Miss Gussie's suggestion.

He was down on his knees between their chairs, carefully picking up the pieces of broken glass. "I . . . I'm sure I don't know what you mean, Miss Gussie," he stuttered.

"I have decided to get married," she announced with great confidence. "It's time and I'm ready and I've decided that Amos Dewey is the husband of my choice."

Rome nodded wordlessly from his kneeling position. Uncomfortable, he hurried to finish his task as quickly as possible.

"Amos and I have been seeing each other for some time," she went on. "We are well suited to each other by temperament. And he is a very appropriate companion for me."

It all sounded pretty cold to Rome. He rose to his feet and carefully set the broken pieces in a napkin upon the table. To his mind, getting married involved things like love and passion rather than temperament and appropriateness. But then, he'd never been in love, which was undoubtedly why he'd never married. That and the fact that the one woman he had asked had turned him down.

He decided to stand rather than seat himself once more and leaned somewhat uncomfortably upon a porch pillar, as distant as he could get from Miss Gussie and still be able to converse with her.

She had said she wanted him to pretend to be in love with her. He was not certain about why she needed that, but he felt sure that he wasn't really going to like the idea.

"I hope you and Dewey are . . . very happy," he said formally.

"Well, we certainly will be," Miss Gussie assured him. "I have every confidence of that or I wouldn't bother to pursue it. But in order to be happily married we have to actually *get* married. That's proving to be a bit of a stumbling block."

"A stumbling block?"

"Mr. Dewey isn't . . . well, I mean he hasn't truly thought it through."

Her statement was obtuse. Rome was a straightforward fellow; he liked the facts set out before him.

"Has he thought of it at all, Miss Gussie?" he asked her.

His question seemed to annoy her. She obviously hoped to enlist him in her plan without humiliating herself.

"Perhaps he hadn't given it a great deal of consideration," she conceded. "But after last night, he is bound to think more than once or twice about it."

"Last night? What happened last night?"

"Last night I confronted him directly."

"What?" Rome could hardly imagine such a moment.

"I asked him, 'Are you going to marry me or not?' "

"And he said?"

"Not."

"Oh."

A long, uncomfortable silence fell upon the porch.

Rome felt a wave of pity for the woman beside him. It was just like Miss Gussie to approach the world on a frank, open, businesslike basis. Unfortunately, there were some things that simply could not be dealt with in that manner.

"You disapprove, Mr. Akers," she said.

"It is not my place to approve or disapprove, Miss Gussie," he told her respectfully.

"That is exactly right," she said. "I'm sure you are looking at this in a very traditional fashion. The delicate, pale young lady must pine away at home while she waits and hopes for the man of her dreams to come to his senses."

Rome made no comment, but he did think that basically, that was the way things were.

"I am not delicate or pale, I'm not even all that young and I have no intention of allowing my life, my fate, to rest upon the whim of a man who clearly does not know what is good for him."

Rome had to admit that waiting for others to take action didn't sound at all like something Miss Gussie would be good at.

"I'm so sorry, ma'am," he told her sincerely. "Surely in time Mr. Dewey will recognize his foolish mistake."

She gave a little puff of irritable impatience.

"I will not sit pitifully praying for a change of heart,

Mr. Akers. I will take steps to make him change his mind."

"A man cannot be forced into wedlock, Miss Gussie," he pointed out. "I mean . . . unless . . . well, of course I . . . you would never . . ."

"Spit it out, Mr. Akers. What are you trying to say?" Rome felt his face burning with embarrassment.

"Has Mr. Dewey . . . ah . . . taken advantage?"

At first she didn't seem to get his meaning; then, when she did, her obvious mortification was surmounted only by her incredulity.

"Good heavens! Of course not. How could you even think—"

Rome wished he hadn't. He had a strong urge to kick himself.

"I didn't think . . . I assure you, Miss Gussie, I didn't think anything. It's just that you spoke of *making* him marry you, and you . . . well, you two have been keeping company for a long time and . . ."

She gave a startled gasp at that statement. He was digging himself in deeper and deeper.

"Mr. Dewey and I are not starry-eyed youths," Miss Gussie stated flatly. "We would never allow passion to exceed the bounds of discretion."

Rome chose not to comment upon that. He was inexperienced with the contemplation of, and motivations for, holy wedlock. He was significantly more familiar with the pleasures of the flesh. And though it was true that many husbands appeared less than lusty where their wives were concerned, most seemed to marry those women in a high fever of desire.

"I am sorry, Miss Gussie," he said sincerely. "I am afraid I am putting everything badly. Frankly, I'm at a loss as to what you plan to do and what my part in it might be."

The woman was sitting in that extraordinarily straight manner again, so that she didn't touch the chair back. And her tone of voice was completely businesslike and matter-of-fact.

"I thought about it all night," she said. "And I believe that the problem here is lack of competition."

Rome raised an eyebrow. "Beg your pardon, ma'am. Did you say competition?"

"Yes," Gussie replied. "That is the problem exactly. People, Mr. Akers, are just like businesses. They act and think and evolve in the same way as commercial enterprise. People want and need things. But when those things are vastly available, they prize them differently."

"Well, yes, I guess so," Rome agreed.

"So when we consider Mr. Dewey's hesitancy to marry me," she continued, "we must avoid emotionalism and try to consider the situation logically."

"Logically?"

Rome was not sure that logic was a big consideration when it came to love.

"Mr. Dewey has been on his own for some time now," she said. "He has a nice home, a hired woman to cook and clean, a satisfying business venture, good friends and me, a pleasant companion to escort to community events. Basically, all his needs as a man are met. He has a virtual monopoly on the things that he requires."

Rome was not certain that *all* of a man's *needs* had been stated, but after his embarrassing foray in that direction, he decided not to comment.

"He is quite comfortable with his life as it is," Miss Gussie continued. "Whyever should he change?"

"Why indeed?" Rome agreed.

She smiled then. That smile that he'd seen often before. That smile that meant a new idea, a clever innovation, an expansion of the company. He had long admired Miss Gussie's good business sense, and the very best of her moneymaking notions came with this smile.

"I can do nothing about Mr. Dewey's nice home, the woman hired to cook and clean, his business or his friends," Miss Gussie said. "But I can see that he no longer has a monopoly upon my pleasant companionship."

Rome raised an eyebrow and nodded.

"This is where it all came clear to me," she said. "In the middle of the night, after hours of going over it in my head, I came to the question of whyever should he change. This is when it all came clear."

Rome listened with interest.

"Tell me, Mr. Akers," she began. "If, say, our customers wanted twice-weekly ice delivery, would we give it to them?"

Rome was momentarily puzzled and then shrugged.

"If they were willing to pay twice as much," he answered.

"Oh, but they aren't," she told him. "Suppose they want to buy exactly the same amount of ice at the same price as before. But they want it delivered in smaller pieces twice weekly instead of once."

"Then we wouldn't do it," Rome said.

He couldn't imagine what this had to do with Miss Gussie's marriage plan, but he went along with it.

"We wouldn't want to do it?" she asked. "You are sure of that?"

"Yes, of course I'm sure," he said. "It would cost us more for no further profit. We wouldn't do it."

"We wouldn't want to. But something could motivate us to do it anyway."

"Like what?"

"Purdy Ice Company," she answered.

Cottonwood's other ice company had never been a very strong competitor. Matt Purdy's operation was quite small, more like a sideline for his farming business. They delivered ice to about half the houses on the far north side of town and a couple of small businesses. Beyond that, they offered no real threat to T.P. Mudd Manufactured Ice.

"I'm not sure I understand you," Rome said.

"If Purdy Ice began delivering smaller blocks twice a week, we would be forced to do the same."

Rome nodded. "Yes, I suppose you are right about that."

"We would be forced to change, pushed out of our profits and complacency, compelled to provide more service for the same money," she said.

"Yes, I suppose that's right."

"That's exactly what we're going to do to Amos Dewey," she declared.

Rome was listening, but still skeptical.

"You are going to pretend to be in love with me," she said, as if that were going to be the simplest thing in the world. "You will escort me about town. Sit evenings on this porch with me. Accompany me to civic events."

That seemed not too difficult, Rome thought. He did not normally attend a lot of public functions, but, of course, he could.

"I don't see how that will change Dewey's mind," he told her honestly.

"You will also let it be known that you are madly in love with me," she said. "And that you are determined to get me to the altar as soon as possible."

Rome got a real queasy feeling in his stomach.

"Amos Dewey will no longer have a monopoly. *You* will be the competition that will force him to provide the service he is not so willing to provide, marrying me."

Gussie raised her hands in a gesture that said that the outcome was virtually assured.

Rome had his doubts.

"I'm not sure this will work, Miss Gussie," he told her. "Men . . . men don't always behave like businesses. They are not all that susceptible to the law of supply and demand."

"Don't be silly," she said. "Of course they are."

He shook his head.

"I'm not sure I'm the right man to be doing this. Perhaps you should think of someone who would seem more . . . well, more suited to the task."

Her response was crisp and cool.

"And should I think of some other man to offer the partnership in my company?"

His mind full and his jaw tight, Rome's thoughts were in an uproar. Miss Gussie always seemed to know what she wanted. And she always went after it with a focused determination. He admired that. But it sometimes made her a very difficult employer. It would make her even more worrisome as a feigned romantic interest.

What on earth made that woman think such a scheme would ever work? And why did he have to be the one involved in it with her?

Because she's the boss, he reminded himself. He worked for her and that was the way life was. A man was always subservient to his boss. Whether it be male or female, young or old, kind or disagreeable, one had to follow his lead. Unless a man was his own boss.

That was his dream. To own his own business, to do things as he thought best, and have his fortune rise or fall based upon his own work, rather than upon the whims of someone else. That's what he wanted. It was his ambition and his hope for the future.

And now Gussie Mudd was handing him that on a silver platter. He could be a partner. Truly a partner. He ran the ice plant now. But as a partner, he would be as much an owner as she.

The offer was tempting, so tempting, too tempting.

"What all would I have to do?" he asked. "How long would it have to last?"

Gussie smiled at him, pleased.

"Very good questions," she said in a tone of praise peculiar to employer and employee. "Every venture needs defined parameters."

She was thoughtful for a moment.

"You will, as I said, need to be seen with me and show preference for me," she told him. "The way rumor spreads in a small town, all you will need to make your intentions public is to let a few words slip to those who frequent the barbershop, and Amos will hear all about it soon enough."

Rome nodded.

"I was hoping for a late-spring wedding," she went on. "When the flowers are at their peak. But I suppose, in this instance, midsummer would be fine. Let's say the Fourth of July—that sounds like an auspicious day for a wedding. It is going to be absolutely perfect. The most perfect wedding this town has ever seen. I do hope you will be there, Mr. Akers."

Rome couldn't even meet her eyes. He was pretty certain that it was a goodly distance from where they stood to wedding bells with Amos Dewey.

"Six weeks, Mr. Akers," she said. "You have six weeks to get me happily married."

2

WEDDINGS OFTEN TURNED A WOMAN'S MIND TO MAR-
riage. Gussie Mudd, however, did not need any assistance as she made her way to the large, prestigious,
dark brick church in the center of town.

Lucy Timmons was to be married that evening.
Keeping the church spick-and-span was the task of the
Circle of Benevolent Service, the foremost ladies'
group at the church. Today the women were combining that work with some special efforts to pretty up the
place for the wedding of the daughter of one of their
most distinguished members.

Gussie had picked the most perfect blossoms in her
garden to arrange in a basket for Lucy's wedding. She
spent much time among her flowers in the early mornings. The soft hush of sunrise and the sheer beauty of
the blossoms gave her a sense of quiet certainty that
helped sustain her. It was as if she were venturing out
into uncharted territory. She needed to gird herself
with calm and serenity to face the challenge.

She glanced down at the basket bouquet she carried
upon her arm. The vivid gladioli and hyacinths caught

the eye, but could not distract from the delicate loveliness of the buttercups and roses. Fresh and pretty and bright, it was the perfect offering for a spring wedding. A symbol of all that was beautiful and new. A life together, two as one.

That's what Gussie wanted for herself. Simply a bond of affection with a man she loved and admired. That did not seem to be asking too much. Gussie loved weddings. She loved the flowers, the bells, the ribbons and the frothy white cake. She had been to many such occasions in her life and mentally she'd taken notes. She knew that when the time came, her wedding would be the most beautiful and perfect one ever.

But before she could have the wedding, she had to acquire a bridegroom. That morning she had seated herself at the escritoire and slowly, thoughtfully, painstakingly made a list of every possible setback or snag her plan might encounter. Though she always kept a positive attitude, especially in front of employees and business associates, she was not naive. It was not going to be easy. Not that Gussie didn't see herself as a very worthy bride. She was a handsome woman, in an ordinary sort of way. More important, she was neither difficult to please nor in expectation of expensive fripperies. She was practical-minded, owned her home and had a profitable business. After years of taking care of her father, she felt confident of being able to accommodate herself to the vagaries and uneven temper that she assumed were typical of gentlemen in general.

But she knew that bringing a man like Amos Dewey to heel would be extremely tricky. An incautious word or a careless error, and he might easily see through her ruse. And her plan involved more than simply lying to one man; it meant lying to the whole town. If everyone found out, it surely wouldn't be appreciated. Any mistake could make her a laughingstock.

That's the way life tended to be, she thought, a lot like business. If something was worth having, it always involved a certain amount of risk. In business, risks could be calculated; in affairs of the heart, perhaps not so easily.

As she made her way up the church steps, Gussie let that last phrase of thought linger over her. *Affairs of the heart.* She would have liked that, but she didn't really expect it. Love was a sweet, pleasant and highly suspect notion. Like magic beans or a fairy godmother, it was a device of children's stories. Not meant to be taken seriously by mature men and women.

Marriage matches, the successful ones at least, were based upon mutual likes and dislikes, similar upbringing and shared moral and religious values. There was nothing magical about those things. And getting distracted by stylish handsomeness was foolish in the extreme.

Still, Amos was quite the looker, no arguing that. Walking at his side was as pleasurable as leading a parade. And just standing next to him made her heart beat faster. She secretly wished he were at her side this very minute. It was very likely, she decided, that she was in love with Amos Dewey. He was handsome, courteous and well spoken. She felt a certain inexplicable tingle in his presence. It was undoubtedly love.

Gussie snorted at her own naiveté. Obviously such feelings were not to be trusted. She must have appeared ridiculous to him. So starry-eyed and dreamy while he was simply passing the time of day. Escorting her in the interim between his grief and the acquaintance of a woman he truly prized.

It was galling, humiliating. But she was no delicate, easily bruised young girl. She was a woman of consequence and value. And if it took the attentions of another man to demonstrate that to him, well, then, so be it.

She had given Mr. Akers a day to, as he put it, "clear up a few things." For the life of her, Gussie couldn't imagine what a single man with no family might have to "clear up" before commencing what was to appear to be a diligent courtship. But his twenty-four hours were nearly up and Gussie would be making her first public appearance upon his arm tonight at Lucy's wedding. Nearly everybody in town would be there. Certainly Amos would be.

They had both agreed to drop a few good hints today. *Gussie's new beau* would make for sensational gossip under any circumstances. It would be better if at least the ladies of her circle and the gentlemen of his close acquaintance had some warning. They, like her, had undoubtedly expected an announcement from Amos Dewey.

Gussie sighed and then deliberately forced a smile to her lips as she opened the door to the little church. With any luck, she thought to herself, they would end up with exactly what they expected. Gussie was just going to have to make an effort.

The interior of the church had the somber elegance of a house of worship. The light from the stained-glass windows was muted. And the scent of incense lingered in the sanctuary. On either side of the aisle were padded pews, intricately carved in walnut, polished and buffed to a shiny gloss.

Several of the women were already at work. Madge

Simpson was fashioning a sateen skirt to drape around the podium. Constance Wilhelm was giving her direction.

Edith Boston and Eliza Penderghast, twin sisters, sat in the front pew chatting loudly. The two elder ladies showed up for absolutely every occasion, although they were a bit old to actually do much work.

Loralene Davies, the elected leader of the Circle and best friend to the mother of the bride, was directing what should be done and how to do it. The official title of the head of the Circle was Benevolent Authority. In Loralene's specific case, it might better have been *Absolute* Authority. Whatever was to be done, it was going to be done her way. Her friend Lulabell Timmons, the Circle's Faithful Scribe, had long ago given up any pretense of having a thought or idea of her own. She didn't need any, since Loralene's thoughts and ideas always prevailed.

Gussie carried her basket of mixed flowers to the front of the building. Though others had also brought blossoms, hers were, by far, the most attractive. She set them upon a dais behind the pulpit, in full view. She had woven lengths of white ribbon into the basket so that they hung from it, giving the arrangement a rich and elegant appearance. Young Lucy deserved that. This was her wedding day, an occasion to recall all her life. Gussie wanted it to be special. The kind of perfect day that she would want for herself.

She fiddled with the ribbons until they seemed to twist around the plain wooden stand like a silken vine. She stood back and surveyed her handiwork.

Helga Shultz, who was married to one of Gussie's employees, and Kate Holiday, the pastor's wife, were dusting the window ledges, nodded with approval.

"They look perfect," Madge reported. "As if they were grown just to be there."

"And the ribbon is a perfect match for this sateen," Constance pointed out.

Gussie saw that indeed it was very alike and smiled with some pride.

Unfortunately, at that moment Loralene was distracted from her discussion with Mrs. Timmons and turned to see Gussie's handiwork on the dais.

"No, no, no, no, no, no, no," she said with certainty. "Remove those flowers from there immediately. We have an arrangement especially styled for there."

Gussie looked at Loralene, who appeared quite ready to march up to the pulpit and toss Gussie's flowers right out the door.

"Where is the other arrangement?" she asked gently.

"Over there," Loralene answered, pointing to the deacon's table on the other side of the church. "They are real hothouse roses, come by train all the way from Longview."

Loralene sounded so impressed with that fact Gussie could only raise her eyebrows. With a smile pasted upon her face, she walked over to the deacon's bench to peruse the actual "hothouse" flowers.

The roses were indeed perfect, pale pink and white blooms about half opened. But they were all cut the same length, stuck in the vase with little greenery and even less thought or attention.

Madge Simpson and Constance Wilhelm stepped up beside her. They too were assessing the train-delivered roses.

"They are very expensive," Madge pointed out. It was basically the only compliment the roses were worthy of.

"Perhaps we should set them outside for a few

hours," Constance suggested. "A little sunshine might perk them right up."

Gussie didn't think so, but she smiled.

"If they are supposed to go on the dais, then that is where we will put them," she said.

Both Madge and Constance glanced over at her as if she had lost her mind. It was true that Gussie was opinionated, and she tended to manage the world to suit herself. This was not a particularly admirable trait, but the other women counted upon her to maintain a certain balance in the group. And she did. Loralene didn't intimidate her in the slightest. In fact, she looked forward to an occasional confrontation. But this morning there was to be no distraction. Loralene might be spoiling for a fight, as she often was, but she'd have to go home to her husband to find one today. Gussie was just not interested.

Dutifully she carried the anemic bouquet of hothouse flowers up to the pulpit. Constance and Madge followed in her wake.

"Put those down on the floor for the moment," Gussie suggested.

The women did as they were bidden with her beautiful flowers, and Gussie set the pale roses in their place.

She stepped back a couple of feet. Madge and Constance stood on either side of her and gave the roses a long, critical assessment.

"Stubby," Madge said.

"Washed out," Constance piped in.

Gussie was in complete agreement, but kept it to herself.

"If this is what Loralene and Lulabell want for Lucy," she said, "then, of course, we should honor their choice."

Both women turned to stare at her.

"So what has happened to you?" Madge asked. "A block of ice fall on your head?"

"Oh no," Gussie answered slyly. "Nothing . . . nothing at all like that." She tried to look as if she had a secret.

From across the room Loralene called out, "That's fine, Gussie. Put the arrangement you brought in the vestibule. Everybody will see it there."

That order brought the building to almost a complete hush. Only Kate Holiday's horrified gasp broke the silence.

Flowers in the vestibule would not even be considered a part of the wedding decoration. Under no circumstances on a normal day would Gussie have allowed Loralene to relegate her offering to such an ill-favored position. But today was no ordinary day. Gussie had a job to do, a rumor to start, an impression to make. And she was not about to let anything Loralene Davies might say deter her from that task.

She retrieved her flowers and began carrying them to the hallway between the church door and the sanctuary. She put a smile upon her face and deliberately began to hum. Every eye in the church was on her and she knew it.

"What is going on?" Eliza Penderghast asked loudly.

"Is she leaving in a huff?" her sister questioned with equal volume.

Gussie stopped and looked back at the two women.

"Certainly not, Mrs. Boston," she answered. "Whyever would I do such a thing?"

Fortunately, neither lady chose to reply.

"I'm simply taking these flowers to the vestibule," she said.

Gussie could hear the murmur of curious speculation as she went on about her task. She set the beautiful arrangement on a small table near the entryway. Unnecessarily, she fussed over the flowers for a few moments. They looked perfect, but she knew she should stay just where she was. And she didn't have to wait long.

She'd expected Madge, who was her closest friend. Instead Constance came. That showed the surprise and seriousness with which they took her strange behavior. Constance was the ear of sympathy and compassion in Cottonwood. A woman could tell her anything and know that she would never be judged.

Unfortunately, Constance could not be relied upon to keep what was told confidential. She shared everything that she knew or heard with Madge. And Madge was an incurable gossip. Absolutely the right friends to assist in Gussie's plan.

"What is wrong?" Constance asked her.

"Wrong? I don't know what you're talking about. Nothing is wrong."

"You aren't acting like yourself," Constance pointed out. "I can't believe you've allowed Loralene to put your pretty flowers way back here."

"Oh, that," Gussie said, chuckling lightly. "Well, you know Loralene. Sometimes it's just better to let her have her way."

Constance gazed at her as wide-eyed and unblinking as a big old catfish that had just swallowed the hook. It was definitely time to reel her in.

"I just . . . I just have other things on my mind," Gussie said.

"Other things?"

"Which do you think looks better on me," she asked, "the blue spring voile or my claret silk?"

Constance stood there mute and staring for a long moment.

"Which do you think?" Gussie prompted.

"Oh . . . I . . . the claret silk," she managed to reply finally. "You look lovely in it."

Gussie nodded slowly. "I do want to look my best."

She finished fussing with the trailing ribbons and turned to walk back into the sanctuary. Constance was glued to her side.

"You always look your best," she said. "What is going on?"

Gussie hesitated and gave her friend a long look.

"I suppose I can tell you," she said. "It's not a secret or anything like that. In fact, tonight everyone will know."

"Everyone will know what?"

"I'm being escorted to the wedding by a new beau," she whispered.

"Amos?"

Gussie dismissively shook her head. "Amos is not a *new* beau. He and I are still friends, of course."

"Then who?" Constance hissed. "Who is he?"

Gussie glanced around as if to assure herself that they were out of earshot of anyone else. She leaned closer to Constance and spoke quietly.

"I'm being escorted to the wedding tonight by Mr. Romeo Akers," she said.

If Gussie had said she was coming with Theodore Roosevelt, Constance would not have been more surprised.

The word spread like wildfire. Constance repeated it to Madge not three minutes after it was told to her. As Gussie concentrated on festooning the pews with love knots of Nile cotton crepe, all around her in little groups the news was repeated. Eventually it even filtered down to Mrs. Boston and Mrs. Penderghast.

"You are keeping company with Rome Akers?" Edith asked loudly.

"The iceman, Rome Akers?" her sister clarified.

"What happened to that young barber?"

"Mr. Dewey?" Gussie pretended to look surprised at the question. "Mr. Dewey and I are the very best of friends, of course."

It all worked even better than Gussie had imagined. By the time they had finished the preparations for the wedding and were making their way outside, the discussion was loud and openly curious.

Gussie lingered for a moment on the steps, speaking with Kate Holiday as the other women, including Loralene and Lulabell, went on their way.

"Oh, I must have left my good jet hatpin in the church," Gussie said, turning to go inside again.

"Do you want me to help you look for it?" Kate asked.

"No, no." Gussie waved her off. "I'm sure I know exactly where I left it."

"We shall see you tonight, then," the pastor's wife said.

Gussie nodded and went back into the church. There was, of course, no jet hatpin. She quickly moved her flower arrangement back to the dais and left the forlorn little hothouse roses on the little table in the vestibule.

For Rome, it had been a very busy week. He'd been trying to teach the delivery routes to the young shute boy, Tommy Robbins. The fellow was smart enough, but Rome wasn't getting any help. The youngster had been on the payroll for a couple of years now, but Miss Gussie had just last week started paying him a man's wage.

Old Mr. Shultz had been genuinely surprised and not generally pleased.

"Why pay a man's wage for a shute boy?"

"He's more than that," Akers told him. "He runs the plant when we're out on deliveries. He's hardworking and dependable. I was thinking that maybe next year, or surely the one after, you could swap out with him. I know that shoulder pains you tremendously."

Shultz's face immediately turned crimson.

"You think I'm getting too old to do my job!"

Rome deliberately remained calm. "It's hard work toting ice day in and day out. It's a vocation for a young man with a strong back."

They were tough words, but they were true.

Shultz had worked for Mudd Manufactured Ice since Gussie's father had started the plant. He was obviously getting on in years. He was still capable and willing to do deliveries, so there was no purpose in rushing into a change. But it was always prudent to have somebody who was capable of taking over in case the old man was injured or laid up.

It was the right decision, but not a popular one. The atmosphere among the three at the plant had been one of stiff silence. The only noise was the grunts of effort necessary for the arduous task of getting enough ice made and wagons loaded.

So Rome was grateful to be out in the sunshine perched, back aching and arms tired, upon the seat of an ice wagon making its slow, lumbering progress through town.

It was not necessary to guide or lead Old Jezzi. The milk-white dray knew the route better than he did himself. A driver could simply point her in the right direction in the morning and the hardworking horse would walk the entire section, correctly stopping directly in front of the right houses.

Not having to do much more than sit on the seat and hold the lines, Rome had a good deal of time to think between deliveries, and this morning his mind was full to near bursting.

He was finally going to be a partner, a partner in the business at last. It would have taken him another five years of scrimping and saving, and now it was to be handed to him upon a silver platter. He toyed with the idea of his name on the building. Mudd-Akers Manufactured Ice. He almost sighed aloud.

Of course, there was the small detail of pretending to be in love with Miss Gussie so Amos Dewey would want to marry her.

Competition, Miss Gussie called it. And spoke of it as if it were a business maneuver. It was simply making the other fellow jealous and was as ancient a female trick as any in the women's bag of wedding lures. And not every man fell for it. That was one fact of which Miss Gussie was obviously unaware.

But how could she know? Rome thought. There was never in the world a lady with more understanding of money or business and less understanding of men or romance.

He would have to take charge of the plan. Make sure that poor Amos was eaten up with jealousy, not resigned to letting the woman go. He had to bring those two together and it had to be soon. He'd never be able to make anyone believe he was in love with Gussie Mudd for any length of time.

Rome wanted that partnership, though he was not completely mercenary. If Rome had thought for a moment that Amos Dewey would not do for Miss

Gussie, he would not have so much as lifted a finger to help her in this crazy scheme.

Miss Gussie deserved a good, hardworking, responsible husband. The two were well suited. They were quiet, respectful, considerate of each other. And a person would have to be blind enough to sell pencils not to notice the way Miss Gussie's gaze followed the man. Of course, tall as he was and with all that black hair, Dewey was the type of fellow who was bound to catch the eye of the ladies. Rome intended to make sure that on forthcoming occasions, Amos would definitely be looking back.

That Miss Gussie was going to take him on as a partner in the ice plant was just a bonus, Rome assured himself, still feeling a little guilty about his good fortune. He had earned that position by his own efforts. He would be putting his cash into the business anyway. Maybe buying a new distiller, which was very badly needed. And he would see to it that the woman would never have any regrets about giving him this chance.

Yet there was still enough underhandedness in the plan to make him a little queasy.

The horse made the turn off Third Street and onto Brazos Avenue. Old Jezzi stopped at the rather large and formidable Richardson house on the corner. Two tall Greek columns stood majestically in the front entry and expansive verandas curved around three sides of two floors. It was a typical house for a cotton baron, perhaps. But it stood on Brazos Avenue, a stark contrast to the modest homes around it.

Grover Richardson might have been the son of the city's founder, but it was cotton, not the town of Cottonwood, that had made him a very wealthy man. That had been his goal and he had pursued it vigorously, to the exclusion of all else. It was not surprising, then, that he had been nearing fifty when he finally got around to taking a wife. He had built her this beautiful mansion, the finest in town. Then he had dropped dead only weeks after they'd moved inside.

Rome jumped down from his perch and glanced toward the front door, where the delivery card was set in its pocket. Each card had four weights of ice to request, two on each side. The numbers were printed on four different colors to represent the four standards. On one side of the card, twenty-five pounds was represented by yellow, fifty pounds by green. On the back, seventy-five pounds was blue and a hundred pounds was vivid red. Each customer had a little pocket by his or her front door and would slip the card into it with the appropriate order weight displayed. It would be impossible to read the numbers from the street, but colors were easy to see.

Rome glanced toward the front door and his face flushed.

"Good Lord!" he exclaimed aloud as he saw the card in the pocket. Guiltily he glanced around, desperately hoping no one else saw what he saw.

He was alone, of course, and no one else would know the significance of a bright red card in the pocket. Though he still worried that someone might glance at it and wonder why a lonely widow with only a twenty-five-pound icebox would be requesting a hundred pounds of ice.

Rome went to the back of the wagon, raised the door and carefully cut a twenty-five pound block of ice. With his tongs he carried it through the front gate. He purposely went up to the request pocket and turned the card to indicate the more appropriate yellow. Then he walked around the length of the veranda to the side door that led into the kitchen. With only one quick, cursory knock of warning, he stepped inside.

He glanced around the room, expecting Mrs. Richardson to be waiting for him. She was.

The handsome forty-two-year-old blond widow of the late Grover Richardson was sitting atop the icebox, attired in an extremely shocking black-and-red lace corset, with satin garter straps holding up black silk stockings that were partially covered to mid-calf with high-button red boots. She held her red silk bloomers in her hand and was using them rather ineffectually as a fan.

"Pansy, don't put the red card in the pocket," Rome scolded. "Some of your busybody neighbors might suspect something."

The woman shrugged. Though she was beyond the prettiness of first bloom, she was still an attractive woman. And the effective use of face powder and paints made her more so.

"They already suspect everything possible of me," she said. "There's not much I could do to lower myself any further in their estimation."

She cocked her head to one side and ran her gaze the full length of Rome's body before deliberately and artfully crossing her legs.

"As for requesting the hundred pounds of ice," she continued in a more throaty whisper, "I just thought you'd want to know . . . well . . . just how really *hot* I am this afternoon."

Rome shook his head and stepped closer to the icebox. He made no attempt at a reply. He'd learned long ago there was simply no arguing with Pansy Richardson. A man would be a fool to even make the attempt.

She smiled up at him now, her expression a soft

challenge. Rome was far from immune to the picture she presented. Her blond hair hung long and silky down the length of her back. Her painted lips pouted prettily, offering things he knew full well that she could deliver. And the red corset she wore was laced so tight that her bosom spilled out the top in voluptuous excess, impossible in nature.

"Hop up now, I need to put this in the drawer," he said, indicating the block of ice he carried, destined for the cold box.

Instead of removing herself as he had requested, Pansy drew her legs up and spread them wide to drape on either side of the polished oak cooler.

"Go ahead, Romeo," she said in a low, teasing voice. "Go ahead and put it inside."

Rome allowed himself one long, appreciative glance at the pale flesh of her inner thighs and the shocking exposure of her intimate parts before dutifully stowing his delivery in the ice keeper.

He positioned the block just right, closed the drawer securely and slowly straightened to his full height again.

Pansy waited, albeit not that patiently, upon her perch.

Rome licked his lips and cleared his throat.

"This is not a good idea," he told her. "It's the middle of the afternoon. The neighbors will notice if the wagon is outside for more than a few minutes."

She raised a challenging eyebrow. "Then maybe you ought to make it quick," she suggested. "I'd hate to do damage to *your* reputation. Although I've heard that being described by the ladies as *quick* is usually not a compliment."

Rome drew off his gloves and stuffed them into his back pocket. He rubbed his palms together vigorously.

"My hands are too cold to touch you," he explained.

Pansy wrapped her legs around his hips and drew him to her.

"Then don't use your hands," she told him.

He was close now and the scent of her tantalized him. It was a mixture of the clean, sweet-smelling innocence of a rosewater bath and the heady, pungent musk of female desire. It was an irresistible combination.

"You'd better kiss me before I do something to hurt us both," she warned.

Rome reluctantly met her mouth with his own.

"Why do you let me treat you like this?" he asked her. "Why do you let me come to you like a whore?"

She pulled away just enough to look up into his eyes.

"Because I trust you enough to know you will never think me one," she answered.

3

THE BRIGHTLY PAINTED RED-AND-WHITE POLE ON THE west side of Cottonwood's Broad Street business district was like a beacon of refuge for the gentlemen of the community. At nearly any time of the day, one could pass in front of the plate-glass window and see a number of occupants beyond the painted identifying script that read: AMOS DEWEY TONSORIAL PARLOR ... SHAVING AND HAIRCUTTING ... HOT BATHS. The customers joked, argued and swapped lies as they waited on uncomfortable slat-backed benches for their turn to sit in the fancy red-leather-and-carved-mahogany barber's chair. Where they lifted up their faces with complete confidence to the steady hand and mild demeanor of Amos Dewey.

Dewey lived his life inside a mind of silences. During the day he could talk and laugh and look as if he were alive, but in his head he kept life quiet. He didn't contemplate the future and he didn't dwell on the past. Silence was simple. Silence was easy. Silence had gotten him this far. Past the anger over the senselessness of his wife's death, past the emptiness of being left alone. Keeping his mind quiet had gotten him from one day to the next for the past three years. But now, suddenly, there were rumblings in the stillness, echoes of life demanding to be heard.

As he stood behind the barber's chair in his shop, shaving and trimming, listening to the incessant talk around him, he could not quiet the clamor that raged inside him.

Gussie Mudd wanted to marry him. It was natural, the expected outcome of being courted. He had courted her, he supposed. Mostly he had just been passing time. Time was empty and it was best to see it pass. Three years was like a lifetime or like a minute. He had passed much of it with her at his side.

He had not thought about what she might think, what she might want. But then, in avoiding thoughts of anger and pain, he'd managed to avoid most any thoughts at all.

It wasn't so very difficult. There was plenty of talk in his barbershop. Enough to distract any man from unwelcome rumination. Especially on a busy afternoon.

A half-dozen men, three of whom were regular hang-arounders, sat in curved-back wooden chairs that lined the far wall and the space in front of the window. Amos's business was thriving. Scrupulously clean and smelling of shaving soap and hair tonic, the barbershop was a peaceful island of male camaraderie, distanced somehow from the complications of women and the screeching of children.

Pete Davies, a slight-framed, balding man in his mid-thirties, was pacing the floor and waxing eloquent upon his decidedly unpleasant marital union. He and his wife, Loralene, were currently living separately. This was not shocking news. Pete got mad and moved out about twice a year since they'd wed. Usually he was on his own for only a few weeks at a time, but occasionally the disagreement lasted for months.

"The thing about women," he was declaring with authority, "is that they don't understand the world at large and have an exaggerated idea of their place in it."

The response included a few chuckles and a couple of nods and a hearty "Amen" from old Penderghast, who was almost stone deaf, generally confused and had been happily wed to his childhood sweetheart for nearly fifty years.

"No smoking. No drinking. No card playing or dominoes. And the Lord Almighty help you if you so much as even catch the eye of some other woman on the street," Pete continued, shaking his head. "I wish somebody would tell me how the home that I built, every board, nail and bucket of paint paid for from the sweat of my labors, every stick of furniture and length of drapery come by the same way—how did that place get to be *her* house?"

"Well, Pete," Amos said quietly, not looking at him but concentrating upon tying the cutting cloth around the neck of Reverend Holiday and reclining him in the big red-leather-upholstered, metal-and-mahogany chair, "it might have something to do with those five children the woman bore you."

A few of the customers snickered.

Pete turned to the barber and shook his finger at him in warning.

"You don't know how lucky you are, Amos Dewey," he said, "to be a man on your own without some woman constantly stepping in to ruin every pleasure you hold dear."

The words were cruel to a man who had doted upon his pretty, delicate little bride. His sweet little Bess,

sickly from childhood, had passed from this world
much too soon.

Amos chose not to take offense.

His grief was intense and at times all-consuming.
But it was his and his alone. He never shared it, not in
word or in deed. Not so much as a whisper. No one
could know. Because he could never bear to speak of it.

Amos carefully wrapped a hot, steamy towel upon
Reverend Holiday's face as the discussion in the
room turned to the president's handling of the coal
strike. Most said bully for Teddy. Texas was not a
state much friendly to unions, but there was always
sympathy for the workingman.

The subject changed abruptly when Perry Wilhelm
breezed in with a bit of hometown gossip.

"I saw Pansy Richardson come to town this morning
for groceries," he said.

A little titter of knowing laughter made its way
around the room.

"Just how much did you see of her?" Clive Benson
asked.

That question really amused the crowd.

Perry shook his head. "Not nearly as much as I was
willing to," he replied. "But more than my wife would
probably appreciate."

The fellows liked that answer as well.

Wade Pearsall added his own news.

"My Vera told me that Mudd's ice wagon was
parked in front of her house today for nearly a half
hour."

That was a scandal for sure.

"Akers or old man Shultz?" somebody asked.

"Maybe the both of them," another suggested.

There was lots of laughter all around.

Benson shook his head, disbelieving. "Your wife

does have a tendency to exaggerate, Wade," he reminded them all. "And she hasn't had a good word to say about the Widow Richardson since that little incident of yours."

Pearsall bristled. "The woman was sitting out on the second-floor porch practically naked," he told them. "I just happened to glance up in that direction."

"And the field glasses just happened to be perched on your nose at the time," Perry added.

That statement produced more loud guffaws. Not everyone, however, found it so humorous.

Reverend Holiday pulled the towel from his face and sat up in the barber's chair.

"That woman is a Jezebel," he proclaimed with equally loud fervor. "She is vile and wicked and a blot of shame upon this town."

His declaration effectively silenced the room. To a man, the occupants looked uncomfortable and guilty.

Amos spoke up for the first time as he eased the preacher back in the chair and began brushing his face with a lavish amount of shaving soap.

"I suspect that most of the things that are said about Mrs. Richardson are untrue," Amos assured him. "A lovely young widow like her, alone all these years and so . . . so spirited. People will talk."

The pastor wasn't completely placated.

"People may talk," Pearsall pointed out, "but Madeline Barclay did name her by name. If the woman lived more modestly and turned her attention to good works, a good deal less would be said."

It was difficult to argue that.

"I can't imagine what Grover Richardson was thinking," Harry Potts, editor of the Cottonwood *Beacon* said, shaking his head. "To marry such a capricious young woman and then to leave her all that money."

"Richardson seemed to like her youth and vitality," Amos said. "She was a good wife to him while he lived. And I'm sure that he never expected to leave this earth as early as he did."

"But what a way to go," Pete Davies whispered under his breath.

Everyone heard his words, but not all were able to stifle their snickers.

Perry couldn't resist adding his own twist to the joke.

"It gives new implication to the longing of most men to die in their own bed."

Most everyone laughed at that. Reverend Holiday did not. And neither did Amos.

"Grover Richardson is probably rolling in his grave to see his wife become such an object of speculation," the preacher told them, shaking a finger at them in warning. "He should have left his fortune to the church or charity. His widow would have been forced to behave herself so she could remarry."

The pastor shook his head. "Instead she is running wild, dressing like a young woman, loud, immodest and hasn't darkened the church door since the day of her husband's funeral."

Reverend Holiday had the discretion not to mention the numerous illicit liaisons the woman was rumored to have.

Amos wondered how she could have done it. Richardson had died only shortly before his own Bess. The widow's reputation was called to question almost immediately.

So soon after the loss, Amos couldn't have . . . well, he still couldn't.

Perhaps it was simply the nature of the man's death that had set the gossip hounds against her. Richardson had been stark naked and in full rut when he succumbed to apoplexy atop his young wife. It was rumored that she'd been trapped beneath his dead body for hours.

An image like that stays with people.

But where there was smoke, there was usually fire, and Pansy Richardson had done little or nothing to quell gossip about her alleged affairs. And the way she looked at men, as if she knew them unerringly and could size them up. It was disconcerting, at the least.

She'd looked at Amos more than once. He had been completely befuddled. His sweet Bess was gone. His life partner was six feet under, rotted and gone. He no longer even thought about the temporal, the carnal. But then, as he reminded himself, he tried not to think at all.

That's why he had not thought about Gussie. He'd not thought about what she might want. About what she might want from him. She had been forced to state those needs to him directly.

And he had rejected her. Clumsily, hurtfully, he had rejected the woman who had been a kind friend and companion to him for the past three years. It was a terrible thing to do. Uncompassionate and ungentlemanly.

If he allowed himself the truth, however, he was relieved that he had done it.

What in the world was wrong with him? he wondered as he scraped the whiskers from Reverend Holiday's chin. He genuinely liked Miss Gussie. She would make a fine wife. And he needed to remarry. He was still young enough to start again, to have children, to live once more.

He wasn't living, and he knew that. Inside, he was as dead as his beloved Bess. He merely continued to work every day and she did not.

"Here comes Rome," Clive announced, capturing Amos's attention once more.

He'd pulled the ice wagon to a stop by the front door. Amos didn't use ice in the shop. Obviously Rome's errand was personal rather than professional.

"Maybe we should ask him how long it takes to make a delivery to the wicked widow," Perry suggested.

The patrons in the barbershop chuckled at that. But when Rome came through the doorway, not a one of them had the audacity to voice the question. Akers was notoriously touchy about women on his route. He spent his days going in and out of the kitchens of other men's wives and mothers. It was bad for business if folks began to dwell upon the inappropriateness of a man, any man, being inside a woman's house without her husband at home.

"Good afternoon," Clive offered in greeting instead.

Rome mumbled a reasonable if distracted response.

His expressive face was a map of purpose, concern and confusion. He definitely looked as if he had something important to say. So much so that he made an unscheduled stop in the middle of the afternoon.

"Hello, Rome," Amos said to him. "You need something this afternoon?"

The man looked ill at ease. He walked to the mirror and gave himself a thorough perusal.

"I need . . . I need the works," he said. "A shave, haircut, the sideburns trimmed."

"All right," Amos told him. "Both Harry and Clive are ahead of you. The wait will be about twenty minutes, I expect. If you are in a hurry, you could come back tomorrow."

"No, no. I have to get it done today," Rome said. "I'm . . . I'm escorting a lady to that wedding tonight."

The silence in the barbershop was all-inclusive. Finally the reverend chuckled.

"Well, well, well, this is good news indeed, Akers," he said.

"Yes," Rome agreed. "Yes, it is."

The other men began to joke and speculate. Rome didn't offer any clues. He had been seen occasionally in the past with ladies who were not necessarily ladies, and more than once his name had been linked to the infamous Mrs. Richardson. But up until now Rome Akers had not singled out any marriageable female for particular attention. It was a novelty. And one that the other men were delighted to tease him about.

"Is this just an evening's fancy?" Amos questioned. "Or are you planning a serious courtship?"

"Why do you ask?"

"The mustache," Amos said, pointing to the man's reflection in the mirror. "Woman hate facial hair. If it's serious courting, the mustache has to go."

"My mustache!" Akers looked extremely displeased. He ran his fingers over his upper lip assessingly.

Rome had worn the long red-gold handlebar for years now. It was as much a part of his face as his eyes, nose and mouth.

"He's right," Mr. Potts agreed. "If you want to win a woman, you've got to do it clean-shaven."

"Yeah, you can grow it back after you're wed," Benson piped up.

"Now, you fellows are getting ahead of yourselves," Amos told them. "He's only thinking to walk out with the woman and you've got him lovestruck and married already."

All of them laughed.

"A happy marriage could do you a world of good, son," the pastor suggested.

The words clearly distressed the man. Amos relented.

"Oh, keep the mustache," he told Rome. "If she agreed to go with you, then she must not mind it very much."

Rome gave Amos a strange look that the barber couldn't quite interpret.

"No, shave it off," he said. "If that's what it takes, shave it off."

Gussie was so nervous her stomach was nearly in full rebellion. Her hands trembled and her voice cracked. And this was before she'd even left the house.

Rome showed up, a little late and a little nervous. His hair was shiny and slicked down in the latest fashion for dapper gentlemen. The width of his shoulders in the gray three-button cutaway coat and the regal grace with which he moved, unencumbered by the weight of a fifty-pound block of ice, made him seem another man entirely from the Rome Akers who was in her employ.

"Will this do?" he asked, indicating his clothes. "I don't have a full-dress suit and the tailor said the soonest they could put one together for me would be next week."

Gussie dismissed his concerns. "It is the twentieth century," she reminded him. "We are not so formal."

She invited him in to stand in the foyer while she pinned on her hat. Gussie was overdressed for the occasion and she knew it. She was gowned in a claret silk walking dress trimmed in tiny gold braid. Her heart-brimmed straw leghorn was festooned with similar braid and clusters of taffeta rosettes pulled together with three elegant cut-steel cabochons.

Most of the women in attendance would be wearing

simple shirtwaist-and-skirt ensembles. And although all heads would be respectfully covered, many would be done so with scarves and bonnets.

She did not feel a bit uncomfortable. It was befitting for a woman of her social rank and means to be very fashionable when appearing in public for the first time on the arm of a new gentleman. Were she to show up in anything less than the latest in style, it would be as if saying to these people that the fine opinion of the man at her side did not matter to her. As a business-woman, as well as simply a human being, she understood that a visible impression often overrode all logic and reasoning.

She gazed at Rome curiously. He did not have the dashing good looks of a gentleman, but he was well enough looking and was sufficiently groomed for the evening. She felt a little ill at ease as she surveyed him. It was almost as if this very familiar man had suddenly turned into a stranger.

"You look different somehow," she said.

"It's the mustache," he said. "I had it shaved."

Gussie was amazed as she recognized the truth. That very long, very red-gold mustache was completely missing on the clean-shaven face that gazed back at her. Rome's handlebar mustache had been a part of him as long as they had been acquainted.

Its absence on his face was startling. The lined, work-ravaged face of Rome Akers would never be classically handsome, but without the long, curling handlebar hanging from his upper lip, he was a fair-looking man.

"You look much better without it," she told him honestly.

He didn't appear convinced. "That's what your Amos told me," he said.

Gussie was surprised. "You talked to Amos about us already?"

Rome shook his head. "No, I went into the barbershop to get cleaned up. I announced that I was headed for a courtship. I figured that was a quick way to get the word out."

Gussie nodded. It was a good idea.

"Amos suggested that if I were *serious* about the woman, I should shave," he said. "I could hardly tell him that I wasn't so serious."

"No, of course not. That would ruin everything."

He came to stand behind her and gazed at himself in the hall-tree mirror, fingering his bare upper lip.

Gussie gazed at him in the glass and a strange jolt went through her. The image in the mirror. A man and a woman in the same small oval was somehow too prosaic, too intimate.

She stepped away from him too quickly and nearly fell. She giggled nervously. It was not an attractive sound.

"We'd best go," Gussie told him.

In truth they had plenty of time, but Rome nodded in agreement.

He held the door for her as she passed through and then proffered his arm when they descended the front steps.

"It's going to be fine, Miss Gussie," Rome told her encouragingly. "Try not to worry too much."

"I am so jittery," she admitted.

"And that is fine," he assured her. "That would be expected for a woman walking out with a man for the first time."

"Do you think . . ."

Gussie hesitated. It was her worst fear and she hated to voice it. Bravely she spoke the words.

"Do you think they'll believe it?" she said.

Rome hesitated and Gussie knew he felt just as she did. The two of them were the most unlikely, mismatched couple ever to promenade down a public street. Everyone would see through the ruse, and their implausible scheme would blow up in a grand humiliation from which neither would ever fully recover. Gamely they kept walking.

"It's very important that you don't overplay your role," Gussie advised. "Don't attempt to hold hands with me or spout poetry or the like."

Rome looked startled. "I would never dream of holding hands with you, Miss Gussie," he assured her. "And the only verses I've committed to memory are the type improper for recitation in mixed company."

She blushed.

"I was just trying to help," she said.

"I know how to escort a lady in public."

"Well, how was I to know that? I've never seen you walking out with anyone and—"

"Smile," he ordered, interrupting her explanation. "The Purdys are on the other side of the street and they are looking this way."

Gussie felt her face flame. This was it. It was really happening. Everybody in town would believe she was being courted by Rome Akers. She just had to hope that the experience would be short, uncomplicated, believable and efficient.

Deliberately she raised her chin high. A asset worth having was worth fighting for, scheming for, even lying for.

She knew the exact moment the Purdys spotted them. There was an audible gasp from Anna. Gussie turned to glance at Rome.

"And they're off!" he said in a teasing whisper.

He smiled at her then. It was the warmest, sweetest smile Gussie had ever seen on his face. It lit up those fine blue eyes, and even though she was aware that it was part of the deception, it took her breath away.

Several other people saw them, but no one actually spoke until they reached the church. Perry Wilhelm was standing next to the steps, rolling himself a cigarette. When he glanced up at them, his jaw actually dropped open in disbelief.

Gussie suffered a moment of panic. Was it that hard to believe that a man like Rome Akers would walk out with her? Fortunately, Wilhelm recovered quickly and so did she.

"Good evening, Rome, Miss Gussie," he said to them.

They acknowledged the greeting. Gussie just nodded, but she heard Rome saying something appropriate, so she smiled.

Sharing wordlessly their secret, she just smiled.

Then, as they went up the steps together, both nervous, scared and edgy, they glanced at each other. In that one friendly, connected instant, something very unexpected happened. Rome Akers winked at her.

It was such a flirty, flighty, man-woman gesture. Innocent yet hinting at all things sensual. To her knowledge, in her thirty-one years of life experience, no man had ever winked at her.

It was somehow reassuring, yet it gave her a strange sort of fluttery feeling in her chest. She swallowed the strange reaction and continued by his side.

They entered the church. On the small table in the vestibule, the anemic hothouse roses greeted the arrivals.

As they approached the sanctuary, Gussie was suddenly aware of the strength of the man beside her.

Somehow the powerful muscles in the arm upon which she so formally lay her hand gave her courage. Rome Akers was a good man to have by her side in any endeavor. She'd known that in business. Now she understood that it was also true when confronted with a personal challenge.

"Smile," he reminded her in a whisper.

She glanced up into his face and did just that. Her knees were quaking, her pulse was pounding, her stomach was near nausea, but she smiled up at the man beside her.

"I'm ready," she told him, not certain whether it was truth or a lie.

He smiled back at her and they stepped through the entryway. There was almost a stunned hush to the crowd. Gussie knew that there could not have been more eyes upon her had she been the bride herself.

Rome was a brave and daring fellow. Gussie would have been very tempted to take a spot in the very first pew they passed. The Mudd family pew, however, was fourth from the front on the right side. She would not have thought that Rome knew that, but he led her unerringly to it. They seated themselves and gazed silently straight ahead.

It wasn't going to be easy. Gussie had known that going into this deception. But she had not realized how conspicuous she would feel. Or how unlikely she would look as the object of attention for a man like Rome Akers.

But Rome, she decided at that rather uncomfortable moment in the pew, was not the kind of fellow who would ever choose a bride based upon the practicalities that the woman offered. Gussie would suit Amos Dewey perfectly. That was obvious both to her and to everybody who knew them.

But Rome Akers? No, there was simply too much . . . too much passion in the man.

Beside her, Rome leaned in closer and spoke to her in a low and private tone.

"Did you see Amos?" he whispered. "He's near the back, sitting with the Bensons. I'm sure he saw you."

It was all Gussie could do to face forward and not glance behind her in the man's direction. Her plan was really happening. Amos had seen her. What had he felt? she wondered. Confusion. Anger. Jealousy. Pain.

Not pain, she hoped ardently. She didn't want to hurt him. She didn't want that at all.

Rome covered her gloved hand with his own. It was then that she realized she was trembling. She looked at him.

"Courage," he whispered.

Gussie straightened her shoulders.

It was at that moment that Mr. and Mrs. Penderghast moved into their pew just in front of them. An audible intake of breath got Gussie's attention. She raised her head to see the Penderghasts, both of them, gazing in shocked incredulity at the sight of Gussie and Rome holding hands in church.

The two schemers realized their breach of etiquette at exactly the same instant and Rome released her hand. It had been a comforting gesture, not a romantic one. But no one else would ever know that.

Gussie had wanted to create talk. She was certainly going to get it now. Nervously she glanced around the room. There was a great crowd of people. Nearly every family in town was represented. And she knew most everyone. Most from her social circle, but also a few from the ice plant, her employees and their families. What would they make of this mismatched pair?

The owner and the manager of their livelihood holding hands together in church. At the very least, it boded upheaval and change. She hadn't given a thought to how this deception might affect her employees.

The minister entered rather noisily from an anteroom, walking from pew to pew, loudly greeting people and discussing the weather, cotton prices and the latest exploits of "Dark Cloaked Avenger," a serial fiction currently being published in *Cottonwood Beacon.*

When he reached Gussie and Rome, he was momentarily struck speechless. He quickly recovered himself and shook Rome's hand in a manner too enthusiastic to be enjoyed.

"I'm so glad you've brought this sinner with you today, Miss Gussie," he said. "We haven't seen Rome in church here since he was wearing short pants."

Gussie was embarrassed by the pastor's attention. It was . . . well, it was so loud. Churches should be quiet, reverent places. And the men who headed them should be likewise. She knew Reverend Holiday to be an upright, righteous and worthy member of the clergy. But for the life of her, she had to bite her tongue to keep from shushing the man.

And now, being the loud focus of attention in the building was almost more public display than she could bear. Anyone who'd missed their entrance, the long walk to the Mudd Family pew or Mrs. Penderghast's gasp could not fail to note the loud comments of the good reverend.

Reverend Holiday continued to gush for several more minutes before he moved on to make his way through the rest of those in attendance.

Why had she chosen this night? Why had she chosen this place? Surely another occasion would have been better for this deception. She quickly met Rome's eyes. He looked as disconcerted as she.

4

ROME COULDN'T IMAGINE HOW LONG ONE EVENING could last. And it had hardly begun. It seemed like a lifetime had passed before the groom and his best man and aide-de-camp appeared up front to wait with the pastor. The music began to play. There was a flutter of anticipation all around the room, as if the wedding might actually commence.

The church door opened and, as one, every person in attendance turned to look. The two young attendants entered one at a time. Leading was pretty, red-haired Betty Ditham. She was the oldest granddaughter of old Shultz, and Rome recognized her from the times she'd visited the ice plant. Behind her was the bride's sister, Becky.

Rome thought the younger Timmons girl must be fifteen or sixteen. But Miss Becky had yet to acquire any womanly curves. Her hips were straight as a board and her bosom more closely resembled a tabletop than a pair of hillocks.

The two made their way to the front of the church. Betty with smiles and flirtatious giggles. Becky with timidity and hesitance. They were in place and facing the back entrance when the bride appeared at the doorway.

The congregation rose to its feet.

Rome put his hand upon Miss Gussie's elbow to help her up. It was a tender gesture he'd often shown to his mother in years now distantly past. It seemed appropriate somehow to extend such a courtesy to his ladylike employer. He accepted a slight nod of appreciation from her before turning his attention back to the dramatic procession.

Lucy looked flushed and lovely, as always. Her elaborate gown might have outshone a less comely young woman, but with her shiny blond hair, bright blue eyes and dazzling smile, she was an unquestioned beauty. And her obvious happiness glowed from within her.

The march to the front of the church was slightly awkward. Her father, a hardworking and capable cobbler, walked beside her. He had a noticeable limp and a thin, wan body bent and twisted by arthritis.

Rome could remember the girl when she was all unkempt pigtails and toothless grin, charging up to his wagon to beg for chunks of ice. It was so strange that she was to be a married woman now, and he was still waiting for the right woman to come along.

Rome hardly had the time to absorb this completely before the congregation was seated and the ceremony commenced.

The preacher, a bit too loud and overenthusiastic, conducted the service with as much solemnity and reverence as he could manage.

Rome did not frequent weddings. In fact, he could not recall the last he had attended. He wondered now why he had not. With the fine music and the sentimental drama of the events, it was, in its way, more entertaining than a traveling vaudeville production.

Of course, marriage itself was a very serious concern. At least it had always seemed so to him. Rome was not opposed to holy wedlock on any level. He thought it to be a very good thing—for Gussie and Amos and Lucy and her beau.

For a man like himself, well, it was hard to even imagine Rome Akers in the position of groom. He accepted the inevitability of marriage. Eventually he would find a woman who didn't annoy him too much and he would settle down with her. He wanted children. He'd need someone to leave his legacy to.

"Who gives this woman in marriage to this man?"

The preacher's words were a bit louder than necessary, with excessive dramatic emphasis on inquisition, as if he truly had no idea who was standing up with the bride.

"I do," old, crippled Timmons replied proudly.

He looked assessingly at the young groom and then shared a quick, almost private glance with his daughter. Then he smiled at the two of them as if he had complete confidence and was wholly in agreement with the match. But in the evening glow of candles, Rome detected a gleam in the man's eyes that could only be evidence of tears.

Reverend Holiday began explaining the duties of marriage. Both the duty of two people to each other and the duty of the couple to God. The bride and groom exchanged brief, intimate glances. The depth of feeling in their eyes said more than anything spoken. They were so young, so attractive, so full of hope.

Rome shot a surreptitious look in Gussie's direction.

She was totally caught up in the solemnity of the ceremony. The expression upon her face was serene and . . . and beautiful. There was no other word to describe it.

Was she daydreaming of her own wedding? Was she imagining Amos, tall and handsome, at her side? Rome would be in the crowd, naturally. As a partner in her company, he would be expected to attend. He would see her looking so serene, so beautiful, so totally and deservingly fulfilled. He would envy her happiness.

When that last thought went through his mind, he was startled by it. What a very strange idea. He shook off the foolishness of it.

"Please join hands," Reverend Holiday said to the young couple.

With the help of the bridesmaid and the best man, the bride and groom both shed the glove upon their respective left hand.

The vows were spoken, his with some stumbling and stuttering, hers with a breathless certainty that was almost inaudible.

Reverend Holiday pronounced the couple man and wife. Theirs was a chaste, sweet kiss. A symbol of their love, not a demonstration of it. The room was filled with delighted smiles. There was some circumspect, muted applause. It was over.

But not for Rome and Gussie. The social triumph of the Timmons family was to be their coming-out party.

They rose to their feet. They received several nods of acknowledgment. The Penderghasts, just in front of them, actually spoke to Rome.

"Good to see you, Akers."

The fact that the man saw him regularly around town and once a week when he delivered ice to the house was notwithstanding.

They shook hands and exchanged pleasantries as if they had not conversed only hours previously.

Mrs. Penderghast was not as easily won over. She'd seen the couple holding hands and she was not likely to forget the shocking sight any time soon.

She did not seem, however, quite so reticent with Gussie. The old woman commented upon the flowers on the dais. Apparently the pretty arrangement was Gussie's.

With great formality, Rome took the arm of the woman at his side. He was a little edgy again and made a special effort to be as well mannered and refined as any man present.

They made their way up the aisle toward the doorway. There was a crush of people and a lot of curious looks in their direction. Rome had known that they would be the subject of great speculation. He had not realized how conspicuous he was going to feel.

Madge Simpson sidled up next to them, her husband in tow.

"I swear, Gussie, that is exactly your color," she said. "It does wonders for your complexion."

The words were spoken to Miss Gussie, but the woman's attention was focused completely upon Rome. It was a test, he realized.

"You are right, of course," he told the woman. "A lovely woman always, Miss Gussie looks especially so tonight." He leaned closer to Mrs. Simpson, as if to share a secret confidence. "But, ma'am, I would warn you of the dangers of swearing in church."

The woman giggled as delightedly as a girl.

She took his other arm and, with some difficulty, they walked four abreast through the vestibule. Madge pointed out some pale, hothouse roses on a table. He remembered the comment from Mrs. Penderghast about the flowers that Gussie had brought.

"I know nothing of flowers, Mrs. Simpson," he

admitted with exaggerated gravity. "These are very fine, I'm sure. But they don't begin to compare with the magnificent, brightly colored ones I saw in the church."

He could see immediately that he'd said the right thing. Madge Simpson was won over. No matter what others might say, she was on his side.

The wedding repast was to be held in the supper room of the Granger Hotel, across the street from the church. After the meal, there was to be dancing. It was, by Cottonwood standards, a grand social event. A banquet table was laid out with a huge side of roasted beef and dishes featuring every root and vegetable currently in season. There were bride's loaves to be kept as remembrances for years. And a white-flour wedding cake baked in geranium leaves and decorated with bows and bells.

The supper room was not like anything that Rome had ever seen. Though he couldn't truly say how unique it was, because he rarely attended any community events. He would most likely have missed the evening had he not been lured into Miss Gussie's scheme.

It wasn't that he disliked the very ladylike social affairs of the town. But they just always seemed something more suited to pairs. A lone man on his own should, more rationally, find relaxation and enjoyment in a smoky barroom or billiard parlor.

He and Joe, Madge's husband, found a table for the ladies and saw them seated before going to the banquet table. Juggling two plates, Rome glanced back nervously several times in Gussie's direction. A number of people had stopped by the table to talk. Rome wanted to be there to help her if things turned sticky.

Having seen Amos at the church, he was fairly certain that the man was in attendance, although Rome had yet to spot him in the supper room. He had no idea how the land might lie there. It was certainly possible that Amos might make a scene. Rome intended to be by Gussie's side if he did.

The noise in the room was growing boisterous. It was a cheerful, happy mood and Rome found himself going along with it, despite the number of speculative glances directed his way.

He and Simpson eventually made it back to the table bearing heaping plates of food. The ladies had been joined by Constance and Perry Wilhelm. The women seemed to have some sort of private joke about the flowers and they laughed together so charmingly, it was a pleasure for a man to watch.

Joe and Rome mostly listened to the feminine chatter while Perry went to procure victuals for himself and his wife. When he returned to the table, a more gentlemanly conversation commenced over the prospects of the new bridegroom. And the need for Cottonwood to become a more diversified community, not solely dependent upon farming and ranching.

Rome was pleased when Gussie joined in the discussion. He knew from long experience that she had a very bright head upon her shoulders. He was glad that she did not see the necessity of pretending a frail feminine ignorance while in public.

After much celebrating, the bride and groom cut the fancy cake with much fanfare. Reverend Holiday, speaking very loudly and looking extremely disapproving, interrupted any ribald suggestions and offered a prayer for the couple, pointing out that *grace* for the meal had not been spoken.

As the band struck up a waltz and the newlyweds took to the dance floor, the guests, more subdued and sheepish, sampled the cake.

Rome took a bite and his eyes widened in surprise.

"Mmmmmm," he murmured in appreciation. It was the lightest, sweetest treat he had ever tasted.

"It's very good, isn't it?" Gussie said beside him.

"It is delicious," he agreed.

"Oh, the man likes sweets," Madge said, her tone teasing. "I think that means, Gussie, that you will have to learn to bake."

There were titters of laughter at that statement. Joe gave his wife a half-reproachful look and the humor faded to an uncomfortable silence.

"I did mean—" Madge began.

Perry interrupted her. "This is like ignoring a bull in the front parlor," he said. "I'm sure not going to act like I don't notice."

Rome said nothing. He had no idea what to say.

"So you two have decided to expand your business dealings to a more personal side," Perry continued finally.

Rome shot a quick glance in Gussie's direction. Two bright spots of color shone in her cheeks. He didn't know if she was embarrassed because she was with him, or simply from lying to her friends.

He cleared his throat. "Miss Gussie has graciously consented to walk out with me," Rome said. "It was a tremendous concession on her part and I would appreciate it if my *friends*"—he emphasized the word—"if my friends said nothing to point out the foolishness of her generosity."

It was, luckily, the right thing to say and just the right tone to say it. The mood at the table immediately turned more carefree and Perry even slapped him upon the back.

"Well, for myself," he announced, "I think it's a

long time coming and not a minute too soon. You two have always seemed a likely pair to me."

The incredulity of that suggestion was so much that Rome's jaw dropped open in shock and he had to quickly cover his action with a faked cough in an embroidered linen napkin.

Rome was completely at a loss as to what to do next. He turned to the woman at his side.

"Would you care to dance, Miss Gussie?" he asked her.

She seemed surprised. "Oh, I . . . I don't dance very much, Mr. Akers," she admitted.

"Me neither, but surely we can manage a one-step," he said.

She rose to her feet and Rome escorted her onto the dance floor. Every eye in the building was on them.

He grasped her right palm in his own and placed his left hand against her waist. The tempo was upbeat and the required step simple. Despite both their claims of ineptitude, it was a special bonus that the two turned out to be quite compatible on the dance floor. Neither was a particularly skilled partner, but they were so well matched that they executed their simple steps in perfect unison.

They rocked along the edges of the polished oak floor. He made a deliberate attempt to keep them in full view of everyone in the supper room.

"Have you seen *him*?" Rome asked her quietly as he leaned toward her in a gesture that would undoubtedly be construed as suggestively familiar.

She shook her head. "Perhaps he didn't come," she said.

"I saw him at the church."

"Me too. And he undoubtedly saw us," she pointed out. "So maybe he chose not to come."

Rome nodded, actually feeling sorry for the man. The sight of them together probably felt like he'd taken a punch to the gut. But it was the fellow's own fault. And Rome salved his conscience with the knowledge that it would all turn out for the best for each of them.

"So while your future bridegroom is out nursing his broken heart," Rome said with a determined smile and a deliberately cheerful tone, "we are free to simply enjoy ourselves."

"Yes," she answered. "Yes, I suppose we are."

"I am bored," Pansy Richardson said aloud.

She sat alone in her parlor, perfectly groomed and gowned for dinner. It was easy, she believed, when a woman lived alone and rarely saw a soul, to fall into careless appearance and sloth. She had no intention of allowing such a fate to visit her. She made efforts to be presentable, though she rarely saw a soul. And she kept busy, though there was not really so much to do.

Tonight she had sufficient leisure to read or listen to the graphaphone or embroider pillowcases. Of course, she had already read every book in her husband's library. She had played all the music cylinders until they were scratchy and she had enough decoratively stitched pillowcases for every sleepy head in Cottonwood.

So she was looking at the Seven Wonders of the World through the stereoscope. She gazed at dusty Sphinx in a landscape of sand, three pointed pyramids in the distances. She sighed. She, of course, had seen all these pictures many times before.

She should go to visit these places in person, she thought. A woman should see Paris. She should stand for herself in the Coliseum. She should view the Taj Mahal at sunset.

Pansy was restless tonight. Restless and lonely. A bad combination for a woman under the best of circumstances. And her circumstances here in Cottonwood were far from ideal.

"I should go," she announced.

She had long since taken up the habit of talking to herself. She decided that a person living a life of enforced solitude should talk to herself, if only to fulfill the need to hear a human voice.

Indeed, she should go. There was no reason not to. She had the time and the money. There was nothing for her here in Cottonwood, Texas. Nothing but the misery of loneliness and the shame of being an outcast.

"I wouldn't give them the satisfaction of my leaving," she stated and determinedly concentrated upon the image in the viewer.

She and Grover had talked of traveling. They had joked and dreamed about wandering through Europe together. Now she knew that without him by her side, she would never see it. It was all right. She didn't really care so much. She would content her restlessness by gazing at faraway places through the lens of the stereoscope.

Usually the pictures held her interest, but tonight nothing would.

It wasn't because Rome was not there. Rome was rarely with her. He was her lover. Her only lover. The only man in her life, despite what her former friends and present neighbors might suggest. But they were so discreet about their affair, it made their meetings infrequent. Perhaps once a week, occasionally twice, he would sneak down the alley and into her back door after dark. It was always risky, because her neighbors were always watching. She was glad when he came, but rarely disappointed when he did not.

Tonight, however, was different. Tonight he was with another woman. He was smiling and flirting and offering his arm to another woman. That bothered her. It bothered her more than she cared to admit.

Of course, she understood that it wasn't real. He'd explained that. As always, he tried to be completely honest with her.

"She just wants to make the fellow jealous," he'd said as he gazed at her across the kitchen table. Her bare foot was in his lap and he was rubbing her instep with deep, strong strokes.

"She wants to make him jealous, so she got you to do it."

He was ill at ease. Pansy knew he didn't much like having to explain himself to her or to anyone. But he was the kind of man who felt duty-bound to do it.

"It's . . . well, it's a business arrangement," he assured her. "It's just a job that she's hired me to do."

"And she's paying you with a partnership in the business?" Pansy was incredulous. "It would have been a lot cheaper if she'd just cast eyes at some stranger and let nature do the rest."

He shook his head with certainty.

"Miss Gussie is not the type of woman to lead some other man on like that. Though I doubt she would even know how to go about it if she did. Giving some other fellow false hope, well, it's dishonest. And Miss Gussie is never dishonest."

Pansy eyed him skeptically. "Well, I don't see anything all that honest in pretending interest in one man to make another one jealous."

But, of course, she had understood. She'd understood both of them. She could almost feel the sting of

Miss Gussie's rejection. And she certainly knew how hard Rome had worked and how long he had dreamed of buying into the ice company.

So she let him do what he'd already decided that he would, and he kissed her toes and ran his tongue along the sole of her foot to say thank you.

She understood, all right. And she didn't mind spending the evening alone. But somehow the combination of the two was unsettling.

"I think your Miss Gussie is barking up the wrong tree," she'd told Rome. "I don't think Amos Dewey can be run to ground."

"What are you talking about?"

Pansy sighed. "That man is not one whit closer to being ready for a new woman in his life than he was the day he put Bess in the grave."

Rome considered her words thoughtfully.

"Not everyone can just get up the next day and start all over again."

From anyone else, such a statement would have been a slap in the face. She knew that Rome had not meant it to be as condemning as it sounded. But the shoe fit, and the whole town intended to see that Pansy wore it.

She set the stereoscope aside and got to her feet. Lamp in hand, she wandered out into the hallway. She considered going upstairs to bed, but it was far too early and she would never sleep. Pansy walked toward the back of the house, stepping into the dining room with its long, majestic mahogany table. Dinner had not been served in the room since her husband's funeral.

She held the light up to near eye level and gazed at the portrait of her husband that hung upon the wall. It was a flattering likeness done the year before his death. The artist had made the man almost handsome. Grover had not been so in life. But what was not captured upon the canvas was the spirit of the man. The lively twinkle that enlivened his eyes as he made some dry, witty comment that only the two of them understood well enough to laugh at.

Many people thought that he'd chosen Pansy because she was young and pretty. And that she'd married him for money and security. Those people would never understand how important it was to find someone in life with whom to share the inside jokes.

Her heart began to ache and she turned from the portrait abruptly.

She walked through the narrow serving door into the kitchen. She wandered about the room for several minutes before breaking off a hunk of cheese and setting it atop a piece of dry, day-old bread. She carried her small meal out the back door. Aimlessly she walked through her yard, eating and thinking. She stopped and gazed up into the darkness of the Texas night. There were a million stars in the sky. Tiny dots of fire in a cool night sky. She just looked. She just wondered.

Was her sweet husband up there a part of the heavens? Or was he just a rotted corpse six feet underground? She wanted to believe the former, but was tortured with the image of the latter.

She had been so cold, so empty inside. She had needed warmth. She'd needed a man's arms around her. She'd not chosen wisely for the job. Judge Barclay had been her husband's best friend. He had been bowed down with grief himself, she had thought. She had turned to him in a moment of weakness. That moment had cost Pansy her reputation.

Perhaps she should have picked Amos Dewey, she mused to herself and snorted in derision. She would certainly have been in no danger of losing her virtue to an unscrupulous man.

Amos was not a man at all these days. Gussie Mudd might not understand that. But Pansy knew that for a fact.

She'd had trouble with a bad tooth last winter and had let him examine her, to see if it should come out. He had, of necessity, looked down her throat and touched her neck, run his fingers along the sensitive flesh below her ear.

He was handsome, male, and he was close. Pansy could not have been expected to be unmoved. She had wanted him. She had wanted his hands to drift down along her throat to her collarbone, his fingers to find the neckline of her bodice and slide beneath it. She had wanted him to cup her breast in his palm, to tease the turgid nipple between his thumb and forefinger. She had wanted . . . she had wanted so much. But she had opened her eyes and saw him above her. Cool and distant. Completely unmoved. Clearly, he had felt nothing.

Pansy had become very knowledgeable about men in the past few years. She knew when a casual brush against her shoulder was dripping with unfulfilled lust. And she knew that a near-intimate encounter could be purely professional. When Amos touched her, it had not been with the careful courtesy of a man doing his job. It had been without any awareness of her as a female.

Pansy lowered her eyes to the world around her once more and shook her head. She and Amos Dewey. They had a lot in common. They had both married for life and lost their spouses far too soon. Pansy's husband was struck down as if like a bolt from the blue. Amos's wife had suffered a long, protracted illness.

But death, no matter how inevitable or unexpected, is always a surprise.

Their tragic losses were so similar. However, their reactions to that fate could not have been more different.

For Dewey, it was as if he had died as well. He allowed his heart to be buried in his wife's coffin and he walked the world with no feelings but hunger, thirst and a terrible tiredness.

Pansy would have none of that. Death had robbed her of her husband, her hope, her dreams. She would not allow it to rob her of her spirit as well. If that made her a harlot and a disgrace to the people of Cottonwood, then so be it. She far preferred living in a scandal than in a sarcophagus.

Amos Dewey, of course, was lauded for his lifeless living. He was a tragic figure whom all admired. Like the fine stallion who had lost his will to run, the husbandman had given up on his bloodline and cut the source of his future to make him more manageable today.

Emotional gelding was what it was. It was a powerful obstacle to be overcome. She didn't envy Gussie Mudd the task.

But she *did* envy Gussie Mudd tonight. She envied Gussie walking with Rome and talking with Rome and being seen with him in public. Something that she would never be able to do.

Since their affair began almost a year ago, her handsome iceman had kept himself totally to her. He didn't even see other women socially. And, of course, he'd asked Pansy to wed him.

Not the most traditional of marriage proposals, she said to herself.

They lay naked in each other's arms on a warm summer night, content and satisfied.

"We could be good together, Pansy," he said. "Marriage to me would restore your reputation. They could still talk, but they wouldn't be able to cut you or treat you with such disdain."

The loss of her good name was a paltry thing when compared to the loss of her mate. But she didn't try to explain that to Rome.

"I'm not the most eligible fellow in town," he continued awkwardly. "But I work hard and I would treat you well."

Pansy had looked over at him. He had a nice face, handsome in its own way, and such strength in his arms and shoulders the sight could make a woman's mouth water.

"Are you in love with me, Rome?" she asked him.

She saw the truth in his face immediately; still he hesitated in his words.

"I don't think I'm the kind of man who falls in love," he told her quietly. "But I would try, if it is what you want."

She rolled in his arms and kissed him then. It was not a sultry meeting of mouths born of hot passion, intent upon enticement, but an honest gesture of genuine affection.

"I have already loved and been loved," she said. "Grover Richardson adored me." She smiled as she added with a teasing lilt, "It was the quality I liked best about him."

Rome's eyes showed real sympathy. Since her fall from grace, many in town had rewritten her personal history to suit her unsavory end. They forgot how romantic her wedding had been and how content and devoted she had been to her husband. Now she was painted as a crass adventuress who had married for money.

Rome, however, understood the truth.

"I can never be him," he acknowledged. "But I would be with you and protect you and try to make you happy."

She had laughed without humor. "This is about as happy as I get, sir. But you, you deserve a woman who loves you. And one that you love so much you just ache from the burden of it."

Pansy swallowed the last of her little snack and dusted her hands together to whisk away any leftover crumbs.

"Yes, that is truly what you deserve," she said aloud.

A sound next door caught her attention. She turned to see the Pearsalls coming up the walkway in front of their house. Most likely they were returning from the wedding party downtown. They had an unimpeded view of Pansy standing in her backyard talking to herself. And if she had heard them, they surely had heard her.

Vera Pearsall, a former friendly neighbor, actively detested her. Probably because Vera's husband spent every free moment at home watching Pansy's house, hoping for a glimpse of the wicked widow. The townspeople had learned that Vera could be counted upon to report every whisper and movement that occurred at the Richardson house.

Pansy almost sighed aloud.

On one of the most boring evenings of her remembrance, she had still managed to do something to keep her solitary life and wild reputation in the forefront of Cottonwood's community gossip.

5

THEY WERE LAUGHING TOGETHER AS THEY MADE THEIR way down the street. The evening had started out nervously and uncertainly. But they had danced and giggled and been surrounded by friends. It was a thoroughly pleasant way to spend an evening.

Gussie had never realized that Rome could be so utterly charming. There had been, of course, several uncomfortable moments. But for the most part it had simply been fun. In fact, it had been one of the most pleasant social events she'd been to in quite some time. That was a delightful surprise. But she couldn't help wishing that it had been Amos at her side.

Rome sensed her disappointment.

"It was too bad that Amos left so quickly after the ceremony," he said.

Gussie nodded agreement.

"But I'm sure he saw us," she said.

Rome chuckled. "Of course he did. Why else would he have taken off so quickly?"

That was undoubtedly true, she thought.

"It's too bad that he didn't stay around to see how well we dance together," Rome said.

Gussie smiled. "He would have been surprised. We've danced together many times and he knows how left-footed I am."

"Well, I thought you were wonderful," Rome told her. "And on such things I always rely on my own opinion."

She was pleased with the compliment. More pleased than perhaps she should have been. But kind words of praise were always welcome, and with Amos they were infrequent. It wasn't that he was not as polite or as gracious. His manners were considerably more elegant than those of Rome Akers. Amos just had a lot of things on his mind, Gussie assured herself. He would say nice things to her if he thought of them. And perhaps after tonight, she would be in his thoughts a good deal more often.

They reached Gussie's house. Her front gate was stubborn, the stiff and rusty bar fastener difficult to manage in the darkness. But before she had a chance to suggest that he allow her to open it, Rome reached over and easily unlatched it from the inside.

"Oh, you did that so effortlessly," she said. "Amos always has trouble with it."

"The gate?" Rome shrugged. "It's just temperamental. I've been coming and going out of it for years. Guess I'm pretty familiar."

"Yes, I suppose so."

He held it open for her as she passed by him and down the front walk. Rome followed.

She reached the steps and then turned toward him.

"Well, I certainly hope our efforts worked tonight," she said.

He was standing a few feet from her, hands in his pockets.

"I hope so too, Miss Gussie," he said. "I hope the guy doesn't sleep all night and is here before breakfast with a proposal on his lips."

She laughed lightly.

"Is that what men do?" she asked. "Have a long, sleepless night and then turn up in the morning with the question on their lips?"

In the silvery moonlight she could see him respond with a shrug.

"It's what I would do if my woman were out with another man," he said.

He used the term *my woman* with a certain emphasis that was unexpected and Gussie wondered briefly what it would be like to be Rome Akers's woman. Had anyone ever been that to him? It was strange that she had known him so well, known him so long, and just now realized how little she really knew about him.

Instinctively, she understood it was better that way.

"So," she said, "on the off chance that tonight's performance was not enough to drive him to bended knee, what should we do next?"

Thoughtful, Rome seated himself on the porch steps. Though there were chairs only a few feet away, Gussie followed his example. Or she did so to a point. Rome was sprawled upon the steps, one foot high, one low, his elbows behind him resting upon the porch. She sat more circumspectly, back straight, ankles together and her hands clasped at her knees.

"I don't think there is much point in my coming to call on you every evening," Rome said. "I'll be sitting on your porch every afternoon to go over the books with you as usual. I'm sure the gossips will be able to come up with a good deal of speculation over that."

"Oh, my goodness," Gussie said. "I'm sure they will."

"Don't let it concern you," Rome replied quickly. "We'll be in plain view of anyone passing on the street. There is absolutely no chance that your reputation will be sullied or that people will begin to talk about you in any uncommon fashion."

"No, of course not."

"But everyone will know that we are together," he continued. "And Amos will have to wonder if all our discussions are . . . purely business."

He said the latter in a deep-voiced whisper and with a dark, dramatic inflection that made Gussie giggle. Across the darkness she could see his teeth gleaming in a broad smile.

"You should be ashamed," she teased.

"I am," he assured her facetiously. "I guess I'd better be careful. This thing between a man and his woman can be as volatile as dynamite. I want him worried enough that it prompts him to ask for your hand, not jealous enough to shoot me dead in a rage."

Gussie laughed out loud at that. The idea of mild-mannered Amos Dewey angry enough to threaten violence was completely absurd.

"I think you will be safe," she said. "But I do hope that the provisions in your will are all up-to-date."

He seemed to warm to her teasing and it pleased her. They had known each other and worked together for a very long time. But they had never been this easy and friendly together. Obviously the scheme was going to create some unanticipated changes in her world. This one, she thought, was perhaps nice and probably due.

Rome had always worked *for* her. Although she trusted his judgment and relied upon his opinion, decisions about the business were ultimately up to her.

Gussie told him what she wanted done and Rome did it. It was important to maintain that type of distance between employee and employer. But once Amos had been brought to the point, Rome was to be her partner. The decisions would be jointly made. So a more equal and amiable footing would be wholly appropriate.

"I think collaborating together on this plan is a fine thing," she told him. "We are getting to know each other better and learning to come up with mutual decisions."

Rome nodded. "I think we will manage very well together, Miss Gussie," he said. "And, of course, you will still have two-thirds of the votes in your own hand."

Gussie was momentarily surprised at his words.

"I meant for you to be an equal partner, Rome. I said nothing about giving you only a third."

It was his turn to look surprised.

"Of course, I understood that you meant to make me an equal," he said. "But I assumed you intended to give the same to your husband. Do you plan on dropping out of the business and handing it over to Amos completely?"

"Why, no, of course not," she answered. "Amos has his own business. I . . . I suppose I never thought . . . yes, certainly I would take him on as a partner as well."

In truth, she had never really considered what interest Amos might have in her business. Many men did not approve of women having their own commercial concerns. Usually those gentlemen were vocal about their opinions. Amos had never spoken of it, so perhaps she had assumed that he had no interest. But husbands always had some sort of say about things.

"Maybe Amos will be more amenable to distillation," Rome suggested.

Gussie glanced at him in surprise.

Rome chuckled lightly. "Perhaps I could spark his interest in a new distiller and the two of us could out-vote you on the subject."

He was joking, but Gussie knew that what he'd said was possible. Taking on a partner, either in business or in wedlock, meant giving up full control of the company. She had known that intellectually, but she had yet to engage her heart in the reality of it.

"I am not completely opposed to a new distiller," she told Rome, not being completely honest with him. "I just wonder about the cost versus the benefit. A new machine will be expensive. And the one that we use now is still working."

"I was teasing you," Rome said. "Let's not talk business tonight." He sat up and opened his arms wide as if embracing the sky. "On a beautiful night like tonight, with the moon high and a gentle breeze in the air, the last thing we should talk about is water distillation."

His manner was so flirty and funny, Gussie couldn't help but throw off her reserve and laugh with the man.

"I've never seen you behave like this," she told him.

He feigned a downtrodden tone. "That's because you always see me working," he said. "And my boss is such a harsh taskmaster."

"Is that what you tell folks in town about me?" she asked, pretending complaint.

"I don't have to tell them," Rome answered. "I'm sure they all observe that you are nearly working this poor man to death."

"You look as strong and healthy as any man in town to me," she remarked.

He grinned. "But as anyone in this town will be able

to tell you by morning, Miss Gussie Mudd looks at Rome Akers through eyes gone glazed with sweet romance."

Gussie's jaw dropped and she was tempted to kick him.

"Indeed they will not, sir," she insisted. "They'll all be saying how you are making a fool of yourself over me."

He chuckled. "All right. Why don't we just agree that my friends will be saying the former and your friends the latter."

Gussie shook her head with resignation. "That will probably be the closest to the truth," she conceded.

"And whatever they say, we're going to be grateful," he added. "The more folks are talking, the sooner Amos will come to his senses and be over here asking the question."

Gussie nodded. That was exactly what she wanted. And the sooner the better.

"What do you think our next move should be?" she asked him.

"What's the next opportunity for us to be in full view of our friends and neighbors?"

Gussie was thoughtful for a moment.

"Well, there is church on Sunday morning," she said.

Rome made an unpleasant face.

"Did you hear what the preacher said to me tonight?" he asked. "I stick out like a sore thumb in that sanctuary. Besides, I'd feel a little guilty about carrying on this deception during Sunday service. It would be kind of like lying in church."

Gussie could see his point. There was a certain amount of the unsavory about it.

"All right," she agreed. "What about Sunday afternoon? There's to be a concert in the park."

He rose to his feet in one smooth motion, turned to her and gave a jaunty salute.

"Would you do me the great honor, Miss Gussie, of allowing me to escort you to that concert?" he asked with marked formality.

Gussie delightedly went along with the game.

"I will await you here, sir, breathlessly and with my heart all aflutter."

"Until Sunday, then, my dear," he said.

She gave him a questioning glance. "Won't you be by tomorrow afternoon for your report?"

He shook his head. "Oh, no, your hardworking employee, Mr. Akers, will be by tomorrow. Your adoring Romeo will not be back to your porch until Sunday."

She smiled at him.

"Until Sunday, then, Romeo."

"Sunday, Miss Gussie," he replied.

He set his hat upon his head and headed down the front walk. He negotiated the gate easily. She listened to the retreat of his footsteps upon the macadamized street.

He began to whistle.

Gussie listened pleasantly for a moment and then realized that he was already at the end of the block and she was still smiling.

The Monday Morning Merchants Association met regularly on Friday afternoons in a back room of the Cottonwood National Bank. There were still those among the membership who could recall those first two or three years that the group had held their meetings just after breakfast on the first workday of the week. But the time had been changed for more than a decade now. They hadn't quite gotten around to changing the name.

That was all right with Rome. In fact, the group's inattention to detail was a quality that had afforded him the opportunity to be a part of it. According to the organization's bylaws, only owners of businesses within the city limits of Cottonwood were welcome to hold membership. Therefore, although he had been a faithful attender for several years, Rome was not, could not be, a member.

Initially he'd gone at Miss Gussie's behest. The organization's goals were civic improvements: better streets, modern waterworks, sanitary sewers. Laudable tasks that Miss Gussie was very interested in supporting. Unfortunately, local businessmen who attended Monday Morning Merchants desired an opportunity to socialize as well. That meant ribald talk, gruff manners and big, smoky cigars. None of those things were appropriate in the company of a lady. So Miss Gussie had chosen to no longer attend. She'd sent Rome in her stead.

At first he'd felt uncomfortable and a little intimidated as well. These were men who owned businesses. That was his bright and shiny dream. To own his own business, to do things as he thought best and have his fortune rise or fall based upon his own work, rather than upon the whims of someone else. That's what Rome wanted. It was his ambition and all that he was working for.

Of course, one thing he'd learned about the world of commerce was that luck played a big part in any endeavor. Luck had not shown any particular preference for him in the past. But now it seemed that things had finally turned his way. And so unexpectedly.

As Rome walked the five blocks between the ice

plant and the downtown meeting, he contemplated his stroke of good fortune and shook his head in disbelief.

If Amos Dewey had simply asked Miss Gussie to marry him, as any fool could see he rightly should, then he and Miss Gussie would be planning a wedding and Rome would still be scrimping and saving in the hope that sometime in years ahead, he'd be allowed to buy in as a partner. How quickly a man's whole future could change! And how fortuitous that it had.

As he reached the wide expanse of Broad Street, the heart of the Cottonwood business district, Rome's mind was much occupied upon that subject. Since their debut at Lucy Timmons's wedding, he and Miss Gussie had been the foremost subject for discussion in town. He'd gotten more than his share of curious, speculative glances. But he refused to take notice. That was what was needed, for folks to be wondering, to be talking. And they would be doing so for some time.

Even after Miss Gussie married Dewey, folks would be curious. Especially when it became known that Rome had been given a partnership. People would be very surprised at that. He wondered what she planned to tell Amos about it. Did she intend ultimately to confess all? Probably so, he decided. Married couples should not keep secrets. He supposed that some did, but were he ever to marry, he'd expect both to speak truth and to hear it.

Broad Street was busy for a Friday afternoon. It seemed almost crowded. More often than not, it calmed considerably as if in anticipation of Saturday, when the town swelled to twice its usual population. Farmers and their families from every direction came to Cottonwood to sell eggs and butter, buy needed provisions and have a bit of fun. But today it was not filled with near strangers, just crowded with folks he knew. Rome almost ran smack into a fellow who was obviously headed in the same direction. It was only after the close call that the two glanced at each other.

"Good afternoon," the other man said rather formally, speaking first.

"A-Amos," Rome answered, stuttering a little. He had known, of course, that a confrontation with Miss Gussie's future husband was inevitable. He just hadn't imagined that it would be so unexpected, let alone on a public street.

The two stood together awkwardly for a long moment.

"I suppose you're headed to Monday Merchants," Rome said finally.

Amos nodded. "Yes, although with all the business on the street this afternoon, I hated to close the shop."

Rome agreed.

He glanced around and saw more than one interested gaze focused in their direction.

"Shall we walk?"

Amos had made the suggestion, but it was a good one. Side by side, they continued through the crowd and toward the bank.

Rome was at cross-purposes. He couldn't help but feel a strong sense of guilt for deceiving this man and manipulating him with a broken heart. Then again, Amos Dewey had called on Miss Gussie for three long years. She had every right to expect a declaration of some sort. It was not at all fair of the man to string her along indefinitely.

And Rome intended to tell him exactly that if he said anything even suggesting that Rome had gone behind his back or stolen his woman.

Amos didn't say anything at all. They walked along

the street to the bank in silence. Amos got to the door first and held it open so that Rome could pass in.

The Cottonwood National Bank was new, gleaming and palace-like in its architecture. It sported shiny white marble floors, huge Greek revival columns and an elegant chandelier hanging from the ceiling. The chandelier had come all the way from New England via the port of Houston. It utilized both long-burning candles and the new electric light bulbs, which were brilliant and modern, if consistently unreliable.

The two nodded informal greetings to those they passed.

Behind the bars of the teller's window, Mr. Viceroy Ditham observed them warily, as if he expected them to break into fisticuffs at any moment.

Rather than that, the two made their way up the elegant stairway to the second-floor meeting room.

"The weather's been good so far this spring," Amos noted.

"The old-timers would say it's still not too late for a freeze," Rome answered. "Though that is very unlikely."

They both attempted, with limited success, to make inconsequential conversation on neutral topics. It was a great relief for each man when he arrived at the meeting room.

The place was already noisy and smoke-filled, but there was a momentary surprised hush as they entered the room together. They quickly parted company.

Somebody handed Rome a cigar. He wasn't much for smoking, but he stuck it in the corner of his mouth and lit it up anyway. Without any mutually understood agreement, he and Amos kept to opposite ends of the room. There were discussions occurring all around him and he tried to keep up a semblance of listening.

He had fully expected Amos to be at this meeting. But he certainly had not imagined to feel so ill at ease. He was doing the fellow a favor, he reminded himself. Without this scheme and the temporary pain it was undoubtedly causing, Amos Dewey was going to miss out on a fine woman like Miss Gussie. It wasn't right to let that happen when a few well-placed lies could prevent it.

Finally the meeting was called to order and the gentlemen merchants took their seats. Huntley Boston was presiding. He was generally known in town as "Mrs. Boston's boy," though he would never see forty again. Huntley was an extremely smart fellow and could figure huge math queries in his head. But he spent so much time thinking his own thoughts that he barely understood what was happening around him. The Monday Merchants was in danger of splintering into several petty rivalries. Huntley not only didn't do anything to stop it, he didn't even seem to be aware that it was happening.

There was the inevitable discussion about mail-order madness.

"People can order whatever they want," Joe Simpson complained. "And it simply arrives on the train with their name on it. They don't need general merchandise anymore."

"The only good use for the Sears, Roebuck catalog," shy Mr. Everhard, the tailor, proclaimed, "is the privy."

Beyond the fear of mail-order madness was the discussion of streets and sewers. The organization was building both as quickly as it could afford them. Unfortunately, that was at a snail's pace. Everybody in town wanted his street to be next, including the gentlemen in attendance.

Macadamization, constructing a road by cementing

small stones together, was the most popular and efficient road-building technology. The merchants association was purchasing cement and combining it with local rock to make dependable, mudless streets all across town.

The proposed Sanitary Sewer Project was a little less successfully managed. Huntley opened up the floor for debate, then apparently got distracted by the treasurer's numbers report and allowed wrangling to go unabated.

The merchants association was laying sewer lines all over the city that were to be connected to a four-pool lagoon system just outside the town. The four-pool lagoon system was the most modern of solid-waste disposal systems. Raw sewage was pumped into one pool and settled. The top ran off into another pool. And then another. By the fourth pool, the one-time sewage was now water clean enough to be released into the river.

The Monday Merchants had invested heavily in the project, hoping to tie every business and residence in town onto the lines. Ditchdigging and pipe laying were everywhere. But, so far not one scoop of dirt for the lagoon system had been excavated.

"Has there been any word from the judge?" Mr. Potts, editor of the *Beacon*, asked.

Judge Barclay had been personally involved with the planning, the handling and the schedule. Under his guidance, the project had run much more smoothly. He had convinced Grover Richardson to donate the land for the four-pool lagoon system. And it seemed as if everything would simply fall into place.

But the judge had left town and Wade Pearsall was now in charge. The line construction continued in a mishmash fashion. Work on the lagoon had yet to start, and for some reason Pearsall was not able to either express their concerns or get an answer from the judge. It was as if they could not discover what was holding up progress.

The mayor, George Honey, was at the meeting, looking as pompous and dignified as a fat fellow barely five feet tall could manage. He suggested that the Monday Merchants turn over the money they had raised for the project and allow the elected officials of the town to take on the oversight of the construction.

This was a very unlikely scenario at best. Wade Pearsall took the proposal as a personal affront and seemed ready to go to fisticuffs with Mayor Honey over the slight to his management abilities.

Rome was listening, but his heart was not truly in it this morning. The same arguments that were repeated meeting after meeting were being expressed once more.

What wasn't being said was what a slap in the face it would be to take the work out from under Pearsall's direction. It would be a public expression of no confidence and the gentlemen of the community were loath to do it, but in Rome's opinion, it simply had to be done.

As with the past several meetings, the discussion was tabled and everyone agreed to allow things to remain in limbo at least another week, hoping that some brilliant solution to the intractable problem would occur to someone.

The next subject up for discussion was equally contentious. The Founder's Day celebration had been an annual event in Cottonwood until the untimely death of Grover Richardson. The Richardsons were the town's first family and for many years the event was nothing more than a small social gathering in the rooms and lawns of the Richardson house.

It had slowly evolved into an all-day community picnic with games and food booths and entertainment. Much of the money for community improvements had been raised then, and Richardson had always matched that amount from his own funds. Since his demise, the planning and implementation of Founder's Day had simply been ignored.

This year, however, was the fiftieth anniversary of the founding of the town. Some kind of celebration marking that momentous occasion had to observed.

"We've been acting like we ain't really a town without Grover Richardson," Pete Davies declared, his tone accusing. "Well, I say we was a proud town then and we're just as proud now."

Casey McCade agreed. "I guess we quit doing the celebration out of respect for the dead. But it would be a better legacy if we kept it up and made it better."

Those sentiments were repeated in a dozen other ways.

"And the more money we make for capital improvements," Wade Pearsall chimed in, "the sooner everybody gets their street paved and their sewer dug."

Pearsall's words produced a groundswell of grumbling, but Huntley quickly reined in the situation before the discussion rebounded to improvement projects once more.

The first order of business was to come up with a date.

"That's easy," Joe Simpson answered. "We should do it on the Fourth of July."

The date momentarily startled Rome. That was the day Miss Gussie had planned for her wedding. Well, that couldn't be helped. She would simply have to pick another date. And truly, it didn't matter. Rome fully expected Amos Dewey to come around long before then.

"July fourth! That's little more than five weeks away," Matt Purdy complained.

"If we can't put this together in five weeks," Perry Wilhelm said, "then I very much doubt that we would be able to put it together at all."

There was a good deal of agreement with that statement.

Immediately Huntley began to press into service one likely gentleman after another. There was no shortage of jobs to be done.

Committees were appointed to build booths and organize games.

Pete Davies volunteered his wife to take charge of the food. It was common knowledge that the two were still estranged. It was not clear if the man was volunteering her to get back in her good graces or to retaliate against her. But she had a reputation for being very organized and capable, so Huntley cheerfully assigned her the task in absentia.

Matt Purdy volunteered his acreage down by the river.

"All my hay should be in by then," he said.

The location seemed a reasonable one. "Most of that ground is low land and prone to flooding," Purdy allowed. "But given the date is in the driest part of midsummer, I think it unlikely that high water would—ah—dampen the event."

The room collectively groaned at Purdy's humor. Despite that, the location, close to town and yet affording the cool shade of the river, was approved.

"What kind of entertainment are we going to have?" Clive Benson asked. "I'm sure the band will want to play, but shouldn't there be something more than that?"

Clive played the tuba in the Cottonwood Community Marching Band. The local volunteer musicians cheerfully paraded down Broad Street on any vaguely appropriate occasion and performed concerts in City Park all summer long.

"Perhaps the ladies of the community would be interested in providing entertainment," the mayor suggested.

"Good Lord, don't get them involved in that," old Penderghast complained, turning to his son for support. "They will do some long-winded elocution about those Greek fellows who wore skirts or make us listen to some fat woman singing in Italian."

The other men in the room chuckled in sympathy. Mrs. Penderghast's preferences for Hellenic myth and grand opera were well known.

"The women will surely come up with something better than that," Benson assured him. "Maybe something with a patriotic theme. We will be observing both the Founder's Day and the Fourth."

"We'll certainly have appropriate speeches," the mayor commented.

"Speeches ain't entertainment," Penderghast complained.

"Then the entertainment should be fireworks," Joe Simpson said with certainty.

"Fireworks!" the mayor agreed excitedly.

Nods all around the room concurred with Simpson's plan. A shower of fancy fireworks was exactly what would make the celebration special. Of course, fireworks were not something that you would expect the ladies to come up with. Fireworks were loud, messy, dangerous; they were clearly the province of men.

"Huntley," the mayor said, "we need a couple of volunteers."

The young banker was busy searching for something in his pockets and looked startled when his name was called.

"Volunteer? Oh, volunteers . . . for . . ."

"Fireworks," the mayor told him, clearly annoyed.

"Yes, of course, volunteers for the fireworks."

No one immediately raised his hand. Most of the men had already committed themselves to other jobs. Rome almost sighed aloud. With all the time that was necessary to devote to Miss Gussie's scheme, he really didn't want any more obligations to fulfill. He should do something, that was certain. Planning and purchasing the fireworks would not involve as much time and trouble as some of the other tasks. But it would curtail what leisure he had left. It required someone sober, deliberate and thoughtful. He was, by nature, a careful fellow. He would rather take the risks himself than see some less steady fellow attempting them. And he was interested in fireworks. It made sense that he should volunteer. So he did.

At the exact moment that he raised his hand, he saw another go up across the room. He stood staring in disbelief at Amos Dewey as Amos stared back at him.

"Oh, good, there's two right there," Huntley said. "Rome and Amos will take care of the fireworks for us."

6

It rained heavily on Saturday night with great bolts of lightning and rumbling thunder. Sunday afternoon was bright and clear, the day seeming to be washed and sparkling in the sunshine.

Gussie gazed in her mirror and was pleased. She felt very well turned out in her new light blue mercerized gingham. She hadn't really needed a new dress and she abhorred the practice some ladies fell into of buying things they did not need simply to have something new. But she was to be promenading in the park with Rome Akers. Every eye in town would be on her. And a woman with a new beau was expected to wear a new dress.

She had to admit it was a lovely dress. Perhaps the style was a bit youthful for a spinster of thirty-one years, but Miss Ima, Cottonwood's most celebrated dressmaker and seamstress, had clearly outdone herself. The sleeves were plain and the skirt had only one flounce. But the bodice was pleated in several dozen quarter-inch tucks which spectacularly enhanced the natural measure of Gussie's bosom. She was excessively corseted, having pulled in her waist to a width not easily bearable since before she was twenty. And she had complained that even standing still she was light-headed. But Miss Ima was right: her inability to get a good breath seemed a frivolous concern when one glimpsed the incredible improvement in her silhouette. She was definitely hourglass, jaw-dropping, male-stopping hourglass.

Gussie turned away from the mirror to get a glimpse of herself from the rear. She was very impressed with what she saw. The skirt was gathered high in the back to fall with great breadth over her wire bustle, making her backside appear stylishly enormous. In fact, she looked so good, she felt almost conspicuous.

The creak of the front gate intruded into her inner fashion debate and she glanced out the window to see Rome coming up the walk. He looked very dapper and handsome himself, she thought. It seemed that the two of them would actually make a rather attractive couple in the park. Which was, Gussie thought, amazing for two people so obviously unsuited to each other.

"Good afternoon," she called out to him.

He stopped in the path and gazed up at her. He was smiling and so very handsome.

"Good afternoon to you, ma'am," he called out.

He left the path and walked to the ground beneath her window, placing his hand on the white-painted rose trellis that was secured from the ground to the eaves at the side of her window. Red climbers grew there in great abundance. She loved being able to catch the scent on a warm spring morning.

"It's a lovely afternoon for a courting couple to take a promenade in the park," he said. "Are you ready?"

"Just let me get my hat," she told him, smiling as she left the window.

In front of the mirror once more, she pinned on her new straw-brimmed leghorn with silk lilies in pale blue. She gave herself one more long, assessing glance at the complete ensemble. Yes, indeed, Miss Ima had outdone herself.

Cheerfully, Gussie hurried down the stairs and then regretted her haste immediately. Due to her tight lacing and inability to breathe properly, she was light-headed before she reached the bottom step.

Again she mused on the intelligence of such tight cinching. Certainly fashion was not as important as health. And nothing that was this binding could be healthy. There was still time for her to change into something a good deal more comfortable.

She went to the door with the intention of telling Rome that in fact she was not ready and that he should wait on the porch.

He was standing there holding a perfect little rosebud that he had obviously pilfered from her trellis. Apparently hearing the sound of her footfalls, he turned his gaze in Gussie's direction.

His expression changed immediately. His eyes widened. His mouth opened.

"Damn!" was his comment.

"I beg your pardon!" Miss Gussie responded.

"I—I'm sorry," he managed to stutter. "I . . . you . . . I mean that dress . . ." He cleared his throat needlessly as if hoping that delay would give him an opportunity to regain his composure.

"Miss Gussie," he said finally, "I have never seen you looking lovelier."

She felt the warmth of a blush stain her cheeks.

"Oh," she said. "Why, thank you, Mr. Akers."

All thought of changing to a more comfortable costume completely fled her mind.

He continued to stare at her. Then, as if just noticing the flower in his hand, he recovered himself and stepped forward.

"Here," he said, thrusting the rose in her direction. "It's one of your own. I didn't think to bring you flowers, but if you wear this, everyone will think I did."

"Oh, yes, of course," she answered.

She took it from him and stepped back into the house. Her sewing basket was in the front parlor and she fetched a pin from it and attached the small red bud to her throat

Her hands were shaky and her heart was beating very rapidly, undoubtedly a further consequence of the tight lacing. She was almost breathless when she returned to his side.

"Very nice," he said, commenting upon the flower. "It brings nice color to your cheeks.

"Thank you," she said and gratefully took the arm that he offered.

He led her down the path, through the gate and into the street.

It was a beautiful afternoon for a band concert. The hot Texas sun was high in a sky of wispy white clouds and a gentle westerly breeze stirred the air.

"I've decided that working together with Amos on the Founder's Day fireworks can be a good thing," Rome said.

She looked up at him questioningly. "I thought you said it would be difficult to live a lie right in the man's face."

Rome nodded. "That part still won't be easy," he admitted. "But I'm thinking what an opportunity it will be to show him how totally unsuited I am to be your mate."

She felt a little tremor go through her.

"You are not *totally unsuited*," she insisted. "I wouldn't have asked you to help me with this scheme if I'd thought for a moment that it would reflect poorly on either of us."

"I'm not thinking to portray myself as a criminal or a bully," Rome told her. "I just thought I'd sort of show myself to be the kind of fellow that wouldn't really make a good husband."

"But I'm sure you would make a wonderful husband," she said. "You have such a thoughtful and generous nature and you're hardworking and dependable. Any woman would be lucky to have you."

He grinned at her. "Well, if I ever need a reference for my employer, I'll know where to come."

Gussie liked his teasing.

"I was just thinking that if what we're doing now doesn't work, that little push of seeing the worst in me might spur Amos to make his decision," Rome explained.

Gussie nodded. "You're probably right. Perhaps we should hold some serious back up plan like that in reserve. We don't know how difficult it may be to make him come around."

Rome patted her arm reassuringly.

"It's not going to be all that difficult," he assured her. "I'm thinking that just catching sight of you today in that dress might bring the man to his knees."

Gussie felt the color rise to her cheeks, but it was a very pleasing and pleasant fluster. His words washed over her, soothing her hurts and her loneliness. It was wonderful to walk beside him. Although with her inability to catch a good breath, she found the pace a little strenuous. At her request, they slowed to a very leisurely stroll.

"This is a good idea," Rome said.

"What?" she asked him.

"Lollygagging like this," he said. "Taking way too much time just to get down the street."

She considered explaining why she couldn't walk faster, but dismissed the idea entirely. She certainly couldn't confess to the man that her corset was laced too tight! Besides, it was fashionable, and there was just no explanation for fashion.

"It makes us look even more like a pair of love-birds," Rome insisted.

"Why do you think so?"

"A courting couple just don't get that much time alone," he pointed out. "They'd be sure to treasure the private moments together, even if they occurred on a public street."

Gussie looked up into the handsome man's eyes and wondered at the good fortune of any woman who would share private moments with him.

They arrived at the main square, where a significant-sized crowd had already gathered. The wide expanse of lawn and trees threaded through interlocking walk-ways, evidence of the thousands of happy, carefree feet that had trod here for generations. Cultivated beds of colorful flowers, hardy enough to withstand the worst of Texas summer, brightened the path in every direction. Near the center of the square was a large open-air gazebo heavily shaded by a couple of tower-ing oaks. Horns tooted and strings whined as the city band was tuning up for an afternoon concert.

The park also boasted a memorial to the War Dead of Both Sides and a small cannon said to be a relic of the Alamo. There was a precious little rose garden tucked away in the far east corner. Gussie had heard it to be a special secret hideaway for young lovers. She had no knowledge of that herself. No man, young or otherwise, had ever attempted to lead her off anywhere alone.

Being on Rome's arm made her feel conspicuous. It also made her feel strangely proud. That was rather silly. Why on earth should she feel any sort of pride just for being escorted through the park by a man who was her employee? Gussie raised her chin even higher and reminded herself how triumphant she would be when Amos Dewey walked at her side, and when her name was Mrs. Amos Dewey.

Feeling a little as if she had run all the way from her house, Gussie hoped that Rome would direct her to one of the dozens of gleaming white benches that made up the seating around the gazebo. Instead he correctly continued to promenade with her upon the busiest paths. The reason to be there was to be seen, and a lot more people would see them walking than merely sitting.

As they strolled along, Rome tipped his hat for every lady and spoke or nodded to every gentleman. No one stopped to talk, but everyone returned his greeting.

There were old folks with walking canes, and younger ones pushing baby carriages. Some were very finely dressed. As well as those whose Sunday best was looking a bit shabby.

Becky Timmons was walking out for the first time with Matt Purdy's son, Matthew. Neither seemed particularly pleased about it. Their stony faces seemed cheerful when compared to Pete and Loralene Davies, who looked more eager to break into fisticuffs than spend a pleasant afternoon together.

The beauty of the spring day was cheerful, uplifting. Gussie felt almost light-headed. Rome entertained her from time to time with little casual comments. He talked about the Monday Merchants, the upcoming Founder's Day; he even repeated the recent discussion on bricking up the well-worn park paths that they sauntered down as they dodged the occasional mud puddle. It was all very ordinary conversation. But when he spoke to her, Rome leaned his head close to hers as if they were engaged in a private, intimate discussion. It was effectively staged and Gussie was certain that anyone watching would believe he was whispering soft, sweet words in her ear.

The close proximity was exhilarating. His face was so close to her own that she could feel the words upon her temples. Her skin prickled with gooseflesh, but she thought it most likely another result of the laced-too-tight corset.

Gussie was certainly having some difficulty catching her breath and there was a certain giddiness that settled upon her.

When they met up with Joe and Madge Simpson, the other couple seemed delighted to see them.

"What a beautiful day for a concert," Madge said.

"And don't you look fine today, Miss Gussie," Joe said. "I don't think I've ever seen you so pretty."

Gussie blushed, again grateful for Miss Ima's new dress.

"Look at the color in her cheeks, Mr. Simpson," Madge said, ostensibly to her husband. "There is nothing quite like a handsome man to bring out the beauty in a woman's countenance."

This was said with a telling look toward Rome.

Gussie glanced in his direction and saw that he was blushing as well.

Perhaps it was his own embarrassment that caused Rome to quicken the pace as they parted company from their friends. They were hurrying along a bit too rapidly for Gussie's good health and she had just opened her mouth to call a halt when Rome squeezed her hand meaningfully.

She followed the direction of his gaze. Walking up the pathway toward them was none other than the purpose of their deception, Amos Dewey.

"Courage," Rome whispered. "And smile."

She felt the former in sufficient quantity and tried to do plenty of the latter. However, she was quite breathless and there was an unreal quality about the moment. Sparkly little stars glittered at the edge of her vision and the earth seemed a bit unsteady beneath her feet.

Amos looked especially handsome this morning, Gussie thought. His long, lean body was perfectly suited to the blue-striped cotton coat. And unlike most gentlemen of his age, the Panama hat was not needed to hide a receding hairline, so he doffed it completely as he stopped directly in front of them. His bow was courtly, formal, stiff.

"Good morning, Miss Gussie, Rome."

The man beside her returned the greeting. Gussie said nothing. She felt strangely disconnected from the moment. As if she were very far away and observing another woman with two handsome gentlemen.

The conversation between the two men seemed cordial, if somewhat reserved. Gussie knew that she should be paying full attention to what was being said, but somehow she couldn't quite focus upon it.

She looked over at Amos. Tall, dark, handsome Amos, the object of all her fondest hopes and dreams. He was the man she was determined to marry.

More stars veiled her vision and she turned to Rome, so familiar and dependable, beside her. He glanced in her direction. His brow furrowed.

"Miss Gussie?"

She heard her name on his lips as if from a far distance. Then the ground swept up and captured her close, warm and so very safe.

Rome had only an instant of time as he realized that she was fainting. But it was long enough for the flash of insight that said, *Let Amos catch her.* That made sense. They were trying to lure the man out of his complacency and what better way than to literally have a woman drop into your arms. It was the reason he was in on this charade. It was the smart thing to do. But as she began to crumple to the ground, instinct overrode the conscious mind and he reached out for her.

It was only when she was safe in his arms that he saw that Amos too had reached out to catch her. He had been an instant too late and Rome now held her braced against one knee, the other upon the ground.

"Is she all right?"

"She's fainted," Rome told him.

"Gussie?" Amos sounded incredulous. "She's not a swoony type of woman."

"Well, you tell me, then, what does it look like?" Rome asked overly patiently. "Do you think she's joking with us?"

Amos looked stunned.

"Go borrow some smelling salts," Rome said.

As the man hurried off, Rome wondered for a moment if Gussie was play-acting, trying to get Dewey's attention.

"Gussie," he whispered gently. "Miss Gussie, are you all right?"

She stirred a little, but didn't open her eyes.

Rome put one arm behind her knees and pressed her more closely against his chest and managed to rise to his feet. The woman was no delicate feather in his arms, but he was strongly muscled from the burdens of his job and carried her easily up the path toward the benches surrounding the gazebo.

If they had been trying to capture attention, they surely had it now. All other motion in the park had ceased and every eye in the place was focused upon them.

Rome stopped beside the first empty bench and lay her out upon it as gracefully as he could. He knelt beside her. She was stirring again. She opened her eyes briefly and looked at him, but it was obvious that she saw nothing and knew nothing.

An instant later, Amos hurried up, clutching a small brown bottle.

"It belongs to Mrs. Penderghast," he said.

Rome didn't care; he grabbed it out of the man's hand and pulled out the stopper, waving it momentarily under Gussie's nose. One good whiff of the aromatic and her eyes opened, she pushed the stopper away.

"Miss Gussie?" he asked. "Are you all right, Miss Gussie?"

Her answer came out in a whisper. He had to lean closely to hear.

"I can't breathe," she told him. "My laces, my laces are too tight."

Being a man of action and the kind of fellow who goes to the source of the problem, it was Rome's first instinct to try to help. He raised her up slightly, seeking the buttons at the back of her dress. One hand quickly released the top one.

He hesitated. It wasn't good sense, propriety or any other reasonable consideration that stayed his hand. It was a sudden, overwhelming, all-consuming aware-ness of Augusta Mudd, his employer, his fellow schemer, his business partner, as a woman, a desirable woman, a woman in his arms.

"Get out of my way," he heard over his shoulder.

He glanced up to find himself being surrounded by a gaggle of anxious, hurrying females.

"What's wrong with her?" Mrs. Penderghast asked.

"She's fainted dead away," Loralene Davies commented.

"Did you two gentlemen have words?" Anna Purdy's question sounded more like an accusation.

Suddenly Madge Simpson was beside him, obviously concerned, but looking calm and efficient.

"Gussie? Are you all right? What happened?"

"She said her laces are too tight," Rome whispered as discreetly as possible.

Madge's eyes widened, clearly scandalized by his words. It was not a thing that a gentleman should be aware of. But her hesitation was only momentary.

"Scat!" she said to him, as if he were a strange cat that had wandered unwelcome upon her back porch. "Both of you men, go tend to your own business. You're not needed here."

Rome felt a certain reluctance to leave, but realized that it was his presence that kept Miss Gussie from the opportunity to draw a good breath. He quickly got to his feet and stepped away. He saw Amos looking unsure and he went over to the man.

"We'll leave her to their care," he said, encouraging him to turn his back as they moved a decent distance away.

"What happened?" Amos asked, his voice full of genuine concern.

Rome looked at the man. He knew the answer as fully as if Miss Gussie had explained herself in great detail. She was trying to get Amos Dewey to come around. She was trying to get Amos Dewey to notice her. She was trying to get Amos Dewey to marry her.

The man's failure to do this was certainly some failing of his own, but Miss Gussie had put it, at least in part, to her lack of feminine charm. Rome remembered his first sight of her this afternoon. She was blushed and pretty and hourglass-curvy. He understood now the price she had paid to look that good for Amos Dewey. He was not about to allow the fellow to have a good laugh at her expense.

"I suppose it was seeing the two of us together," Rome lied. "She probably feared it might come to blows. This has all been too much for her."

Dewey's expression was so incredulous, Rome was tempted to plant him a facer. It was as if he thought fighting over Miss Gussie were beneath his dignity. Rome didn't know why that made him so angry. He wasn't a man to sink to that level. But at this moment, with the woman lying faint just a few yards away, he could have cheerfully pummeled the man.

Rome glanced around to see who was watching and what they might be saying. Everyone within sight was looking in their direction, with as much interest focused upon Rome and Amos as upon Miss Gussie. Even the band seemed to be looking instead of tuning up.

He was tempted to start yelling at the whole crowd to mind their own business, but fortunately, he recalled that getting attention was part of the plan. He hoped that sacrificing Miss Gussie's health was not.

"She's a fine woman," Amos said beside him.

Rome turned abruptly toward the man.

"Yes, she is," he answered, the tone of irritation still unmistakable in his voice. Miss Gussie should not have to plot and scheme and lace herself too tight to breathe just so that Amos Dewey could be persuaded to do what any fool could see was the smartest move to be made. The day she cast her eye in the barber's direction, the man should have got down on his knees and thanked his lucky stars. She was smart and hard-working, generous . . .

"She deserves a man who genuinely cares for her," Amos pointed out.

Rome couldn't have agreed more. His thoughts trailed off somewhat. She was his employer and as such, he'd often thought of her as difficult and stubborn. When had he changed his opinion of her? When had his part in this scheme changed from a mercenary one to the concern of a friend? He didn't know. But somehow it had. She did deserve a man who could really care for her. He was no longer completely convinced that man was Amos Dewey. And Dewey apparently didn't believe it was Rome.

"Miss Gussie should have someone who is devoted, faithful and besotted by her," Amos continued.

"And you think that I am not?" Rome asked the question made obvious by his tone.

The expression on Amos's face was judgmental and vaguely disapproving.

"I don't know if you care for her or not," he said. "You certainly came onto the scene as gentleman caller very quickly."

"Perhaps I was just waiting for you to step aside," Rome said.

The other man's eyes narrowed and his tone became clipped. "But you managed to hold off loneliness in the meantime."

It was more the way he said it than what was said that called out a warning to Rome.

Dewey's eyes were cold as steel. "Since my wife's passing, I often wander the darkness late at night. It is amazing what secrets a person can happen upon in a dark alleyway in the glow of moonlight."

A stillness settled upon Rome as the words were spoken. He was wary now, extremely wary. He had always known that his illicit affair with Pansy Richardson might be found out, might catch up with him. But now was not at all a good time. The people of Cottonwood would be scandalized by such behavior and Gussie would be forced to publicly shun him. The scheme would be completely ruined. Even the hope for him to ever become a partner in her business could be lost.

"I don't know what you mean," he lied admirably.

Behind them, only a few yards away, the ladies crowding around their fallen sister began to stir. The movement caught the men's attention and they turned in that direction. Rome saw that Miss Gussie was now sitting properly upon the bench. She looked more flushed and embarrassed than pale and drawn.

His impulse was to rush to her side. But he glanced over at Amos. Surely the man felt the same need to make sure she was all right. Maybe this was the moment that he would act upon it. Rome deliberately held himself back, waiting for the man to make a move, willing him to go to Miss Gussie's side.

The fellow did not portray even so much as the slightest inclination to do so. He caught Rome looking at him and momentarily seemed uncertain.

Rome knew he was staring the man down, but he simply couldn't seem to stop himself. The moment was drawn out nearly to infinity.

"I just . . ." Dewey hesitated. "I just want what is best for her. I'll do whatever is necessary to protect her."

It was a threat, plain and simple. Rome couldn't

interpret it as anything less. And he could make no reply. There was nothing to say.

Without another word, Amos nodded a good-bye and turned away.

Rome gazed after him, angry for a moment, and then, unwilling to neglect Miss Gussie another moment, he hurried to the woman's side.

From the little bench, she smiled up at him shyly.

"Feeling better?" he asked.

She nodded.

"It must have been this awful humidity," Madge Simpson fibbed gracefully. "It's worse than the summer heat for stealing a woman's breath."

"Yes, it is," Rome agreed affably.

He seated himself beside Gussie and quite naturally took her hand in his own. Her eyes still held that luminous, dazed quality as he gazed into them. He'd always thought her so strong, so self-reliant. He had never thought about her heart, her feelings. There was a vulnerability about her that he had never noticed before. Rome didn't want to hurt her. And he didn't want to see her hurt.

Quickly he glanced back in the direction of Amos Dewey's retreat. The man was no longer anywhere in sight. Rome felt bad. He wanted to apologize for Amos, to apologize on his behalf for not being the man he should be. Rome wanted to apologize for being the man by her side instead of the man she dreamed about.

"Are you all right?" he asked. He had meant to voice the question in quiet concern. But the words came out low and intimate. They were too close and they knew each other too well.

"I'm fine," she answered, though she sounded a little shaky.

He quickly rose to his feet, grateful to be able to put some distance between them.

"Shall we move closer to the gazebo?" he suggested. He wasn't sure why. Certainly they were after attention, but nobody could have missed her fainting spell, and even those who might have been looking the other way at the time had focused in on his discussion with Amos. Maybe they should move down to the front because they actually were the show!

Gussie walked with perfect steadiness on his arm. She had recovered her composure completely. Any lingering pallor was disguised by the bright brush of embarrassment in her cheeks.

The gown that had shown off her figure to such perfection was now slightly ill-fitted, evidence that within the closed circle of concerned matrons, someone had loosened her stays. Rome didn't like knowing that. It felt wrong somehow to be privy to such intimate information.

A lot of this whole scheme was beginning to feel wrong, he decided. Making Amos jealous was turning out to be downright dangerous. Not just to him, but to Pansy as well. He owed the woman at least discretion.

"What did you and Amos say to each other?" Miss Gussie asked him quietly as they seated themselves upon the front bench.

Rome hesitated only a moment.

"I think it's working," he said honestly. "I think the man definitely does not like the idea of the two of us together."

Miss Gussie smiled at him, so pleased, that he could not even worry about what the repercussions of this scheme might mean to him. He cared only about what they could be for her.

7

PANSY RICHARDSON STEPPED OUT OF HER BATH RELUC-
tantly. The water had already cooled and her skin was
pruney, but she was hesitant to give up the most pleasurable activity she had planned for the day.

Sundays were always unpleasantly long. When
Grover was alive she had risen early and excitedly.
Eager to wash and dress and wear her newest hat to
church; to sing and pray and be among friends. That
was what Sundays were all about. Not anymore. These
days she woke long before she wanted to and deliberately ignored the bells that called for her. A house of
worship was no longer a sanctuary for her.

She picked up a piece of thirsty cotton toweling and
began to dry herself. Her movements were slow, careful. There was absolutely no hurry. The only bright
spot on Sundays for her now was that Rome did not
have to work. Usually he managed to sneak down the
back alley and into her house. They would loll around,
in bed and out. Living the day as if it were their last
together. She liked that about him, that he understood
how temporary everything could be.

Rome wouldn't be making his way to her house today. He'd told her all about his bargain with Gussie Mudd and his mission to get her set back up with Amos Dewey. It was a waste of time, Pansy thought, though she hadn't voiced that opinion to Rome. Why discourage him when he was so hopeful? And perhaps if Miss Gussie saw how hard he'd tried, she would take pity upon him and give him the partnership anyway.

That was Pansy's hope. As far as she was concerned, there was absolutely no chance that Amos Dewey could be brought to his knees by Augusta Mudd.

Gussie was not a bad sort of person. Pansy actually liked her spirit and her drive. But her experience with men was extremely limited and she was ill-prepared for a challenge like poor Amos Dewey. Why else would she have chased the man unsuccessfully for so long?

Dry now, Pansy hung her damp towel upon the edge of the bathtub and put on her wrapper. The spring sunshine was bright outside. She considered sitting out on the second-floor porch and allowing those warm, comforting rays to smile down on her. But she decided against it. The last time she was caught outside in her wrapper had thoroughly scandalized the neighbors. Now they were all watching her, hoping she'd see her way to shock them again. Pansy wasn't about to give them that satisfaction. But neither was she willing to be a prisoner in her home. She had as much right to enjoy the sunshine as anyone else.

Drawing back her sleeve, she reached through the cold, soap-skimmed bathwater to pull out the drain plug. The houses on Brazos Avenue were not yet connected to the new sewer-pipe system being laid all over town. But Pansy wouldn't be inconvenienced if the sewer system was never completed. When her house was built, Grover Richardson had a covered pit dug in the far back corner of his lot to allow his home the convenience of modern plumbing. This was how he'd developed his interest in a public sewer system. And why he'd prodded Judge Barclay to lure the Monday Morning Merchants Association into investing in the project.

Lure.

The word was an appropriate one. Barclay was so open, so friendly, he could entice with words, draw you in before you realized you were even interested. That's what he'd done to the Monday Merchants. It was what he had done to Pansy as well.

She sighed. A wealthy and comfortable life was not necessarily a happy one.

Pansy went up the narrow steps from the basement bathroom to the kitchen and then to the stairway in the main hall. She would dress and go out, she decided.

Pansy Richardson could no longer avoid the truth about herself. Despite everything she did to please herself, she was not happy.

It was Sunday afternoon. Half the community, sated with a pleasant dinner and family togetherness, would be promenading through City Park. They would be laughing with friends, sharing time with spouses, tending children. Pansy had no children, no spouse, nor even a friend.

Of course she had Rome, but Rome was . . . Rome was . . . he was her lover, she supposed. Although that description was not all that finely accurate either.

He certainly made love to her. And in a generous,

giving way that was more friendship than romance, he was in love with her. But in her life he was more of a convenience than an object of affection. He fulfilled her desires. He was the bright, shining moment in her endlessly bleak landscape. He was a fine, loving, generous man. But she could offer him nothing in return. She had nothing of herself to offer.

Perhaps someone else could.

Rome Akers and Gussie Mudd. She allowed the names of the couple to drift through her thoughts slowly and methodically. They would undoubtedly spend the afternoon in the park. It was public, proper, and at least the place was familiar to both of them. Pansy considered the couple carefully. The ingenious match they'd come up with might in truth be very good for both. A marriage like that would hand Rome respectability on a silver platter. Forget the partnership—he'd have his own business and a certain standing in the community that only family connections could provide. It would create an immediate improvement of his lot in life, the kind that could otherwise take a generation.

And it could be good for Gussie as well. She would have a hardworking, devoted husband who could be extremely gentle and would be, Pansy was certain, absolutely faithful.

She smiled when she thought of that. Rome would be a much smarter match for her than Amos Dewey. And it would take more than the small bite of a green-eyed monster to bring him back to life.

Up the stairs and into her bedroom, Pansy retrieved her underclothing from the highboy chest and began to dress. Lawn drawers with a matching camisole were soft against her skin after much washing. Her corset, however, was not a pleasant companion. She laced it herself on a dress form that had not changed since her trousseau. She wrapped it around her and lay upon the bed, holding her breath to hook the front fastenings. Once the closures were secured, she lay there for a long moment accustoming herself to the tight cage and her diminished lung capacity.

Yes, that was what he deserved, Pansy reiterated in her mind as she slipped her arms into the sleeves of her bright green walking suit. She considered the love and devotion of a good woman. Rome deserved that. And she wondered if Gussie Mudd could be the woman to give it to him. It was possible, it was keenly possible, if the right things occurred at the right time. Pansy thought that perhaps she could help. No one could ever make things happen for someone else. But one could do much to aid in the timing of things that had the destiny to be.

She swept her hair up in a loose topknot and covered it with her wide-brimmed leghorn decorated with sweeping green and blue peacock feathers. The hat also sported a lip-length veil of dark green net. A veil should have spelled modesty for the wearer, but this particular one drew attention directly to her pretty pink mouth. People thought her to be the wicked widow. She did them a service by playing the part.

Attaching her beaded chatelaine bag to her belt, she headed downstairs, stopping briefly in front of the hall-tree mirror for one last check of her appearance. What she saw in the glass was a woman, still young, attractive and eminently presentable. If the good, churchgoing folks of Cottonwood found the sight of her abhorrent to their sensibilities, then let them look away. It was a beautiful Sunday afternoon and she intended to enjoy it.

The short walk up Brazos Avenue to Third Street

and then straight toward the town square invigorated her. Spring was indeed in the air, along with the scent of the dark purple laurel and yellow jasmine. The sun shone down upon her, warming her like a dear friend.

She needed to get out more, to see more. Of course, it was always a problem when she did. Women on their own would cross the street to keep from coming eye to eye with her. The men, on the other hand, were all eyes all over her. And if she chanced upon a couple, the wife would grab her husband by the sleeve as if she feared Pansy would try stealing the man away on a public street. As if she would want their paunchy, balding husbands!

Pansy could already hear the music as she approached the park. The town band made a valiant effort to belt out the strains that resembled "Beautiful Isle of Somewhere." They were amateurs, much in need of practice, but full of enthusiasm.

She avoided the park generally. And especially so when it was crowded with people as it was today. For all her own bluster and brashness, she preferred not to put herself in the way of her detractors. Confrontations were extremely rare, but they had happened. She would not seek them out.

But her evasion of the park was rooted in more than steering clear of her fellow Cottonwood citizens. One of the lesser-traveled byways led across to the north side of the park through a heavily treed area toward the rose garden. Pansy never went there. And she never would. It was the Richardson Rose Garden in honor of her late husband, whose family had founded the town. He had donated the land for the park and money for all the amenities and improvements around her.

Grover had loved this place. His childhood home was near the river. This shaded floodplain, no good for farming, had been his playground. It had become his grown-up legacy. He was buried under a huge slab of slick black granite in his rose garden.

Pansy pulled her thoughts away immediately. It was too pretty a day to be sad and angry and regretful. Grover was gone, gone forever. He would have wanted her to be smiling on a pretty Sunday afternoon. So she did, deliberately. And if the people who saw her stared at her, wondered about her pleasant expression, let them.

The crowd around the gazebo was growing steadily. Pansy definitely wanted to avoid the crush. And the way skirts were pulled aside on the pathways, the crush was equally as interested in avoiding her. She turned in the direction of the more deserted south section of the park. Here lantanas and trumpet vines grew in profusion. Huge stands of blooming sage and crepe myrtle gave a serene sense of privacy to the place.

The path curved around a big magnolia tree, its thick, leathery green leaves pointing in every direction. As she rounded it, her breath caught in her throat at the sight of one giant white flower in bloom, undoubtedly the first of the season. The sound that came from her lips was almost a sigh. Pansy loved the big, gaudy, almost indestructible blossoms, too big to be worn on a lady's hat or to adorn her bosom. She far preferred them to the tiny, brightly colored blooms of her namesake, so easily crushed underfoot.

She slipped off her glove and ran her hand along the smooth softness of the petals. An old story told to children was that the magnolia was the first flower God ever created. He was so impressed with the beauty and majesty of it that the other plants were envious. So He made flowers for all of them, in every shape and color.

But the magnolia was His first and always remained His favorite.

Closing her eyes, she gently caressed the blossom with the tips of her fingers. Feeling the anther, she drew the heady scent of it into her nostrils. She was alive. She was so very much alive.

A sound to her left startled her eyes open.

A man had rounded the path and was standing there, looking at her. Her mind registered neither a face nor a name, only the realization that she had been caught. She had been caught with her mask removed. Caught with her self exposed.

"Excuse me," she said hastily and turned to hurry down the path in the opposite direction.

Her cheeks were bright and hot with embarrassment. She had been seen with her heart in her eyes and somehow felt far more naked than being spotted on her porch in a wrapper.

"Mrs. Richardson!"

He was following her.

"Mrs. Richardson, wait," he called out.

She was tempted to break into a run and allow her feet to find their freedom back to the safety of her house.

Pansy would not give them, him, the satisfaction of seeing her scurrying like a scared rabbit. Abruptly she stopped and turned to face her pursuer. Her mask firmly back in place, she raised her chin and presented herself as the wicked widow. Beautiful, desirable, dangerous to any who tried to get too close.

The man who followed her was Amos Dewey. Pansy almost sighed in relief. If a man was to catch her naked, it was far preferable that he be a near eunuch.

Deliberately she let her eyes roam with prurient interest from his face down the length of his body, lin-

gering long upon the front of his trousers. It was easy
to see what Gussie Mudd might find attractive about
the man. He was tall, but had none of the rangy slim-
ness that made men awkward. Thick black hair
showed neither any hint of gray nor any sign of receding. His dark eyes were very handsome behind his
spectacles and there was something about his voice, a
low, soothing quality, that was somehow more alluring
than the words he spoke.

"Good afternoon, Mrs. Richardson."

Pansy held her shoulders back and kept her chin
raised as if readying herself for battle.

"Ah, Mr. Dewey," she replied in a low, throaty voice.
"You . . . ah . . . want me?"

It was not a question. It was spoken more like a
threat. A dangerous double entendre that she delivered
with a lusty smile and a risqué glance at the front of
the man's trousers.

Dewey was at least alive enough to blush brightly
from the roots of his hair to where the flesh disappeared beneath his collar.

"You . . . you dropped your glove, ma'am," he said
and held it out to her.

Pansy had the almost uncontrollable impulse to giggle nervously, but managed to stifle it.

"My glove?" she answered, her words honeyed.
"And you have returned it to me, Mr. Dewey. How
charming. Most men would have kept it under their
pillow to warm them on these cool spring nights."

The implication was obvious. Amos Dewey's
already red face went almost florid. He might not be a
man anymore, but he apparently could still remember
when he had been.

"You'd best give it to me, sir, and hurry back to the
crowd," she told him, her voice low and enticing

enough to drip honey. "It will do your reputation no good to be caught alone with me, secluded in the hedges."

Her words had brought out an unexpected reaction in him. He actually laughed out loud.

"I believe, Mrs. Richardson, that my reputation is sufficiently stalwart to survive it."

Her defense, her armor, her protection against the world was the powerful facade of seduction that she drew around her. It was a less-than-perfect shield against him.

"My dear man," she said in a voice just above a whisper, "the most noble and virtuous have been known to miss the mark when encountering the right temptation on a deserted park path."

She took the glove he offered and with slow, studied movements eased it onto her hand as if she were carefully covering nakedness that was too intimate to see.

His eyes were wide now. She saw him swallow nervously. Amos Dewey did want her. The truth of that was abundantly clear.

She smiled at him. It was the knowing smile of an experienced woman putting a man considerably less so in his place.

To her surprise he didn't cower. He didn't run. Behind the round spectacle lenses he was surveying her curiously.

"My Bess told me once that you and Grover were the most devoted couple in Cottonwood," he said.

Pansy blanched at his words. She couldn't talk about Grover now. She couldn't let her defenses down.

"Your wife must have been mistaken," she replied, her chin cocked in defiance. "Everyone in town knows I married Grover for his money."

Amos shook his head. "No, I agree with my wife.

I'm convinced you loved him. At least you loved him then."

The wrench in her heart was genuinely painful.

"It doesn't matter," she told him, her anger rising. "Grover's dead. Your wife is dead. I'd be better off dead. And you practically are."

Not waiting for a reply, she jerked the glove completely in place and turned to hurry away. Inexplicably she felt the sting of tears in her eyes.

Amos Dewey. Amos Dewey. Amos Dewey was not going to live happily ever after with Gussie Mudd. She deserved better and so did Rome. Pansy would see those two together if it was the last thing she ever did.

Gussie liked music. She always had. Music was like business. It varied widely in form and structure, but it made sense. Even when it was unpredictable and slightly discordant, as the Cottonwood Community Marching Band could be, there was a surety to it that was familiar and somehow comforting.

Listening to Sunday's selections, "Ta-Ra-Ra Boom-De-Ay!" "The Band Played On" and the ever-so-appropriate "Fountain in the Park," Gussie began to recover more fully from her unanticipated and not so very genteel swoon. Rome had moved them to a bench very near to the gazebo. While this certainly put them in the public view, it was a little too close to Clive Benson. Benson played a very enthusiastic tuba, and sitting near it on the right side, Gussie felt it overwhelmed all the other instruments. She enjoyed the music nonetheless. The shined-up gentlemen in their spiffy band uniforms with the bright gold braid and fringed epaulets were visually stirring, if not audibly perfection.

She turned to smile at Rome beside her. At first he'd seemed a little ill at ease and she blamed it upon the fainting spell. But he'd recovered himself enough to entertain her through most of the concert. Gussie often saw humor in things that other folks might politely pass over. Casey McCade had grown a girth that was unfamiliar to his band uniform. Every time he blew his trumpet, the button just above his belt strained, making a small gap that revealed his undershirt. Gussie caught herself keeping time to the music by way of the shirt gap. She nearly exploded in giggles when Rome leaned over and mentioned this unconventional metronome. Apparently he had been doing the very same thing.

Little Missy Holiday, her lacy pink pinafore stained and her reddish pigtails festooned with grass, ran up to the steps of the gazebo to perform a dance for the audience. Thinking herself a prima ballerina, the chubby five-year-old, looking much like her boisterous father, the reverend, lifted her skirt to reveal two grimy knees and a torn stocking. The girl ignored a dozen beckoning hisses from her mother and the low rumble of her father's disapproval before one of her older sisters came forward to bodily remove her, with plenty of noise and complaint, from her makeshift stage.

"I'm sure the reverend was exactly the same way," Rome whispered in Gussie's ear.

The two shared a very pleasant but ungallant laugh at the pastor's expense.

Being with Rome was fun and easy. He was perfectly polite and, though perhaps not possessed with polished manners, he was easily respectful and treated her with a gentleness a gentleman might envy.

He had said nothing to her about her swoon. For that she was grateful. She certainly didn't wish to talk about it. The whole incident was pretty hazy to her. One minute she was standing with Rome and Amos, feeling somewhat breathless. The next she was in Rome's arms, surprisingly strong and safe, and he was laying her upon the bench.

She remembered his face over hers and then it was Madge, bending there talking to her. Thank goodness the woman had been able to loosen her corset a bit so that she could catch a lungful of air and recover herself. It had been foolish in the extreme to bind herself so tight. She almost deserved to faint for her foolishness. But what must Rome think?

He, of course, could not know how tightly laced she had been and undoubtedly attributed her lightheadedness to the close proximity of Amos Dewey. She really ought to assure him about that, she thought. She was not a dizzy, vaporous schoolgirl overcome by passions. Her love for Amos was thoughtful and practical. In the three years they had kept company, he had only rarely kissed her. And then only upon the cheek.

Of course, she would expect a full married life with him. She was certainly ready to do her duty as a wife. But only as a wife, of course. Passion should not, and could not, be catered to outside the bonds of matrimony. Once she and Amos were legally wed, they would have a lifetime to explore the physicality of their love. Gussie had no urgency to do so prior to that time. It was her perception, from the little unmarried women were allowed to hear, that the act necessary for the procreation of children was basically messy and uncomfortable for women, although men apparently enjoyed it well enough.

Rome undoubtedly thought her to be a silly schoolgirl swooning within sight of her swain. She did not like the thought at all. But she certainly couldn't admit to him the truth, which was in some ways worse. She had so desired to be attractive that she had laced herself too tightly for even the slightest exertion.

The dress she wore was now way too tight in the waist and fit very ill. She hoped that he did not look at her too closely or he would undoubtedly notice the difference. But at least she could draw breath.

When the last strain of the afternoon concert faded away, the applause rang through the crowd. Rome and Gussie rose to their feet, as did most others within the immediate vicinity of the gazebo. The band took their bows.

Rome offered his arm and Gussie took it.

"That was a pleasant way to spend a Sunday afternoon," he said to her.

"Do you never come to the concerts?"

"No, I never have," he admitted.

Gussie was genuinely surprised. "What do you do on Sundays?" she asked.

A strange expression crossed his face momentarily and Gussie had no idea what he might have answered. He was spared a reply as Wade and Vera Pearsall stepped up to speak to them.

"It was a lovely musical entertainment," Vera announced. "Simply lovely. Did you and Mr. Akers enjoy it, Gussie? How could you not? Are you quite recovered from your swoon? Well, of course you are."

Gussie smiled admirably. Vera was one of those rare persons for whom conversation did not require another person.

Rome and Pearsall seemed to simply ignore her, starting up their own conversation about fireworks and the Founder's Day celebration.

"Don't let them sell you just a bunch of glittery stars like the ladies want," Pearsall told him firmly.

"We're looking for lots of boom and bang. Fireworks aren't fireworks if your ears aren't ringing in the aftermath."

Vera took the opportunity of their distraction to inch Gussie away for a very short but very private dialogue. Her words were low, gushing and furtive.

"I think it's an absolutely fine idea and you should snap him up as quickly as possible," she whispered. "I know, I know what you're thinking. He doesn't have a lick of fortune or property to recommend him, but a woman of your age can't afford to be so picky. It was unfortunate that Amos Dewey couldn't be brought to the point, but you can be grateful you don't have to compete with Saintly Bess. And who knows why they didn't have children. Everybody thinks it was her, being so sickly and all, but it could have been that he wasn't all that he should be in that respect. After all, it's been close to three years and he . . . well, there hasn't been a word of scandal about him and believe me, I'd know if there was one. He doesn't seem too eager to marry either. We can only imagine what that must mean."

Gussie had no idea what it must mean or what it had to do with his wife's barrenness, but there was no need for her to respond, Vera kept up the conversation without her. She pretended to be listening, though her attention was actually focused upon what was being said between Rome and Wade.

"Everybody thinks that the judge did such a fine job," Pearsall was saying. "He's a likable fellow, I admit that myself. But folks ain't seen the books like I seen. They are a pure puzzle going absolutely nowhere. And I write the man letter after letter about when to start construction on the lagoons. He only responds about half the time and then seems to misunderstand everything I say and every question I ask.

Everyone blames me for that, but I can't schedule construction until I get the paperwork. He set it up just that way, and then he's too busy to do what becomes necessary."

"He set it up that way?" Rome sounded surprised. In truth, Gussie was too.

"Yes indeed," Pearsall answered. "Folks think that I ain't doing my part, I'm not trying to get the lagoons built as the lines are laid, but the way I see it, Barclay's just lazy about turning over the land and following through with the permits. He's probably busy with some gal down in Austin as well. Once a fellow gets a taste of something like that Richardson tart, he ain't fit for ordinary females."

Gussie felt her face flush at the implication and tried harder to appear intent upon Vera's conversation.

Rome's response was long in coming. The length of silence was strange enough to make Gussie glance in that direction. His face revealed nothing, but his expression was hardened. Somehow the softness of his tone when he spoke sounded almost dangerous.

"I think more was made of that scandal, Pearsall, than was ever verifiably certain."

Wade made a snorting sound, dismissing the suggestion. "His wife filed for divorce. He left town. Seems to me that says it as loudly as if they'd been caught bare naked together on Broad Street."

At that moment, Vera, apparently sensing Gussie's wandering attention, grabbed her by the arm to ensure that she was listening.

"Be very careful in your dealings with Akers," Vera said. "Don't reveal your heart, no matter what is in it. You must string him along. It is never good to seem too eager, even at your age."

The last statement disquieted Gussie. Her immediate reaction was to haughtily tell the nosy know-it-all that she did not play games with a gentleman's tender feelings. That if a man did not love her on his own, she would never stoop to trick him into doing so. But that was exactly what she was involved in. Using Rome to play games with Amos. She could cloak it in business terms and economic theories, but it was a deceptive mating game as old as lies and equally as deceitful.

She was saved from making any comment at all by the arrival of Perry and Constance Wilhelm.

"Are you feeling better?" Constance asked, her warm tone tempered with concern.

"I'm perfectly fine," Gussie assured her. "It was just the heat."

"Yes, the heat," Constance agreed, though having been in the circle of women who surrounded Gussie, she was well aware of the restrictive laces that were loosened.

"It's perfectly miserable already," Vera piped up. "And it's not even June."

An amiable discussion of the vagaries of weather in east Texas generally, and in their little town specifically, commenced. In truth, there was nothing out of the ordinary for the season. But it was such a benign subject matter that it suited casual Cottonwood conversation perfectly.

Joe and Madge Simpson joined them and entered easily into the talk of excess heat and damp, sticky air.

When after several moments it was generally agreed that indeed summer was almost upon them and that the rain last night was welcome if the storm was not, Rome took Gussie's arm and they began a careful inching away from the crowd. No one made any attempt to stop them. But everyone seemed to have one last word that they wished to say. Finally it was just the two of them, making their way arm in arm down the park path and out to the street.

They walked in silence for a couple of moments. As the time lengthened and became uncomfortable, Gussie struggled to think of something to say.

"The music was . . ."

"I thought that . . ."

They spoke simultaneously and then hesitated.

"Please, go ahead."

"No, you first."

"I was just going to say how pleasant the afternoon has been," she told him.

Rome nodded. "I think we're making real progress as well," he said. "Amos sounded downright belligerent when I talked to him."

"He did?"

Rome assured her that it was so. Gussie couldn't help but be pleased. In a business negotiation, a little blustering and belligerence from your adversary usually meant having the upper hand and frequently proceeded a concession.

"So it's working," she said.

"It seems to be," Rome answered, grinning at her like a mischievous boy. "I think he could come around very soon."

Gussie smiled at him. She was pleased. She was sure that she was pleased. But there was a stab of disappointment in it as well. She enjoyed being with Rome. He was fun and funny and interesting to be with.

But, of course, he could continue to be her friend.

That thought fluttered through her mind rather surprisingly. She had never been friends with Rome. She had never been friends with any man. Her dealings with men had been either business or social. In neither case could she ever actually let down her guard and be genuinely comfortable or natural. What a pleasure and a relief it was to be able to do both.

They would be working together, business partners, not employer and employee, actual partners. A friendship should be the natural outgrowth of that.

They reached the picket fence in front of her house. In truth, Gussie was a little loath to go in. She'd enjoyed herself tremendously and in comparison, the evening before her looked long and lonely.

"So when is our next outing?" she asked him.

Rome was thoughtful for a moment.

"The committees for the Founder's Day are to meet one night next week," he said. "The married men usually bring their wives to these things and they have food and take on a party atmosphere. Amos will have to be there and will have to see me, since we are on the same committee. I'll bring you as my companion."

Gussie's brow furrowed. "You think I should attend uninvited?"

Rome shrugged with unconcern. "It may be noticed, but that's what we want, isn't it? Bring a dish and we'll simply do it. Just because it hasn't been done before doesn't mean we can't do it."

"Ah, innovation," Gussie replied, teasing him. "Businesses grow and change through innovation."

They walked up to the porch steps. Rome hesitated and Gussie turned to him. She was on the first step, he still on the walk. They were equal in height now, looking straight into each other's eyes. He was smiling.

"You can always find a business excuse for everything, can't you?" he said.

Gussie laughed lightly. "I suppose so. Though I am hard-pressed to explain my fainting spell."

"That one is easy," Rome answered. "Supply and demand."

"What do mean?"

"The supply of air you could get through your corseting was less than the demand that your lungs required."

Gussie's face paled and she felt as if she might faint again. He had actually said the word *corset* to her. He'd said it aloud. And he'd been aware that she was laced far too tightly.

"How . . . how did you know that?" she demanded.

"You told me," he answered. "When I laid you on the bench, you told me your laces were too tight."

Humiliation welled up in her, almost too horrifying to bear. Her face flaming in embarrassment, Gussie had no idea what to say. She had told him. She had admitted that very intimate fact to him. He was looking at her as if he had no idea what was wrong. The man was a crass idiot, a completely crass idiot.

"I . . . I . . ."

She was simply to mortified to speak. She turned and ran into the house without ever once looking back.

8

THE COTTONWOODS, FOR WHICH THE TOWN WAS NAMED, were sloughing off seed in the morning sunshine. The fluffy white spores gathered along the ground like small winnows of picked cotton and floated aimlessly on the air, catching the gleam of sunlight.

At the loading dock of the Mudd Manufactured Ice plant, Rome Akers took little note of the beauty of the day as he loaded the wagons. The pressure valve on the water distiller had been acting up and he'd spent the better part of the morning trying to find the problem and remedy it.

If this were his business, he would have long ago replaced the ancient piece of machinery with a newer, more efficient and dependable system. But Miss Gussie was far enough removed from the actual everyday working process to be less easily convinced to make capital improvements. Labor was cheaper than equipment. So a few extra hours' effort to get the same benefit was simply a necessity of doing business and the longer that major purchases were postponed, the better.

Once he became a partner, Rome assured himself,

things would be a good deal different. Miss Gussie was a fine business thinker, but he was the man with his hands on the day-to-day operations of the plant. In that way he was better qualified to see the whole effect of deteriorating machinery and lost productivity. When he became a partner, she would be forced to listen to his assessment.

Old man Shultz urged the hundred-pound blocks of ice down the ramp. To make sure that it didn't get away from him and slide off onto the ground, Rome placed his body at the end of the long, slick slope. Then, using much of the momentum created by the downward movement, he grasped the block with the heavy ice tongs and slung it into the wagon.

Inside, Tommy Robbins, the plant's shute boy, stacked it tightly and carefully to ensure minimal loss from melting. The stacking was, in fact, the job of Shultz, who stood now at the top of the shute. But it was the toughest job, requiring the youngest back and the strongest muscles. The older man could no longer do it with any ease. With absolutely no fanfare and hardly a word of explanation, Rome had switched the positions of the two men.

Rome laid another ice block on the wagon floor and turned back to the ramp to see Shultz hesitating. His attention focused beyond Rome, the old man tipped his hat in deference. Rome followed the direction of the man's gaze and found himself looking directly into the eyes of Miss Gussie. The woman was all dressed for town, her dove-gray walking suit neat as a pin, her parasol unopened in the morning sun and a silly little hat, useless for any purpose but decoration, perched upon her head.

"Good morning," Rome said, noting with some surprise his own pleasure in seeing her. Usually he considered a visit from *the boss* somewhat of an intrusion. It always slowed the work and this morning, when they were already late, the sight of her should have been very unwelcome. But somehow it was not.

"You're still loading the wagons?" She had every reason to be surprised.

"The pressure valve on the distiller is acting up again," he told her. "It's not only troublesome and a time waster, it's dangerous."

She was, just as he had anticipated, not overly concerned.

"I was hoping to have a few moments to talk to you," she said.

Rome was fairly certain that what she wanted was a private word, but that was impossible. Normally at this time, the wagons would be loaded and he'd be able to take a few minutes to catch his breath before beginning his route. But today's deliveries were already late and he hated even a brief hesitation in getting the ice on the road.

"You'll have to talk to me here," Rome answered, giving a meaningful glance at the other men.

It was back to work and Shultz dutifully slid another cold gray block down the ramp.

Miss Gussie hesitated. Rome expected her to simply walk away. Or to remind him to stop by the house after his route was complete. She certainly didn't owe Tommy or Shultz any explanation of her presence at the plant. But looking a little nervous and unsure, she apparently thought that she did.

"I have some . . . papers for you to look at," she said.

It was a blatant excuse. She was obviously embarrassed to request even a few moments of private talk. Rome supposed things were looked at differently now that he was thought to be courting her.

She widened her eyes a little, hinting that deception was necessary and that he should go along.

"I . . . ah . . . yeah," he answered a little lamely.

Miss Gussie was an honest, straightforward woman, unused to dissembling and unfamiliar with the necessities of intrigue. Her halting explanation and his uncertain answer incited more curiosity than it dampened. The men around them said nothing, but they were looking and obviously wondering what the two might have to talk about.

Rome continued his loading as he searched his brain for a subject worthy of an important business discourse. Money and real estate were both out. Everyone knew that he possessed neither. Progress and mechanization were good, but Miss Gussie might mistake it for a real discussion spurred by the problems with the distiller. Transportation was always up for debate, but Rome could not think, on such short notice, of anything the railroad had done lately. Of course, there was always those *progressives* in Washington.

"The papers about this Pure Food and Drug Act?" he blurted out. "Yes, I've been wanting to talk to you about that."

Her hesitation was so slight, only the most careful observer would have even noticed it. It was impossible that anyone interested in business might be completely unfamiliar with this particular piece of pending legislation. It had caused a flurry of discussion and argument.

"Yes, yes, we need to discuss it," she agreed. "They are pushing it through Congress now. It could affect every tonic or can of beans sold in America."

Rome almost smiled with pride at her.

"If . . . if it is passed into law, it wouldn't be just a

tremendous undertaking for the government," she continued. "It would affect, to some degree, every one of us, including the operation of the ice plant."

The woman knew what she was talking about. Not everyone in Cottonwood did. If the law passed, the federal government would be taking on an entirely new role, beyond the defense of the nation and the printing of money. A lot of folks couldn't understand this. But then, it was perfectly clear to Rome that Miss Gussie was not like a lot of folks. She'd had to work doubly hard and know twice as much as men in business. And she was a woman equal to the task.

Rome slung another block of ice from the dock ramp to the wagon bed.

Young Tommy butted in. "Well, I purely don't understand it."

Both Rome and Miss Gussie turned to look at him. Tommy was not yet twenty, but he was a likely young fellow who had never been shy about offering his two cents on a subject. Though he didn't truly give much thought to anything beyond what his ma might be stirring up for supper.

"Why would those people back East care what we eat?" he asked.

"They don't really care what we eat," Miss Gussie explained with the patience of a teacher. "They are just trying to control the quality of food and medicines that are sold. The law would try to ensure that anything sold to be consumed by the body would at least be clean and wholesome."

"But how could they do that without watching what each and every one of us puts in his mouth?" he said. "And that ain't the business of government."

"The boy's got the right of that," old Shultz called out in full agreement.

"You wouldn't want anyone to get away with selling Tommy something that was rotted, tainted or poisonous?" Rome asked the man.

"Of course he wouldn't," Tommy answered for him. "But it's my responsibility to see that don't happen. *Let the buyer beware!*"

The statement was made with such final certainty that one would have thought he was quoting the Good Book.

"But what if the buyer is injured?" Miss Gussie asked him. "What if he was innocently injured by something that he couldn't know was bad? Shouldn't a law protect him from people who would profit from injuring others?"

There was no immediate answer from any of her employees.

Rome continued her conjecture. "That kind of thing happens all the time in many different kinds of businesses, including the one we're in," he said. "Just two years ago hundreds of people were infected with typhoid and many of them died when they consumed ice cut from contaminated water. That's why at Mudd Manufactured Ice we make our product only from pure, distilled water. The science is there to make ice safer. It's the right thing that the science be used."

"But they shouldn't have to make a law about it," Shultz declared. "The businesses themselves should take on the burden of what is wholesome and what is not."

"And some do take that on," Rome said. "Companies with conscience, like Mudd Manufactured. But not all do and it is hard for the ones with public concern to compete with the lower prices offered by those with no concern at all."

"Those are just bad people," Tommy piped up.

"Ain't no way to make a law that those intent upon it can't get around."

Shultz agreed. "If you got a law, you've got to have enforcement," he said. "Is the sheriff going to quit chasing train robbers so he can chase meat packers?"

That brought a spark of laughter to the group.

"The bill calls for the hiring of inspectors trained to do the work," Rome said.

"And how do we know that the inspectors won't just take bribes from these unscrupulous men and we're no better off?" Shultz asked.

"That might happen," Miss Gussie admitted. "But at least we have to try to protect ourselves, to protect our families. This is a way for us to do that."

"Sickness and death are God's will, that's what Reverend Holiday would tell us," Tommy declared. "No earthly Caesar can protect man from the fate for which sin has doomed him."

"If it is God's will that an innocent child die of typhoid, I'm sure He can manage it without giving profit to some greedy businessman in the process."

Miss Gussie's words were impassioned, immovable, and when Rome looked into those bright eyes, he felt an inexplicable sense of pride. He felt pride and . . . and something else entirely.

"Let's go have a look at those papers," he said quickly. "I'll be right back, fellows," he told his crew.

He took Miss Gussie's arm and ushered her, a bit hurriedly, away from the loading dock and around the building toward the side entrance. As soon as they had cleared the corner and were within the privacy of the narrow alleyway between two brick structures, Rome pressed Miss Gussie back against the wall. It was not until that instance that he realized he intended to kiss her. But, of course, he could not.

He stepped back from her, shaken, attempting to recover his wits. Did she realize what he'd been up to? he wondered. Did she know how close he'd come to overstepping his bounds? He was her employee. Even with a partnership likely in the near future, such familiarity was unconscionable. Another moment and he would surely have had his face slapped.

Miss Gussie's cheeks were deeply flushed. His unseemly action must have been noted. She must be embarrassed. But she said nothing.

"Sorry about the deception," she said. "I just thought I needed to make up a reason for why I would be here in the middle of the morning."

Rome shook his head. "You have every right to oversee your business at any time for no reason at all," he told her. "But I understand what you're thinking. I think I am . . . I think I am getting a little confused about what is part of the deception and what is . . . well . . . real."

Gussie nodded as if she understood.

She glanced around almost nervously. Rome realized once more how very alone they were. Too alone. It was almost intimate, broad daylight a few yards from a public street, but it felt very intimate.

She began to fumble for something in her pocketbook. "I had to tell you what's happened," she said.

"What?"

She held up a folded piece of fine white papeterie. "Amos has sent me a note," she said, smiling at him. "He has requested permission to call upon me this afternoon."

For a moment Rome didn't quite understand the meaning of her words. Then he felt suddenly as if someone had slugged him in the stomach.

"This could be it," he said, forcing a smile to his

face. "Seeing us together yesterday must have brought him around."

"Yes, it seems so," Miss Gussie agreed. "What else could it be?"

Rome couldn't imagine anything.

"So you will have your partnership right away," she told him. "And I will be married by the Fourth of July after all."

"I . . . I never doubted it," he mumbled.

They stood there together in the privacy of the quiet morning.

Rome cleared his throat. "I am so very happy for you, Miss Gussie," he told her.

"I am very happy myself," she assured him.

It occurred to Rome that if they were both so happy, why did the moment seem like such a melancholy one?

Gussie wished she had saved her new dress for today. She certainly did not relish being bound up and breathless once more, but she knew that she had looked her best and she could have used some of that confidence this afternoon.

First there had been that horribly embarrassing moment after the band concert. And her silly, childish reaction of running into the house. Then this morning she'd hurried down to the plant without a thought of what excuse to give for her presence, but then her presence surely hadn't needed an excuse. She'd been uncomfortable and foolish and ended up discussing politics. How incredibly unattractive! She tried never to do anything like that in public.

If those things had not been enough to make her nervous, that strange discussion she'd had with Rome at the side of the building had been even worse. She'd felt very giddy and foolish. The way he'd ushered her out of sight, she'd almost thought . . . well, she'd almost thought that he'd wanted to be alone with her. What a ridiculous idea! Naturally that was just some sort of silly female reaction.

Now Amos was coming, apparently to propose to her, and she felt skittish. It was not a state of mind that sat well with her.

She had settled upon the idea of seeing him in the yard. There was a little bench there, not a bench exactly, but a sanded half log that stretched between two stumps. It was shaded in the warmth of the afternoon and Gussie was certain that it was a lovely place to receive a proposal. It was a good deal more proper than allowing him unchaperoned into the parlor. And more private than simply receiving him on her front porch.

A proposal surely involved a kiss and Gussie wanted to be kissed. She'd never really thought much about it before. But somehow now it was very important to her. She would not allow modesty or concern for her reputation to stand in the way of it.

She had thought Rome was going to kiss her.

The thought popped into her brain, for perhaps the hundredth time since that morning. When he'd pulled her around the corner and pressed her back against the hard, rough brick, she had thought he was going to kiss her. What an astonishingly improbable idea!

Gussie tutted to herself and shook her head. She was spending entirely too much time in the company of her employee. She was beginning to believe the deception herself. Thank heavens it was almost over. In a few short weeks she would be Mrs. Amos Dewey and she could forget all the conniving and deception that had brought it about. Of course, someday she and Amos would look back upon this and laugh. As she straightened the cameo at her throat, she couldn't honestly imagine how a woman would ever explain to a man that she had tricked him and have no bad feelings.

She heard Amos fumbling at the gate. He always had trouble getting it open. She stood making last-minute adjustments in front of the hall tree mirror. She assured herself that though she was past thirty and never the loveliest lady in town, she was as pretty as God had intended her to be. That would certainly have to be enough. She forced a broad, welcoming expression on her face before hurrying to the front door.

He was coming up the porch steps. He was so tall, so handsome, his lean features enhanced by the thick dark hair and brown eyes behind neat wire-rimmed spectacles.

"Good afternoon, Amos," she said.

He looked up at her. His expression was solemn.

"Hello, Gussie," he said. "Thank you for agreeing to see me."

She smiled brightly at him. He wasn't looking at her.

"May I come in?"

She hesitated. The plan had been for the yard, but somehow the privacy of the parlor seemed more suited to the mood.

"Certainly," she answered and led him into the front parlor, where he immediately seated himself on the most formal and uncomfortable seat in the place.

Gussie almost took a chair herself, but then primly sat on the edge of the fainting couch. Once the proposal was accepted, he could move beside her without seeming overly familiar.

She smoothed her skirts down nervously and then clasped her hands together to keep them still. Amos was not looking at her. He held his hat in his hand and appeared fully engrossed in the job of straightening the brim. Gussie focused on the part in his hair. In the latest fashion, known as the half shingle, it went from the middle of his brow to the middle of his nape. It was, as always, perfectly straight. He was, as always, perfectly groomed and eminently fashionable.

Now he was also hopelessly silent.

Gussie tried to think of something to say. He had come to see her. It was not her place to start the conversation. Besides, what could she ask him? *Excuse me, sir. Did you come here to make me an offer of marriage?* Even hearing her own words in her head made her fidget. Her knees began to tremble.

Amos looked up.

She smiled at him. He did not smile back. His expression continued to be sober and reflective. She wanted laughter, she wanted joy. They seemed very far from it now.

The silence between them seemed unreasonably long and almost loud. Gussie couldn't stand it. The anticipation was unbearable.

"It's certainly been warm the last few days," Gussie said, feeling a little damp at that very moment. She could wait no longer for him to pick up the conversation. "Summer is surely almost upon us."

"Yes," he agreed. "Summer is hot. Usually very hot."

"Very hot indeed."

"Yes, yes indeed. It's hot."

There really was no more to say about that. Gussie searched her brain for another topic of conversation. Amos was a quiet man. Not at all prone to lengthy discussion. She had forgotten that about him. She'd forgotten that when they were together, any talking done was mostly done by her. Amos was back to straightening his hat brim.

"How is your business?" she asked him.

"Good," he answered. "It's always good this time of year. When it starts getting hot, men want to shave their beards and get the hair off their necks."

"Yes, and it has been hot."

"Yes, it's been real hot so far."

They were back to that. She had to think of something else. Or he had to start making his speech. She preferred the latter, but it was only the former of which she had some control.

Gussie tried again. "I understand you're on the fireworks committee for the Fiftieth Anniversary Founder's Day Picnic."

He looked up suddenly, his face animated with interest.

"That's what I came to talk to you about," he said.

"The fireworks or the Founder's Day Picnic?"

"No, no, neither," he replied. "I came to talk to you about . . . about Rome Akers."

"Oh?"

"I don't think you should see Rome Akers," he said simply, not looking at her.

"What?"

"I don't think you should see Akers," Amos repeated. "He's not the right fellow for you."

Gussie was a little surprised at his choice of direction. Certainly jealousy had led him here to her door, but it simply made more sense to start with his own feelings, not with those of others.

"I've known Mr. Akers for a very long time," she said. "We are friends."

Amos looked back at her then. The line of his mouth was as straight as if the taste of his words were bitter.

"You can know someone for many years," he said. "You can know them and work with them and have a high opinion of them and still not be aware of important aspects of their character."

"Well, yes, that's certainly true," she allowed.

The conversation halted. She had no idea what more to say. Her palms were sweating. Why didn't he just get on with it?

"I have known Rome for a very long time myself," Amos continued finally. "And I have always liked and respected him. He's honest and hardworking. He's ambitious as well, perhaps in this case too much so."

Gussie was momentarily startled. Could Amos know about the partnership? She relaxed. He could not know unless she or Rome had told him. Neither of them would be foolish enough to do so.

"I admire Rome a great deal," Gussie said. "But surely you did not come here to discuss him."

"Yes, in fact, I did," Amos told her.

"You did?" Gussie was now very confused.

"I . . . well, I couldn't help but notice that you've been walking out with him," Amos said. "And I'm not at all sure that he is the right man for you, Miss Gussie."

She didn't exactly know what she should say. She couldn't insist that he *was* the right man, because then it would sound as if Amos had no chance with her. But she couldn't simply agree that he was not and negate everything in her scheme thus far.

"I like Mr. Akers very much," she said. "It remains to be seen whether our feelings for each other can grow."

Amos cleared his throat. It was a nervous, constricting sound.

"I think it would be best, Miss Gussie, if you make certain that your feelings for him do not grow at all."

Gussie could not fathom Amos's tack at all. If he wanted to present himself as the better candidate for her husband, then he rightly should be apologizing for having spurned her earlier. And he should be on his knees at that very moment, asking her to give him another chance. Instead he persisted in discussing his rival. Gussie found herself being unexpectedly annoyed.

"I have known you for a very long time, Miss Gussie," Amos told her. "And we have been, I believe, close friends. I would never want to see you hurt or disappointed in any way."

Gussie frowned.

"Mr. Dewey," she stated forcefully, "would you please stop beating around the bush and say what you have to say."

He hesitated, as if he truly did not wish to explain himself. Then he leaned forward slightly and lowered his voice as if relating some sort of secret.

"Rome Akers is not the man for you," he said with certainty. "There are things about him you do not know, things about him that a lady such as yourself should not know. I've come . . . as a friend . . . to warn you about him."

"To warn me about him."

"Yes. I feel . . . because of our long association . . . a certain protectiveness toward you. If you had a father or a brother, I would have been able to voice my concerns directly to them. But as you have no one else but your friends, Miss Gussie, in this you must rely upon the knowledge and judgment of your friends."

Gussie sat staring at him for a long moment. He hadn't come to propose. Once again he'd disappointed her. And this time he'd managed to insult her as well. To suggest that she needed his guidance and judgment in selecting an appropriate suitor! She could manage to support herself financially and run a successful business, but she still was not considered equal to the task of choosing her own gentleman friends. Gussie was absolutely livid. She rose to her feet.

"Thank you for stopping by," she said, as coldly as civil society would permit.

Amos immediately stood as well.

"I've upset you," he said.

"How could you think that, sir?" she asked, her jaw set tightly. "Who could not welcome the unsolicited interference of an erstwhile friend whose motives are completely inexplicable?"

"Miss Gussie, please I—"

"You have your hat, Mr. Dewey," she said. "I won't keep you. You know your way out!"

9

THE AFTERNOON SUN WAS TEMPERED BY A PLEASANT southeasterly breeze that still held a trace of salt and sea, a fragrance from the Gulf. Rome pushed Gussie in the shaded swing beneath a towering river oak. Her skirts ruffled with the activity, giving him an occasional glimpse of a female ankle clad in white calf boots with brass buttons.

Several sets of strolling citizens made their way through this end of the park. Though the number on a weekday afternoon in no way compared with the Sunday afternoon promenades, many, like Rome and Gussie, could not resist the mildness of the summer day.

The two had cut short their business briefing to take a public turn together. They wanted to be seen, of course. And Gussie seemed particularly keen to get away from the confines of her home. They needed to talk and the park was as good a place as any. Especially since no one in Cottonwood was so rude as to venture close enough to listen in on the couple's private chat.

"So Amos came to see you, but he didn't propose?"

Rome posed the question when the swing was near to him.

Gussie shook her head negatively, but didn't get an opportunity to speak until she had traveled out almost over the edge of the water and then all the way back to where Rome stood ready to push her again.

"He's not one bit closer to proposing than he was before," she said.

Rome let that thought sink in as she swung away from him and back once more.

"What on earth did he want if not to make you an offer?"

Gussie was away again without an answer.

Rome was positive that a formally paid call must mean something.

She was back again.

"We simply discussed inconsequential things and then he left."

Rome continued to watch her. He didn't quite believe it, but he couldn't imagine any reason for her to lie. She was back for another push. Carefully he made sure that his hands touched only the seat of the swing, never the derriere of the lady.

"He made a special request to see you," he said. "Why would he do that and then not have anything to discuss?"

Again he had to wait upon her reply. When it came, it was no answer at all.

"I don't wish to discuss it further," she said simply.

Her words were firm and brooked no argument. Rome felt a stab of guilt. Of course she didn't want to talk about it. She must have been very hurt. She'd thought Dewey was going to propose and he didn't. Twice now, the man had rejected her. Rome found himself feeling increasingly annoyed. The fellow flatly didn't deserve such a fine woman as Gussie Mudd.

Rome thought about something Pansy Richardson had told him. Something to which he'd not paid much attention at the time.

"I'm not sure if this fellow is really right for you," he said, voicing Pansy's words in his own doubt for the first time.

"Oh, but we are!" Gussie insisted immediately and with almost too much certainty.

Rome gave her a long look as the swing took her out to its farthest distance. One of the most common adages of business truth is that people are the most adamant when they are the most unsure. Gussie's hasty declaration flew in the face of thoughtful, balanced objectivity. He was not certain if love could hear the voice of reason.

"I'm sure that he's really lonely and alone," Rome said as she came closer once more.

"Of course he is," Gussie replied. "And he needs a woman to take care of him."

Rome couldn't help but agree with that. Though it did seem to him that perhaps Pansy had had a point. Amos didn't appear to have gotten over his wife's death. Maybe Miss Gussie couldn't see that. Perhaps she was so taken with him that she wasn't able to.

Rome eyed his boss and co-conspirator critically. Was she all that taken with Amos Dewey? He really hadn't noticed it. When the man's name came up, you couldn't see any change in her complexion. She didn't get flustered or giggly, the way women in love were supposed to. She didn't seem to pine for his presence. And he could not recall hearing her say anything particularly fawning about him.

But then, Miss Gussie was not a soft, girlie kind of woman. She was thoughtful, businesslike. Not just any man could move her emotionally. Amos Dewey did not do that. Maybe no man ever could.

He glanced at her and saw her eyeing him with speculation.

"What are you thinking?" she asked.

"Nothing," he answered too quickly.

"That worried frown always means something," she insisted.

She had known him too long.

"Is it possible for a woman to be attracted to a man who is all wrong for her?" he asked finally.

Gussie allowed her foot to drag on the ground. Rome grabbed the ropes, assisting her in bringing the swing to a stop. She twisted the lines as she turned to face him.

"How could he be wrong for me?" she asked Rome incredulously. "We have known each other most of our lives. We come from similar backgrounds and upbringing. Both of us have successful businesses. And we're suited in demeanor and temperament. There can't be anything wrong about that. We are obviously perfect for each other."

Rome thought about disagreeing with her. But he didn't. Gussie Mudd always knew what she wanted. Why was he even questioning the wisdom of her choice? There was not a clearer head for business in town. And not one person's judgment that he trusted more. She ran her own life and she obviously knew her own heart and mind.

"You must be right," he said, trying to convince himself. "You certainly must be right."

He nodded and she did too, but they didn't meet each other's eyes.

"You two should be married," he continued. "We just have to find a way to make that happen."

Rome reached out, offering his hand. She put her gloved one in his and rose to her feet.

"I think my plan is a good one," she said. "I don't know why it hasn't worked."

"I thought so too," Rome admitted. "I thought that when he saw us together, it would spur his jealousy and he'd come around."

They stood together by the swing, each holding onto one of the ropes as if it were a lifeline for both.

"Maybe he's not quite jealous enough yet," Rome suggested. "Do you think it's time to throw a little more wood in the firebox?"

"What do you mean?" she asked.

"We should see if we can really raise the heat on Mr. Dewey," he said, raising his eyebrows meaningfully.

Gussie looked at him, all curiosity and speculation.

"It does seems that the jealousy is having an effect. Dewey did come calling," Rome observed. "But obviously it was not enough. We'll have to give him a more intimate meeting with the green-eyed monster."

He made a silly, spooky face at Gussie and she giggled.

"And how are we going to do that?" she asked him.

He laughed and shook his head. "I don't know," he said. "We'll have to come up with something."

Gussie was thoughtful for a long moment.

"I wonder what he would do if he caught you giving me a kiss."

Rome held his body perfectly still. Unbidden, the memory of the previous morning assailed him. It was a guilty memory. He had practically dragged her around the building and then pressed her up against the wall.

He had wanted to kiss her. He had really wanted to kiss her. It was totally, totally wrong.

The level of his bad feeling about it served only to illustrate his current confusion. The very idea of kissing her tantalized him. He felt obligated to resist it.

"I'm sure we shouldn't have to go that far," he said. "I couldn't *kiss* you."

The statement was made with such resolute dread that Gussie momentarily paled, struck by his apparent distaste.

"No, no, I didn't mean for it to come out exactly like that," Rome said hastily, apologizing. "What I meant to say was, it would be so . . . unwelcome to your person. Surely we will not need to go so far as to . . ."

His words drifted off and were waved away.

"I am not averse to having you kiss me," Gussie assured him. "And I think it would move things along very nicely. Nothing provokes jealousy like seeing another fellow kissing your woman."

That seemed reasonable logic. Though he was still reluctant to play with such a dangerous type of fire.

"When you say *kissing*," he asked. "what exactly do you mean?"

Gussie wore a puzzled expression. "Why, I just meant . . . I just meant the usual kind of thing," she said. "One mouth against another. You know, my mouth against yours."

There was a strange, almost high inflection to her words. Rome barely took notice of it. He was more acutely aware of the blush stealing up his neck.

There was no cause for him to be embarrassed. She was just a woman, a woman soon to be married to another man. They were surely mature enough to talk about something like kissing.

"You think this kissing will . . . will help bring Amos around?" he asked with as much matter-of-fact tone as he could manage.

"Yes, I believe so," she answered. "What do you think?"

She seemed so open, so innocent of the dangers.

"Without a doubt," he assured her. "When Dewey sees us kissing, he won't be able to ignore it."

Gussie smiled, pleased. Then a moment later, she looked doubtful once more.

"How on earth could he ever see us kissing?" she asked Rome. "Couples don't . . . well, they don't do that out in the open."

"Of course not," Rome agreed. "But sometimes they do get caught. I suppose we've got to work toward getting ourselves caught by Amos Dewey."

Miss Gussie sighed and shook her head.

"I can't just go around kissing a man on a public street," she said. "What if someone else besides Amos saw us?"

Rome nodded. "That wouldn't be good. We need to figure out a way to have him see us without exposing you to any censure or criticism."

Miss Gussie laughed lightly and seated herself once more in the swing. "I think the only way to do that is to install me in the kissing booth at the county fair!"

Rome's eyes widened and then a big grin split his face as grabbed the ropes on either side of the swing and pulled back excitedly before sending it flying out ahead.

"That's it!" he said, laughing delightedly. "That's exactly it!"

"What?"

"The kissing booth," he said. "It's perfectly acceptable for a woman to be seen kissing if it's for a good cause."

"Kissing for a good cause?"

"Yes," he told her. "A woman donating her lips for charity is perfectly acceptable."

That was certainly true. Rome had seen kissing booths crop up even at church socials.

"The county fair isn't until the fall," she pointed out.

"I know, so we can't wait for the fair. We've got to set up a kissing-for-a-cause plan that occurs right away."

Gussie seemed to consider that as she swung back and forth.

"Maybe we could set up a booth at the Founder's Day Picnic," she said. "To support a charity like the orphanage or the library."

Rome was hesitant. "Aren't there plenty of supporters for those causes already?"

Gussie nodded. "Both the Circle of Benevolent Service and the Monday Morning Merchants Association raise money for them every year."

"So it might seem contrived if we tried to do it as well," he said.

"Perhaps," she agreed.

"And that's too long to wait," he pointed out. "The picnic is on the last day of our timetable. The day you wanted to get married."

"Oh, well I suppose I wouldn't have to get married that day," she said.

"No, that was our agreement," Rome said. "We can't let this deception drag on interminably. We want you married on the Fourth of July, and waiting to do the kissing booth until then would be cutting things too close."

"You're right. We really don't want to wait that

long. And if we did, what would we do between now and then?"

Once more Gussie brought the swing to a stop. She continued to sit in it, thoughtful. Rome stood beside her, then spoke in a more modulated and private tone.

"We need to do the kissing booth soon," he said. "So we need a reason to raise money right away."

"We can check the newspaper on Saturday," she suggested. "Surely some terrible calamity has occurred somewhere where emergency donations are needed."

"I can ask around the firehouse and the bank," Rome said. "Maybe somebody has been burned out or gone bankrupt."

The two looked at each other for a moment and serious faces suddenly turned to smiles as they both giggled guiltily.

"We can't be wishing for something terrible to happen to somebody," Gussie said.

"We can start calling ourselves the charity vultures," Rome said. "Soaring overhead waiting for a disaster until we can swoop down and do good work."

They laughed together for a few moments and became thoughtful.

"There is bound to be a cause that needs us," Gussie said with certainty.

Rome suddenly realized exactly what it was.

"We'll raise money *for* the Founder's Day Picnic," he said.

Gussie looked at him, not quite understanding. "What do you mean?"

"We only have a few weeks before the picnic," he pointed out. "I'm on the fireworks committee."

"Yes, you told me."

"We have a very small budget to work with," he

explained, "so we were going to purchase some fireworks and do the display ourselves."

"That sounds like a good idea," she said.

"Thank you," Rome replied. "It was actually mine. But now I have a better idea."

"And what is that?"

"If we were to raise sufficient funds," he said, "we could have a professional fireworks company come and do a display."

"A professional fireworks company would come to Cottonwood?" she asked.

"They travel all over the country," he told her. "They put on displays that are safer and better than anything that we could do. I saw one a couple of years ago up in Fort Worth. I swear it was half an hour of rockets shooting off, stars exploding overhead. They even had a big, fiery sign with the Texas flag and the name Fort Worth burning in a half-dozen colors. It would be the best entertainment the people of Cottonwood have ever seen."

He hesitated before offering a slow grin. "And it would give us, Miss Gussie, a chance to kiss-for-a-cause."

She met his smile with one of her own.

"We'd have to raise the money to pay the fireworks showman," Rome told her. "And Amos would naturally have to be involved. He's on the committee with me."

"Of course," Gussie agreed, a hint of pride in her voice. "That's a fabulous idea."

"We'd have to raise the money soon," Rome continued. "I'm sure we'd have to pay most of it up front to get someone to be here on such a busy day for fireworks as the Fourth. The sooner we have to raise the money, the sooner we'd have to set up the kissing booth."

Gussie nodded, but she was concerned. "We can't just set up a kissing booth on Broad Street."

"I don't know why not. But you know what would be better? The park on Sunday afternoon. Think of all the people who are here. Practically the whole town shows up for their afternoon promenade. And we'd get more than usual once word of our plans spread around."

"Do you think the Monday Merchants would agree to let you do it?" she asked.

"They are going to be very enthusiastic," he said with certainty. "And we'll make a lot of money. We'll get some pretty, young girls, maybe that Betty Ditham and the mayor's oldest girl. They'll be primped and pretty in their Sunday best and the young blades will be lined up all the way to the railroad tracks."

"They certainly would. It is a very good idea, Mr. Akers. And I know that it will make money. But I . . . I couldn't be out there will all those young ladies."

"Why not? That's what the whole plan is about."

She was blushing and embarrassed.

"Betty and the mayor's daughter . . . they are young," she managed to get out at last. "And I'm . . . well, I'm not."

"That shouldn't matter," he said. "It doesn't have anything to do with being in a kissing booth. You are as unmarried and eligible as they are."

"Yes, but it wouldn't be dignified," Gussie countered. "And I would stick out like a sore thumb."

"So we'll get some women your age for our kissing booth as well," he said.

"Now that's silly," she said. "Women my age don't volunteer for kissing booths."

"They will for ours," Rome assured her with

absolute confidence. "I think I can find a way to recruit some of the most well-bred, dignified women in town."

"You're joking."

Rome just grinned at her. "You're not the only one in this partnership that can come up with a plan," he said.

"Even if your plan works. I'm afraid I would be far too conspicuous," she insisted.

Rome laughed, apparently delighted at her discomfiture. Then he raised a teasing eyebrow.

"Where is the brave leader of the Mudd Manufactured Ice company?" he asked. "I have never known her to allow shyness to stand in the way of a good business deal."

"Mr. Akers—Rome, I . . ." Embarrassed, she lowered her voice to just a little above a whisper. "None of the young blades would stand in my line."

Her blushing admission only solicited an amused chuckle.

"I would absolutely see that they don't," he promised.

"What!"

"It will be perfect, Miss Gussie," he told her. "Can't you see me? I'm standing there in front of the kissing booth all day, having to plunk down coin after coin to make certain that nobody else gets a chance to come close to kissing my girl."

"Oh, my heavens!" Gussie exclaimed. "That could cost you a fortune!"

"It would be the very best investment a man ever made," he assured her. "And I'd be kissing you all afternoon in front of the whole town. If that doesn't set Amos Dewey on his ear, nothing will."

Rome's heart was beating like a drum. Amos Dewey might not be the only person affected.

* * *

The barbershop was not all that busy on Thursday mornings. Old man Penderghast sat in one of the chairs by the window. He was ostensibly waiting for a shave, but he'd begun snoring fifteen minutes ago and Amos didn't bother to wake him up.

Amos carefully soaked his combs in soapy water and washed and dried his brushes with great care. A barber was only as good as his equipment. And a barbershop was only as good as its barber.

In a fancy-carved walnut tool bracket that hung upon the wall, he stowed his cutting implements, razors, scissors, clippers and cutlery. He pulled the two-and-a-half-inch Perfecto out of its slot. It was his favorite razor to use. He owned a Henry Sears & Sons Queen that he utilized on a regular basis. But his favorite was the much more ordinary Perfecto. It was the right length, it had the right balance, it was curved at exactly the right angle and it could hold an edge. Therefore it was the most often used and required the most care.

Amos opened it up with a motion born of much practice and certainty. He drew the blade across his thumbnail. It was smooth, but made no impression. He grimaced so slightly that it was hardly noticeable.

He picked up his hone, a hand-sized rectangular cut of fine-grit yellow stone, and began the delicate process of sharpening. It was not a task that could be taken on without care. A razor's edge was a difficult perfection to get or maintain. And the hands of a careless workman could ruin a beautiful shaving instrument.

Amos lay the blade perfectly flat on the hone. He drew it forward, edge-first on a diagonal stroke. Every part had to make contact with the stone with equal pressure, honing evenly from heel to point.

He then turned the razor in his hand to the opposite side, taking care not to touch the hone in a backward stroke. Drawing the edge just right was a skill acquired only with much practice. But Amos could always tell when he was doing it correctly. It was almost as if the hone were sucking the blade to it, unwilling to be apart from it a moment longer.

He was careful to test again after every few passes. An underhoned edge would not cleanly cut a beard, but an overhoned one could be as rough as a file. When he had it honed to perfection, he would strop it with leather until it moved across the flesh with no more bite than that of a feather.

He focused his mind on the task, but his thoughts drifted, as they had all last night and this morning, to the confrontation with Miss Gussie. He had been obliged to do it. She had been his friend and companion for three years. It was not honorable to know, without a doubt, that she was making an untenable alliance and not at least warn her that there were things about Rome Akers that she didn't know.

He liked Rome. He always had, he probably always would. If he had not seen him leaving the Richardson house under cover of darkness, he might have thought the man a fine enough choice for Gussie Mudd.

But he had seen and he did know. So he could not in good conscience allow the man to trifle with the innocent affections of a decent, well-bred lady while he cavorted with a woman of questionable reputation.

Amos had handled it badly, of course. He had known that he would. Women were so hard to talk to, so hard to explain things to. There were so many truths they simply could not be allowed to know, any discussion with them always involved evasion and deception. His beloved Bess had been the same way. He had had to guard her, shelter her, protect her from the hard facts of life.

He had not been able, however, to protect her from death.

Amos tested the razor's edge once more against his thumbnail. It was almost right, almost perfect, but not quite good enough. A couple more sharpenings would easily do it.

As he set the blade against the hone once more, the door opened. He looked up casually and was then so startled that he pushed the edge too hard and cut himself cleanly on the heel of his palm.

He swallowed the curse that sprang to his lips and dropped both the hone and the razor onto the counter shelf with a clatter. He grabbed a towel and wrapped it quickly around his injury.

"Good morning, Mrs. Richardson," he said formally.

"Good morning to you, Mr. Dewey," she said. "I hope that I'm not interrupting."

"No, no."

He glanced over at old man Penderghast. The man was wide awake now and looking at Mrs. Richardson as if he'd never seen a woman before. Of course, in some ways that was entirely true. There weren't a whole lot of women in the world who were like Mrs. Richardson. At least there weren't in the world of Cottonwood, Texas.

She wore a startling black dress, but this was no widow's weeds. It was trimmed in pale blue and crimson braid, which gave the somber style a festive appearance. Amos did not keep up with the fashions in ladies' gowns, but the cut of the dress was like nothing he had ever seen before and could be nothing less than the very latest style. Its high collar, long sleeves and trimly gored skirt were all in themselves perfectly respectable, but somehow they were put together in a way that made a man's thoughts fly to what was beneath the thin covering of flimsy cloth.

She was smiling at him as if she knew exactly the direction of his thoughts. Deliberately Amos kept his mind blank and his body still, though he could not completely control the stirring of his loins. She was an attractive woman, there was no denying it. But it was more than simply that which kept men on edge. It was as if she were the embodiment of all things sexual and forbidden.

He could remember her when she had been a young girl, and even as Grover Richardson's new bride. Her erotic sensuality had not been apparent then. Or had it? He had been so in love with Bess, he probably had just not noticed.

But he noticed her now. He had seen her in the park on Sunday and he had been jolted by the experience. She had not so much as touched his hand, yet every word she said, every movement she made, every minute he was in her presence had been rife with carnal awareness and sensuality.

Now, even as he tightened the pressure on the towel he'd wrapped around his cut hand, he was very aware of Pansy Richardson. He didn't like it one bit.

"Can I help you, ma'am?" he asked, forcing civility into his voice.

The barbershop was a bastion of male privacy. Women never intruded. It was often a place of low conversation, bawdy humor and coarse language. Ladies were naturally excluded from that. Of course, some would have said that Pansy Richardson was no lady.

"I just stopped in for a shave and a haircut," she told him, joking. Her laughter had a low, sultry quality that no decent woman would have been cursed with.

Amos didn't even smile. He refused to give her that satisfaction.

Penderghast, however, was extremely entertained. The decrepit codger couldn't hear it thunder, but his ears were perked up like those of a hound dog on the scent and his rheumy eyes were bright with expectation. He guffawed as if Mrs. Richardson were some vaudeville wag.

The woman gave the old fellow an appreciative glance. His tongue practically hung out of his mouth in response.

"I assume you do have some purpose in being here," Amos said.

"Yes," she answered, turning back to him. "I desire some professional service from you, Mr. Dewey."

She said the word *desire* in such a way that Amos could feel the blush creeping up his neck and ears. He hated how she made him feel. He hated the loss of control. In fact, maybe he hated her.

"I can't imagine what service I might provide, Mrs. Richardson."

"Can't you?" she asked.

He didn't care for the banter. He didn't care for the suggestiveness. She should just say what she had to say and get out of his place of business.

"You will have to speak forthrightly, ma'am. I am not good at guessing games."

"No," she said, "I'm sure you're not. In fact. I would go so far as to suggest that you are probably not good at games of any kind."

She turned her back on him and walked over to the mug case. Every man in town who came in for a regular shave had his personal mug for mixing shaving soap. Some mugs bore only the man's name or initials. Others had pictures depicting his livelihood or avocation. Joe Simpson's had a picture of a lathe. Pete Davies's showed hounds on a chase. Clive Benson's proudly displayed a tuba.

"It's like looking into the soul of every man in town," the woman remarked.

Amos had the ridiculous urge to throw his body between her and the mugs to protect the privacy of his patrons. Women were supposed to be innocent and ignorant. Pansy Richardson knew far too much. She was a threat to any man who came near her.

"What is it that you want, Mrs. Richardson?" he asked her.

She turned in his direction and with a slow, deliberate regard, she let her eyes drift down him from head to toe.

"I just need for you to take a look at me," she said.

"What?"

"My neck, Mr. Dewey," she clarified. "I believe I have a carbuncle on my neck." Her eyes widened in feigned shock. "Oh, dear, what were you thinking?"

He didn't answer. He was not quick or clever enough to make the witty reply.

"That is part of your job, is it not?" she asked him. "Lancing boils, removing cysts. You have to learn to do those things to get a barber's license."

Amos nodded. "Yes, of course."

"Then you will offer me relief?"

Her question was so strangely phrased as to make him more wary and ill at ease.

"Have you been feverish?" he asked. "Suffered aching? Swelling?"

"All of those," she answered. "And I've beheld the awful thing in my mirror. You simply must help me."

He could hardly refuse. The insidious infections

were not only painful, but dangerous. The sepsis could be loosed inside the body and cause serious illness or death.

"I can't tell anything without an examination," he said.

"That's why I'm here."

Amos would have been very happy to tell her to go elsewhere. But there was no one better qualified to help her in Cottonwood. She would have to take the train to Millville or Longview in order to see some other barber. Or perhaps a doctor, though they were certainly not known for their finer cutting skills. Most surgery involving *materia medica* was for removing a limb. The more delicate art of taking a knife to an angry boil was left to those of the barbering trade. Amos was not only the best barber in town, he was especially well schooled and experienced in treating infections. When a man spent his whole life getting a close look into the faces of other men, he learned a good deal about pus and infestation—the two biggest culprits of disease.

Yet there was a delicate question he had to ask her. But he was loath to ask it, even of a woman of questionable morals like this one.

He turned away from Penderghast, making the moment as private as a public place would allow.

"Mrs. Richardson," he said quietly, "is it possible that you have . . . that you have the syphilis."

Her initial reaction was to stare at him in puzzlement.

"Do you know what syphilis is?" he asked.

Her expression changed to incredulity, then anger. For a moment Amos thought the woman might slap him.

"Yes, Mr. Dewey," she answered quietly, definitively, "I do know what it is. I know how a person gets it. And I know that I do not have it."

"Sometimes the very first symptom is a chancre that can be very much like a carbuncle."

"This is not that," she said through clenched teeth.

Amos didn't pursue the subject further. He had seen several of the venereal sores and believed he would recognize the disease when he saw it.

"Please sit in the chair," he suggested and made a courteous invitation with his hand, hoping to placate her displeasure.

He stooped down to the lower cabinet to retrieve the small leather kit that he referred to as his surgical bag. It contained a tin of salve, some boric acid, rubbing alcohol, sterile bandages and castor oil.

From his tool bracket he took a narrow probe and a small, thin scalpel.

When he turned back to the chair, he was surprised to see it empty. Mrs. Richardson continued to stand in the middle of the room, showing no indication of following his order.

"I need you to sit in the chair to examine you," he said.

She was looking at him stone-faced and straight in the eye.

"I couldn't possibly do that," she said.

His brow furrowed in question.

"Why not?"

"Surely you know," she said.

Amos didn't have the vaguest idea.

"No, ma'am," he answered. "I do not."

She gestured toward the expanse of plate-glass window in the front of the shop and to old man Penderghast, who still sat wide-eyed in his seat.

"Are you thinking to put me on display, Mr. Dewey?" she asked. "Do you want every person in Cottonwood to have a nose pressed against that glass?"

"I . . . well, I . . ."

"Do you have any idea about how I am treated in this town?" she went on. "Everything I do is up for speculation and everything I do is watched. These people would like nothing better than to see me in that barber's chair. They would undoubtedly come to the same erroneous conclusion that you have."

The woman closed the distance between them, coming to stand directly in front of him. She was close enough for Amos to catch the scent of her. She was not heavily perfumed and musky, as he would have expected. She smelled clean and fresh, floral and almost innocent.

He took a retreating step backward.

She followed him. Her voice was low, meant only for his ears.

"I cannot, will not, allow myself to be a public spectacle, displayed for the amusement of the fine, upstanding citizens of Cottonwood," she declared with conviction. "I've had more than my share of that, thank you very much, and I will not consent to more."

His back to the counter, Amos could get no further away from her.

"I suppose I could look at your neck from a standing position," he said. "I could even do it in the back room. There are no windows at all there, but the light is not too good."

Mrs. Richardson stood in front of him for what seemed like an inordinately long time, hesitating as if to consider all of the alternatives. She glanced back at the barber's chair and then at Amos once more.

"No, I think you were right the first time," she said. "I should be seated. But the windows will have to be covered."

"I can close the shades," he said. "They are mostly for keeping out the heat of the afternoon sun. They would keep anyone from glancing in easily, though you can see through them."

"The shades won't be enough," she said thoughtfully. "I want the window covered with paper before they are drawn."

"All right," he said.

"And I don't want anyone else in here."

"Of course not," he agreed.

"Since there are gentlemen coming in and out all day," she added, "I think it should be after regular business hours."

"Okay."

"The door will have to be locked and we will have to have complete privacy."

Her demands were excessive; still, he continued to accede to them.

"I'll let you know when would be the best time for me," she said. She stepped back from him and smiled pleasantly. "Thank you very much, Mr. Dewey. You have been very helpful and I am certain that you will be able to cure what ails me."

"I . . . I can't know until I've looked at it thoroughly," he told her.

"Yes," she answered. "Isn't that the way it always is."

Her voice was throaty now and full of meaning. Amos had no idea what that meaning might be.

She turned from him and headed toward the door.

"I'll be back soon," she said.

Amos wasn't sure if it was a threat or a promise.

She stopped in front of Penderghast and leaned forward to loudly say good-bye. The woman was practically shoving her bosom in the old man's face.

When she walked out the door, the grizzled codger was still grinning like a fool.

Amos snapped at him.

"So do you want a shave or are you just loitering!"

10

THE KISSING BOOTH WAS AN IDEA THAT TRULY APPEALED
to the gentlemen of the Monday Morning Merchants
Association. As soon as Rome brought it up for discussion, he was roundly applauded. And the fact that
the money raised was going to be used to pay for a
professional fireworks display at the Fourth of July
Fiftieth Anniversary Founder's Day Picnic was even
better.

"You just simply take the cake," the mayor told him
loudly, giving him an enthusiastic slap on the back.
"You just simply take the cake."

Most of the other men were equally congratulatory.

"I always say you got a good head on your shoulders," Matt Purdy told him. "If you get tired of fetch-
ing and carrying all that *Mudd-y* ice, you can sure have
a job toting ice that's a lot more *Purdy.*"

The man guffawed, clearly enjoying his own little
joke. The fellows around him laughed as well, including Rome, who found more humor in the man's behavior than his words.

"I think it's bound to be a very successful venture,"

Huntley Boston said. "What young ladies are you recruiting to man the booth?" He chuckled. "Or perhaps I should say woman it."

"I thought I would ask the mayor's daughter," Rome answered, "young Becky Timmons, the Benson girl and Betty Ditham."

"Ah . . . Betty Ditham," the banker said thoughtfully. "The daughter of my teller. She is certainly quite lovely and a sweet girl as well."

"Betty is the prettiest girl in town," Rome agreed. "So we'd sure want her. With the others we have a blonde and a brunette and a redhead, which should cover the preferences of just about every fellow in Cottonwood."

"Except the misters who like their gals baldheaded," Purdy piped up and then laughed uproariously at his further attempt at humor.

"My boys will be digging out their hoarded pennies for this, I'm certain," Wade Pearsall announced to the room, proudly intimating that his shy, pimply sons, just out of knee pants, were now debonair swains.

"I may have to make an extra trip to the bank myself," Pete Davies told them with a wink, evoking a good deal of knowing laughter all around.

"Maybe Pete won't be the only one," Rome said. "I've got some special surprises for some of you."

The suggested mystery prompted a lot more interest and even more questions. But Rome was finished talking. He'd done about all the talking he could manage that morning at the impromptu meeting of the Circle of Benevolent Service, Miss Gussie at his side.

"We're married women," Lulabell Timmons informed him as if he didn't know. "We have husbands. We can't participate in a kissing booth."

"That's the beauty of it, ladies," Rome explained.

"Your husbands can't possibly allow other men to kiss you, so they will have to occupy your time. And they have to pay for your kisses."

"Why should they pay for what they can get for free?" Kate Holiday asked.

"Or what they couldn't get for love or money," Loralene Davies put in cynically.

The married women all laughed knowingly.

Rome smiled with them and shot Miss Gussie a quick conspiratorial glance before he continued.

"I just think that a kissing booth would be more fun, and more fair to the single gentlemen like myself," he said, "if the married men were forced to step up to the counter as well."

"I doubt seriously if you could keep my husband away," Loralene complained with some bitterness. "He's got his eyes on those young girls all the livelong day."

"Well, if you're standing in the kissing booth," Rome told her, "he'll have to keep his eyes on you, or risk having half the single men in town sample a little smooch."

Loralene's jaw dropped in shock. All around her the other women tittered and giggled at the idea.

"All of your husbands will be standing in the front of your line, trying to keep the other men away," he said. "And they'll have to pay a pretty penny to do so."

There was a good deal of scandalized mumbling and concerns about proprieties. Rome was confident. The fact that Miss Gussie was on his side and that Loralene appeared to be leaning his way suggested success. If both of the lady leaders of the community were for it, who could be against it?

"What do you think, Kate?" Vera Pearsall suddenly asked. "I'm not at all sure that the reverend would approve of such shenanigans."

Rome looked toward the pastor's dainty and demure young wife with concern. Reverend Holiday could be a stodgy stickler at times. He might not approve of such a scheme.

Surprisingly, Kate Holiday answered with a grin so mischievous it sparkled up her whole expression.

"I certainly hope that you will find a spot for me in that kissing booth," she said.

There were several shocked gasps at the audacity of the pastor's wife.

"Surely you don't mean to participate yourself?" Vera asked.

"I can hardly wait," Kate answered.

"But the reverend . . ."

"My husband is a fine, clean-living, godly man," Mrs. Holiday stated. "But the truth is, he's so tight his teeth don't even chatter in a snowstorm."

A couple of the younger women giggled. Most, more circumspect, hid a smile behind a hand.

"I'd like to see him spend a little money on me," Kate Holiday said. "Even if all I get for it is a kiss."

Her agreement truly broke the ice. If the pastor's wife thought it would be a fun trick to play on her husband, then the rest of them were more than willing to do the same. And they immediately entered into a serious discussion about organizing, selling the tickets and decorating the booth.

They decided upon signs and bunting, with ladies kissing by shifts through the afternoon. It was going to be the busiest, and hopefully the most profitable, kissing booth ever. The loyal husbands at the Monday Morning Merchants Association were going to make it so.

As Rome now glanced around at those unsuspecting

merchants, so enthusiastically supporting the booth, he couldn't help but smile.

"I can't imagine that we'll make enough money to completely pay for professional fireworks."

The statement came from Amos Dewey, who had quietly walked up to Rome's side. His was the only dissenting voice and Rome was grateful that at least he kept it quiet and private. Being a member of the committee, he might well have felt left out, not having been asked his opinion beforehand. Of course, Rome couldn't risk his knowing of and perhaps opposing the plan before he'd assured its success. It was a perfect plan to kiss Miss Gussie in public. No man in love would ever be able to tolerate such a show.

"Don't worry," Rome told him. "We'll make more money than we'll ever need."

Amos appeared skeptical. "I think it will be successful," he agreed. "But the young fellows who are going to be lining up couldn't come up with enough ready cash to pay the bill if they spent everything they have on kisses."

"I know," Rome said. "Wait till you hear the plan."

The meeting was breaking up. There were a couple of details to go over with the fellows who'd volunteered for the building crew. Matt Purdy stopped to tell them a ribald joke.

"Did you hear the one about the buck-toothed gal who went on her honeymoon?" he asked.

Rome and Amos listened to the whole story, laughed politely at the appropriate time and were then able to make their escape.

They walked down the long stairway into the main part of the bank, retrieving their hats from the rack near the door. Nodding cordially to Viceroy Ditham, they went out together into the street.

Still Rome didn't speak. They crossed to the far side and up the walk. Rome waited until they were in a deserted area in front of the greengrocer's alleyway and completely out of earshot of anyone else before he spoke.

He, of course, had no intention of revealing the personal agenda of Miss Gussie and himself. But he delightedly, even proudly, revealed the rest of the plan. Rome enjoyed it so much, he laughed out loud just telling it.

Amos didn't laugh at all. In fact, as the explanation went on, he began to look considerably displeased. His brow was furrowed with worry.

"I picked the women carefully," Rome said, attempting to pull a rein on his own hilarity. "I didn't choose anyone who would create a hardship. All of the wives are married to men well heeled and perfectly able to make a fine little contribution to the fireworks fund. So we're going to encourage them to do so."

The expression on Amos Dewey's face grew darker. He folded his arms across his chest and shook his head.

"The ladies will never agree to this," he said.

"They already have," Rome told him. "We've got Madge Simpson, Kate Holiday, Constance Wilhelm, Loralene Davies, Birdie Honey—even dear old Eliza Penderghast has volunteered."

Amos looked genuinely shocked.

"Well, they are very ill-advised," he said. "And when they speak to their husbands about it, I'm sure that they will be forbidden to participate."

"Speak to their husbands?" Rome looked at him, puzzled. "They can't speak to their husbands about it. That would destroy the element of surprise."

"You expect these women to participate in such a public folly without the permission of their husbands?"

Rome put his hands upon his hips. He was becoming more than a little annoyed.

"The young girls will be expected to ask their fathers," he said. "But these wives are full-grown women. How much permission do they need to play a joke on their husbands?"

"They might not need it, but they should have it just the same," Amos said. "I don't like this. I don't like it at all."

"Why not?" Rome asked. He was definitely put out now.

"The whole thing smacks of prostitution," Amos declared.

"Prostitution?" Rome was incredulous.

"Paying a woman for her kisses. What else would that be?"

"They are not paying the women." Rome's voice held all the calmness and patience he could muster. "They are donating money for charity."

"A negligible difference," Amos argued. "Money is being paid for a lady's favors and that is morally abhorrent."

"It's not morally anything," Rome assured him. "It's a fun joke the wives are going to play on their husbands to make money for the fireworks."

"I certainly would never have allowed my wife to be involved in anything like this," Amos stated unequivocally. "And she would never have gone behind my back to do so."

Rome had no idea what to say. He stared at Amos in disbelief.

Dewey eyed him coldly and spoke with rapier intent.

"I think your own questionable standards are creeping into your public obligations."

"Questionable standards?"

Rome finally understood. This was not about the kissing booth. This had nothing to do with wives or jokes or raising money for fireworks. This was about Pansy Richardson. This was about himself and Pansy Richardson.

"You know exactly my meaning," Amos said.

Rome tried to come up with a suitable reply. He had very few choices.

He could admit it. They were both men. Men understood that illicit relationships sometimes occur. Neither he nor Pansy had a spouse to be unfaithful to, so while their actions were scandalous, they were not adulterous. Amos might not approve, but he could not have Rome either arrested or excommunicated. Rome could simply admit it and let the chips fall where they may.

Or he certainly could deny it. There was so much lying and deception going on already, one more wouldn't amount to much. He could claim that it was over. Which was not a bad suggestion.

What he chose to do was neither of those alternatives, and the best course in his estimation. He did not deign to reply. His life was in no way the concern of Amos Dewey.

Rome turned and walked away without a word. He crossed the street and kept moving. Head high, shoulders back, angry inside as well as concerned. A jumble of thoughts seething in his brain. It took a concerted effort to sort them out. Once he did, he felt somewhat better.

If it had been Dewey's intent to expose him, he would simply have done so. Instead he had spoken to him face-to-face. That was a good sign. It was a warning. Amos was telling him that he had the power to expose him. He would do so if Rome didn't . . .

Rome smiled. This was not about the kissing booth. This was about Miss Gussie. Dewey was warning him away from Miss Gussie. It was working. The fellow was jealous. He was as ripe and ready as a blackberry drooping on the stem. Miss Gussie could pluck him off and make him into a pie at her leisure.

It was going to work. It was all going to work. Rome was going to get his partnership. Miss Gussie was going to get her perfect wedding. And Amos Dewey . . . Amos Dewey was going to get more than he'd bargained for.

I certainly would never have allowed my wife to be involved. And she would never have gone behind my back to do so, Amos had said, giving a lot of insight into his marriage. Being wed to a woman like Miss Gussie was going to be a good deal different.

Suddenly it seemed to Rome that the two were not particularly well matched at all.

He reached for the latch on the gate and hesitated, realizing where he was and what he'd done. He'd left Amos heading for home. But he was not standing in front of McCade's Boardinghouse. It was Miss Gussie's gate and garden that he'd come to.

11

PANSY HEARD ABOUT THE KISSING BOOTH WHEN ROME came to make his regular ice delivery. She met him at the back door with a big smile. She was, however, fully dressed, which seemed fine with him. He kissed her and hugged her close, but there was something distant in his touch. She could probably have convinced herself that it didn't mean anything, but she was hoping that it did.

He was extremely pleased with the whole idea of the kissing booth. Pansy laughed with him at the plan to make the married men cough up money to kiss their own wives. And she listened intently to his special bonus strategy with Gussie Mudd. Rome was convinced that Dewey was writhing with jealousy and this one small gesture would put him over the edge. Pansy wasn't at all certain that would happen, but the possibility deserved consideration.

"So by next week at this time, your life ought to be pretty much back to the way that it used to be," she said. "You and Gussie will once more be to each other what you always were."

He looked a little surprised at her words.

"It will never really be what it used to be," he said. "I'll be a partner and have a lot more say in the running of the business. And Miss Gussie and I know each other a good deal better now than we ever have. That changes things."

Pansy smiled. "Yes, of course it does," she said.

She watched him stow the ice in the lower drawer of the icebox and she felt an overwhelming sense of sadness. She had not loved him. She did not love him. But she would miss him just the same.

"Are you all right?" he asked her.

"Oh, yes, I'm fine," she assured him. "It's . . . it's just the heat. Summer must really be upon us."

"Uh-huh," he said, not quite believing the excuse. "I was going to tell you that I couldn't see you for a while. That I felt like we need not take any risks to visit until all of this is over with. But if it's over by Sunday, as I think it might be, then I can still show up here late Sunday night."

"No, you needn't come here on Sunday," she said. "I . . . I've just been so busy, as I'm sure you have too. I'm just going to rest, I think."

That surprised him.

"Well, all right, then," he said. "I'll wait until the next week, but we will have to celebrate my success: Rome Akers, a partner in Mudd Manufactured Ice."

"You seem pretty sure about what you want," she said.

"Shouldn't I be?"

"Do you know the story about the peddler who prayed for a mule?" she asked.

Rome shook his head negatively.

"There was this peddler man whose old horse died,"

she said. "He needed an animal to pull his wagon, but he had no money to buy one."

Rome leaned against the icebox, folding his arms across his chest, listening.

"He saw this ancient toothless mule that had been put out to pasture as far too old to work," she continued. "And the peddler thought it might be able to pull the wagon for a few months at least. But the peddler couldn't afford to buy even him. So he began to pray."

Pansy put her hands together as if imploring Heaven.

"Night after night the peddler prayed. 'Lord, give me that mule to pull my wagon.' Day after day he prayed. 'Lord, give me that mule to pull my wagon.' "

She looked at Rome once more.

"Finally one day up in Heaven, God called Saint Peter over and said, 'Peter, see that the peddler gets that old mule.' Saint Peter said that he would take care of it. 'The peddler's been praying for a long time,' Saint Peter pointed out. 'He will surely be happy to get that mule.' God sighed and told him, 'Yes, I suppose he will. I had a crack team of chestnut geldings in mind for him, but the man just seemed to have his heart so set on that tired old mule.' "

Rome chuckled and shook his head. "That's a funny story, all right, ma'am," he said. "But what is it supposed to mean?"

She walked over to him. He opened his arms as if to embrace her, but she took his hands in her own and held him, looking him closely in the eye.

"It means, Mr. Romeo Akers, do not set your sites too low in this world," she said. "God may have bigger plans for you."

Rome squeezed her hands and planted a gentle kiss on her forehead.

"I should call Reverend Holiday," he teased, "and tell him that you're maneuvering for his job."

Pansy shook her head.

"Not me," she said. "God and I haven't been on speaking terms since Grover's death. But I trust Him to look out for the people I care about, even if I choose to look after myself."

Rome's expression grew serious, as if he wanted to say more. Pansy was pretty sure that she didn't want to hear it.

"You'd better get on out of here," she said. "Vera Pearsall is probably timing your visits and it wouldn't do business any good to have folks thinking that you're spending far too much time with me."

He kissed her again, this time on the lips, but it was as chaste as the other had been.

"You're right, I've got to go," he said. "And a week from Sunday is a very long time away."

Rome picked up his ice tongs and headed for the door.

"I'll let you know what happens on Sunday," he promised. "For all I know, Amos Dewey may challenge me to fisticuffs right there in the middle of the park. The fireworks kissing booth could be as explosive as the fireworks themselves."

Pansy smiled and waved as he walked out the door and then whispered to herself, "Not if I have any say in it."

After he left she hurried upstairs to change her clothes. The royal blue would be the gown to wear. It was perfectly modest and yet cut in a way that showed her figure to fine advantage. Of course, she knew from experience that wearing it uptown would have every man in Cottonwood turning to get a better look at her.

But that was all right, she decided, as long as she was able to capture the attention of the man she sought.

She didn't truly know Amos Dewey's heart. Only a couple of weeks ago she would have said she thought him incapable of love. But she was not so sure anymore. He was not exactly the cold, dead shell of a man she had thought him to be. Pansy knew that he was aware of her. And if he was aware of her, he *could* perhaps become jealous, as Rome intended. He could run back to Gussie Mudd with a marriage proposal. And the silly woman would accept it, never imagining how much better off she could be. Pansy was determined to see that didn't happen.

She dusted her face with La Blanche powders and tinted her lips and cheeks with Blush of Roses. Her hair was neat and tidy. Deliberately she pulled loose a couple of strands around her face. She looked a little tousled, a little wanton, a little bit more than Amos Dewey would be able to ignore.

The man had suggested that she had syphilis. That infuriated her. The insufferable conceit of believing that you know all and understand all made her furious. But she recognized that she was as much to blame for his misunderstanding as anyone. She had dared the community to think what they would. And they certainly did. Now she had to suffer the consequences. If things went her way, she would at least redeem herself in her own eyes.

A quarter hour later, her blue parasol with the black lace trim overhead, she made her way up Brazos Street toward the center of town. She felt a rather surprising case of the nervous jitters. It was a condition that rarely bothered her. She cared so little about her life that risks no longer held much fear. Being trampled by runaway horses or struck down with a fatal disease seemed a fair enough end to a sad, broken life. She would never seek out calamity. She wouldn't throw herself from a cliff or drink poison. But if something tragic happened to her, she wouldn't really mind it so much either.

She supposed that was why she was willing to make this sacrifice. Why, after all that had happened, after all she had done to maintain her own self-respect, she was willing to lower herself to what people believed her to be. Somebody deserved to be happy. She was fairly certain that she never would be again, but she didn't want that fate for Rome Akers. In fact, she didn't even want it for Gussie Mudd.

Pansy reached the barbershop to discover that it was not nearly as empty and deserted as it had been upon her last visit. All along the wall and in front of the window, the chairs were full of men, each and every one of whom had both wide eyes focused directly upon her.

She hated it, but it played into her hands as well. Nothing could make a man act more foolishly than knowing other men were watching.

Joe Simpson sat in the big, fancily carved red-leather-and-mahogany barber's chair. His face completely obscured by a lather of shaving soap, he was recognizable only by the bald spot on the top of his head. Above him, Amos stood poised with razor in hand, ready to make the first draw.

"Mrs. Richardson," he said by way of acknowledgment and seemed far too displeased and disconcerted to say anything further.

"Mr. Dewey," she answered. "If I could speak to you privately for a moment, sir."

He plainly did not like the idea. He gave a quick,

almost guilty glance toward the men all dutifully cooling their heels in uncomfortable chairs. However, she knew that under no circumstances would he ask her to take a seat and wait her turn. No woman would be expected to linger in a barbershop. And one with Pansy's reputation would incite far too much interest and speculation if she did.

Every other man might well be willing to take that chance. She knew Amos Dewey would not. Pansy gave only a cursory glance around. Each and every fellow in the place was staring at her and Amos in turn, and grinning like a fool.

Dewey perused the room as well, as if hopeful that he might see a private spot. There was, of course, not one available.

Finally, reluctantly, he gestured toward the rear door.

"If you'd care to step into the back room, ma'am," he said.

Pansy crossed the room, head high, with every movement closely observed. She didn't exaggerate her movements or swivel her hips when she walked. She didn't need to. She simply moved slowly and the men's imaginations managed to do the rest.

Amos politely held the door for her, but it opened inward. To hold it involved stepping halfway inside and narrowing the entry. As she came up beside him, she saw his Adam's apple move when he swallowed. Pansy was tempted to brush against him as she went past, but did not give in to the evil temptation, knowing it would not ultimately serve her purpose and might completely frighten the man off.

The back of the barbershop was primarily used for bathing. It was a small area, damp and steamy with a closed-in, musty smell. A dazzling array of lead-lined pipes ran through the room, pumping in both water to be heated and that coming directly from the tank. The large japanned bathtub took up much of the space, but was almost overshadowed by the huge heating tank on the fuel-burning hot boiler.

The boiler was rather noisy. Amos went to stand by it as if its very formidable bulk could bolster him. Pansy had no choice but to follow him.

She stood in front of him at arm's length. Close enough for him to hear, but far enough away that he could still get a good look at her. He'd left the door open, so that they were in full view of the men by the window. But no one could possibly hear what they had to say.

"What do you want?" he asked, immediately coming to the point.

"I'm ready for you to look at my spot," she said. "I don't think I can bear the pain much longer."

The last was added to elicit his sympathy. She could see by his expression that it worked, but not particularly well.

"You really must help me," she implored.

"You want me to look at it now?"

"No, not now, of course not," Pansy said, wondering if she had perhaps overplayed her hand. "With all these men here, I couldn't possibly let you examine me."

Amos glanced back in their direction.

"You do see what I meant about noses to the glass," she said.

He didn't answer, but he did offer a reluctant nod. Pansy didn't have to turn her head in that direction to see that every eye there was looking straight at them.

Amos was silent for a long moment. She knew that he didn't want to do it. He wanted to just send her away. But she also knew that he wouldn't. He was not the kind of man who could do such a thing. She counted on that.

"All right," he said. "How about tonight after closing? I'll put paper on the window and draw the drapes."

"But how will you see what you're doing?" she asked. "Lamps are such weak lighting. Wouldn't it be better in daylight?"

"Well, yes, certainly it would, but—"

"Then I'll come on Sunday afternoon," she cut in.

"Sunday?"

"You are closed on Sundays, of course."

"Of course."

"And everyone should be busy promenading in the park," Pansy pointed out. "There will be plenty of daylight through the papers on the windows and you'll be able to see perfectly well."

"Yes, I suppose I could, but actually, I have another engagement on Sunday," he said.

"Oh, I am sorry," Pansy told him, apologizing. "That is perfectly all right. I do understand. I'll come back sometime next week and see if we can set up another day."

The idea of her returning in front of his customers elicited exactly the response she expected.

"No, no," he said. "Let's go ahead and get it over with, shall we? I can miss my other commitment. Sunday will be fine."

"I hate for you to cancel your plans," she lied smoothly.

"It's no trouble," he assured her. "I don't believe anyone will miss me."

The crew to construct the kissing booth arrived early in the morning on Saturday. It was only a two-hour job. But the fact that a half-dozen men showed up to work turned it into a half-day project.

Joe and Perry had agreed to help Rome. Pearsall and the reverend showed up to tell them how they should do it. Pete Davies was there to complain about his wife. And Amos was on the committee, but kept his thoughts and words to himself all morning.

Completely unexpected was the arrival of Viceroy Ditham, carrying an eight-foot one-by-twelve to be used as a counter edge for the booth.

"If my little girl is going to stand here giving out kisses to fellows all afternoon," he said, "I intend to make dang sure those young bucks ain't going to get too close."

"We'll put the wide counter on this side," Rome told them. "And put all the young women behind it. I'll need another counter on this side."

"Another counter?" Perry asked. "What for?"

Rome didn't answer.

"We won't need a one-by-twelve for this side," he asserted. "A two-by-four laid flat will be plenty good enough."

Perry looked at Joe questioningly.

"You're not going to let us in on it?" Joe asked.

"I told you, there were a few big surprises," Rome answered.

"I just hope you haven't lined up the employees from Nellie's," Perry said, referring to the dance hall/saloon on the far side of the railroad tracks.

Rome chuckled. "You know, I didn't think of that," he said. "But there is still time, Perry. Why don't you go down there and talk to the girls? Joe and I will build a separate booth for them. One that's more like a shed, closed in on all sides and with a latch on the door."

That brought a spate of ribald laughter all around.

"What's the joke, gentlemen?" Reverend Holiday asked, coming up behind them unexpectedly.

Joe and Perry both looked guilty. But Rome refused to be shamefaced.

"Just a little low humor, Reverend," Rome said.

"Ah . . ." the pastor said, nodding. "I do understand. Sometimes a story is far beneath the level of Christian decency, but it's so deucedly funny that it just has to be told."

The men relaxed somewhat. Perry maybe relaxed too much.

"So, Preacher, did you hear the one about the buck-toothed gal who went on her honeymoon?"

Reverend Holiday eyed him critically. "That one may have to be told," he said. "But it does not have to be told to me."

The little building project went up with few problems or setbacks and no injuries, unless you counted Wade Pearsall hammering his thumb. The booth was eight feet square with a wide, overhanging slant roof to protect the complexions of the ladies. It had a nice counter on the east side and a narrower one on the north. The south side was open as the point of entry and the west was low and latticed to cut down on the sun but allow the breeze to blow through.

Just before noon, a delegation from the Circle of Benevolent Service, consisting of Kate Holiday, Madge Simpson, Constance Wilhelm and Miss Gussie, showed up with bunting, streamers and signs. Even more welcome, they brought lemonade and lunch.

They spread a couple of tablecloths on the ground and had an impromptu picnic. There was much laughter and good-humored gluttony.

The women showed the signs they'd lettered. Madge's had a very large F on one side and then the rest of the words—'IFTIETH ANNIVERSARY, 'OUNDERS DAY, 'OURTH OF JULY and 'IREWORKS— on the other.

Constance went for the more factual, gaily decorating the words KISSING BOOTH and TWO BITS, the latter indicating the price.

Kate Holiday's sign was a good deal more dramatic and had the reverend coughing down a naughty chuckle. It read: KISS A GIRL, SET OFF SOME FIREWORKS.

The ladies were roundly praised for their efforts, and accepted the accolades with good humor and exaggerated humility. It was all much fun. Not the least of which was the little private picnic.

"I can't tell you how long it's been since we've done something like this," Madge observed as she handed her husband another chicken leg.

"We go for a lot of picnics," Constance said. "But we have children underfoot all the time. It's just not the same."

"It's sure not," Pete Davies agreed. "Once a woman has children, she just has no need for a husband, except to bring home the paycheck."

"I'm not sure about that," Madge Simpson replied. "Children take a lot of time and energy. It may look like a wife doesn't need her husband, but I think she may need him more than ever."

"But children do change things," Wade Pearsall pointed out.

"Oh, but they'll be grown and gone before you know it," Reverend Holiday told them all, waving away both complaints and concerns. "And once they are out on their own, you miss them."

"Of course," Constance agreed.

"And you'll hope that you and your husband can still remember why it was that you wanted to spend your life together," Kate Holiday added.

The pastor looked over at his wife, apparently a little surprised at her words, but he made no comment.

Rome had nothing to say either. He'd made a point of seating Miss Gussie directly opposite Amos Dewey. Then he sat down next to her, closer than propriety would normally allow. He was pretty sure that no one could fail to notice. Dewey was certainly looking daggers at them.

With his fingers, Rome plucked out a nice tender piece of white meat. He held it up to show Miss Gussie. She looked at him, puzzled. He held her gaze, willing her to trust him. He brought the piece of chicken to her mouth, never breaking eye contact. As he neared her lips, she opened them for him, showing a pretty pink tongue and white, even teeth. She took the offered tidbit with her teeth and he watched her as she chewed it.

"Good?" he asked her.

"Very good," she replied.

Rome glanced over at the group and noted that several people were actually watching. Amos Dewey, with his back now to them, was deliberately not.

"Who fried this chicken?" Rome asked. "It's perfect."

"It's my chicken," Constance answered. "I'm glad you like it. Perry still says it's not as good as his mother's."

"Your mother makes better chicken than this?" Rome asked him. "Isn't she a widow woman now? Maybe I should go sit a Sunday or two on her front porch."

The idea of young Rome courting the ancient and disagreeable Mrs. Wilhelm brought delighted chuckles all around. Except for Amos Dewey, who turned back around to make a joke that had no hint of humor in its tone.

"Seems to me the right widow woman might suit you perfectly," he said.

"Maybe so," Rome told him, grinning amiably.

"So, Rome," Pete Davies asked, "when are you going to let us all in on this big surprise that's coming tomorrow?"

Rome studied the group. A couple of the women looked guilty and sheepish, but not so much that their mates would take notice.

"The surprise tomorrow," he said. "I'll tell you all about it . . . tomorrow."

Everybody laughed.

"Joe and I think we've figured it out already," Perry said. "We think he's invited the girls down at Nellie's to participate."

That statement brought guffaws of laughter from the men and little titters of embarrassed giggles from the ladies.

"More likely," Wade Pearsall put in, "he's asked the grieving Widow Richardson to participate."

The gathering found that remark equally humorous. Rome did not. He glanced toward Amos Dewey. His jaw was set grimly.

Rome took another swig of lemonade and sidled up a little closer to Miss Gussie. If the idea that he was seeing Mrs. Richardson and courting Miss Gussie didn't sit well with Amos, then so much the better. The more he was disturbed, the sooner he'd be brought to the point. Besides, it was nice to be next to Miss Gussie. She was warm and cheerful and smelled really nice. And she made him feel at ease. Rome hadn't realized until he was talking with Pansy how much had actually changed between them. A few short weeks ago she was his employer. Liked and respected, certainly, but he had not thought her capable of finer, gentler feelings. He did now. He understood how lonesome and filled with longing she must have been.

He felt some of that too. Someday he wanted to be settled down like the couples around him; he wanted to be making a life with someone, dreaming of the future ahead, persisting through the adversities of parenthood. He wanted that. Every man did, sooner or later. Once he was settled with his partnership and his life was his own, Rome decided he might begin looking for the right woman.

She would have to match him in ambition and intellect. That was more important to him than a pretty face and a fine figure, though he certainly could appreciate those as well. But he didn't think he could bear being tied to someone who didn't strive or didn't think. He wanted a woman who would truly be able to share his life, he thought. To share it the way Miss Gussie could share it. A wife who could talk with him and laugh with him and allow him to be just the man he was, without shame or pretense. That could be a heaven on earth. And if she could move beneath him like Pansy Richardson, that would be even better.

"What are you smiling about?"

He looked into Miss Gussie's trusting brown eyes and realized that some daydreams were never meant to be shared.

He leaned close and whispered, "I'm just thinking about tomorrow."

She blushed and lowered her eyes. He had meant that he was thinking about the great trick they were playing upon the husbands. He realized Miss Gussie must think he was referring to their personal plans, sharing kisses in front of the whole town.

That could be very frightening for her. Rome wondered if she had ever been kissed. Surely she had. The woman must be getting close to thirty. In all that time some man must have found his way to those sweet pink lips. He glanced over at Amos. Had he kissed her? They'd kept company for nearly three years. Could a man resist a woman that long? Rome suspected that if any man could, it might be Amos Dewey.

He realized, however, that it didn't matter who had kissed or when or not. She had never kissed him and that made what they were going to do tomorrow distracting.

He observed that she was daintily wiping her mouth on a napkin.

"Walk with me," he said, rising to his feet.

He offered his hand and she took it. He helped her up and then kept hold of her arm, weaving it with his own in such a way that he appeared to be an elegant escort, but he could, with virtually no effort, brush the side of her breast with his forearm and elbow. It was a trick boys learned when they were just out of knee pants, when no other contact with the female gender was remotely possible.

The gentlemen in the group, if they were paying attention, would undoubtedly notice the less than sterling handclasp. The ladies, he hoped, would remain ignorant.

"I'm going to show her our handiwork," he announced and began walking toward the little booth.

"Don't be telling her you did all the work yourself," Joe called out. "We all know how men in love are known to lie."

There was some good-humored laughter behind them. Rome chose not to make a retort.

"Men in love," he repeated quietly to Miss Gussie. "We've certainly come a long way in a short time if that is the kind of thing they are saying about me."

"Yes," she agreed. "I remember worrying that nobody would believe it. Now it seems that everybody does."

Rome smiled down at her.

"I wish I could have seen Dewey's face when I fed you that chicken," he said. "The fellow was so put out he turned his back to us completely."

"Yes, he did," she said quietly.

Her tone was not light or victorious. She sounded worried, or maybe confused.

"Are you all right?" he asked her.

"Oh, yes, I'm fine," she assured him. But he didn't think it was true.

He released his grasp upon her arm and took it again in the more traditional and respectful manner, thinking he might have offended her. She didn't seem to notice.

They reached the booth and he walked her into it through the open south wall. She dutifully admired the solid workmanship and listened to his explanation of the design. She even laughed at the two separate counters, wide for the young unmarried girls, more narrow for the wives intent on costing their husbands a pretty penny.

"I suppose I should be here at the corner," she said, standing at the joining to the two counters. "I'm neither one of the young girls nor a married woman."

"You'll be a married woman soon enough," he promised. "Remember, you wanted the Fourth of July to be your wedding day."

She smiled for the first time since they'd left the group.

"Are you nervous about tomorrow?" he asked her.

"Tomorrow?"

"Kissing in front of all the people in town."

From the blush that stained her cheek, it was clear that even the idea of it was embarrassing.

"You don't have to be afraid," he assured her.

"I know," she answered. "I know you would never . . . take advantage."

He was silent for a moment, surprised as he took in the import of her statement. Then he smiled.

"Well, I might actually," he suggested mischievously. "But probably not in front of every man and woman in town."

She jerked her head up, startled. When she saw that he was teasing, she gave him a clench-fisted blow to the belly.

"Oh! You've wounded me, woman," he complained. "It's a knockout punch. I don't think I can stand."

She giggled at his exaggerated reaction until she realized that he had backed her further into the corner, clutching the wooden counters to maintain his footing, and had a supporting, entrapping arm on either side of her.

Miss Gussie gazed at him, wariness in her eyes.

"I'm going to kiss you now," he warned her quietly. "I'm not going to hurt you or take advantage of you. I'm just going to kiss you."

"Now?"

"Dewey is probably watching us," he said. "But even so, I think that we should get past the awkwardness of this first kiss in relative privacy."

She swallowed bravely, as if she were readying herself for some terrible ordeal.

"All right," she said.

Closing her eyes, she pursed her lips tightly together and raised her chin to offer them to Rome.

He thanked his own foresight in getting her alone for this. It would have been downright shaming had she tried to kiss him like that tomorrow. The whole town would know that she was no sweetheart of his.

It should have been humorous, but it was not. It was an unpardonable world in which this sweet, warm woman with so much to give should have been surrounded by babies already, but didn't yet even know how to kiss a man.

He laid his hand upon her jaw. Her eyes opened.

"That's not quite how you do it, Miss Gussie," he said.

Her brow furrowed. "Oh, I'm sure it is, Mr. Akers," she answered. "I have seen people kiss and they do their lips just like this."

"Perhaps when they kiss an aunt or a mother-in-law," he said. "But a man doesn't kiss a woman like that."

She wasn't convinced. "Are you certain?"

"I am absolutely certain," he assured her.

His hand still upon her jaw, he allowed his thumb to caress the very edge of her lips.

"You need to open your mouth," he said.

"Open my mouth?"

"Just a little bit. Not a big O, like you were visiting a dentist. Just a little *o*, as if you were drinking from a narrow-necked bottle."

"What kind of woman would drink from a bottle?"

"The kind who would like to be kissed," he replied. "Now come on, try it."

Courageously, with brow furrowed in concentration, she attempted just the right opening. It was nearly perfect.

"That's good," he praised her. "That's very good."

She didn't acknowledge his words but held her mouth firmly in place, as if concerned that she might be unable to achieve the same result again.

Rome raised her chin a little higher and leaned forward, angling his head slightly and bringing his lips down upon her own.

"It's just me," he whispered a hairbreadth away. "You don't need to be nervous or afraid with me."

His lips touched hers. That was all he intended. Just a touch of mouths, a very tender gesture, intimate but not impassioned. But as he tasted the warm sweetness of her mouth, he lingered. The reality of her nearness was so much more beguiling than he'd expected. For a moment he forgot that he was only favoring a friend and became entranced by the absolute perfection of Gussie in his arms. And she *was* in his arms. He would never know if she had stepped forward or if he had pulled her into his grasp, but somehow his hands had ceased their grip upon the counters and she was pressed close against him.

He took a gasp of much-needed breath and deepened the kiss. Her mouth was eager and infinitely ardent. The soft curve of her bosom against his chest was enticing. His hands trembled with the need to clench her buttocks and grind her body into the aching erection in the front of his trousers.

That thought stopped him in his tracks. He jerked away immediately and turned his back from her so she would not see what, perhaps, she had felt. He was as inappropriately hard as if he were a boy in knickers hiding under the meeting-house steps to get a glimpse beneath the ladies' skirts.

"Oh, my!" Miss Gussie said, behind him. "Oh, my goodness, I . . . well, I never imagined it was like that. No wonder people make such a fuss about it. I always wondered. It just never seemed . . . my goodness, I'm tingly all over."

Rome was regaining his control and composure. Her

last statement caught so in his throat that he was forced to cough. He turned back to her.

"Are you sure we should be so . . . so shocking in public?" she asked him.

"I am sorry, Miss Gussie," he told her. "No, we should not do that tomorrow. I . . . I lost control. I did take advantage. I cannot apologize enough. I . . ."

"Oh, that wasn't what you intended," she said.

"No, ma'am, I assure you it was not. Tomorrow I promise I will be a good deal more circumspect and my kisses won't—they won't be anything like that."

"Oh, that's good, then," she answered.

"I am sorry I was so offensive," he said.

Her eyes were bright with excitement, passion.

"I wasn't offended, Mr. Akers," she assured him. "I was . . . well, I was simply so . . . so pleasured that I thought perhaps we had it all wrong. It should be the ladies paying the money."

Rome's jaw dropped open. He was speechless.

"What are you two doing up there so long?" Joe Simpson called out to them from the picnic spot.

They both turned guiltily and waved to him.

"Rome, you aren't trying to get a free sample, are you?"

Simpson laughed uproariously and most of the rest of the group found his remark quite humorous as well. Rome and Gussie smiled at each other, but neither thought it was nearly as funny as it should have been.

SUNDAY DAWNED BRIGHT AND EXPECTANT. IT WAS barely three weeks until the Fourth of July, three weeks until Gussie Mudd planned to be a married woman. But her focus as she sat in church listening intently to Reverend Holiday was on the city park and the kissing booth.

Every time her thoughts drifted to the day before and Rome's lips on her own, little thrilling shivers traveled up and down her spine. Deliberately she tried not to think about it while seated in church, but the more diligently she tried to avoid the memory, the more often her ruminations went off in that direction.

She had been meeting Rome Akers almost daily since her father's death. But she was meeting him this afternoon and somehow everything about it had changed. Gussie found herself looking forward to his arrival. Their scheming had brought them closer together. They had become more friends than employee and employer. Gussie had always admired Rome's hard work and his honesty and thoroughness. Now she discovered that she enjoyed Rome's company. She liked the sound of his laugh, the twinkle that sparkled in those clear blue eyes and the way he said *Miss Gussie* as if it were just one long word.

She had chosen to wear the dress Miss Ima made for her. She'd been up half the night, with a good deal less skill than that of the seamstress, loosening the waist so she could wear it without such drastic lacing. It fit her now, and though certainly not as stunning as it had been, it did look very nice on her.

She hoped that Rome agreed. If Rome thought she looked nice, then, of course, Amos would think the same. She'd worn the dress for Amos. Because she knew Rome liked it.

The whole town seemed to be buzzing with excitement and anticipation. All the women seemed to be in on the wonderful joke. Though not a word was spoken carelessly. With children all around, it was understood by mothers that a secret kept was one never mentioned. The husbands remained blissfully in the dark about the vaguely mentioned *surprises* in store.

She had hoped that Rome would have come to escort her to church this morning, but he had not mentioned it and she had not asked him. He had seemed strangely thoughtful and subdued yesterday after their visit to the kissing booth.

He'd said that he had "lost control." Gussie was not entirely sure what he meant by that. He had certainly seemed very much in control to her. He had been demonstrative and masterful, as if in complete command of his faculties, as well as of her own.

With her thoughts heading in that direction once more, Gussie resolutely forced them on to a more Sunday-morning plane.

The pastor's message was an important one on the duties of marriage. She admonished herself to pay close attention. It was still her plan to shortly join the ranks of wedded wives. She should be very interested in what that job entailed. But it was not the *duties* of marriage that occupied her mind, it was the potential delights of it.

She sighed aloud and then covered her mouth, horrified that perhaps someone had heard her and knew that she carried her heart in her hand.

Surreptitiously she glanced around; no one seemed to be looking at her. That was good. It was good for now. But this afternoon she wanted everyone looking at her. Especially Amos Dewey. She wanted that particular pair of dark brown eyes peering out from round-rimmed spectacles to be focused directly upon her.

She allowed her imagination to wander. In her mind's eye she saw herself leaning over the narrow counter, her lips dangerously close to those of Rome Akers. Suddenly, Amos Dewey comes pushing through the crowd. He grabs Rome by the shoulder and jerks him away from her. Then he pulls Gussie into his arms and kisses her, he kisses her exactly the same way that Rome had kissed her.

An excited little shiver ran through her again. She was grateful to stand for the benedictory prayer.

As the congregation bustled out the front door, Gussie received several conspiratorial winks from her friends. It was as if everyone simply wanted to get the midday meal over with and rush to the park. Gussie felt exactly the same way.

Her stroll home was more of a jaunt and her hastily put together meal was hardly tasted, she was so anxious to get on with the day. She forced herself to take tiny bites from her plate and chew eat one slowly and thoroughly. But when she finished, it was still nearly a half hour before Rome was to arrive.

When she heard the creak of the front gate a full fifteen minutes early, it was all she could do not to go running out the door and down to the gate to meet him.

He looked surprisingly sporty and fashionable in his blue-striped seersucker coat, dark blue trousers and polka-dot vest. His collar and cuffs were celluloid, but they had the look of linen. And he'd left his driver's cap at home, replaced by a straw *Mustang* sombrero with a four-inch brim and braided ribbon band.

"You look very nice."

He grinned, removing his hat.

"I think that is what I am supposed to say, Miss Gussie," he told her. "You look very pretty. I do like that dress. But I hope you're not feeling faint today."

She blushed a little, but actually enjoyed his teasing.

"I don't think I'm likely to faint today," she said. "But I suppose I could carry smelling salts in my pocketbook."

"Maybe you should," he suggested. "Just thinking about spending the afternoon kissing you makes me feel a little faint myself."

It was a joke. A further attempt to tease her. And they both did laugh, but there was more underlying it. Gussie heart was pounding like a hammer. Rome couldn't quite meet her gaze and both of them were slightly awkward.

"Are you ready to go?" he asked.

It was actually very early. They could most likely be the first people in the park, but Gussie simply could not wait another moment.

"Yes, let's go," she said.

He led her down the steps and through the front gate.

"I like the way that you hold my arm," she told him.

"It's different somehow from the usual grasp of an escort."

"I'm sorry," he said hastily and quickly changed to the way that was so much more familiar.

"No, don't change it," she said. "I do really like the other way. It just seems so . . . so much more friendly."

There was something strange about Rome's expression. Something she couldn't quite interpret. But he smiled at her and offered his arm again in the unconventional manner.

They walked together side by side in silence. For the first time in a very long time, they didn't seem to have anything to say. The little shivers of nervousness that she'd been fending off all morning now seemed to be coming in waves of giddy trembling.

Gussie suddenly couldn't bear the silence another minute. They talked all the time. What on earth did they talk about? At that moment she couldn't think of a single thing. But there had to be something they could talk about right now.

"How is the pressure valve on the distiller?"

"Huh? Oh, yes, uh . . . well, it's not any better," he said. "It's not going to get any better. These things don't get better, they just get worse. But it's not any worse. It's not any worse yet. But it won't get better. It will have to be replaced. Uh . . . that's how it is."

"Oh, well, that's good," she said and then wasn't sure if it was.

The conversation dragged once more. He seemed to be scrounging his brain for a subject as frantically as she was herself.

"How was church?" he asked.

"Very good," she told him. "Very good. Everyone looked their best. Loralene had a new hat."

"Oh, that's nice," he said.

Gussie was astounded at herself. He'd asked her about church. A subject that could be expounded upon for hours, and she'd spoken only of clothes and hats.

"Reverend Holiday preached a very good sermon," she said.

"Oh, good," he said.

"Yes, very good."

"What . . . what did he preach about?" Rome asked.

"The sermon was on marital duties," she said.

Rome nearly tripped on something that wasn't there and his voice came out in an almost squeak.

"What?"

"Marital duties," she repeated.

"The preacher talked about that in church!"

Gussie looked at him curiously.

"Of course he did," she answered. "It's in Ephesians. You know, wives and husbands submitting to one another. A wife is to her husband as to the Lord and the husband is to love his wife as he loves his own flesh. That one."

"Oh, that one," Rome said. "I guess I don't know that one."

The silence returned.

"I wonder what Reverend Holiday will think about all that after Mrs. Holiday puts him through this afternoon."

The two exchanged glances and both burst into laughter.

"It's going to be a great joke," she said.

"What an afternoon," he agreed.

They both nodded.

"Maybe our last afternoon together," he said.

That thought brought them pause.

* * *

She didn't knock. She simply opened the door to the barbershop and walked in. He had been waiting for her, expecting her. Still, her arrival was a surprise. Somehow every time he looked at her he was surprised.

"Mrs. Richardson," he said, nodding.

"Good afternoon, Amos," she answered.

She closed the door behind her. The key was in the lock. She turned it and then pulled the shade down over the door, sealing off the rest of the world outside.

When she was in the room, it was as if she took up all the space and all the air. Amos had noticed that about her the other times she had come here, but today it was even worse. He felt as if she were all around him and he could scarcely draw breath.

Her clothing was mannish in style, dark blue with a short puffed-sleeved jacket. The white, pleated shirt-waist displayed narrow, crisply pressed pleats. At her collar was a little bow tie. Somehow, together it served to make her look more womanly, more desirable. Amos pushed that thought away. He did not desire her, he reminded himself. He no longer felt those things.

"I have everything ready," he told her. "It shouldn't take too long."

He hadn't told a soul about his plans to examine Pansy Richardson in order to protect her privacy. He would be late for the kissing booth in the park, but with all the uproar that was surely to result from Rome's wild idea, he doubted that anyone would even notice his absence.

He sincerely hoped Mrs. Richardson was not afflicted with a venereal disease, but if she were, Rome was sure to be infected. He could never marry. It was unfair to get Gussie's hopes up if the man was unfit for marriage. Amos had already disappointed the woman once. It would be too cruel a fate for her to set her affections again, only to have them dashed once more.

"Should I go ahead and remove my things?"

Her words startled him, caught him unaware. He glanced quickly at the front windows. He had covered them in a week's worth of newsprint and then he'd drawn the drapes anyway.

"Should I remove my things?" she repeated.

"Leave your things on," he said.

She put her hands on her hips and eyed him critically.

"You want me to sit in that chair with this hat on?" she asked.

Her hat. Her silly, undoubtedly expensive little hat. It couldn't keep the sun out of her eyes, or, for that matter, even out of her hair. But it did stick up on the top of her head with an expanse of ribbon and a great long feather.

"Remove your things and get in the chair," he said. "I want to get this over with as quickly as possible."

She gave a little laugh.

"A good many gentlemen think just that way," she said, her voice sultry and teasing.

Amos didn't like the sound of it.

She reached for the long jet pin that held her hat in place. The movement seemed to emphasize the long, sleek curves of her body. Everything about her was feminine and alluring. Amos turned his back on her, untempted, he told himself. He would keep his mind clear. He would keep his mind empty. He was determined to do that. But his eyes drifted up to her reflection in the mirror and he watched her. He couldn't help but watch her.

She removed her hat, setting it carefully upon an empty chair. Slowly, very slowly, she began peeling down her gloves. Revealing inch after inch of the pale flesh of her forearms, then the heel of her hand, her palm and finally five delicate feminine fingers. Then the baring of her other hand.

Amos swallowed hard and forced himself to look away. His hands trembled as he gathered his tools. The probe and scalpel were clean and had been sterilized in boracic acid and boiling water. The skin was supposedly full of germs, but he was not going to be guilty of adding any.

He glanced into the mirror. She was standing right behind him. She was just standing there looking at him. She'd removed her jacket and her silly little bow tie. In shirtsleeves, the top button undone, she seemed strangely small and vulnerable. There was no particular expression upon her face, but he found her somehow threatening.

He didn't know how that could be. Small, vulnerable, yet threatening. It didn't make sense. Amos stood head and shoulders taller. And she was a slightly built, delicate woman; even holding a knife or a gun, she would be no match for him. Yet he was wary of her. Some deeply buried native instinct warned him that Pansy Richardson was very, very dangerous.

"If you're ready, then get in the chair," he said.

"Oh, I'm ready, Amos," she replied. "I'm ready and I've been ready. The question is, are you ready?"

Her answer didn't alleviate his wariness.

He indicated the barber's chair. It was a beautiful piece of modern equipment and he was very proud to own it. It had come by train all the way from the East Coast, Koch & Son, New York, and it was as fine and fancy a barber's chair as any in this part of Texas. It was carved mahogany and finished in solid brass. It had an amazing hydraulic mechanism that allowed the barber to raise or lower it to the height most advantageous to him. It also revolved and reclined, which allowed for the best possible position for any job to be done.

Mrs. Richardson held out a hand to him.

Amos stared at it as if he didn't know what it was.

"Aren't you going to help me up?" she asked. "This chair looks very difficult for a woman to mount."

It didn't seem that difficult to Amos, but he offered his hand.

Pansy stepped upon the footrest and then pivoted, carefully seating herself on the slick red leather. She held his hand for what seemed like just an instant longer than necessary.

When she freed him, she ran that same hand along the upholstery, making sounds of obvious approval.

"This feels so nice," she said, stroking the smooth cowhide.

Amos swallowed uncomfortably. There was something so sensual about her. She was so difficult for a man to resist. But he had to resist her. He had to get this over with. He had to get her out of here.

Amos pumped the hydraulic-lift peddle three times in rapid succession. She jolted upward in inch-high increases. The jerking motions of her body were somehow erotic, filling his mind with images of pounding sexual climax.

"Is it on the back of your neck?" he asked.

"What? Oh, yes, it's on the back," she said.

Amos pulled the long brass lever on the side of the chair, reclining it as far as it would go.

"Is it on the left side or the right?" he asked her.

She hesitated. "It's . . . it's rather in the middle," she answered.

"Turn on your right side, then," he said.

He adjusted the mirror to catch the sunlight from the upper windows and focus it upon the occupant in the chair. His heart was beating faster than it should. Deliberately he calmed himself. A steady hand would be necessary and he must maintain one.

A couple of stray tendrils had escaped her elegant upsweep and curled around her neckline. Carefully he smoothed them out of the way. At his touch, she gasped audibly.

"I'll not hurt you," he promised. He considered himself very skilled and his scalpel was very sharp. "I'm going to relieve your pain, not add to it."

As he turned back her collar, he tried to avoid any direct contact between her flesh and his own.

He didn't see the carbuncle. The skin he encountered was perfect, unblemished and glowing with good health. He assumed the boil must be lower, but her clothing made it impossible to proceed.

"Could your loosen your shirtwaist a bit, Mrs. Richardson?" he said.

"Of course." She began fumbling with the buttons.

A moment later, Amos peeled the shirtwaist down her back. Even with it lowered, he did not see the carbuncle.

"I thought you said that it was on your neck," he told her.

"Oh, no, you misunderstood me," Pansy countered. "It's on my back."

Amos shook his head. He was certain she had said it was on her neck.

She wore a surprisingly high-necked corset cover and when he tried to pull it down, he discovered that it fit snugly. He couldn't examine the flesh beneath it. Perhaps he could locate the boil through the thin silk covering. He moved his hands tentatively across her back, feeling the smoothness of the material warmed by the flesh beneath it.

Pansy sighed and his heart caught in his throat. It had been so long since a woman had sighed at his touch. So long since he had touched.

He tried to pull his thoughts away. He didn't want a woman, he reminded himself. He especially didn't want this woman.

Amos stepped back from her. "I think you'll have to remove the corset cover," he said.

"All right," she answered, not seeming nearly enough concerned with her own modesty. She rolled over onto her back and sat up, pulling the shirtwaist out of her skirt. She handed it to him. He hung it on a peg at the edge of the washstand.

Amos stood dumbfounded as she crossed her arms over her chest and grabbed the hem of the corset cover with both hands. Despite some difficulty, she managed to pull it up and over her head.

Her corset was black and very tightly laced, showing ample décolletage. Amos looked away. He told himself it was gentlemanly reserve. But the unwanted stirring in the front of his trousers was equally causal. Even after looking away, however, he saw the image indelibly ingrained in his mind.

What was he doing here? Why didn't he make her go? They should not be alone together with her half dressed.

"Perhaps I should take this off as well," she said.

His back to her, he glanced up into the mirror. She was looking right at him. Looking right at him as she slowly unclasped the front hooks. The bottom one first. And then the next.

He couldn't breathe. He couldn't think. He was watching her. She was watching him. He was not supposed to be watching her. He was not supposed to be thinking about her. He should be thinking about Bess. His Bess. Bess whom he loved so dearly.

Bess seemed suddenly very far away and very long ago.

There was one hook left. One small impediment to his seeing her bosom naked, exposed. Amos's mouth was dry, his brow sweating. He was looking at her.

"Turn around, Amos," she said to him, so low, so seductive, it was almost like the words of a spell.

He turned and looked at her. There was no guile or trickery in her gaze. She spoke to him with honesty, forthrightly.

"I want you to make love to me, Amos," she said.

"What? Why?"

"Why not?"

"Bess . . ."

"Bess is dead, Amos," she said. "But you and I are not."

Bess was dead. His wife was dead. He hadn't been able to stop it. And he hadn't been able to change it. All the waiting for her had not brought her back to him.

"You don't have anything wrong, do you?" he asked. "There is not so much as a blemish on your skin."

Those blue eyes teased and taunted him now.

"You'll have to see for yourself, won't you, Amos." She lay her forefinger atop the lone hook that protected her modesty. "Won't you just have to see for yourself."

His hand trembled. His whole body trembled. He reached out and unfastened her corset. It fell away from her body, leaving her naked from the waist up.

His heart, his breath, his life caught in his throat.

"Perfect," was the word that came out of his mouth.

And perfect was an apt description of the two graceful, upward-tipped breasts before his gaze. He looked at her; feasting his eyes upon such beauty was like sustenance to his being. For the first time in a very long time, Amos Dewey felt alive.

"Shouldn't you touch me?" she suggested. "Just to make sure you're not dreaming."

Amos did touch her. He reached out to caress the pale, rosy-tipped mound. He tested the slope with two fingers. The flesh was so exquisitely soft. The nipple so incredibly hard. He cupped the breast in his hand; the weight and firmness were exactly what he thought they should be. She was absolutely and totally, in every way, exactly what she should be.

"Shall I lay back down now?" she asked him. "I should lay down so you can examine me."

Amos was too befuddled by desire to even answer.

Slowly, languidly, she lay back in the reclined barber's chair, drawing up her right knee and her skirt at the same time. She pulled the hem of her skirt nearly to the waist, revealing a flat belly and long legs covered by black stockings and red silk bloomers.

"Take your time, Amos," she whispered. "Examine me."

The blood was pounding through his brain, making it very difficult for him to think clearly, but it was also pooling in the front of his trousers. He was fully erect, almost painfully hard and aching. He shouldn't touch her. He knew that he shouldn't touch her. He no longer had feelings like this, he reminded himself. He no longer wanted this. He trembled all over, trying not to want it so wholly, so desperately. At that moment he couldn't remember why he shouldn't.

Pansy Richardson was reaching out to him.

"What's this?" she asked, her sultry voice teasing.

"Do you think you're going to be able to hide behind a big thing like this?"

She touched him. She merely touched him. Her hand rubbed him over his clothes. It was too much. He grabbed her hand and pushed it away.

He planted one knee beside her on the chair and bent down to kiss her. The taste of her was sweet and he wanted to savor it, but he was far too greedy. He buried his hands in her hair, holding her firmly and securely in his control as his mouth pursued the secrets of her own. With much eagerness he trailed his lips down her jaw and her throat to take her breast in his mouth.

Amos knew he was moving too fast. He knew he was rushing too much. But he was like a starving man offered a feast. He could not hold himself back. Pansy's hurried passion seemed to match his own.

He felt so jelly-legged he didn't know if he could stand. Somehow she got him seated beside her in the chair. She was holding him, caressing him. Meeting him touch for touch. Kiss for kiss.

She wiggled up into a sitting position upon his lap.

Amos jerked off the red silk bloomers, finding the flesh beneath them smoother and softer than the fine fabric.

In a near frenzy, four hands clawed and pulled at the buttons on his trousers. When they were finally loosed, she drew him out and caressed him. It was so wonderful, he simply could not stand it.

He drew her up to her knees and she straddled him. He touched her intimately and groaned aloud at the hot, welcoming wetness of her, opened wide as a blossom in summer rain.

As she lowered herself down upon him, he tried to take his time, to go slowly. He knew how big he was and how painful that could be to a woman.

Pansy would have none of his hesitance or trepidation. She did not cringe from his raw physicality but gloried in it. She buried him deep inside her. It was a tight fit that stretched and filled her. Yet she was so wet and slick that his entry was made easily and her only words of complaint were "More" and "Faster."

He grasped her buttocks, directing her, guiding her as they moved in lusty, hurried, desperate concord. Her whines of pleading and moans of pleasure were sounds more welcome to his ears than the finest music or most glorious oratory.

"Love me! Love me!"

She wrenched out the words through clenched teeth. He was certain he understood exactly what she meant.

He grabbed her around the waist and pulled her down tightly against him. Holding her rigid against him, he gripped her buttocks and pounded inside her again and again and again until they were all and everything. Nothing and no one existed beyond the mahogany-and-leather barber's chair and the two people straining toward bliss upon it.

"I can't wait," he groaned through his teeth. "I want and I can't wait."

"Amos!" she cried out as the inside of her body jerked and clenched him, racheting down upon his most heightened spots of sensation.

He came inside her, screaming against her breast. He came and came until he thought it might never stop. Years of pain and shame and aloneness poured out of him.

"I'm sorry," he began repeating over and over as soon as he could talk. "I'm sorry."

"It's all right," she whispered to him. "It's all right."

He continued his apology. "I'm sorry. I didn't

mean . . . I was so rough. It was so fast. It has been so long. I . . ."

Inexplicably, he felt himself tearing up. He was going to cry. He didn't want to. He tried not to. But when his eyes welled up, he closed them tightly to keep the tears at bay and they spilled out the sides of his eyes and down his face.

"That's all right," she said beside him. She was kissing his neck, caressing his shoulders. There was no passion in her actions, only comfort. "It is not all that strange to be a little out of practice and lose control. And the crying . . ."

Her words drifted off as if she were loath to continue.

"What about the crying?" he asked her.

"It just means you still miss her," she said. "I've . . . I've cried every time. Every time."

Every time, she'd said. But he looked in her eyes now and saw no tears.

13

THE PARK WAS AS CROWDED AS ROME HAD EVER SEEN IT. He and Gussie had arrived early, but so had nearly everyone else in town. He supposed that the excitement and anticipation that plagued him were the same for everyone. Promenades were a good deal less adventurous. Everybody was walking, but most were unwilling to leave the immediate area of the kissing booth for fear they might miss something.

Rome glanced over at Miss Gussie and she smiled broadly at him. They didn't have to even share the words, for they knew that their idea was going to be a big success. Like a positive completion of a commercial venture or a business opportunity well utilized, there was the tingle of euphoric fulfillment.

It was a wonderful, almost intimate moment between them and Rome was grateful for it. They had both felt ill at ease together this morning. And it was all his fault. Yesterday he had kissed her in a manner that was totally uncalled-for. He had kissed her like a lover. Now, with a day of kissing ahead, they were both naturally concerned that he might do the same again.

Rome was determined not to. He couldn't imagine what had come over him to behave like that. He was, and always had been, a man of strong passions, but he was never a man lacking in control. And he was certainly not the kind of fellow to take advantage of a woman's vulnerability. Vulnerability was the only explanation for the response he'd elicited from Miss Gussie. She had a purpose she was striving for and a plan to be carried out. The unfortunate necessity of his nearness was merely part of the plan. She certainly had no intention of luring him with feminine charms or responding to his unwelcome advances.

The kissing booth was going to raise money for the Founder's Day fireworks. But the main goal for him and Miss Gussie was to raise the green-eyed monster in Amos Dewey. Today, it was Rome's utmost resolve to do exactly that.

"I don't see him anywhere," he told her as he perused the crowd of jauntily clad gentlemen and fashionable ladies with bright parasols.

Miss Gussie looked around as well.

"He must be here," she assured him quietly. "The whole town is here. Nobody is going to miss this."

Rome nodded. It was absolutely true. It was doubtful that anything less than the Fiftieth Anniversary Founder's Day Fourth of July itself could garner more sense of thrilled expectation.

None of the ladies had taken up places in the booth. Even the young misses, the known participants, seemed to be waiting for some sort of announcement. Anxiously he checked the watch in his pocket several times.

With Miss Gussie at his side, he stood around talking with friends, discussing the weather, speculating on the chance of rain. He smiled, he laughed, occasionally he squeezed Miss Gussie's hand. She was still uneasy with him. And the waiting wasn't making it any better.

Finally, at three minutes before two, he could wait no longer. He gave Miss Gussie a last brave smile and then got up in front of the kissing booth and held up his hands for silence.

"We are so glad that you all turned out for this fireworks fund-raising," he said. "We want you to do a lot of kissing, spend a lot of money, and you'll make the Founder's Day Fourth of July more fun and spectacular than we've ever seen here in Cottonwood."

There was a little spate of polite applause.

"We have a number of lovely ladies who have agreed to trade their kisses for your quarters," he said. "So many, we even have a couple of shifts. So if at any time the lips of the lady you're most interested in are not at your line, let me encourage you to try another set."

That statement brought hoots of laughter.

"It is all for a good cause," Rome reminded them. "The Founder's Day Fourth of July fireworks will be bigger, brighter and safer because you made the estimable sacrifice of paying two bits to kiss a pair of pretty lips."

The applause was louder now, more enthusiastic.

"Now, if the citizenesses of Cottonwood participating in the kissing booth would please take your places," he said.

The next few moments couldn't have been more dramatic if he and Gussie had planned and rehearsed them. The young girls, whose identities were already known, went up to the booth first. There were a couple of moments of expectant hesitation. Then Miss Gussie walked across the empty grass with every eye upon her. There was some murmuring. It wasn't entirely pleasant being so much the center of attention.

Fortunately, a moment later, Madge Simpson stepped out of the crowd and met up with her path. The surprise was audible. When Constance Wilhelm started moving in the same direction, the excitement heightened and the noise level surged. The mayor's short, fat wife stepped into the cleared area, obviously intent on joining her daughter at the kissing booth.

"What the devil!" Pete Davies swore as Loralene followed the other women.

Eliza Penderghast wasn't too spry, but she set out with enthusiasm. The look on her husband's face was so completely dumbfounded that the crowd burst into laughter.

Reverend Holiday's merriment, with his big bold voice, could be heard over just about anyone. And when it stopped suddenly, the silence drew attention.

"You mind your father today," his wife was admonishing their children. "I'm going to be very busy, so you must promise to behave."

The two oldest nodded eagerly, not completely understanding the game but knowing that it was very much fun. The youngest, five-year-old Missy, relinquished her mother's hand reluctantly and then grabbed her father's coattail.

The preacher was caught off guard and sputtered his dissent.

"Mrs. Holiday, I . . . I don't think . . ."

Kate turned and gave him a raised eyebrow and a glance full of feigned reproach.

"Faith, hope and charity," she quoted the New

Testament. "These three, but the greatest of these is charity."

The pastor had no quick comeback. He watched his wife take her place in the kissing booth and for one of the very few times in his life, he was completely speechless.

However, no one else in the park seemed to be suffering from that problem. The noise of the crowd had grown to a crescendo that roused the whole area. The brightly decorated booth with its draped bunting and barrage of colorful signs was the focus of every man, woman and child who stood in the warmth of the early-summer afternoon.

The young women took their places first, and lines began to form almost immediately. Especially so in front of Betty Ditham. The queue of eager, pimply-faced youths might have daunted less determined girls. But Betty was extremely self-possessed and -assured, easily eliciting deference and good manners from the young gentlemen. The other blushing unmarrieds emulated her example and quickly appeared equally in control of their string of admirers.

The first shift of wives consisted of Constance Wilhelm, the mayor's wife and Loralene Davies. All three appeared exuberant and excited about the opportunity to participate. The reactions of their respective spouses varied.

Perry Wilhelm took it with great good grace. He walked up to stand in front of his wife and she gave him a very cheeky grin.

"Pay your two bits, mister," she challenged. "Or get out of the way."

His threatening look was completely feigned as he drew a quarter out of his pocket and laid it upon the narrow counter in front of her.

She smiled at him with undisguised wifely approval.

"I hope I'm going to get my money's worth," he said, leaning toward her.

Rome grinned as he turned his attention away. He suspected it might be the wisest quarter Perry ever spent, but he wasn't about to watch.

The mayor seemed almost completely befuddled, not quite comprehending the meaning of the event.

"You are going to kiss other men, Birdie?" he asked his wife in a whisper that sounded genuinely distressed.

"No, Georgie," she answered, consoling. "You just have to donate your money and I'll kiss you."

"Oh. Oh!" A giant grin swept his face. "What a splendid joke on us! Rome Akers, you take the cake," he called out. "You simply take the cake."

Not everyone, however, accepted being the butt of the jest with such amiability.

"I'll be danged if I'm going to pay for something that's mine by right of religion and law," Pete Davies declared adamantly to his wife.

Loralene didn't even appear insulted.

"You just haven't got two bits in your pocket," she said. "Now, would you step aside for the paying customers?"

There wasn't a soul in line behind Pete, so Rome quickly stepped into the breach, pulling a quarter out of his trousers and secretly hoping he wouldn't be obliged to use it.

Pete turned around and saw him and his eyes narrowed.

"What do you think you're doing?" he asked.

Rome smiled. "I'm standing in line to buy a kiss," he answered, showing his quarter.

"I don't think this was much of a dang good surprise," he complained. "I've got half a mind to knock your teeth out."

Rome smiled again. "You might have to stand in line for that too," he said. "Maybe we could set up another booth for the husbands to punch me. Of course, if you're going to have to spend your money anyway, I'd think you'd prefer smooching to slugging."

"Humph!" Pete was disapproving but defeated. Loudly he slammed his coin upon the narrow counter and reached for his wife. Loralene was stiff and reluctant. Pete was belligerent and demanding. When their mouths met, like magic they both softened toward each other; the air around them sizzled.

Rome's eyes widened. If he'd ever wondered how those two had managed to acquire five children, it was no longer a mystery.

He glanced over at Miss Gussie. She was watching him. He was glad that she was on the second shift. By then everyone would know the drill and the first shock of surprise would be gone. He wanted to stir up a lot of gossip, not to mention the ire of Amos Dewey.

He glanced around, looking for the man, but didn't see him. Everyone in town was there. Dewey was undoubtedly as well. And he would pop up out of the woodwork as soon as Rome started buying rights to Miss Gussie. The man had better have a pocketful of money if he tended to outbid Rome.

But, of course, Amos would get to kiss her, and propose to her, and marry her. That was the plan. Rome felt the tug of something very unwelcome. He pushed the unexpected resistance away. Everything was going according to plan. Rome would be instrumental in making Miss Gussie's most romantic dream come true. In a pique of jealousy, Dewey would realize that he couldn't live without her. And the fellow would, after three years of hesitation, finally come forward and claim her as his true love.

Rome wouldn't watch while Amos kissed her. And he wouldn't be there when the proposal was offered. Or when she joyously, tearfully accepted. He'd make it a point to miss the wedding. Somehow the sight of them living happily ever after was not that appealing.

He glanced over at Miss Gussie once more. Their eyes met. Hers were bright, shining, full of warmth and intelligence and humor. Unbidden, the memory of the kiss they'd shared the day before filled his thoughts. He let his eyes linger upon her lips. The bottom one trembled. If he got only this one chance to touch her and taste her, should he not have his fill? To remove this ill-timed and unreciprocated desire for her from his system, should he not have just this one day to *be* the man he had pretended for her?

The afternoon sun was slanting low through the slits of the paper-covered windows of the barbershop as Pansy Richardson, clad only in her black silk stockings and shoes, lay in the arms of Amos Dewey. They spoke little. Words seemed the most uneasy communication between them. They kissed and caressed until they were drunk with desire. Pansy didn't quite understand her need to touch him, to move him. Her intention had certainly been to seduce him. She was determined to see the barber estranged from Gussie Mudd forever, leaving the way open for Rome to pursue the woman. That had been the extent of her motive. Or at least she thought it had been. Somehow, once in his arms, she was no longer sure what it was that she wanted from Amos Dewey.

He raised his head and looked at her. Inexplicably she felt safe and certain and somehow so very right in his embrace.

He shook his head disbelievingly and tried to disengage her from him, but she wouldn't let go. She held him fast. He wasn't sure if it was for his sake or for her own.

"I . . . I don't know what to say," he managed to mutter. "I never, never intended this. I never intended to touch you. I would never . . . I would never try to touch you."

"I seduced you, Amos," she told him quietly. "You have no cause to reproach yourself."

"No cause?" he asked. "First I throw all my moral superiority to the wind by engaging in unsanctified sex with a woman I hardly know. I lose control like a green schoolboy and then I burst into tears." He took a long, deep breath. "I don't know what your life has been like, ma'am, but I believe this counts as one of the most humiliating experiences of mine."

Pansy laughed out loud. Somehow he didn't sound humiliated, regretful or even slightly displeased. He was looking at her, his dark eyes bright and handsome, naked without his spectacles.

"I see," he said, his tone feigning affront. "My humiliation can only be topped by your ridicule."

"I have no reason to ridicule," Pansy assured him, tenderly caressing his neck and chest. "The . . . ah . . . shall we say . . . precipitant cannon shot is not all that surprising," she said. "It has been over three years since you've been with a woman."

"Closer to five," he admitted. "My Bess was ill for a long time."

She nodded and then laid her cheek against his shoulder. She undid the buttons on his shirtfront and allowed her hand to burrow inside, caressing his skin and thick mat of dark hair that grew there.

"Perhaps now," she said, "since it has only been a few moments since your most recent encounter, you can show me how clever and considerate you know how to be."

He took up her challenge with a long, lingering kiss, followed by a teasing exploration of her bosom. There was no hurried passion in his touch now. It was as if, for both of them, time would go on forever and these moments would simply extend out into eternity. There was no ceremony or solemnity between them. They laughed and joked as they took turns sucking each other's nipples and searching out the secrets of the flesh beneath their clothes.

He took down her hair, exclaiming with wonder at the beauty of it. She took off his rumpled white shirt and marveled over the strength of his rangy muscles and the powerful width of his shoulders.

Like mischievous children, they toyed with the mechanisms of the hydraulic chair. At times the results were laughable. At other times they became breathless.

Slowly, leisurely, languidly, they made love through the long length of the summer afternoon. And it was love, truly love. Touching the heart and loins with equal intensity.

As the climax neared he pressed her beneath him, powerfully claiming her with each sensual stroke. Pansy felt the tension rising in her. Her vision blurred and yet focused intently upon him, upon the man above her, upon the man she loved.

With a cry of ecstatic fulfillment she called out his name. A moment later, he was screaming her own. It was perfect. Absolute. Beyond any emotion she had ever felt. And it was elation.

Pansy waited for tears that never came. They did not plague her. She was home at last, the past buried with the love and respect that it had always deserved. But the future was now before her like a bright beacon of hope and promise.

She gazed into his eyes. There was joy there as well. Joy and contentment. Amos Dewey had found his way home as well and she was so very, very glad to be there.

Pansy snuggled in his arms. Silently she offered a prayer of thanks. For so long she had been angry. For so long she had not understood. She still could not fathom the reasons, but her heart was in the present once more and that was a gift.

"It feels so wonderful to be here with you like this," she told him with unguarded honesty. "It is heaven, just like heaven."

"Mmmm, heaven," he agreed. "I'd forgotten it was like this." He pulled her more closely against his chest. "Or maybe it was never like this."

"It was never like this," she said. "With different people it is always different. Our pleasure today is something unique. It is you and me and can never be the same with anyone else."

As Pansy voiced the words, she realized how very true they were. She also realized how intensely special the past hours had been. She felt more alive, more intensely happy, than she could recall in recent years. Certainly not since Grover's death. She wanted to jump to her feet, dance around the room, laugh until her belly ached. But she was not sure what Amos might be feeling. She'd understood the tears in his eyes earlier. She'd known that feeling of being sad-dened by the pleasure because it contrasted so sharply with the pain. But he was smiling at her now, smiling as she was smiling. Could he too appreciate the miracle that had just occurred between them? Pansy thought that it must be so.

"I am so . . . happy," she said, almost loath to use a word so inadequate for what she was feeling. "Are you happy?"

His laughter was deep and throaty and full of emotion.

"I am very happy," he said.

"I never expected it would be this way," she admitted. "I came here to seduce you, but I never expected I would be seduced in turn."

Amos gripped her more tightly in his arms and pressed a kiss to the top of her head. He did not move away but stayed there, breathing in the scent of her hair as if it were a life-giving restorative.

"I can't imagine why you seduced me," he told her, his deep, resonant voice so close. "But I am so very glad that you wanted to."

Pansy laughed again, lightly. She felt so happy, so satisfied, so perfectly content with this man. It was as if all the hurts and heartache and humiliation of the past had been swept away in one sweet, brief moment of unity and pleasure.

"Oh, I didn't *want* to seduce you," she told him, teasing. "I did it for a friend."

"You did it for a friend?" he repeated, his tone incredulous.

"Yes," she said. "I did it for Rome Akers. It was clear to me that he and Gussie Mudd are perfect for each other. The only thing that stood between them was her infatuation for you. I knew that you didn't love her or want her. Allowing me to turn your head would convince you of that fact. It would nail the coffin lid on that romance for good."

Pansy continued to snuggle up against him, giddy with her good fortune.

"I came in here to seduce you for completely altruistic reasons," she said. "People have always believed the worst of me. I decided that for such a worthy cause I would prove them right after all. But I was the one who was fooled."

She breathed in deeply. The warm, clean, masculine smell of bay rum mixed with the musky odor of sex was a fragrance so heady that she was drunk with it.

"I came here to perform for you, to conquer you, to take you as my lover," she admitted. "I had no inkling that you would show me such love and passion that I would be as starry-eyed and dreamy as a virgin bride."

She was laughing again, but realized, rather suddenly, that he was not. He was, in fact, holding himself inordinately still. Cold and distant and still. Perhaps it was a reaction to the power of what they had found together. Or maybe it was residual sadness from the life, the love, that had gone on before.

"Of course, what we shared here could never diminish what you had with your wife," she said, more tentatively now.

"No, no, naturally not," he replied. "The duties of the marriage bed should never be compared with purely carnal pleasures."

His words sent a chill through her, causing her shoulders to tremble. She felt the need to cover her bare breasts with her arm.

"There was more than *pure carnal pleasure* here," she told him. "There was trust and tenderness. There was healing."

He sat up then, his relaxed composure disappearing. "More likely it was ordinary immorality couched as such," he said.

Pansy felt a sudden, extreme discomfort at his nearness and her nakedness. She awkwardly rose from his lap and began searching for her clothing. Deliberately she tried to keep her mind blank. After what they had shared, the sexual intimacy, the emotional closeness, the friendly laughter, she could not truly believe that he was purposely insulting her, making ugliness out of the beauty they had just shared.

She found her red silk drawers and hurriedly stepped into them. Her corset was hanging from the edge of the chair's footrest. Pansy grabbed it and pulled it around her.

Amos had risen to his feet and was readjusting his clothes and buttoning his trousers.

Pansy couldn't look at him. She couldn't meet his eyes. In all these years while she had lived upon the edge of the community, these years when so many thought the worst and rumors followed her every move—through all of that she had never felt embarrassed. She had flaunted herself in front of all their lies and speculation, she had lived as she had chosen to do so and she had never felt embarrassed or ashamed. Now she felt shame. Now, after opening her heart to him so easily, so fully, now when all she offered was pure and true, now she was made to feel tainted, unworthy, unclean.

"I've decided to remarry," he said.

The words jolted her. She had managed to get her skirts on and was tucking her shirtwaist into them.

"What?"

"I've decided to remarry," he repeated. "This unholy tryst has at least brought some good. I see now that I have been too long a widower and that it's time to put aside my mourning and fulfill my province as a husband and perhaps one day as a father."

Pansy's brain felt fogged.

"Is this some sort of ill-framed proposal, sir?" she asked him.

He looked straight at her then, his eyes once again guarded by round, wire-rimmed spectacles.

"Certainly not," he answered. "I may be inexperienced and easily led, ma'am. But I am not so ignorant as to imagine that I would owe marriage to a female who offers her charms so indiscriminately and with such largesse."

Pansy flinched as if she'd been slapped.

"I had thought that only a pure and true love, such as I had with my Bess, would suit me," he continued. "But I see that I am capable of performing sufficiently, even with a woman I do not admire in the least. Therefore, I will choose a wife suited to me in temperament and moral fiber. And at the very least, I will be able to stop your lover from deceiving and despoiling a fine woman like Gussie Mudd."

14

GUSSIE WAS A LITTLE BIT NERVOUS. IT WAS DIFFICULT not to be. All around her there was laughter and good humor and kissing, lots and lots of kissing. It was sweet, but still it was men and women with mouths together in such an intimate way it made her feel all melting inside.

And there were some interesting and unanticipated developments. Huntley Boston lined up with the young lads in front of Miss Betty Ditham. When his turn came, he not only paid his two bits, he continued to buy, discouraging the fellows waiting behind him. Viceroy, Betty's father and Huntley's boss at the bank, was not in the least pleased with these developments and pleaded to Rome to set limits on how many kisses a man could purchase from a woman other than his wife.

Gussie could tell that Rome sympathized with the man's impotent outrage, but to give in to him would have ruined their own plans for later. Rome shook his head and said that as long as the banker had quarters, he could continue.

For her part, Betty, always confident and self-possessed, seemed content to allow the men to make a fuss. She complained about neither Huntley's attentions nor her father's disapproval of them. Her serene and enigmatic smile would have done credit to the "Mona Lisa."

Gussie wished she could conjure up a similar composure. She was jumpy as a cat in cockleburs. Her eyes returned time and time again to Rome, seeking the reassurance of his glance or just the comfort of his presence. Occasionally she thought to peruse the crowd for sight of Amos Dewey. He was, after all, the object of this scheme. And no market manipulation could ever be achieved if the competition remained completely ignorant of the moves made. Only if she were attempting to corner some commodity would stealth be an asset. As it was, forcing Dewey to action was essential and Gussie was having trouble keeping that part of the plan in mind.

All around her, teasing laughter began to swell as Perry Wilhelm got down to his last quarter and was trying to make the final kiss last long enough to end Constance's shift.

Gussie giggled along with everyone else as Perry continued to lengthen the kiss and Rome very obviously counted down the time with his pocket watch. When he gave the cease notice, there was applause all around. Perry actually took a bow as Constance, blushing, gladly gave up her place in the booth.

Gussie was as charmed as everyone else, but also extremely mindful of what came next: her own public spectacle and private exposure. The second group of ladies was taking its place. Becky Timmons took young Miss Ditham's place, clearly attempting to emulate the latter. If the lanky-legged, pimply-faced fellows who'd waited in vain behind the banker were disappointed, they, at least, had the good manners not to show it.

The mayor's daughter showed a bit less confidence and when no young bucks lined up in front of her, her father stepped forward himself. That action disconcerted the young lady even further.

"Daddy! No!" she whispered to him frantically.

The mayor was too thickheaded to correctly interpret her plea.

"Don't worry, little princess," he said. "I've still got a few quarters I haven't spent on your mother."

The girl's humiliation was short-lived, however, as one of the older Pearsall boys moved from Becky's line to her own.

Kate Holiday was practically giddy as she stepped up to the narrow counter. The reverend had made an impromptu trip home to raid the sugar bowl. The preacher's natural exuberance was significantly toned down by what was obviously an unfamiliar public duty, kissing his wife. Gussie was pretty sure that he was uncertain as to a pastor's participation in such an activity. But for all his boisterous behavior, he clearly loved his Kate and wanted to go along with any scheme she came up with.

Madge Simpson was a good deal more matter-of-fact about the matter. She and Joe had had a whole hour to celebrate the joke and were now primed for a dual performance that was both cute and comedic. Joe was painstakingly counting out his coins as if he were loath to part with any of them. Madge pretended disinterest, as if kissing her husband for an hour from a booth in the park were no more fascinating than any other wifely task.

The clink of her husband's quarter in the glass jar was like a starting gun. The two pressed their lips together in a noisy, hurried fashion that was hilarious. The crowd around them applauded, appreciating the joke.

Gussie swallowed her nervousness and stepped up to her position. She was very aware of the awkwardness of her choice. She was not young and sought-after like the unmarrieds, nor was she a matron like her friends. She was Gussie Mudd, the town spinster. And she was about to turn the local gossips upon their ears.

Rome immediately came to stand in front of her, his eyes telegraphing a message of reassurance. This was all part of the plan, she reminded herself. This was going to get her married to Amos Dewey. And that consequence would be worth whatever momentary risk and discomfiture were required.

A little flutter of gossip swept through the crowd as people began to realize what was happening.

Rome loudly jingled the money in his pocket. He brought out a quarter and laid it upon the counter in front of her.

"Unlike the other fellows, Miss Gussie," he said, loudly enough that the words were clearly not meant to be private, "I knew who was going to be selling kisses today and was able to secure sufficient financing for the occasion."

"I'd call that cheating!" Joe Simpson declared with feigned fury.

"Mind your own business," Rome told him. "And kiss your wife before somebody else does."

Simpson laughed, but took his advice.

Rome turned to look at Gussie once again. He was pretending humor for the crowd, but she saw in his eyes the seriousness and nervous intent that she felt herself.

She grinned at him, hoping to appear reassuring.

He returned the look with equal confidence. They would do this just as they had planned, and it would bring Amos Dewey to his knees at last.

"I'd like to buy a kiss, Miss Gussie," he said.

She felt every eye upon her. And her name swept through those assembled like a whisper in the wind. She looked down at the shiny, gleaming quarter sitting in front of her. Two bits a kiss. That was all that was required. Two bits was not a lot to invest for a lifetime of happiness. And that was what it was, she reminded herself. That was exactly what it was.

With a grand gesture, everyone watching, she picked up the money and dropped it into the big glass jar.

"Thank you for your donation, sir," she said and then leaned forward toward him. She pursed her lips before she remembered she wasn't supposed to. As his mouth came closer, she relaxed as he had taught her and opened for him. Rome was there. So very close. The scent of him so familiar, so masculine.

He turned his head slightly and Gussie closed her eyes as his mouth opened over hers. It was a sweet and tender kiss, a self-conscious kiss. Both parties were fully aware of the numerous pairs of eyes upon them. Gussie felt the warmth of his shirtfront so near to her bosom. She trembled slightly as he pulled his lips away.

"Thank you, ma'am," he said politely.

"You're welcome," she answered.

She saw him swallow nervously.

"We're going to have to do better than that to drive a certain someone to jealous rage," he whispered.

"I know," she said. "I'm ready. Do your worst."

"Well, I hope it won't be the worst," he told her as he retrieved another coin from his pocket. He was already moving in toward her when the quarter clinked in the jar.

This time he took her chin in his hand, angled her head slightly and put his mouth on her own. Her lips melded against his as if they were meant to be together, firm but yielding. There was a gentle tugging and a joining that touched more than the physical. Gussie was drawn into its sweetness, giving as well as getting. Suddenly she could no longer hear the people around her. She was no longer aware of being on display. The world beyond the two of them faded into obscurity. With eyes closed and hands at her sides, there was only the scent of him, masculine and almost tangy, that surrounded her. It was the most alluring fragrance ever known to womankind, finer than the floral gifts of nature or the most luxurious of perfumes. And a taste that completely defied description. It was not sweet or piquant, but rather a zest of jewels, without flavor yet lingering, unforgettable. His mouth pulled at hers. It was as if he were drawing her inside, as if she were now not so much herself anymore as a part of something totally new. Something that was part him, part her and completely neither of them as well as both. Without hesitation she gave herself up to it, willingly transformed.

He began drawing away, but she was not quite ready to release him, not quite ready to give up that sweet suction that so pleased her. As he moved back she leaned further toward him, reaching out to grasp his shoulders.

It was only when she heard the hoots and whistles of those around her that she recalled her public exposure.

Gussie jerked away from Rome. Her face was flushed with embarrassment. How could she have forgotten where she was and what she was about? This was no romantic tryst; this was a business maneuver. At least she'd intended it to be so. Or she'd thought that was what she'd intended. A flutter of tiny magical wings set off within her midsection, letting her know that it had been more, much more. She lay her hand atop her chest, hoping to still those flutters. Such a feeling would not be so easily caged.

"Oh, my," she murmured.

Rome's heart was in his eyes. There was apology and determination and . . . and something else that Gussie didn't immediately recognize. It was something fiery and ardent. She couldn't help but wonder if it was the same strange ailment that suddenly plagued her.

Everyone there was looking; everyone was laughing. Gussie Mudd had made a spectacle of herself and she was somehow beyond caring.

"Akers should have to pay extra for that one," Pete Davies called out.

His words were followed by some hearty guffaws and a lot of backslapping.

"A kiss like that's worth six bits if a penny," Clive Benson agreed.

Gussie was blushing furiously now. She glanced over at the reverend and Kate. They too were eyeing her as if she'd just swallowed a mule as well.

She was unsure of what to do or what to say. The kiss had been meant to make Amos jealous. Gussie didn't see him anywhere and what she was afraid had happened was that she had managed only to make herself look foolish. As she glanced through the crowd, almost every face was turned in her direction.

She was drawn to the one that offered the most comfort and understanding. Rome was smiling at her, looking a little chagrined, but content. He was obviously not worrying overmuch about the gossip swirling around them. If he did not worry, she decided, she would not worry.

He pulled two quarters out of his pocket and dropped them in the jar.

"I don't mind paying a little extra to kiss the woman of my dreams," he said.

There was some cheering and good-natured ribbing that accompanied that statement. Gussie felt almost giddy. The phrase *woman of my dreams* somehow skittered across her skin, raising gooseflesh. She reminded herself that he was only pretending, that she was not at all his ladylove. That she was his employer, he her employee. For one moment she felt a distinct stab of envy. How wonderful it would be to actually be loved by such a man.

Perhaps it was that thought alone that emboldened her. Or maybe it was just the high jinks of the moment. Gussie reached across the narrow counter and grabbed Rome by the shirtfront. Angling her head slightly, she pulled him to her, this time kissing him with a brazen abandon that was all passion and no purposeful plan.

He did not preempt her control, or what control she had. She felt foolishly exuberant and completely willing to go with the moment. When the moment passed, she moved only inches away to look into his eyes. The smoky response she saw there told her what she knew already. This was a dangerous game they played. And they were playing it far too well.

"I definitely think that Miss Gussie should have to pay for that one," Joe Simpson declared.

The titter of nervous laughter seemed to agree. Though not even that could break through the spell that had fogged up her clear thinking.

Gussie reached down into her skirt pocket for her purse. With a feeling of unreality, she retrieved two bits and gladly added them to the jar.

* * *

The afternoon had been a resounding success. The clink of quarters had gone on and on, until the fireworks extravaganza was absolutely guaranteed. Rome's own private fireworks seemed equally as certain to explode.

He sat on Miss Gussie's front porch with her at his side. Ostensibly she was helping him total the contributions, but every time their hands accidentally brushed, they both trembled.

Joe and Perry had stayed late to take down the booth. Rome was grateful to leave the job to them. And they had been very happy to take it on. Laughing about the good time they'd had and reliving the most exhilarating moments of the afternoon.

Rome could simply not get his thoughts in order. He'd spent the most pleasant hour of his life kissing Gussie Mudd and he couldn't get back to the way they had been before, the distance they had always maintained.

He stopped the counting as he laid his hand atop hers. She looked up at him, her eyes and heart so open. He kissed her. It was a kiss almost tentative, very tender, testing. She did not turn him away. She kissed him back so lovingly, so willingly. She kissed him back as she had done for the crowd. But there was no coin involved here. No performance to be done. She kissed him because she wanted to and for no other reason.

As their lips parted, she too had a momentary look of confusion. What were they doing? What were they thinking? He'd pushed those questions from his own mind and now watched her brow furrow and then smooth as she did the same.

"I've lost count again," she told him, indicating the money.

"I don't think we're going to get it right," he said. "At least not tonight."

She nodded, wordlessly agreeing to the obvious. She made no move to commence counting again. She only looked at Rome. She looked at him as if she had never seen him before. What she was thinking, he did not know.

For his part, Rome was trying not to think, trying not to plan. He only wanted to be with Gussie. He only wanted to be with Gussie, alone.

The evening shadows covered the porch, making their unchaperoned presence there a little bit scandalous. They had been alone so many times before. They had been on this porch so many times before. But it had never been like this. It had never felt like this.

"Come sit on my lap, Gussie," he said.

It was a shocking suggestion. The sort that should have got his face slapped.

Instead she rose from her chair and hurried toward him. She hesitated beside him as if uncertain what to do or how to proceed. Gingerly she lowered her backside to his knees.

Rome refused to allow her such reticence. He was sure that at any moment they would both come to their senses. He was not willing to waste these few fleeting moments by faltering.

With one hand on her hip and the other upon her thigh, he pulled her close against him. It felt right. It felt perfect. So naturally her arm slid around his shoulder. The side of her bosom was against his chest. Her round, firm buttocks were atop his erection. This was how it felt good. This was how he wanted her in his arms.

"Kiss me," he told her. "Kiss me like it will cost you everything that you might ever possess."

She did. After a long afternoon of practice, their mouths sought each other with welcome and confidence. She tugged and playfully bit at him. He answered with equivalent urgency.

Rome wrapped his arms around her, pulling her close in a way that he could not have done in the park. She didn't show any reluctance. In fact, as the kiss deepened, she pressed herself to him.

Lovingly he ran his hand upward from her waist to the side of her breast. He wanted to touch her, but he dared not. He smoothed his way back to her waist again, only to retrace his journey once more. Finally, as she opened wider for him, allowing his tongue its will to exploration, he moved his hand across the top of the smooth roundness of her.

In truth, he could feel virtually nothing. There were so many layers of clothing between his hand and her flesh that he had no clue to her shape or size, the warmth of her skin or the site of her nipple. But she gasped, from modesty or pleasure he did not know, but the sound of it went through him like fire, stirring his loins.

Gussie ended the kiss, hiding her face against his neck.

He squirmed in the chair.

She sat up. "Am I too heavy for you?" she asked him.

"Oh, no," he answered truthfully.

His movements were more an opportunity to press himself against her than to relieve himself of her weight. Relief was not what that offered. The more pleasurably he sawed himself upon her, the more need for relief was required.

They kissed once more, expressing with their

mouths the things they were afraid to say in words. Rome loved the taste of her, he loved the feel of her. She had become his in a way he had not expected. It was a dream and he didn't wish to awaken from it.

He continued to caress her breast. But the frustration of all the clothing began to grate upon him. With his other hand he began undoing the buttons at the back of her dress.

"What are you doing?" she asked him, her lips against his neck. "Are you removing my clothes?"

She hadn't told him not to. She'd simply asked if that was what he was doing.

"Of course not," Rome assured her. "I'm . . . I'm simply going to loosen your corset a little."

"You're going to loosen my corset?"

Once more it was not a protestation.

"Yes, you . . . you are breathing heavily. I can't have you fainting as you did that day in the park."

"I don't feel like I'm going to faint at all," she said, bringing her lips eagerly to his once more.

Her enthusiastic passion was so unexpected, so lustful, he feared he might faint himself. His whole body seemed to have turned to jelly. That is, except the part that was a throbbing, aching ramrod.

Once the buttons on her shirtwaist were dispensed with, he began peeling the garment down her arms. He'd had enough experience with women's clothing to know that while a corset could be loosened from the back, it could be done away with entirely if a man could get his hands upon the front hooks.

Naturally she would never allow him to do such a thing, he reminded himself. And she certainly shouldn't. If he were a true friend or even just a gentleman, he should stop right now. He behaved as neither.

He pulled the pretty blue dress down off her shoulders, baring her arms. Her corset cover was virginal white, lacy and pretty. Nothing sensual and seductive about it. The sight, however, had him adjusting in the chair once more.

She looked down at what he had done. And then looked up to meet his gaze. In the dim light he could see her lower lip tremble and the glow of perspiration upon her brow. But it was the expression in her eyes that held him. An expression of both desire and doubt. She wanted him, but she was afraid as well.

"I should let you go in, Gussie," he said. "Someone could come by and see."

She didn't even glance toward the road. "We should go in," she told him. "You should take me. Take me, Rome."

He did not need to be asked twice. With one arm beneath her knees and one behind her shoulder, he rose to his feet in a swift, sure motion. She wrapped her arms around his neck, clinging to him closely as if to protect her modesty from the eyes so intent on assailing it.

When they reached the door, it was her hand that opened it. He crossed the threshold with Gussie in his arms and then slammed the door loudly behind him with his heel.

She was trembling again, this time clearly in fear. Either of them might awaken to good sense at any time. It was paramount that he reassure them both while they were still so foolishly out of their minds. He kissed her. Long and lovingly, he kissed her. She returned the gesture with equal fervency and pressed her bosom to his chest.

"I have never . . . never felt like this," she whispered.

"Neither have I," he answered and realized as he heard the words that he spoke the truth.

He glanced toward the stairway. He wanted to take her up to her room, to lay her across her bed and show her such pleasure, she would never see the end of it. But he didn't want to scare her, or to presume too much. Undoubtedly she would call a halt to his advances soon. She had not said she would allow such liberties and certainly she shouldn't. It was best not to behave as if he thought that she would. Instead he carried her into the front parlor, the most formal part of the house. The room where circumspect young women would meet gentleman callers who were not so much as allowed to unbutton a coat without permission.

He lay her on the wine velvet fainting couch in the near corner of the room. Rome sat beside her as she reclined in the darkness. He touched her lips with his own, lightly, gently, three times. Then he kissed her again, this time with the passion they'd shared on the porch. She met him, his equal in devotion and desire.

He smoothed the thin, girlish corset cover over her breast, swallowing the desire it evoked. He wanted to see her bosom. He wanted to kiss it, caress it. He had no right. He knew she would not let him, should not let him. The past hours had been time out of time. They had not been reality. They must come to an end. But in his heart he pleaded that it would not be so soon.

"Miss Gussie, if you don't want me to touch you . . ."

"Touch me," she answered, guiding his hand beneath the lacy covering. "Please touch me."

Rome couldn't deny either of them. He made hasty work of the three strong hooks that kept her bound so tightly. He pushed the offending garment away as he clasped her breasts in his hands. Finally flesh against flesh.

Her breath came through the depths of her throat, deep and impassioned. Rome caressed her naked bosom, marveling at its size and firmness. Nothing she'd worn had shown her to such advantage as the bare skin he could glimpse through the thin shafts of light from the curtains. Her nipples were thick and hard, begging him to handle and tease them, begging him to taste them. He did.

She gasped at the touch of his tongue upon her, drawing up her knees. It was a fortuitous move. Rome slipped in between her thighs, spreading her before him.

He took turns suckling one breast and then the other as she squirmed and writhed beneath him, moans of earthy carnality emitting from her throat. Never had any woman felt so sensual, so desirable in his arms. Never had he wanted a woman as he wanted this one.

He whipped her nipples with his tongue. A sensation that she greatly enjoyed, judging by the flailing of her head from side to side and her inability to keep her legs stilled.

Rome grabbed her knee and bent it, curving her leg around his waist. He allowed his hand to traverse the length of her thigh. Her black cotton stocking was gartered a few inches above her knee, only a short distance from the legs of her drawers. He slipped his hand inside the latter. The flesh there was so soft, so welcoming, he nearly moaned aloud.

She did exactly that. Begging for more with phrases like, "Oh, please!" "Yes, Rome." "Please, Rome." "Yes! Please! Oh! Rome!"

He knew what she needed. He knew what she wanted. Even if she did not know herself. He brought his thigh up tightly into the crux of her legs.

At first she didn't seem to know what to do. It was as if she were waiting for him to explain the rules. In her innocence, she did not know that desire has no rules. He leaned down to nibble lightly upon her neck. Ever so gently, he rubbed against her and then whispered into her ear.

"Do what feels good," he told her. "Move as it feels good."

She hesitated.

He swirled his tongue into her ear and then whispered again more breathily, "Find pleasure, Miss Gussie," he said. "I want you to find pleasure with me."

Tentatively she began to move. Ever so curiously, she eased herself against the hardness of his thigh. Rome urged her on with words and caresses and kisses.

"That's it," he praised her. "Yes, my precious, my darling, my love. Yes, that's it."

Little whimpers of needs were escaping from her. He held her fast, glorying in her. He slipped his hand between them. Down past her waist, along the seam line of her bleached lawn drawers to the firm, pouty lips so near his knee. She was close. She was very close. Just a little push would send her over the edge. Just a tiny push and she would know pleasure the way a man could give it to her. The way Rome could give it to her. He wanted to give it to her. He wanted to do it. He knew a lot about women. Amos Dewey would never have the sense to offer her this; he wouldn't have her live without it no matter how she chose.

Her cries and words and pleas were coming faster now. Her body was squirming beneath him, riding him.

As his hand moved lower she fought between the desire to spread herself for him and the urge to clutch him to her more closely. He understood what she wanted. He wanted it too. He wanted it so badly, he ached from it. There could be nothing more pleasurable than being inside her. Buried deep inside her.

Being one with her. That was what he wanted. But he wouldn't take it. He wouldn't take it now.

He moved his hand lower and lower along the front of her drawers until he caressed her intimately.

She whimpered his name. Begging for what she did not know. But he did. Softly, gently, he touched her, mapping her, appreciating her. Then he pressed her labium together between his last three fingers and the ball of his hand, forcing the tiny nubbin to squeeze outward and reveal itself to his touch. He grasped her between his thumb and forefinger and manipulated her with painstaking tenderness.

Her orgasm was like a lightning bolt, sudden and intense. Then, like in an earthquake, there was more in the aftermath. She cried out.

She looked up at him, eyes wide, unbelieving. He took her in his arms, holding her, comforting her as she reassessed the world they lived in. His own pleasure denied, he held tight to her, tamping down the desire that he felt, cradling her in his arms as he tried to think.

For the past few hours he had tried not to think, but now was surely the time. Now was, at the very latest moment, the time to think.

She was trembling and he pulled her closer. Kissing her eyes, her cheeks, her chin, her lips. He unfurled the corset cover that had ended up around her neck and drew it down over her bosom. He removed his trousered leg from the wet warmth it had so recently awakened and straightened her skirts more modestly. He sat beside her upon the narrow fainting couch. It was full darkness now and he could not see her face. But he could hear her breathing and he comforted himself that there were no tears or recriminations in the sound.

"Miss Gussie," he said finally, his own voice sounding strange to his ears. "Miss Gussie, I want to marry you. But I won't ask you tonight. So much has happened. I know I haven't given you time to think. I'm going to give you time tonight. I'm going to leave you now. And tomorrow afternoon I'm coming back. I'm going to get down on one knee and ask for your hand. I would be so overjoyed, so honored, if you would say yes."

With that he rose to his feet.

"I'll see myself out," he added. "Good night."

15

PANSY RICHARDSON SAT AT HER KITCHEN TABLE, STAR-
ing at the bold stripes of her tablecloth. She could not
quite get her mind around all that had happened. She
had gone in to seduce Amos Dewey and been seduced
herself. Amos had not lured her into some romantic
tryst, that had been her forte. But somehow during that
afternoon in his arms, she'd been coaxed into seeing a
new vision of what her life could be. She had thought
herself independent, in control of her own destiny.
Now she realized that the opposite had been true.

Fate had taken her husband from her. Will Barclay
had ruined her reputation. And the community had
prescribed her life from that point as one of sinner and
outcast.

Pansy had thought that she was living her life, but
now saw clearly that the first action truly of her own
making was the altruistic attempt to help Rome.

The fact that her efforts had blown up in her face
was disappointing. The reality that she had made a
deep-seated connection with Amos was frightening.
But the truth was that she now saw the possibility to

change her life. For that she could not be anything but grateful.

There was a light tap on the kitchen door before he stepped inside. She had known he would come. He had not said that he would and, in truth, she had not invited him. But somehow she had known he would come and had been waiting for him here in the kitchen.

They gazed at each other from across the distance separating them. He looked troubled. She felt that way exactly. Smiling at him, she indicated the other chair at the table. He crossed the room and seated himself.

"How was the kissing booth?" she asked him.

"We did well," Rome answered. "We made enough for a first-class fireworks exhibition with maybe even some funds left over."

"That's good," she said, nodding. "That's very good. I knew you would do it."

"Of course, Miss Gussie and I had other intentions," he reminded her. "But I . . . things have changed, Pansy, and I . . ."

"Things have changed for me, too," she said. "I want to be on the speaker's podium at the Founder's Day Fourth of July Picnic."

"What?"

"I want to be on the podium," she repeated. "No, more than that, I want to speak from the podium."

"Why would you want to do that?"

"I am the last of the Richardsons," she said. "Grover's family founded this town fifty years ago and I am Grover's widow. If I want the Richardson name to be kept alive, I am the only person able to do it."

Rome was speechless for a long moment, simply staring at her as if he had never seen her before.

"You've never been too concerned about the Richardson name in the past," he pointed out.

Pansy nodded, acknowledging that truth. "I haven't been thinking about it," she admitted. "I suppose it could be said that I simply haven't been thinking."

There was a silence in the room. It lingered as Pansy considered how much she should say, how much he deserved to know.

"I didn't break up Judge Barclay's marriage," she told him.

It was the first time the man's name had been mentioned between them.

"He was a dear friend of Grover's," she explained. "I was hurt and scared and I turned to him for comfort. I needed the warm arms of a friend to console me. I had no idea that he was a womanizer."

She looked up and met Rome's eyes. They were full of sympathy and understanding. She'd always known he would not condemn her. She didn't know why she had not trusted him with the truth.

"It only happened between us once," she murmured.

Pansy felt the sting of tears in her eyes, but she refused to give in to them. It was time to say it aloud. It was time to speak the truth, if only so that she could hear it herself.

"I was horrified at what I had done," she confessed. "I was wretched and ashamed. It was not a misstep or a fall from grace. It was a vileness. A disgusting, horrible vileness. And I was guilty. I knew that I was the one who was completely and totally guilty."

Her hands were trembling. She clasped them together to keep them still.

"It was not just the adultery," she continued. "I saw my sin as much deeper than that. Grover was making love to me when he died. My lust for him, my need for him, had cost him his life. And then he was not a month in the grave and I was in the arms of another man."

She stared at Rome, willing him to understand.

"It was as if I had murdered him," she said. "And then moved on as if nothing had ever happened."

"Don't say that about yourself," Rome implored her. "It's just not true."

"What's true is what we believe to be so at the time. I was disgusted with myself. Certainly I was still grieving, still confused and bewildered by what had happened. But I believed myself solely at fault. I believed that I had lured the man against his will. And that I deserved to be punished."

"So you purposely took upon yourself the mantle of a harlot?"

Pansy smiled humorlessly and shook her head.

"That was not the punishment I intended," she replied. "I wanted to apologize. To make restitution to those I'd injured. I was the one who confessed all to Madeline Barclay."

Rome's eye's widened. That piece of information genuinely surprised him.

"I went to her, penitent and guilty, taking all the blame upon myself," Pansy said. She shook her head again and gave him a self-deprecating grin. "I can assure you that she did not thank me."

Rome nodded, comprehending perfectly.

"The judge had always been a womanizer," he said. "I suspect she'd always known about it."

Pansy agreed. "It wasn't until afterward that I realized that this was not the first time the judge had strayed. But because I admitted it out loud, she had to do something. And that something included publicly naming me in her divorce."

"I am so sorry," Rome told her.

Pansy shrugged. "I wasn't particularly. I was still guilty. And what I did was still wrong. The punishment, the shunning that I received, felt justly deserved."

She watched his brow furrow. She was not certain that anyone else could truly understand her motives.

"Everyone thought the worst of me," she continued. "So I cultivated that opinion. I nurtured it and enhanced it at every turn. I believed I was living my life as I pleased, despite the disapproval of my neighbors. But the truth was, I was living my life intentionally to foster that disapproval. It was what I wanted. But it's not what I want anymore."

"What's changed?"

"I have," she said. "I've stopped looking at who I am based on a single series of actions. I was Pansy Richardson before I was the wicked widow. I can be Pansy Richardson again."

Rome's expression was worried. And she knew why. She knew that it was hard for him to imagine her change of course. She knew it was hard for him to believe that her fellow citizens would allow such a turnaround.

"I have to speak from the podium at the Founder's Day Fourth of July Picnic," she told him again. "I want you to speak to the Monday Merchants about it."

"I will certainly try, Pansy," he promised. "But I don't know if they'll let you speak. I don't know how I'll convince them."

"Oh, I think you can convince them," she said. "Tell them I know why the construction on the lagoon system can't get started."

That certainly got his attention.

"What do you know about the lagoon system?" he asked, startled.

"I know that the Monday Merchants keep sending paperwork to the judge about getting the digging started and nothing happens. You've all blamed it on my neighbor here. Poor Mr. Pearsall is not the sharpest knife in the drawer, but his incompetency is not the problem."

"What is the problem?"

"I am the problem," she told him.

"You?"

Pansy nodded. "Construction can't begin, won't begin, because the people of Cottonwood don't own the land."

"What do you mean, we don't own the land?" Rome asked. "Your husband gave it to us."

"Not quite," she replied. "He intended to donate it to you. It had been announced that he was signing the land over to the town. Judge Barclay was drawing up the papers. But Grover died before the papers were signed."

Rome gazed at her with undivided interest.

"I had no idea that it hadn't been taken care of," she told him. "Not for months after. Not until the terrible scandal had broken and the whole town had turned from me in disgust. Then one day I got a visit from the judge."

"I'd heard around town that he continued to visit you," Rome said. "I never believed it."

"He came here once. No matter what the story, people always make it bigger than it really is."

Rome nodded in agreement.

"Judge Barclay said that the land was still mine," Pansy told Rome. "And he asked me if I would like to get a little bit of expensive revenge against the good people of Cottonwood."

She folded her hands together and looked Rome directly in the eye.

"He would keep the secret of the land's ownership while local investments were made and the lines were laid," she explained. "The longer he stalled, the more money the people would tie up in the project, the more they would lose. Then, when it finally came out that I owned the land outright, they would have to buy it from me at top dollar or lose everything they had already spent."

Rome's jaw dropped in disbelief. His expression was one of incredulity.

"You and Barclay came up with this idea?"

"Actually, it was the judge's idea," she said. "Since he was forced to leave town, he's been strapped for cash and very lacking in capital. For his part, he wants half of what the town pays me. No small bit of his enthusiasm for the plan is that a goodly portion of what his wife received in the divorce is invested in municipal bonds. She'll lose heavily."

"This is how you intend to turn over a new leaf, by revealing that you were willing to cheat us?" Rome was in a state of shock.

"I haven't cheated anyone yet," she assured him. "If the community is willing to give me another chance, I'm willing to give them one as well."

Slowly Rome shook his head. "I don't know, Pansy. I don't know if this will work."

"I don't know if it will either," she said. "But from my perspective, I've got nothing more to gain and nothing left to lose."

"I'll talk to them," he promised. "I'll talk to them."

"I want to be on that podium," she insisted. "I want my chance to confront my accusers."

There was a long silence between them. Pansy knew that the truth might well have ruined their friendship. Rome was a kind, open, honest man. He could forgive many things. She was not sure that such an unsavory intrigue, however, was within the scope of what he felt to be pardonable.

"So that's what I wanted to tell you," she said. "What was it that you wanted to tell me?"

He looked at her almost with surprise.

"Oh, I . . . I came to say I can't see you anymore," he answered.

"Oh. Did you mean to say that before you heard the truth about me?"

"Yes, yes, I did. Although I didn't intend to just blurt it out like that. I meant to be more solicitous and gentle. I'm sorry."

"No, it's all right, truly," she assured him. "I intended for this to be an end to us as well. I really have decided to change. I'm not just trying to force people to treat me differently. I am different from what they think they know about me."

"You're different from what I know about you as well," he said.

"I suppose that if I was never as bad as they thought," she said, "I was also never as good as you hoped."

"I'm not usually wrong about people," he told her.

She laughed aloud at that.

"At least I'll have one person on my side because they believe in me, rather than in their own best interests."

Rome rose to his feet and bent forward to kiss her on the forehead.

"I'll talk to the Monday Merchants," he said. "You are probably right. They won't want to jeopardize their investments just for the honor of continuing to brand you as a scarlet woman."

"You do understand the moral barometer of the average businessman," she teased.

She watched him walk out the back door and sighed. It was a sound that was almost melancholy. He had not touched her heart or shaken her soul the way that Amos Dewey had done that afternoon. But during the months of their affair he had proved himself a sweet and vigorous lover. One who treated her with kindness and respect. In the long future of self-imposed chastity that lay ahead of her, she would very much miss him.

Pansy walked to the window for a last glimpse. The moon was bright and she could see him clearly as he retreated across her backyard and into the shadows of the alley. It was only after he disappeared that a movement from the corner of her eye captured her attention. She turned to see Wade and Vera Pearsall standing upon their porch, their eyes gazing in the direction that Rome had taken.

Amos had no intention of waiting for a more convenient time to call. If he didn't do it this morning, he might lose his nerve and never do it at all. There was a special "called meeting" of the Monday Morning Merchants at ten o'clock. He didn't know what it was about, but he couldn't imagine a more inconvenient time to get together for discussion than on Monday morning! But he was not going to allow his civic duties to supersede his intentions today.

He had vowed to speak to Gussie and he was going to do it no matter how inconvenient it might be for him to come calling on her right after breakfast. He was determined.

Amos reached inside the familiar gate and opened the latch. He walked right up the path and knocked upon the door.

Unwillingly, his mind was drawn to another woman

who would undoubtedly be at her breakfast as well. He wondered if her conscience had kept her up at night. Or if she even had a conscience.

Determinedly he knocked upon the door.

Pansy Richardson had certainly shown him that he was alive. For that he supposed he should be grateful. But he didn't feel grateful. He felt angry. She had used his weakness for her to manipulate him. For one short, so-precious moment he had thought her to be special to him, to be a new beginning in his life. But she was not. She had proved indisputably that she was not. Every touch, every kiss, every embrace she had given him was a scheming lie, done for the sake of another man, another lover. It would have been lowering under any circumstances. The fact that he had given her his heart, his all, in exchange for such a tarnished offering was beyond any acceptance. He had to get away from Pansy Richardson. She was dangerous to him. And around her, he was dangerous to himself. He was determined to tie himself to a safe mooring. Gussie Mudd was that.

From the other side of the doorway, Amos could hear the unexpected sound of fleet footsteps. She was *running* to the door. Amos hardly had time to take in the idea before the door was jerked open. Her bright, excited smile and exuberant manner immediately dimmed upon the sight of him.

"Oh, Amos," she said. "Ah . . . what a surprise."

"Good morning, Miss Gussie," he said, removing his hat. "May I come in?"

There was a tiny moment of hesitation, as if she were perhaps unwilling or uninterested. Amos hastily stepped into the breach.

"I realize that it is quite early for calling, but it is imperative that I speak with you now and I have other obligations later in the day."

"It's certainly all right," she assured him in a tone that was deliberately hospitable. "Do come in."

She invited him into the front parlor and then balked at the entryway as if she were uncomfortable with having him in the room. Amos glanced around, expecting to see some cleaning problem. However, there was none. The room appeared perfectly in order. Gussie was an excellent housekeeper, he reminded himself. Another perfectly fine reason to choose to marry her.

"Please, make yourself comfortable," she said finally, apparently deciding that the front parlor was the correct room for receiving him.

She seated herself in a small, overstuffed rocker and indicated for Amos to take the large, comfortable wing chair across from her. He chose instead to sit on a low-backed seat next to hers. It was nearer and more intimate, both conditions more conducive to the words he had to say.

He glanced over at her and swallowed. She was looking very nice this morning. Her hair was clean and shiny. Not so severely coiffed as he recalled from the past. Her eyes were sparkling and her complexion simply glowed with good health. Amos had never thought her an unattractive woman. But he supposed that he hadn't thought much about her looks at all. He'd not been thinking about women or their attractiveness. He'd not been planning to marry again. Now he knew full well that he must plan on it.

Better to marry than to burn, the Bible had stated clearly. A wicked temptress had ignited a fire of passion in Amos. A sensible, honorable marriage to the right sort of woman would surely keep him from being consumed by the flames.

"There is a matter of deep importance that I wish to speak to you about at this time," he said.

Gussie raised her chin a little defiantly. "If you are coming to give me more vague warnings about Rome Akers," she replied, "I will tell you right now that I am not in the least interested in hearing them."

Amos was a little startled by her vehemence. Of course he remembered counseling her against any liaison with Akers, and he was even more certain now that the man's motives were in question. But there was no reason to mention that now.

"I'm not here to talk about Rome," he assured her. "I'm here to talk about you . . . ah, I mean about . . . about us."

"Us?"

He cleared his throat nervously.

"You cannot be unaware that I have been . . . that I have been . . . ah . . . aware of you for some time," he managed to tell her.

"What?"

Her response bordered upon impatience. Amos knew that he must make himself perfectly clear.

"I have been hopelessly distracted by grief since the death of my dear Bess," he began. "I have kept my focus most unthinkingly upon the mere basics of life, the living of one day to the next, without due consideration to the future and all the possibilities that might be pursued there."

He hesitated and drew a breath.

"But now as I look toward the horizon once more, I have become convinced that I am not the kind of man to face the road ahead in single harness, but that as part of a team, I might better fulfill my duty and destiny."

That actually sounded very good, he thought. Fulfilling destiny in team harness; it was almost poetic.

"With an appropriate woman at my side, I feel that I

would be both a better and a more productive citizen. We could easily look forward to a good many years together and even possibly a child or two, though I will not be insistent upon that, leaving such monumental decisions completely in the hands of the Almighty."

Amos tried to gauge Gussie's manner with regard to his declaration. Her expression was totally blank. And when he continued looking at her, she startled as if perhaps she had not been listening.

"I'm sorry," she said, confirming her inattention. "What were you saying?"

"I was asking you to marry me," he answered, annoyed.

"Marry you?"

The incredulity in her voice suggested that such an idea had never occurred to her. As if she had not, only a few short weeks ago, practically asked him herself!

A little awkwardly, but with great ceremony, Amos lowered himself to one knee on the floor beside her.

"Yes, Miss Gussie, I am asking you to marry me," he said. "I believe you professed it as *what everyone in town has been expecting for some time.*"

"Well . . . ah . . . yes, but that was before . . ."

The woman seemed completely dumbfounded. It was clear to Amos that her aspirations in his direction had changed. Undoubtedly Rome Akers figured prominently in that alteration. He realized that it was likely that she would turn him down flat. He didn't want that to happen.

"I have surprised you with this," he acknowledged. "We haven't been seeing much of each other these past weeks and you have perhaps forgotten how well it is that we get along."

"Oh, no, I haven't forgotten," she told him. "It's just . . ."

"Just that it is rather sudden after so many years," he finished for her.

She opened her mouth as if to make further explanation, but then didn't. Her expression turned very serious and businesslike. Amos had seen that look before, but never focused upon him.

"I don't think—" she began.

"That's right," Amos interrupted. "Don't think. At least not right now."

His interruption was timely.

"I know that you are about to refuse me," he said. "And it's because you haven't had time to really consider my proposal thoroughly."

"I'm not sure—"

"With a thing like marriage, no one can ever be sure," he injected quickly. "But a decision like this one deserves due consideration, and I would ask you to give me that."

He took her hand in his. There was no spark of trembling anticipation, no thrill of nearness. Amos felt no desire for her at all. The absence of that emotion spurred him to be even more insistent.

"I am willing and able to spend the rest of my life being a partner and companion to you," he said. "I believe that we are highly suited in both station and temperament. I beg you to at least do me the honor of taking my offer under advisement for a time. Please do not dismiss me out of hand."

Amos could see in her eyes that she was obviously still thinking to do so. But for the mere sake of good manners, she could not.

"Please do get up, Mr. Dewey," she told him finally. "You surely should save your knees for weeding or praying."

"I'm doing both," he assured her as he took his seat

once more. "Weeding out your excuses and praying that you will accept me."

His little joke didn't seem to bring her much humor or advance his suit one iota.

"I . . . I will think about it," Gussie agreed, almost grudgingly. "However, I do not want you to get your hopes up. I am not so certain that we are as well matched as you say."

"We are, Miss Gussie," he replied. "We are very much indeed."

"I'm not so certain," she said. "We lack . . . we lack passion, sir."

"Passion?"

Amos was genuinely surprised at the mention of the word. Ladies did not often speak of such things.

"I'm not sure that passion is a meaningful measure for potential matrimony," he said.

"But surely it is essential for the bliss of such a union," she countered.

"It can be very misleading," Amos said, his thoughts unwillingly drawn to those very wonderful hours he'd spent in Pansy Richardson's arms. "It is ofttimes powerful enough to obscure good judgment. To cause one to mistake desire for honor."

Gussie looked skeptical, but she didn't dispute him.

"I suppose so, but that would surely be in extreme cases," she said.

Amos felt his own situation could easily be considered extreme.

"All I am asking is that you give my offer due and sincere consideration. Though we may not feel . . . overly ardent toward each other, I believe that we could complete a fine partnership together that would be beneficial to us both."

Her expression was doubtful.

"Simply tell me that you will think upon it," he urged.

"All right, I will think about it," she agreed.

"Good. Now I really need to be going," he said, rising to his feet and retrieving his hat. "There is a special *called meeting* of the Monday Morning Merchants."

"Today?" she asked, surprised. "How strange that nobody mentioned it yesterday."

Amos shrugged.

"I wouldn't know," he replied. "I was unable to attend the little fund-raising event in the park. Was it successful?"

"You weren't even there?"

Gussie's tone revealed her disbelief.

"No, I . . . I had a . . . a patron in my shop," he said.

"All afternoon?"

"It—it was a s-surgical case," he lied nervously, stumbling over his words.

He bowed formally, taking his leave.

"Good day, Miss Gussie," he said. "I will be speaking to you again very soon."

16

ROME KNEW THAT THE GENTLEMEN OF THE MONDAY Morning Merchants Association were not going to be at all pleased to hear how their former member, Will Barclay, and the most notorious woman in town had bamboozled them. The piece of land Richardson had donated for the lagoon was absolutely essential to the grand design of the sewer system plan. Finding a new site or coming up with money to meet a purchase price would cost the investors dearly. Rome only hoped that the gentlemen would be willing to allow Pansy her moment on the podium and that bit of revenge would be enough for her.

Most everyone arrived with good-natured grumbling. The Monday Merchants should definitely never meet on Mondays or in the morning, everyone agreed jokingly.

That small piece of humor vied for attention with jovial reminiscences of the previous day's so-very-successful kissing booth. Huntley Boston took a good bit of ribbing about standing in line all day with the whippersnappers so that he could kiss Betty Ditham.

The banker accepted the teasing with good grace and no explanation.

Pete Davies was still protesting that it had to be some sort of thievery to make a man purchase what he already owned by right. The other husbands, however, didn't seem to have either complaints or regrets.

Huntley was just calling the meeting to order when two latecomers entered the room. Rome hardly noticed Wade Pearsall, but he did take note of Amos Dewey's sober countenance. Perhaps the barber was still reeling from the scene at the park yesterday. He had been morally opposed to the gentlemen buying kisses from their wives. Rome could only imagine what he'd thought when he'd seen what was going on between Miss Gussie and himself.

Miss Gussie.

Just bringing her name to mind eased his worries somewhat. He had left her house last night walking on a cloud. He couldn't believe how lucky he was. And he couldn't believe how blind he had been. All this time the perfect woman for him, the perfect mate for his life, was next to him every day on her own porch, and he had been too mule-brained to see her. Certainly it wasn't going to be easy, he reminded himself. Miss Gussie had for years now seen him only as a loyal employee. And she'd thought herself set on Amos Dewey. But clearly that had changed. He'd felt her love for him, her need for him, her oneness with him last night. He knew she was not a woman to give her heart so lightly.

He'd gone straight from her house to see Pansy Richardson. He wanted no lingering ties to any woman in his past. This afternoon, as soon as his business here was completed and his ice deliveries were all caught up, he was going to stop by her house as usual. But unlike times past, today he would talk less about business than about love. He was going to ask Gussie Mudd to marry him. He could hardly wait.

But before he could do that, he must explain to the men in this room, who'd invested their hard-earned dollars in the town's future, that they had been cheated. Rome hated to dampen the high-spirited mood, but he had no choice.

There were not enough seats for everyone. Some sat. Others stood, and along the back of the room most leaned indolently against the walls. Once Huntley had the room quieted down, he turned it over to Rome.

"Mr. Akers, who is responsible for our very successful fireworks fund-raising yesterday, has asked to speak to us this morning," the banker said.

He gestured to Rome, who moved to the front of the room. He had no notes. In truth, he had no plan of how he was going to tell these men what was going on. He simply had to blurt it out and let the chips fall as they may.

"I'm not here to talk about the fireworks for our picnic," he declared immediately. "And what I have to tell you is not very good news at all."

The smiles around the room became more serious expressions as the men listened.

"I have just discovered why construction has not begun on the lagoon system," he said. "And why our repeated letters to Judge Barclay in Austin have gone unanswered."

"Has something happened to the judge?" the mayor asked, concern in his voice.

"I suppose you *could* say that something has happened to him," Rome answered. "He has conspired to swindle us."

"What!"

Murmurs of disbelief spread about the room.

"It seems that Grover Richardson never got around to signing over the lagoon-system land to the city," Rome explained. "The judge and Mrs. Richardson have kept quiet while you invested your money in laying the lines. Once we were thoroughly committed, they could ask top dollar for the lagoon land and we'd have to pay it or lose what we've already put in."

The reaction to the news was as bad as Rome had expected, perhaps worse. There were several men present whose modest fortunes could be wiped out by the scheme. Almost everyone there would lose money. Investing in a modern, sanitary sewer system for the city of Cottonwood was considered a civic duty for local businessmen.

The questions flew fast and furiously. How did it happen? How were they going to stop it? Should they call the sheriff? Could they simply seize the land? And the inquiry most dear to the hearts of a group of businessmen: Who was to blame?

Several looks were shot in Wade Pearsall's direction. He'd been in charge of the project since the judge left. The merchants were silently wondering why he hadn't noticed something, why he hadn't ferreted out the facts.

Rome couldn't help but feel sorry for the fellow. He had done the very best that he could. He was not an especially bright man, but he was eager. Personally, Rome doubted if any of the Monday Merchants could have discovered the truth on their own. They all knew and trusted Judge Barclay. One friend, untrue, could cause more trouble and heartbreak than a dozen strangers.

Several of the men stood quietly, almost in shock,

stoically contemplating what this could inevitably mean to them.

Others were openly angry, eager to smash a fist in the nearest doorjamb or somebody's face.

Most couldn't stop talking. Couldn't stop questioning. Couldn't stop hoping that something could be done.

The mayor stood off to one side of the room, his hand upon his cheek, repeating the phrase "Oh, my heavens! Oh, my heavens!" over and over again.

"Gentlemen, gentlemen," Rome called out, trying to get their attention once more. "You have not heard all I have to say and you're missing an important piece of the puzzle."

Slowly the room quieted.

"I just found out about this last night," he said. "Mrs. Richardson told me herself."

"That scheming, low-morals hussy! We should run her out of town on a rail!" Pete Davies declared.

There were voices of agreement throughout the room.

"Not if she is the one person who could possibly help us," Rome asserted. "And I think that's what she wants. I think she wants to help us."

"She wants to help us get rid of our money, it seems like," Clive Benson declared adamantly.

He was not alone in his opinion.

"Let us listen to what Rome has to say," Huntley insisted, quieting the room once more.

"Mrs. Richardson wants her reputation back," Rome said to them. "She is the last member of the Richardson family, the founders of this community, and she wishes to be treated that way. She wants to speak at the Fiftieth Anniversary Founder's Day Fourth of July Picnic."

That revelation silenced the men for a long, thoughtful moment.

"That's all she wants?" Huntley Boston asked, his relief visible. Not only was he personally invested in the sewer system, but the bank held notes on many of the businesses of the men around the room who stood to lose heavily as well.

"That's all she's indicated to me," Rome told him. "She says she wants to speak at the picnic."

"So we let her speak at the picnic and she signs the land over to us." Joe Simpson's statement was phrased more as a question.

"No, she didn't say that," Rome clarified. "She said she wanted her reputation back and she said she wanted to speak at the picnic."

"Speaking at the picnic, that's easy," Perry said. "But getting a reputation back—it seems to me that's not within our power."

"Yeah," Pete Davies agreed. "We could name her the town virgin and it sure as heck wouldn't make it so."

Rome hated being in agreement with the man.

"She believes that we could make some difference," he said. "She thinks that if we start treating her better and insist that our wives treat her better, that equals the restoration of her reputation."

"Well, it sure doesn't," old man Penderghast piped up. "Folks smiling in your face don't mean nothing if they are still talking about you behind your back."

Rome shrugged. In truth, he was of the same opinion.

"But maybe it makes you feel better if they just try to hide their contempt," he said.

"I don't get it," Joe said. "She's got the whole town over a barrel and all she wants is for us to make nice to her. Why would she go to all this trouble just for that?"

"I don't know that she did," Rome said. "The way

she told it, the swindle was the judge's idea. He needs money and it's a way to get back at Madeline. He knew how much of the money she got was invested in the project."

"But she went along with it," Clive pointed out. "She was willing enough to take advantage of us."

"Why wouldn't she be?" Rome answered. "The whole town has treated her like an outcast."

"She did that to herself," McCade said. "With her loose living and outrageous behavior."

Rome nodded. "She did it to herself and this is her way of trying to undo it."

"Well, is she going to give us the land?" Perry asked. "Is she going to sell it to us at a price we can afford?"

"She didn't make any promises," Rome admitted. "My guess is that she will let construction begin on the lagoon, but keep control of the land to hold you to her bargain. I don't speak for her here. That's only my opinion. All she required of me was that I ask you if she could speak at the picnic."

"And how much of a share of this swindle are you getting for your help?"

The question came from Wade Pearsall. It stunned Rome into silence, and the rest of the room as well.

"How much is that whore paying you for your part of this deal?" the man asked again.

"I am telling you all this because she asked me to do so," Rome stated. "I know nothing about it beyond what I'm telling you. And what I'm telling you, I learned last night."

"Yeah, you learned it last night," Wade said. "Last night in her bed."

The room was completely quiet.

"Vera and I have been watching that house," Wade went on. "We've seen a man coming and going at late hours. We knew something was going on, but we could never see his face. Last night we saw him clear in the moonlight. It was you, Rome Akers. You're her lover and you have been for months. Are you going to deny it?"

Rome stood there staring at the man, wondering what to do, what to say. Rome was her lover, or he had been until last night. The affair was over. But was a thing like that ever over? Could a man just accept the favors of a woman and walk away unchanged, untouched, without consequences?

"Do you deny that you're her lover?" Pearsall demanded once more. Rome glanced around the room. Every eye was upon him. Every expression was questioning. If Judge Barclay, whom they had known and relied upon, could have proved to be untrustworthy, was it so hard to believe that an upstart among them, a man without business or property, might be equally as guilty?

"How much money do you have invested?" Wade asked.

Of course, Rome had not contributed so much as a penny. What money he'd saved was in the bank, gathering interest so that he could buy his way into Mudd Manufactured Ice. He'd not felt obliged to put his pittance on the line. Miss Gussie had put in more than her share. He'd kept his savings in cash because she had not. But how could he explain that? How could he make them believe that?

"You tell us that you haven't been her lover and that you stand to lose as much as the rest of us," Wade said. "Then maybe we'll believe that you're not in on this flimflam like she is."

Rome understood Wade's venom. He understood Wade's motive. They were going to have to deal with

Mrs. Richardson. And Judge Barclay was in Austin, too far away to be a scapegoat. Someone had to be blamed. Wade would be a good person at whom to point the finger. He'd been in charge of the project. He should have checked the paperwork to see that everything was in order. He should have tried harder to find out what the holdup was with Barclay in Austin. He should have found out months ago what was going on. It would be easy to find fault with him.

Pearsall was determined not to be at fault. It was Rome who was going to be held responsible. It was Rome whose reputation was to be traded for thirty pieces of silver.

"I have nothing to say about any ties that I may or may not have had with Mrs. Richardson," he answered finally.

The silence in the room was palpable. Rome could almost feel his friends withdrawing from him. He had never been one of these men. To achieve that status had been his grandest ambition. He had seen it, almost felt it within his grasp, but it had never truly happened. And now as seconds ticked by, the potential slipped away as if it had never been.

"Mr. Akers." Huntley Boston spoke up at last with a rhetorical inquiry. "You are not in fact a merchant or business owner in this community, are you?"

"No, I am not," he answered.

"Membership in this organization is actually limited to businessmen in the community," Huntley said. "I think I speak for our entire organization when I say how grateful we are to you for bringing this problem with the lagoon system to our attention."

The man's formal tone was colder than any ice Rome had ever sold.

"When we have made a decision, we will be talking

to Mrs. Richardson directly about it," he continued. "As this is Monday morning and you have deliveries to make, I'm sure your employer would appreciate having you get on about your work. You are dismissed, sir, and thank you."

Rome clenched his fists impotently as he looked at the men around him. Joe appeared stricken with disbelief. Perry wouldn't meet his eye. Old Penderghast was disappointed; Benson disapproving. The mayor was dumbfounded. Strangely, only Amos Dewey seemed sympathetic.

There was nothing to be said. There was nothing to be done. Begging, pleading, prostrating himself before them and declaring his innocence would not make any difference. He was dismissed. The shreds of his pride were all he had left. He would take them with him.

Head held high, he walked out of the room without looking back.

They had not arrived as a group. Constance came first, alone. It was Constance who told Gussie the story. Madge and Kate, Eliza and Edith, Loralene Davies and Lulabell Timmons, all found their way to her front parlor. Each with her own secondhand version of what had happened, what was going to happen and how that unrepentant hussy, Mrs. Richardson, should be dealt with. They said less about Rome, out of deference to their hostess, but his part in the scandal was made clear.

At one point Gussie excused herself to use the privy. She walked the long length of her backyard with deliberate steps and perfect composure. Once inside the narrow little building with the door firmly shut against the outside world, she vomited and then burst into tears.

Rome was Pansy Richardson's lover. He had left Gussie's arms to go to her. He had touched Gussie, kissed her, brought her pleasure through skills no doubt learned in another woman's bed. Her heart was shattered. Her dreams were destroyed.

She could hardly even work up any anger about the swindle. Despite what the rest of the town believed, she knew Rome was not involved with that. He was too honest, too forthright, to be involved in such deceit. If Rome were not part of it, then it was simply about money. And money could not bring happiness, contentment or meaning to life. Money was merely a measure for business. For things that mattered, it was only green paper and cold metal.

She made her way slowly back to the house. These women were, and had always been, her friends. But their presence now was far from welcome. Like an injured animal, she wanted to crawl into the solitude of her lair and lick her wounds. She knew she would not be allowed to do so. They all knew that she had been keeping company with Rome. They undoubtedly thought she must be disappointed and hurt. They could not know that she was in love with the man. That she had waited all morning for him to come to her. That she had even sat through Amos Dewey's most inopportune marriage proposal, wondering vaguely what she had ever seen in the man.

"I suppose they'll expect us to invite *her* to join the Circle of Benevolent Service," Loralene Davies had reflected, horrified.

"And have *her* inside our homes as if she were one of us," Lulabell had added.

"I don't suppose the place would have to be fumigated afterward," Madge joked. Her comment was accepted humorlessly.

"Perhaps she is genuinely sorry for her sins," Kate suggested. "Maybe she is just hoping for a new start."

"And to get it she is going to blackmail the whole town?" Edith Boston asked. "That doesn't seem to me to be the best way to go about it."

The arguments had gone on for what seemed like hours on end. Nobody wanted to give Pansy Richardson another chance. But only those with little or nothing invested in the sewer project could afford not to do so. The woman would be allowed to speak and she would be invited back into the fold, with the hope that she would not ruin them all financially and bring the town to financial collapse.

Gussie stepped through the back door and into her kitchen. She could hear the women all whispering in the front parlor. She was loath to go in and sit with them once more, but it was her house. She had no choice.

She dipped a rag in cool water from the big crockery drinking jug and wiped it across her brow. The air was hot and her head ached. Her stomach still churned with nausea and she wanted just to lay her head upon the kitchen table and cry a bucket of tears. She soothed her eyes, hoping to disguise any redness or swelling.

She was a businesswoman, stalwart and unemotional. The only time these women had seen her cry was at her father's funeral. She was determined to keep it that way.

Bravely she returned to the front parlor. The furtive whispering ceased as soon as she stepped through the doorway. They were all looking at her. And they were all looking very ill at ease.

"What is it?" she asked.

They looked at each other as if no one really wanted to be the person to have to answer. Constance took on the task.

"Rome Akers has come calling on you, Gussie," she said. "We didn't know if we should send him away or . . ."

She glanced around at the other women for help in finishing the sentence. None was available.

"We told him to wait on the porch," she said.

"Oh."

Gussie was completely at a loss as to what to do or what to say. All morning she had eagerly awaited Rome. Now there was nothing to see him about. But of course there was. He worked for her. She couldn't choose not to see him. But she certainly couldn't talk with him while a whole flock of women sat listening in the front parlor.

"We can send him away," Madge suggested.

"No, no," Gussie told her. "I must see him, of course. Perhaps it would be best if . . . if you took your leave."

There was no truly polite way to ask people to leave your house. Gussie did it as gently as she could.

Kate Holiday jumped up as quickly as a jack-in-the-box.

"Look at the time! It is getting so late," she said. "I'll hardly have an hour to get the reverend's dinner on the table."

"I need to be getting back to the children as well," Constance said.

Quickly, but with perfectly kind excuses, the women took their leave. Madge was the last one out. Gussie followed her to the door.

"If you need me, send for me," she whispered just before she stepped out onto the porch. "Why don't you come to dinner later in the week? It's been so long since we've done that and you know how much the children miss you, and Joe and I enjoy your company so much."

"Thank you," Gussie said. "Perhaps I will."

She saw Madge glance toward the end of the porch where Rome was undoubtedly waiting. Her barely perceptible nod was not much of an acknowledgment for a former friend, but at least she hadn't cut him completely.

Gussie watched Madge go down the walk and out the gate. Old Jezzi stood there hitched to the ice wagon; sturdy and dependable, just like yesterday or the day before. But this was not yesterday or the day before, this was today. Terrible, terrible today. There was no getting away from it and it had to be faced.

Gussie glanced at herself in the hall-tree mirror. Her hair was not as tidy as it should be, and if one looked closely, it was obvious that she had been crying. She smoothed her hair as she headed up the stairs. Rome would certainly wait for her, and a little Blanc de Pearl powder could hide a multitude of female emotion.

She seated herself at her vanity and carefully disguised the pain that was in her heart. In a secret dream, she imagined that he would tell her it was not true. That he had never loved another woman. That he had never kissed Mrs. Richardson as he had kissed her. That he had never held Mrs. Richardson and touched her and made her feel the way he had made Gussie feel. That was what she wanted to hear. That was what she *needed* to hear. But she knew such words would never be spoken. If Rome could have denied it, he would have. It had been clear, both from what the women had said and from what they hadn't, that Rome had been summarily cast out of the Monday Merchants meeting. Had his own guilt not condemned him, he would never have allowed them to do so.

Gussie smiled at herself in the mirror. A smile for practice. It didn't look completely real, but perhaps it

was near enough. She rose to her feet and picked up a
floral silk fan and secured it with the attached bracelet
to her wrist. The afternoon was quite warm, she told
herself. But she knew it was more for barricade than
cooling that she carried the fan with her.

After descending the stairs, she headed for the
kitchen. A pitcher of lemonade was cooling in the icebox. She had made it this morning while she waited
for him. She'd made it before she knew. Gussie set the
pitcher on the usual tray with two glasses. From the ice
drawer she chipped off a few small pieces and added
them to the cool liquid. The lemonade and the tray
looked just like always. They looked just like they had
on any other day on her porch. Who was to know that
everything in the world had changed?

She carried the refreshment down the hall and out
onto the porch. The screen door slammed behind her.
Rome rose to his feet. Dressed in his work clothes, hat
in hand, he looked as handsome as Gussie could ever
remember him being. But then, she hadn't seen him in
daylight before—she hadn't seen him in daylight since
she had come to love him.

"Good afternoon, Rome," she said cheerfully, as if
this day were really not different from a hundred others they'd shared on this porch. "I'm sorry that I was
otherwise detained when you arrived."

He hurried over to take the tray from her. She was
almost reluctant to give it to him. It was like armor, like
her shield. She was about to do battle for her own self-
respect and she needed to gird herself like a warrior.

Politely Rome set the lemonade upon the small table
between the two chairs and waited until she had seated
himself. It was to be a quiet, civil affray.

He sat down as well.

"I suppose you've heard," he said.

He was looking at her. He was looking at her very closely. Gussie hoped the face powder was doing its job.

"Of course I've heard," she said, feigning unconcern. "You have today's report?"

He looked momentarily confused and then nodded hastily, retrieving his tally book from his shirt pocket.

"Please, go ahead," she told him.

He hesitated for a long moment, uncertain. She continued to wait, expressionless. Finally he opened his tally book.

"Manufacturing was thirty-seven hundred pounds since Friday," he read. "We had one hundred fifty pounds remained undelivered from the previous week. That makes three thousand eight hundred and fifty. We delivered three commercial accounts at one thousand pounds. There were four residential deliveries of seventy-five pounds each, five at fifty pounds and eleven deliveries at twenty-five weight."

"That's cutting it pretty close, isn't it?" she asked.

She knew full well that it was always this close early in the week. But she always commented, so she felt she should again.

"Monday is our biggest day," he answered. "We'll have more surplus left in storage tomorrow."

She nodded.

He began reading the accounts collected and uncollected. Gussie feigned interest, but she did not hear a word. She forced herself to look at him. The sight was painful. It was very painful to look at someone whom you loved so much, whom you wanted so desperately and whom you knew, without question, you could never have.

She fanned herself, glancing away, ostensibly listening to his report.

It was only when she noticed the silence of the porch that she realized he had finished. She was trying to think of something appropriate to say when he spoke up himself.

"I can't imagine what you must be thinking of me, Miss Gussie," he said.

"Why, I'm not thinking any more or less of you than I ever have, Rome," she told him.

"I'd . . . I'd like to tell you my side of it."

She waved his words away with her fan.

"It's not necessary," she said. "I have the gist of the story, I believe. Even rumors have aspects that are undoubtedly true as well as those that certainly are not. You should trust me to know the difference."

The man's whole expression changed. His visage, dark and brooding, lightened with hope. His shoulders rose as if a huge weight has just been lifted from them. He almost smiled.

Gussie knew it was cruel to give him any impossible expectations.

"After all the years you've worked for me," she continued, "I am absolutely certain that you would not involve yourself in any scheme to cheat, defraud or extort money from anyone. I would be willing to swear in court that you have never so much as attempted to pocket a penny from my business. So, no matter what is said on that account, I am completely confident of your honesty."

His wavering smile faded completely.

"Thank you, Miss Gussie."

"I have no great abhorrence of accepting Mrs. Richardson back into polite society," Gussie went on. "She was a devoted wife to her husband while he lived. And as for the nature of her alliances since, I simply do not care to know."

Gussie fanned herself and smoothed down the pleats in her skirt. Between them the lemonade remained untouched, the pitcher sweating profusely in the afternoon heat.

"I do, however, find her methods for acceptance rather high-handed," she said. "But I trust that she will do the right thing when it comes down to it."

He nodded.

"She will," he agreed. "She is not a bad person, but she's made some bad mistakes."

Rome was studying her. The intensity of his gaze was positively nerve-racking.

"As you are . . . her confidant," Gussie told him, "perhaps you could suggest to her that there is a faster and more foolproof method of setting one's reputation to rights."

Deliberately she attempted to sound worldly-wise and knowledgeable.

"Please tell her that it is my highly considered advice that she marry with all due haste. A respected gentleman of the community would be a perfect choice. A business owner or perhaps a partner in a business. Someone . . . someone like . . . like yourself, Mr. Akers."

Rome's brow furrowed. His whole body seemed to tighten as he gazed at her, puzzled.

"Gussie, I . . ."

"It has been a busy day," she said, fanning herself and feigning a light laugh. "I know you will certainly be surprised. I admit that I was myself. But apparently our little ploy yesterday worked perfectly. Amos Dewey walked right into my parlor this morning and proposed marriage, just as I had hoped he would."

She attempted a cheery little laugh. It fell flat, but she went on without it.

"Please don't say anything to anyone, of course. Certainly not to Mr. Dewey, for I haven't given him my answer yet. A day or two on pins and needles will do the fellow a world of good after what he has put me through."

Gussie looked into Rome's eyes and saw raw pain. She didn't know if it was his alone or her own reflected. She ignored it and kept talking.

"It seems at last as if all my dreams have come true. I can be married by the Fourth of July and you, Rome Akers, will have your partnership in my business just as I promised."

He was stunned into silence for several long moments and then the painful truth burst from him.

"The partnership no longer matters to me," he said.

"For heaven's sake, don't say such a foolish thing," she scolded him. "You've worked very hard for this and you deserve it. Besides, it will go a long way to getting you out of your current predicament. With a partnership in Mudd Manufactured Ice, you can walk right back into the Monday Merchants meeting and not a soul can question your right to be there. Once you and Mrs. Richardson are wed, they'll be treating you with the same cautious deference with which they will treat her. If you are both careful, if you live right, in a few short years that deference will turn into respect. You both will rise to prominent positions in the community and all of this current little whirlwind will be yesterday's gossip. Only dredged up for recall on the most boring of cold winter nights."

"I don't love Pansy Richardson," Rome stated with absolutely certainty.

Gussie fanned herself and lowered her eyes. The shards of her broken heart cut her to the quick.

"Not everyone is lucky enough to marry for love,"

she told him quietly. "A companion suited in both station and temperament might actually be better. Love is not a meaningful measure for matrimony. It can be very misleading and ofttimes powerful enough to obscure good judgment, to cause one to mistake desire for honor."

They looked at each other as if across a chasm a thousand feet wide. It was like business, Gussie reminded herself. Never show fear when your note comes due. Never let them know when you're broke. Whatever you're selling, pretend you're loath to even part with it.

"Rome Akers," she said. "Look at you! You've got a new partnership in a growing company and soon a lovely wife who is wealthy, influential and lives in the finest house in town. Perhaps you should stop wearing that long face, sir. This is undoubtedly the luckiest day of your life."

17

IN THE WEEKS PROCEEDING THE FOUNDER'S DAY Fourth of July Picnic, there was more gossip in Cottonwood than the entire half year prior. There was, of course, the tremendous hue and cry over what had come to be called the Sewer Swindle. The very afternoon that the news came out, Madeline Barclay had boarded a southbound train for Austin. She confronted the judge in his room at the Grand Hotel and, according to rumor, shot him dead, straight through the heart, with a smoking, pearl-handled pistol.

Mr. Potts at the Cottonwood *Beacon*, keen to get the facts right, reported that Mrs. Barclay had actually smashed her former husband over the head with a convenient whiskey bottle and that the man had required twelve stitches. But that story didn't make the rounds in Cottonwood nearly as efficiently as the original tale.

This exciting piece of news was actually good, Rome thought. Madeline Barclay might have done her best to ruin Pansy's life once, but this time her quick temper and drive for revenge had made her ex-husband the focus of attention. Giving people more to talk about than the wicked widow.

But Mrs. Richardson's turn of leaf had plenty of attention from local townsfolk as well. And counter to everything Rome knew about her, she used that notoriety to her advantage. She was, in essence, blackmailing the town. But instead of her usual daring behavior, she showed herself sober, thoughtful and penitent. She didn't force herself into anyone's circle and she kept her own company almost exclusively.

She attended church for the first time in years. Rome wasn't there and didn't see her, but the story he'd heard at the barbershop was that she was dressed plainer than a Mennonite. Some people didn't even recognize her.

Rome began to wonder if he would recognize her himself. She refused to see him except in broad daylight, standing in her garden in plain view of the Pearsall house. She even waited outside while he carried ice into her kitchen.

Her attitude was exactly opposite of his own. Although he was not guiltless, he felt betrayed by his friends. His liaison with Pansy was immoral and unsanctioned, he could not deny that. But both were unmarried. There were no spouses or children injured and they had been judiciously discreet. That didn't make it right, of course. It should, however, have made it forgivable.

What galled Rome more was the demise of the rumor that he was somehow involved in the swindle. Gussie Mudd had made him a partner in her business. That was interpreted as indisputable evidence that he was not involved in any nefarious business practices. Huntley Boston apologized to him personally and politely asked him to allow the Monday Merchants to reinstate his membership.

"I was completely out of line," Huntley said to him, backed by Joe Simpson and Perry Wilhelm. "I jumped to conclusions that were totally erroneous. My behavior was unforgivable, but I am asking you to forgive me."

Rome didn't want to forgive him. He didn't even want forgiveness for himself. His whole world had turned upside down and maybe he liked it that way better.

It was all very much as Gussie had predicted. But then, Gussie always did understand the secrets of commercial success. It was the secrets of the heart for which she had little understanding.

The formal announcement of her engagement to Amos Dewey was met with shock, surprise and ultimately congratulation. They were clearly, in the opinion of the people of Cottonwood, the perfect couple. They were both a little older, a little wiser than most betrothed. They both were financially secure and ran successful businesses. They were prominent in church and community, interested in civic affairs and local politics. And, except for a small lapse early that summer, they had been keeping company for some time.

If the two seemed a little less giddy and ecstatic than typical young lovers, that could be accounted for by their sensible natures and temperaments and maturity.

Seeing them together was painful for Rome. Jealousy certainly played a part, but it was more than that. He loved Gussie. He loved her and he believed that he understood her. He wanted her to be happy. And though he liked and respected Amos Dewey, he no longer believed that the man was capable of making her happy.

He was convinced that only he, Rome Akers, was the one to do that. That short, sweet time when he and Gussie had been out of their senses and into their dreams had convinced Rome that the two of them were meant for each other.

He wanted to talk to her, to plead with her. She acted as if that special night had never happened. She talked as if marriage to Amos Dewey were the choice she had wanted to make. Rome was not convinced.

She was certain that he'd had nothing to do with the swindle, but she was hurt by his relationship with Pansy Richardson. He wanted to explain himself. But perhaps there was no way. The town was going to forgive his indiscretion because it was forced to. Miss Gussie had no reason to forgive him. And obviously, she could not.

She was going to marry Amos Dewey as she'd planned. And cast their perfect night of love, the most sublime moment of Rome's life, into the rubbish heap as if it were of no lasting value, a trivial folly, best forgotten.

"She will never find happiness married to Amos Dewey," Rome stated with certainty.

Pansy Richardson agreed with him.

"They will stay faithful and true to each other and have a long life," she said. "And it will seem even longer than it is. He will never bring out her humor. She won't ever inspire his imagination."

Rome didn't know much about humor or imagination. But he had learned a lot lately about love. And those two would never find it together.

"Well, can't we do something to stop it?" he asked.

Pansy looked at him as if he had lost his mind.

"I am through plotting and scheming," she told him. "And the way things have turned out for you, I would think you have had enough of it as well."

"I love her, Pansy," he admitted.

She nodded sorrowfully. "I was afraid that you did," she said.

"I can't let her marry him."

"I don't know how you can stop her."

Rome didn't know either.

"She told me that I should marry you," he said.

Pansy raised a questioning eyebrow and laughed lightly. "She does understand the game. She's a smart woman. But she lacks my experience."

"What do you mean?"

"She's right that having us wed would suit folks here in town. It would be nice and neat and acceptable," Pansy explained. "Making an illicit alliance into one blessed by God and community would be a smart move if getting back in everyone's good graces could actually make someone happy."

"But it can't?" he asked, already knowing the answer.

Pansy shook her head.

"Gussie Mudd has never been married," she pointed out. "She hasn't known what it is like to live with a man you love. If she did, she'd never consider anything else."

Pansy's mood had turned melancholy; purposely she forced a smile to her face.

"I was loved once," she said. "I want that again. But I'll live alone the rest of my life before tying myself into a marriage without it."

That was exactly what Gussie was doing and Rome felt powerless to stop it.

She never saw him alone or gave him an opportunity for a private word. Since the announcement of their upcoming nuptials, Amos Dewey was close by her side on every occasion.

The barber began closing up his shop early in order to sit on Miss Gussie's porch while Rome made his report. Ostensibly this was done so that Amos could learn the business.

"I'm turning the company over to Mr. Dewey as soon as we are wed," she announced one afternoon.

Rome was dumbfounded. He glanced over at Amos. The declaration was no surprise to him and apparently gave him no cause for concern. Rome would run the company and Amos would oversee it.

"Miss Gussie assures me that I can count on your expertise, and I know that I can count on your cooperation," he said.

Rome couldn't believe it. Mudd Manufactured Ice without Gussie Mudd? It was inconceivable.

"What will you do, Miss Gussie?" Rome asked her.

She seemed startled by the question and did not immediately have an answer.

"She'll be my wife," Amos replied, as if that were obvious. "I can provide for her even without her business."

Rome looked at Gussie again. Still she said nothing.

"This should be good news for you," Amos continued. "Miss Gussie has told me how you've been saving money to buy into the business. I would be perfectly willing to allow you to gradually buy me out completely."

Rome was stunned into silence. It should have been good news. His own business, wholly his at long last. And a very lucrative and exciting business as well. He should have been shouting for joy. But he found that he could not muster any enthusiasm for his good fortune at all. What possible pleasure could a profitable business bring to an empty life?

"Thank you," he managed to get out.

He felt no sense of elation, only loss.

* * *

It was always good when a plan worked out like you thought it would, even if it took some unexpected twists and turns along the way. That's what Gussie told herself as she went over the list of details for her wedding to Amos Dewey. It was to be the perfect wedding. The wedding she had always planned.

Miss Ima had been commissioned to construct a dress that could show Miss Gussie's figure to its finest advantage, without corseting her into collapse. She was busily stitching up a confection of frothy lace and white silk that would be the dream of every young girl in town.

With the help of Constance and Madge, every invitation had been handwritten and hand-delivered. Phrases like *request the honor of your presence* and *to be united in the bonds of holy matrimony* flowed with flourishes from their ladies' fine pen points with the ease of grocery lists.

Gussie was carefully watering her garden in the early-morning hours. And shading it in the worst of the afternoon sun. She wanted to ensure an abundance of beautiful flowers decorating the church as well as a stunning bouquet to carry. There would be no puny hothouse blooms arriving by train for her, she insisted.

A grand cake in the Greek-temple style was ordered for the event. Mrs. Boston, who retained a fine reputation as a confectioner, had volunteered to make a marzipan bride and groom to adorn the white butter frosting layers and represent the sweetness of the wedding day.

Bubbly champagne shipped all the way from France was an extravagance that raised eyebrows among the ladies of the Circle of Benevolent Service. Reverend Holiday even appeared a bit ill at ease with serving spirits, and imported ones at that, so soon after a religious ritual. He suggested to Gussie, privately, that she limit her guests to one glass apiece.

In short, it was to be the finest, the fanciest wedding that the town of Cottonwood had ever seen. And why not? Gussie asked herself. When a woman has waited thirty-one years, she certainly ought to celebrate with more than a simple ceremony.

She was to be a married woman at last. After all the long, lonely years, she would take a man's name, meld her life with his own, share his bed, perhaps bear his children. It meant monumental change and tremendous challenge. It was everything that she had hoped for!

And yet, it was so much less than what she really wanted.

July 5th was the date she'd set upon. The wedding was to take place on Sunday afternoon. Close enough to her original plan that it felt as if she'd achieved her goal, but avoiding any conflicts with the Fiftieth Anniversary Founder's Day Fourth of July Picnic.

It was all going to be absolutely wonderful. A beautiful wedding, marriage at last and maybe a family—it was a happily-ever-after by anyone's definition. Still, Gussie found herself sighing, almost sadly.

"A penny for your thoughts."

Amos sat across from her in the porch shadows of a summer evening. They had shared a nice meal in the dining room and had come outside to escape the heat.

He was spending almost all of his free time there these days. He closed up the shop early and came straight to her house. They ate dinner together almost every evening. And they sat upon the porch until nearly bedtime. Amos would then politely take his leave and Gussie would retire. It was ordinary. It was easy. It was almost as if they were already wed. Almost.

"My thoughts are hardly worth a penny," she told

him. "Perhaps you should wait until I'm on my high horse about something. Then I'll give you more than you'll want, absolutely free."

They smiled at each other pleasantly. He had a nice smile, straight, white, even teeth, full lips and crinkles in his cheeks all the way back to his ears.

Amos was a thoughtful and generous suitor and showed every indication of being a good husband. She was lucky. She was very lucky, she reminded herself, not for the first time.

"How was the shop today?" she asked. "Did you do much business?"

"A typical day," he told her. "Most of the regulars stopped by to get a word or two in."

"And a few of them had more than a word or two, I suspect."

He chuckled lightly.

"Pete Davies was in," Amos said. "He asked me if it was true that Mr. Everhard was tailoring a cutaway coat for my wedding."

"Ah . . . I'm sure Mr. Davies didn't approve," Gussie said.

"He didn't voice his opinion one way or the other, but he did tell me that his father was buried in a coat just like that."

They enjoyed each other's company. A long association had made them easy with each other, friendly, complaisant.

"Has Rome mentioned anything to you about a new distiller?" she asked him.

"Distiller?" Amos shook his head. "No, he hasn't said anything to me."

"He will. We've been making do with the old one for quite some time now. The valve is in a perpetual state of repair and disrepair."

"Ah," Amos replied, rather disinterested.

"So when he does ask," Gussie said, "you must put him off."

"Oh?"

"I want to surprise him," she explained.

"Surprise him?"

Gussie nodded eagerly.

"With the passage of that Pure Food and Drugs Act in Congress, I'm thinking that the demand for new mechanical processes may foster some new inventions," she said. "I'm hoping we can streamline the plant, maybe with new, modern machinery. I don't want us investing in any old-fashioned equipment."

Amos was looking at her strangely. But then, the man knew nothing about ice production or the manufacturing process.

"If he asks about replacing the distiller," she said, "try to stall him until after the first of the year."

"You want to streamline the plant?" He sounded surprised. "I thought we were going to sell it to him."

"Oh, yes. Yes, of course," Gussie replied, recalling that she'd tacitly agreed to that. "I suppose Rome can streamline it himself."

She felt a sinking sensation in her heart. It was a keen sense of loss. One that she willed herself not to give in to.

"Will you talk to him about it?" she asked.

"I will if that's what you'd like, Miss Gussie. But really, you should talk to him about it yourself," Amos said. "You're the person who actually knows something about it."

It was true, of course. She should be discussing the business with Rome. Amos wasn't even interested in ice manufacturing. He was a barber and all of his experience and expertise was in the tonsorial arts. His fledgling participation in the company was at her request and his own reluctance. Gussie didn't want to talk with Rome. She couldn't bear to talk with him. It was painful just to have him sit on the porch and make his report.

To touch someone's heart and give him your own so totally, so intimately, was a dear and special thing. To then pretend that it had never happened was a torture. To know that their lips would never meet again, to forever be exiled from the shelter of his arms, to recall with perfect clarity that moment of immeasurable bliss that he had given her and insist that it never be repeated.

Gussie loved her business. She had nurtured and cared for it as she had her home and her garden. It was her last connection to her father, her family, her heritage. It was as dear to her as if it were a part of herself, an extension of who she, Augusta Mudd, was in the world. However, she was prepared to give it up. To give it up forever rather than live with the pain of seeing Rome every day, wanting him and knowing that he was eternally beyond her grasp.

"Amos, would you like to kiss me?" she asked suddenly.

He raised an eyebrow, perhaps surprised at her boldness.

She was startled herself at her question. He had kissed her cheek when she'd accepted his proposal. And they brushed each other's lips at every meeting and parting. But there had been no passion between them, no lusty lovers' tryst, no danger of anticipating the vows to be spoken.

"Of course I would like to kiss you," he answered.

He rose from his chair and approached her. Taking her hand, he urged her to her feet. They stood awkwardly together for a long moment.

Gussie felt nervous, ill at ease. They had kissed before, but it had never seemed so deliberate, so intentional. It had never before been so important to her.

Amos leaned down and put his lips against her own. It was a gentle meeting of two mouths. Friendly. Chaste.

He stepped back and they stared into each other's eyes. It was as if they were brother and sister. Affectionate cousins. Platonic companions.

"That won't quite do, will it?" he said with refreshing honesty.

He didn't need to explain himself further. They were both fully aware of his meaning.

She watched him swallow his reserve as he gave her an encouraging grin.

Amos slid his arms around her waist and pulled her closer to him. Gussie wrapped her arms around his neck. He was taller than Rome, she noted against her will. He was taller but not nearly as muscular. Not nearly as warm. Not nearly as welcome.

This time when he brought his mouth down on hers, it was open. She parted her lips for him as well. Willfully she put all she had into her response, remembering the feeling that she'd shared with Rome and replicating it to the best of her ability.

Amos was trying very hard to please. He moved his mouth on hers. His tongue lapped and explored, teased and tasted. His fingers combed up into her hair at the nape of her neck. He held her fast as his kiss deepened desperately. Their bodies were flush, tightly together, but no heat emanated from them. No flame burned. Amos brought a hand up to grasp her breast in a burst of feigned passion. But it *was* clearly feigned.

They broke apart, not meeting each other's eyes, then they seated themselves in the chairs once more.

The silence between them was all-enveloping. There was nothing to say. No excuses to make. It was as it was and they had no power to make it different.

Is it Bess? she thought she should ask him. *Are you still in love with your late wife? Is it me or is it anyone?* That was how she should be questioning him. That was the correct course of inquiry. But she demanded nothing. She didn't really care. And what if he turned the tables on her? Was she a woman lacking in desire? Did she not love him? Or did she love someone else?

Gussie didn't want to answer, so she posed no questions of her own. If she felt no carnal needs, perhaps it was best that he felt none either.

They got along very well, Gussie reminded herself yet again. He was quiet and respectful. She was serious-natured and hardworking. Their marriage would never be explosive or imprudent or . . . or even passionate. But they could be . . . content. That surely would be enough, she told herself. Simply content.

Resolutely she turned to Amos and smiled. She had lived without fiery romance for thirty-one years. Surely she could resolve to do without it for thirty more.

"So have you heard any rumors about Rome and Mrs. Richardson?" she asked by way of making conversation.

He looked momentarily shocked and she realized that she had phrased the question quite incorrectly.

"I mean—I mean, have you heard anything . . . lately?" she amended. "I was actually hoping for an announcement from those two."

"An announcement?"

"Yes," she answered. "I advised Rome that the most efficient and time-tested method of restoring a reputation includes hasty nuptials followed by uneventful matrimony."

Amos appeared genuinely puzzled.

"Surely you can't think that Rome should wed himself to her," he said.

"Why not?"

"Mrs. Richardson has . . . well, she has . . ." His voice trailed off and he cleared his throat. "Miss Gussie, her sullied reputation was fairly earned," he explained.

She blushed, but refused to be embarrassed into silence.

"You mean that she has . . . she has been with men other than Rome," Gussie clarified.

"This is not a proper topic for our discussion," he replied.

"We are to be married in less than a week, Amos," she pointed out. "Surely we can relax some of the proprieties."

"I'm not certain a matter such as this should be discussed even between a married couple," he said.

"Don't be silly," she said. "I'm a woman grown. I know . . . I know babies aren't found under cabbage bushes."

He smiled at her, his stern facade melting somewhat.

"Certainly not in this part of Texas," he said. "The heat would scorch them."

She answered his smile with one of her own, but didn't give up her train of thought.

"Why do you think that Rome shouldn't marry Mrs. Richardson?" she persisted.

Amos seemed genuinely annoyed at having to explain. But did his best in his own, rather stifled way.

"Nobody sells fruit at a peach picking," he said with great emphasis.

Gussie rolled her eyes.

"Next you'll be talking about free milk and cows."

Amos nodded. "My point exactly," he told her.

"Well, my understanding," Gussie responded, "is that Mrs. Richardson is . . . shall we say . . . out of the dairy business."

"Miss Gussie!"

"She has vowed to turn over a new leaf," she said. "She shows every evidence of doing so. And I personally believe her."

"The future cannot change the past," Amos replied. "Rome is a smart, ambitious man. He would not wish to tie himself to a woman who has proven to be faithless."

"Faithless to whom?" Gussie asked. "You knew her when Grover was alive. So did I. Was she not a devoted, loving wife?"

"Yes, yes, she was that."

"Doesn't that part of her past exist as well? If she was a good wife once, why would she not be again?"

"Perhaps she would be," he said. "But a man might not be willing to take such a chance."

"Marriage is always a chance," she said. "There are no guarantees of happiness anywhere. It's a wonder that wedlock still exists, that anyone is willing to step up to the challenge of it."

"But when you're in love," Amos said, "you're willing to risk everything."

The words were out before he could stop them. Gussie watched the expression upon his face as he realized what he had said. He'd been speaking of his own marriage, his love for Bess, sweet, sickly Bess. He married her for love, cared for her during her short life and mourned for her years after she was gone. He'd done that all for love.

Now he was about to marry Gussie and none of that emotion, none of that fine feeling, none of it was a part of their plans.

"You've proved my point exactly," Gussie said quietly. "If Rome loved her, none of that would matter. Not her past, not her reputation, not even other men. If he loved her, as you loved your Bess, then nothing could stop him from going after what he wanted."

Amos swallowed. Slowly he nodded.

"Obviously Rome does not love her," he said.

"Could a man . . . be with a woman, touch her, lie with her and not love her?" Gussie asked.

"It happens all the time," he answered.

"Could you?" she asked him.

He didn't answer. He turned his attention away from her, gazing intently upon the fireflies in the garden.

"I suppose we will see," she whispered quietly to herself.

"What?" He turned back to her. "Did you say something?"

Gussie felt a strange lethargy settle upon her like a weight on her shoulders.

"I said that July is a very hot month to plan a wedding."

18

THE AFTERNOON OF THE FOUNDER'S DAY FOURTH OF July Picnic was hot as any Independence Day could be expected to be. Or so Harry Potts, editor of the newspaper, had commented that morning in the Cottonwood *Beacon*. The long-dry weather and a slight western breeze were the only things that made it bearable. But it was a day for socializing and celebration. Not even the most climate-complaining of Cottonwooders were willing to miss it.

Matt Purdy's new-mown hay field at the edge of town was resplendent in bright colors, swarming with activity and wafting the wonderful odors of roasted corn and peach pie.

The city band had been placed on a hastily constructed platform that held the podium. Shaded beneath a dark tarpaulin, its members would be protected from the weather, whether inclement or seasonally scorching.

Following the fine success of Rome Akers's kissing booth, several local organizations had set up stands to entertain, intrigue and generally lighten the pocketbooks of charitably inclined citizens. There were games of chance, ladies' art, fancy preserves and needlework for sale. There was even a seed-spitting contest, the cost to enter being five cents, the price of a slice of fresh, ripe watermelon.

Most of the businesses in town were represented as well. Some were simply showing their wares. Others were all decked out in patriotic paraphernalia, flags flying and slogans ablaze. The tobacco shop was giving away mechanically rolled cigarettes, one to a customer. Timmons Shoe Shop offered a free booting consultation involving putting one's bare foot on a piece of inked paper. The unshod, with blue soles, stood around waiting for their results. At McCade's Livery, there was horseshoe pitching. All over there were plenty of giveaways, demonstrations and play-pretties for the little ones and their parents. Everyone found something to hold his or her interest.

All morning old man Shultz had driven a hay wagon from Main Street to the festivities and back again, providing fun and old-fashioned transportation to those who had neither buggy, horseback nor bicycle to bring them.

The length and width of the hay meadow was dotted with family picnics. Children chewing on fried chicken legs were more common than bluebonnets in April. Loosed from apron strings, they ran wildly with the freedom of hot summertime. And the call of scolding mothers was more shrill than the incessant cawing of field crows.

Pansy Richardson had adorned her clothes as if they were sackcloth and ashes and she were headed for her own stoning. This was the day she had waited for, this was the day she had asked for. If occasionally she asked herself why, there were a million reasons. And every one of them had to do with herself.

She probably should thank Amos Dewey for that, she thought in her more generous moments. She had given herself to him. Not in the way that she had allowed men to use her body. She had given herself to him wholly as a person to love and be loved. She had given herself to him as she had once done with Grover Richardson.

Amos Dewey had not gloried in her gift as Grover had. He had thrown it back in her face as something tarnished, worthless.

It was in that moment, that oh-so-painful moment, that she had realized the truth. She had thrown away all that was valuable and was left with the dregs of a life that was bitter with disappointment.

Pansy Richardson intended to get that back.

Many of the gentlemen of the Monday Merchants had quizzed her on what she planned to say. Most were gently suggesting that she could formally donate the lagoon land, just as her husband had, even signing the papers right there on the spot. A few of the more cynical worried that her moment at the podium might be used to further blackmail the Cottonwood community into both financial and moral ruination.

Wade Pearsall had openly threatened her that there would be those in the crowd ready to defend themselves against her scurrilous tyranny. If her intent was to strike out at her neighbors, they would return the gesture in kind.

Pansy hadn't enlightened any of them. Her agenda was her own and she would fulfill it without any advice or opinions from the town fathers.

She was coming before her accusers, sorrowful and penitent. It was said that forgiveness was good for the soul. Today, the soul of a whole town might improve.

Certainly she was doing her part. She was living quietly and behaving modestly. She was as chaste as a nun and channeled her energy into good deeds and hard work. Her house was spick-and-span, her garden blooming and her grounds well tended. All her daring new fashions were packed in cloves of camphor in the attic. And she had attended church three Sundays in a row.

In truth, it had not been so terribly difficult. She found that the life of the wicked widow seemed to have run contrary to her more basic nature. She was not really the type of person who enjoyed an excess of attention. The wicked widow turned heads wherever she went. When she spoke, her words must always be pointed, witty and risqué. In many ways, it was a lot easier and more comfortable to be ordinary Pansy Richardson once more.

Of course, she was never going to be completely ordinary. She still loved to flirt and giggle and think inappropriate thoughts. She still loved to spin around in the moonlight until she was dizzy. And she would greatly miss the strong arms of a lover beside her in bed. But if she could regain her self-respect and the respect of this community, it would be well worth the sacrifice.

She had been loved once, she reminded herself. A man had loved her and cherished her for five years. There were many women in the world who didn't know that adoration for five minutes. She would not be greedy. And if sometimes in the lonely, loveless future ahead of her she thought about a long, slowly wondrous afternoon in a barber's chair, that would be her own weakness, her own fantasy. No one else need be the wiser.

"Good morning, Mrs. Richardson."

The female voice called out and Pansy turned to see whose it was. Kate Holiday and the reverend were walking in her direction.

Pansy thought Mrs. Holiday to be a cute little button of a woman with a keen sense of humor and a lot of natural style. Her wardrobe, however, was serviceable and much mended and the hat she had on today, while perfectly good for keeping the sun off her face, was surely several years old and meant for a dowager, not a young mother. Pansy wondered to herself what the clever pastor's wife might manage to make out of that trunk of daringly fashionable clothes in Pansy's attic. She smiled to herself as she resolved to find out some day soon.

"Good morning to you," Pansy answered. "And you as well, Reverend. It looks like a fine day for a picnic, doesn't it."

She directed the last comment to the couple's young children, who were wide-eyed and eager with the excitement of the day.

"It *is* a wonderful day for a picnic," Reverend Holiday agreed in a loud, booming voice that was impossible to ignore. "But any time that man can commune with God and nature is a moment blessed and fortunate."

"Yes, I suppose so," Pansy said.

"It's been so good to see you in church these last few weeks," Kate said. "I understand that you used to attend regularly before the death of your husband."

They had been talking about her, of course. But how could they not? She had practically dared the whole town of Cottonwood to talk about her for years. It was the sort of thing once started, very hard to stop.

"Yes, my late husband grew up in your church," she

answered, focusing attention on the reverend and his wife in turn. "I attended as a young woman."

"And we gave abundant thanks to God for bringing a lost lamb back into the fold," the pastor declared.

"Yes, well, thank you," Pansy replied. "I've . . . I've enjoyed your sermons very much."

The reverend looked like he was about to say more when his wife waylaid him.

"I was wondering if you would be interested in joining the Circle of Benevolent Service," Kate said. "I don't know if you are familiar with the ladies' organization, but we do a lot of nice things for the people of Cottonwood and we have such a fun time."

Pansy was surprised.

"Have you discussed this with the other members of the group?" she asked Kate quietly.

The minister's wife looked concerned.

"Why, no," she said. "All the women of the church are welcome. And I am Vigilant Servant at the Gate. It's my job to seek out and welcome new members."

Pansy wasn't sure if the young woman was naive or bursting with warmth of generosity. Either way, she was touched and grateful. The preacher's wife might be the easiest woman in town to win over, but clearly it was a start.

"Thank you very much," she said. "You have been kinder than you have to be."

Her words seemed to puzzle Mrs. Holiday. And from his expression, they might have worried the reverend.

Pansy took her leave and began making her way through the crowd. A young boy nearly ran into her, followed by a big, yelping yellow dog that practically knocked her down. Laughing uproariously, she had just regained her balance when she spotted Rome.

Under a banner proclaiming them to be the province of Mudd Manufactured Ice, he and Tommy Robbins, with some assistance from old man Shultz's wife, Helga, were busy making and serving up ice cream. Rome, in his shirtsleeves, sat on a three-legged milking stool as he turned the crank on the freezer. The motion turned the wheel dasher inside the two-and-a-half-gallon freezer can that held the sweet combination of cream, sugar and eggs. In the pine tub surrounding the tin container, the rapid cooling of melting ice, accelerated by the use of salt, froze the contents into a smooth taste treat chilly enough to send shivers up a child's back on the hottest day in July.

Rome looked up and saw her. With immediate welcome, he smiled. Pansy smiled back at him, but kept her distance. In all that had transpired, she felt the most regret for what had happened to Rome. Certainly he had been her lover and was as guilty as she for that indiscretion. But it was her pride and her arrogance that had brought them to this pass.

Of course, most people would say that he had not suffered overmuch for his sins. His humiliation before the community would be well remembered, but had been short-lived. He'd gotten his partnership in the business that he loved. And he hadn't been obliged to marry Pansy. Though she had thought it a sweet gesture that he had been willing to do so.

To those who did not know his heart, it appeared that Rome Akers had emerged from his part in the Sewer Swindle unscathed. But Pansy did know his heart. She had known it long before he himself had. And she had plotted to repay his friendship by allowing him to win his heart's desire.

But everything had gone badly. She tried to lure Amos away from Gussie. Instead she drove him into her arms. And what felt worse, she couldn't even confess her failure to her friend. She could never reveal Amos Dewey's fall from grace. There were already far too many men whose names had been dragged through the mud for the sake of Pansy Richardson. She would take that secret to her grave if necessary.

As if her thoughts had conjured the vision, she felt the hairs prickle on her neck and turned to meet eyes with Amos Dewey. The sight of him, so tall and handsome, so solid, resolute and steady, sent a rush of pure, selfless joy flowing through her being. And she smiled, delighted to see him, before she remembered that they were nothing to each other.

It was then she saw Gussie bearing down on her, obviously with the intent to speak.

"Good afternoon, Mrs. Richardson," she said.

Her voice was deliberately civil and perfectly acceptable, but Pansy could hear the tone that was not there. The anger, the jealousy, the hurt that poured out of the heart of a woman politely encountering the lover of the man she loved.

"Good afternoon to you, Miss Gussie," she replied. "Mr. Dewey." She nodded almost imperceptibly in his direction as well.

"Has Rome offered you some of our ice cream?" she asked. "It is absolutely the best you will ever eat. The recipe is my own, cream and eggs from our local farmers, and frozen with genuine manufactured ice produced right here in our hometown."

Gussie was being purposely warm and welcoming, but Pansy could hear the stilted tone in her voice. Her affair with Rome, which was physically pleasant and selfishly unrestrained, had injured this woman. There had been no intention for her or anyone else to suffer, but it was the nature of sin to bring suffering. Pansy liked and admired Gussie. But because she had slept with Rome Akers, they would never be friends.

How much more would the woman be mortified to know that her fiancé had been Pansy's lover as well.

"Rome," Gussie called out. "Do bring Mrs. Richardson some ice cream."

"I'll get it for her," Amos Dewey said behind Gussie, surprising both women.

He walked over to where Tommy was scooping out the last freezer can, leaving the two women standing together. It was awkward, uncomfortable. Pansy felt an almost overwhelming compulsion to apologize, but she knew she must not. Atonement and amends would be for this evening at the podium. And anyway, the wrong she had done this woman could never be made right.

"I walked by your house the other evening," Gussie said finally. "I see you've started a little flower garden."

Pansy nodded. "It's not much and it's late in the year," she said. "It could never be as lovely as your own. But I thought I might try it anyway."

"With the right care and plenty of attention," Gussie told her, "the plants that spring forth in the worst heat of summer can be the sturdiest and most beautiful."

There was nothing more to say and thankfully, Amos had returned to stand beside them. He held two bowls of ice cream, one in each hand. Pansy assumed that one was meant for her and the other for Gussie. Gussie obviously thought the same as she reached out to take one from him.

Amos did not relinquish it.

"This is mine," he told her. "You did say that ice cream gives you a headache."

Gussie blushed, confused.

"Well, yes, in fact it does," she admitted.

"Mrs. Richardson," he said, "why don't we go take advantage of that little patch of box elder shade and enjoy our ice cream?"

What Gussie might think about that, Pansy had no idea. But her own heart leaped inside her at the prospect of being alone, or even partially alone, with the man she loved.

"That sounds like a lovely idea," she answered, amazed at her own composure.

Side by side, at an arm's-length distance, they walked to the small patch of shadow made by the young tree, little more than a sapling. He said nothing until they reached their destination. They turned, keeping the occupants of the Mudd Manufactured Ice location in sight. He handed over her bowl of ice cream.

"Don't do it," he said to her simply.

"Don't do what?" she asked.

"Whatever it is you are planning," he answered. "Haven't you done enough already to punish people and ruin lives?"

Amos was well aware that he deserved whatever ill befell him. But he wanted the ax to fall upon his neck alone. He'd been trying to figure out what Pansy's plan was since he'd first heard about her "new leaf." He didn't believe for one moment that she was really trying to change. He didn't believe it. He wouldn't believe it.

"You are up to another scheme," he said as they stood together by the box elder tree. "You schemed to defraud this town, you schemed to seduce me into your bed and you schemed against Gussie and me."

Her mouth was a thin line of disappointment.

"I schemed *for* Gussie and you," she said. "She's in love with Rome, in case that slipped your attention. And you're not in love with her, in case you've deluded yourself into believing otherwise. Also, if I can recall the afternoon correctly, I never seduced you into my bed. We managed to get it all done in a barber's chair."

He hated her words. He hated the weakness in him that they represented.

"Just tell me what you are up to," he said. "I think you owe me that much."

"Owe you for what?" she asked him. "I owe you because I awakened you from a living death and showed you that there was a whole world going on around you? Or do I owe you because I touched your heart? You can't let anyone do that, can you? You're going to marry a woman who does not, cannot, ever love you, just so you won't be in any further danger of having someone touch your heart."

His jaw tightened in anger.

"Maybe I am protective of my heart," he said. "I've had it broken and I don't want to go through that again. But I'm much better off than you. You're positively heartless."

"Is that what you think?" Her tone was almost humorous. "That I have no heart?"

"How else could you so easily forget the husband you were wed to? And go from man to man without looking back?"

"You think your loss was greater than mine. You think that you must have loved more," she told him. "You're just deceiving yourself. You sought solace in isolation. I sought it in the arms of strangers. We were both wrong. But I suppose we both did what we had to. The goal of grief is to live through it. Now I've chosen a life of chastity and you're marrying a woman in love with another man. We're both probably wrong again."

"I've simply made a highly appropriate life choice," he said. "It's you who seasons your witch's brew with plots and schemes."

Her eyes narrowed and her jaw tightened.

"You're so interested in plots and schemes, Mr. Dewey," she said, genuinely angry, "why don't you ask your fiancée about her little matrimonial machination?"

"What are you talking about now?"

"Ask Gussie Mudd about the plan to use Rome Akers to make you jealous and win over the man of her dreams."

Amos just stared at her, puzzled but cautious.

She handed him the bowl of ice cream.

"Thank you very much," she said. "But I've somehow lost my appetite."

He watched her walk away. She headed away from the ice-cream booth as if she wanted to ensure that she made no further contact with Rome or Gussie.

She'd said those two were in love with each other. It was undoubtedly just more of some diabolical plot. Something she and Rome had undoubtedly hatched together to gain control of Miss Gussie's company. But Rome was going to buy the company from Gussie. And she seemed to very much want Rome to have it.

Gussie was without any doubt about Rome's innocence in the Sewer Swindle. She was so unshakable in her faith in his honesty, she'd turned the whole town to her way of thinking. Perhaps she was right. Maybe he wasn't part of any moneymaking scheme. And maybe his pursuit of her was genuine as well.

Amos glanced over at the two of them. She was now

helping him prepare another batch for the freezer. They stood apart, as if unwilling to get too close or to converse with each other more than was necessary. It was as if they were uncomfortable in each other's presence.

They had not always been this way. He had seen them together many times, both before their ill-fated courtship and during it. They had always been at ease with each other. But now they were not.

Amos watched as Gussie ignored Rome to strike up a conversation with Tommy Robbins, the shute boy. Having attempted to talk to the young fellow several times himself, Amos knew that Miss Gussie must be desperate for the distraction to even attempt it.

Could she be in love with Rome?

Did it matter? After all that had come out concerning his illicit behavior, she could never choose him for a husband. Not even if she were free could she align herself in marriage to a man who was widely known to have carried on a secret liaison with another woman.

Or could she?

What had she told him? *If you're in love, nothing else will matter. Not the past, not reputation, not even other lovers.* If Gussie loved Rome as he had loved Bess, then nothing could stop her from going after what she wanted.

"But if she's in love with Rome Akers," he ruminated aloud, "why is she marrying me tomorrow?"

Amos walked back to the booth carrying the ice-cream bowls. Gussie was washing up the dishes in the makeshift kitchen. Two tubs of wash water sat upon a long bench. The freezer cans and dashers, as well as all the serving bowls and spoons, had to be kept clean.

The cream mixture was stored in two ten-gallon milk cans, kept cool by the wall of straw-covered ice beneath a protective awning. The little area was surprisingly cool for such a hot part of the afternoon.

"Can I help?" Amos asked as he brought her the dirty dishes.

She smiled up at him, though her expression was a little uneasy.

"Have you decided to alter your poor opinion of Mrs. Richardson?" she asked him. "The woman really cannot be as bad as some people say."

"Perhaps she's no better than she should be," he replied absently.

He rolled up his sleeves and picked up a dishtowel. Fishing a freshly washed bowl out of the rinse tub, he dried it and stacked it with the others on the bench.

"Did you find out what she's going to say this evening?"

Amos shook his head.

"She's refused to say anything to anyone."

"Well, maybe she just wants to say it one time," Gussie suggested.

"Maybe so," he agreed.

"We certainly are passing out a lot of ice cream," she told him proudly. "Rome has just started cranking our fourth batch. I wouldn't be surprised if we ended up serving all twenty gallons."

Amos smiled at her. He liked her enthusiasm.

"You enjoy this sort of thing, don't you?" he said.

"It's fun and it's good for business," she said. "We give away ice cream. Our customers acquire a taste for it and want to make it more often. That means they'll be buying more ice and we'll be making more money."

"Was this Rome's idea or yours?" Amos asked her.

"A little of both, I guess," she answered. "It was Rome who came up with giving away something cool, since it was obviously going to be so hot. He thought maybe chilled lemonade, because he likes it so much. I came up with the plan for ice cream."

"You and Rome sure do think alike," Amos remarked. "You seem to like the same things, dream the same dreams, understand each other perfectly. I suspect that you might even be able to finish each other's sentences."

"Don't be silly." There was a slightly nervous timbre to her voice.

"Gussie," he said very quietly, "are you in love with Rome Akers?"

She gasped and the soap-slippery bowl she held dropped from her hand.

Amos handed her his dishtowel and leaned down to pick up the unbroken bowl. Wordlessly he took her place at the washtub.

"Why on earth would you suggest such a thing?" she asked him, sounding horrified.

"I know how much you like him," he said, "and how much you want him to succeed in the business."

"Well, I like most everyone in town," she assured him. "And I've been helpful and encouraging to practically every young man in the Monday Merchants."

"That's true," he allowed. "But then, of course, there is the fact that you two were seeing a good deal of each other before all this scandal broke. I can't help but wonder if maybe there was more to your feelings for him than you let on."

"No, of course not!" she replied so adamantly that

her denial seemed almost excessive. "I have no feelings of that kind about Rome at all!"

That couldn't possibly be the truth. It was more than obvious that there was something between the two of them. Perhaps it was over, maybe it was awkward, but something was there.

"You must have cared for him at some time," he said. "You two did keep company for several weeks."

"There was nothing between us," Gussie insisted. "Nothing. You have absolutely no cause to worry."

"I wasn't worried," he told her. "I would only worry if I thought you were trying to keep something secret from me."

That statement stopped her completely. Clean dishes were beginning to pile up in the rinse tub.

"There is nothing between Rome and me that you should know about," she said finally. "The truth is, we were only pretending to be sweethearts."

"Pretending?"

"Yes, pretending." She laughed a little bit too cheerfully. "I can see that here on the very eve of our wedding, I'm going to have to confess everything."

Amos waited, listening.

"After I delivered my—my ultimatum about wanting to be married and you decided not to see me anymore," she began, "well, I just couldn't take no for an answer. I tried to look at it like a business merger. I wanted to merge my life with yours, but you were resisting. I decided that if I brought in more competition, you'd get concerned about your margin of profit and would be forced to reevaluate your position."

"What?"

"I—I asked Rome to let people think he was courting me," she said. "We acted like we were sweethearts.

I decided if you saw me with another man, you would want me for yourself."

Amos could hardly believe his ears. Pansy had spoken the truth. She was not the only woman who was capable of deception.

"And I guess it worked," Gussie said. "You must have gotten jealous. After the kissing booth, you did come and propose to me."

"I didn't even see you at the kissing booth," Amos answered. "I wasn't there, remember?"

"Oh, yes, that's right," she said. "But anyhow, you did propose. And so you can see that you have no reason to worry about Rome and me. We were only pretending to care for each other."

"Rome did this as a favor to you?"

She blushed. She'd already said more than she wanted to.

"No, I . . . I promised him the partnership."

Amos stared at her, trying to take it all in.

"You gave Rome Akers a partnership in your company so that he would help you make me jealous."

It was a statement, not a question.

"Yes, I suppose you could put it that way," she said. "You aren't angry about it, are you?"

"Angry? No, no, I guess I don't feel angry," he said.

"I realize that it is a little dishonest to try to maneuver things your way," she said. "But life can be so complicated and out of control. Sometimes it is very hard to just let things happen when they don't seem to be inclined to do so."

"And you did this because you are in love with me?" he asked.

"Well, of course I . . . I . . ."

They were looking each other directly in the eye. He saw the lie there. And he saw the truth.

"I think you are a very good and fine man," Gussie told him. "I thought . . . I thought that it was time I married and that you might make me a perfectly acceptable husband."

Amos stared at her for a long moment.

"I proposed to you," he said, "because I thought you would make a perfectly acceptable wife."

She lowered her eyes and nodded slightly before looking up at him again.

"I knew that you weren't in love with me," she said. "I'm willing to settle for that."

"You shouldn't be. I loved Bess. I loved her with all my heart and my being and my soul. I was thinking that I could never replace that and maybe I can't, but I'm not going to settle for anything less and neither should you."

"What do you mean?"

Her face was stricken, but he couldn't think about how he was hurting her. He reminded himself of Bess, sweet, smiling Bess, and how much they had loved each other. There was no substitute for it and no lesser terms on which matrimony was acceptable.

"I was wrong to ask you to marry me," he admitted. "I was hurt and angry about something else and I have almost dragged us into a lifetime of unhappiness. I don't want to marry you, Gussie," he said. "I'm breaking off the engagement."

"Are you sure?" she asked him.

Her voice was surprisingly calm. There was no hint of hysteria, fury or even disappointment. She did not even mention the elaborate ceremony, the most perfect wedding the town would ever see, scheduled to take place in less than twenty-four hours.

"Yes, I'm sure," Amos told her. "I don't love you.

And I care enough about you not to allow you to marry without love."

Gussie handed him the dishtowel.

"I'm going home," she said simply.

She walked away.

19

ROME LOOKED UP FROM HIS ICE-CREAM CRANKING TO
see Miss Gussie walking across the hay meadow.
Strangely enough, she was not walking through the
other booths, meeting people and socializing. She had
taken off on the diagonal, making a beeline for the
road to town. She hadn't said a word. It was curious.
Enough so that he stopped cranking and rose to his
feet. He intended to follow her, but a small sound
behind him reined him in. Amos Dewey was washing
dishes in the back of their area. Amos was a good fellow. He seemed to genuinely care for Gussie. If someone needed to go after her, surely he would. Perhaps
she'd forgotten something at home. Or had thought of
an errand that simply could not wait. She was, after all,
getting married very soon.

That fact churned inside him like sour milk. He felt
as if he were trapped with his foot on the tracks, a train
bearing down upon him at top speed. There was little
chance of escaping the inevitable. Yet he was somehow frantic to die trying.

"Have you got that other batch ready yet?" Tommy called out to him. "This one is nearly empty."

The words pulled Rome back to reality immediately.

"Almost," he answered and sat down to resume his task.

He was going to be cranking ice cream all day. That was what Miss Gussie wanted from him and that was what he was going to do. If Miss Gussie were ill or needed help, the man she was going to marry would be hurrying to her side. Amos Dewey would be racing after her. He was not, so all must be well.

Still Rome worried. As the afternoon dragged on and she did not return, he became even more concerned.

The shadows lengthened, his arm and shoulder aching from his endeavors. He'd cranked eight freezers of ice cream. Amos was helping him unload the last. With the worst heat of the day behind them, the demand for their cold confection had diminished. There was no line waiting for this share. Most folks were already beginning to gather around the stage near the center of the grounds. The special entertainment was ongoing. The city band had played several sessions. A quartet contest had pitted different groups of harmonious gentlemen against one another. And a children's choir had delighted parents with recitations of "One, Two, Buckle My Shoe" and a noisy rendition of "Pop Goes the Weasel."

The speeches would be coming up very soon. Typically the least popular entertainment. But today every man and woman in town was anticipating Pansy Richardson's speech. No one intended to miss it.

Tommy was antsy not to miss anything and Rome sent the boy off.

"We might as well leave this here and go on over ourselves," Amos told him. "Anyone wanting ice cream can scoop it out, and we can come back and get the rest of this cleaned up during the fireworks."

"You go on over," Rome said. "I guess I should stay around here until Miss Gussie returns."

"I doubt she'll be coming back here," Amos said.

Rome was concerned. "Is she ill?"

"No, not at all," Amos replied. "She'll feel a lot better tomorrow."

Tomorrow. Her wedding. The wave of disappointment that swept through Rome was sickening. Miss Gussie, his Miss Gussie, would be forever separated from him by marriage to another man.

Everything he had worked for, his own business, respect in his community, those things paled in comparison to the prize that would soon be far beyond his reach. He couldn't let it happen. He couldn't just stand by and allow her to walk down the aisle into marriage with another man.

Gussie had schemed to get herself a husband. Pansy had schemed to get vengeance against the town. Rome found that he was no better than either of them when it came to something that was truly important.

"It looks like they are about to get started," Amos pointed out. "Let's go hear what Mrs. Richardson has to say."

"You go ahead," Rome told him. "I'll clean up and be over in a few moments."

"Are you sure?" Amos asked. "I don't want to leave you here with this."

"I'll be finished in a couple of minutes," Rome replied. "I won't miss a thing."

"All right," Amos said. "I'll see you there."

"Right," Rome answered.

He was smiling brightly into Amos Dewey's face, but there was nothing but guile in his heart.

Whistling, he continued his task, gathering up the dishes and packing the freezer can in a tub of ice.

Rome kept one eye on the back of Amos Dewey. The moment the man disappeared into the crowd, the whistling abruptly stopped. He set the dishes down on the ground at the spot where he was standing, and as if shot like a sky rocket, he took off diagonally across the field toward the road to town.

He ran, one foot in front of the other. He left behind him the responsibilities of his business. The concerns of his community. The people of his acquaintance. He was running away from all of them, toward the only thing that really mattered. The woman he loved.

Loping across the meadow was made more dangerous by the gray onset of evening. He risked it anyway. He ran as if pursued. But then, he was being chased by time itself. Tomorrow she would be out of his range completely. Beyond his grasp for all time. If he was to ever have another chance with her, it would have to be tonight. Another chance. A chance to apologize, a chance to explain, a chance to beg another chance.

When he reached the road, he was able to pick up speed. He followed the hard-packed ruts made by innumerable wagon wheels as he hurried into town. He had no plan of what he would do, what he would say. He knew only that he must get to her side.

The roadway was deserted. The small town that was his home was dimly lit in sunset before him. He had always gone after what he wanted. He had struggled all his life to get ahead, to amount to something. Rome saw now with clarity that perhaps he might never have understood otherwise that the things he had most valued, respect and success, would be empty achievements to him were Miss Gussie not there to share them. The two of them had been partners of the mind and spirit long before they were so in business. Somewhere along the way they had become partners of the heart as well. It had not been only an untamed moment suspended from reality. They had found mutual love. He was not willing to allow her to simply cast it off as if it were an inconvenience.

He reached the edge of town. It was almost eerie in its silence. Everyone was at the festivities. It was as if the whole of Cottonwood were his alone. His and Gussie's. He traversed the empty streets, his footfalls audible on the macadam paving. He went to the crossing of Broad, around the corner of the park, down the way so familiar to him, to the modest home that was so very dear.

The house was dark, completely dark. Only the flutter of fireflies lit up the garden. Rome ignored the gate and jumped the fence, scanning the porch. She was not seated there. He took the steps two at a time and pounded, a little overenthusiastically, upon the door.

"Gussie!" he called out. "Gussie? Are you at home?"

He was winded from the run and bent forward, drawing in breath as he waited impatiently for her to answer the door.

She didn't come. Minutes ticked past. He waited upon the porch.

Had Amos been wrong? Perhaps she had gone to hear the speeches after all. He'd come all this way to speak to her and she was not here. He was just thinking to leave when he heard the creak of a footstep overhead.

She was in her room upstairs. Was it possible that she had not heard him on the porch?

He pounded more insistently upon the door once more.

"Gussie!" he called out. "It's me, Rome. I've got to talk to you."

There was only stillness and quiet inside the house. Too much quiet. She knew he was there. Why didn't she answer?

He banged upon the door again.

"Gussie! I know you are there."

No response.

He walked out into the yard and gazed up at the open window of her bedroom.

"Gussie! Gussie, are you all right?"

"Go away!" she answered finally. "Would you just go away."

Rome hesitated, thinking he should do just that. She was to be married tomorrow. Maybe he was being selfish. Maybe he was just thinking of what he wanted. Perhaps she loved Amos Dewey and truly wanted to marry the man.

He recalled with perfect clarity how her lips had felt upon his own. How she'd trembled in his arms as he'd touched her intimately. Had it been only a carnal pleasure? The kind of physicality that any male and female might find together. The lust-filled release of tension such as he and Pansy Richardson had engaged in with such frequency. Had it been only that between himself and Gussie? Or had it been something on a higher plain, something deeper, richer, more meaningful?

It had been all that for Rome. It had been love. And he was not willing to give up on it without a fight.

He called out to the darkness of the open window.

"Gussie, I'm not leaving," he said. "I'm not going away unless you talk to me."

"There is nothing to say," she called back.

"There is everything to say," he countered. "That is what is wrong. I still have everything to say to you."

She came to the window then; he could see her only in silhouette.

"I'm not really up for receiving visitors," she said.

"I'm no visitor," Rome told her. "I am your friend and your business partner and . . . and I am a man who loves you, Gussie. Can you turn away so callously a man who loves you?"

"Go away. Come back tomorrow."

She walked away from the window. Rome was bereft. It was her house. It was her choice. He should leave because she had told him to. He should leave and come back tomorrow. Tomorrow. Tomorrow was too late. Tomorrow she would be married.

"Gussie!" he called out to her again. "Gussie!"

She didn't answer.

He turned to leave, but then couldn't. It would be as if he were walking away from his only opportunity for happiness. And a good businessman never walked away from an opportunity.

Rome turned back and surveyed her house. He saw the front door shut against him. He saw the bedroom window wide open. Without another thought, he barged through the impatiens and the hibiscus bushes. After he made his way to the sturdy rose trellis that went past her window all the way to the roofline, he began to climb.

He'd gone up only a few feet when he grabbed a handful of thorns in the darkness and cursed loudly. He stopped for a moment to suck the bleeding injury to his pierced palm and then he was headed upward once more. Within a few more steps he did it again, only an arm's length beneath her window.

"Damn!" he cried out again.

This time the sound of bare feet scurrying across the floor was unmistakable.

"What are you doing?" Gussie asked, horrified, as she leaned out and spied him on the trellis.

"I'm not going away, Gussie," he declared with certainty.

"Get down from there before you fall and kill yourself!"

"I will not," he told her. "I am Romeo and I am assailing your balcony."

He couldn't see her face, but he heard the anxiety in her movements as she hastily attempted to shut the window.

Rome hurried to reach it before she did. He'd just placed his hand on the edge of the sill when she slid the window closed. She'd missed his hand by a mile, but she didn't know that.

"YEOW!" he screamed.

Immediately there were sounds of distress coming from her room. Abruptly the window reopened.

"Are you hurt?" she asked anxiously.

He grasped the inside of the sill with both hands and heaved his body halfway through the window.

"I am hurt, Gussie," he told her. "I'm hurt because you won't see me. You won't talk to me. You won't let me tell you how much I love you."

"Go away, Rome," she told him, backing away from the window.

"Too late," he answered. Using the strength he'd gained handling huge blocks of ice, he raised his torso until he could brace himself with a knee and then he swung a leg over and climbed into her room. "I'm already inside."

Across from him, he heard the scratch of a match against sandpaper before it illuminated the room. She lit the coal oil lamp on her vanity table and he could see her clearly.

Her summer wrapper was thin and gauzy, a sheer nod to convention to cover her nightgown. Her hair hung unbound down her back, surprisingly thick and wavy. She looked young and vulnerable.

"You've got to get out of here," she said. "If someone sees you from that window, it won't do either of our reputations any good."

Rome had already been through town. He could have told her that there was not a soul to see them for miles around. But he did not. Instead he went to stand directly in front of the window and called out into the darkness.

"This is Rome Akers," he announced to the empty street. "I'm up here in Miss Gussie's bedroom."

"What are you doing?" she demanded, horrified.

"Just what you suggested," he answered. "I'm trying to ruin your reputation."

"What!"

"You see, Miss Gussie, I remember exactly what you said," he told her. "Hasty nuptials and an uneventful married life are the most foolproof remedy for a bad reputation."

"What are you saying?"

"I'm saying, Gussie, that I love you and I want to marry you."

That was not enough, he thought. Amos Dewey also *wanted to marry* her. Half the men in Texas would *want to marry* her if they knew her. He had to be more resolute than that.

Rome crossed the room to stand in front of her. Her eyes were wide, questioning, as he dropped to his knees before her.

"Gussie Mudd," he declared with indisputable authority, "by fair means or foul, I *am going* to marry you!"

Before she had an opportunity to disabuse him, he reached out, wrapped his arms around the backs of her knees and slung her over his shoulder as he rose to his feet.

His unexpected move either startled her into silence or knocked the wind out of her. For a moment she said nothing. And then her words were demanding and profuse.

"Put me down! Put me down this minute!" she ordered, jabbing her fists into his back. "Put me down!"

He did.

Rome dropped her diagonally across her high feather bed. Her gauzy wrapper flew open, revealing a curvy, nicely bosomed female in a thin cotton night-dress. He grabbed the hem of it and promptly pulled the garment up to her neck.

She gasped and would have hidden herself from him had he not seized her wrists in his hands.

"Marry me, Gussie," he said. "You were meant to marry me."

The very last thing Gussie Mudd would have expected on the night before she planned to be married to Amos Dewey was to find herself naked in her own bed with Rome Akers leaning over her.

"What do you think you are doing?"

He held her wrists securely and she struggled against him.

"I don't know, Gussie," he answered. "I don't know what I'm doing."

He lowered himself atop her, covering her exposed body with his own.

"I haven't known what I was doing since the after-noon I came to you, planning to offer you a proposal of marriage, only to have you advise me to marry someone else."

"It's the right thing to do," she told him, trying to wiggle out from under him.

He released her hands and wrapped his arms around her shoulders, crushing her chest tightly against his own.

Rome rested his head in the crook of her neck for a moment before he raised up and looked her squarely in the eye. "I don't love her," he said.

It was an excuse. But not enough of one to suit Gussie's ideals.

"Then you shouldn't . . . you shouldn't have gone to her bed," she answered.

"No, I know now that I shouldn't have," he admitted.

He sighed long and thoughtfully, a little line of worry cropping up between his brows.

"I can't change that, Gussie. I can't alter the past. I can't do anything to make it better."

"No, you can't," she agreed, her heart aching. It was the truth and the truth was often painful.

"But, Gussie," he continued, "you are so willing to give Pansy Richardson a second chance. You found it so easy to believe that she would put that opportunity to good use. Will you not allow me the same consideration?"

"I cannot," she said with certainty as she trembled against him. "I cannot."

"Why?" he asked in a whisper against her ear. His warm breath raised gooseflesh along her skin.

The tears welled up in her eyes. Gussie wanted to cry. She wanted to cry and scream and rail against him. But she did not. Instead she answered his question.

"You kissed her just like you kissed me," she said. "You touched her as you touched me. You showed her pleasure the same way you did me. That's what you did, Rome. You can't deny it."

"I can deny it," he answered.

"Don't lie to me," she pleaded.

He ran a caressing palm down the length of her hair and wound it around his hand like a rope.

"I won't lie to you, Gussie," Rome said. "You can believe me when I promise that I will not lie."

She believed him.

"I kissed Pansy Richardson," he said. "I touched her. I lay with her without benefit of marriage. But nothing, nothing that I did with her was anything like what you and I did together."

"And how was it so different?" she demanded.

"Because it was love between us, Gussie."

His eyes were so close. He was looking at her with such intensity.

"It was love," he repeated. "You can't tell me that it was not. It was love when we embraced. It was love when we kissed. And it was love when you shuddered in ecstasy against my hand."

Aghast, she turned her face away from his gaze, too humiliated to look him in the eye.

"Must you remind me of my weakness?" she reproached him.

He kissed her temple and tenderly ran two fingers from the spot to her jawline.

"It wasn't weakness, Gussie," he told her. "It was power. The power of love. The very consequential power of our mutual love for each other."

"Oh, Rome," she complained.

She tried to pull away from him, but he wouldn't let her go.

"You cannot deny that you love me," he said.

"I do love you," she admitted. "But I cannot forget

that you've been in her arms. I forgive it, Rome, because I do love you. But I cannot forget it."

"I can't forget it either," he told her. "And I wouldn't want to. It was a terrible, hurtful mistake. A mistake I intend to learn from and keep before me always as a reminder of how casually I can head down the wrong path and how dangerous that can be to my happiness."

He took her face in his hands and gazed into her eyes.

"But I also vow to limit my mistake to that, not complicate it by a marriage that was never meant to be. I don't love her. And it's wrong to wed someone you don't love. Are you listening to me, Gussie? It's wrong for me. It's wrong for you as well."

"You men all seem so very sure about that," she said. "You should learn to see wedlock more in terms of a diversity product line. Not necessarily exactly what you might want, but a profit margin that you can live with."

He chuckled lightly and lay a tiny peck upon the end of her nose.

"The union of two people involves more than gain and loss," he told her. "It is the only thing about human existence that makes the rest of it worthwhile or even bearable."

He angled his head above her mouth. She knew he was going to kiss her.

"Forgive me, Gussie," he pleaded. "Forgive me my mistake and make my life bearable once more."

Somehow she couldn't resist him. She didn't want to resist him. As he lowered himself to her, she wrapped her arms around his neck. Openmouthed, she met his kiss with her own.

It was just as it had been between them. Sweet and hot, matched and matchless. The taste of him was oh, so familiar and her body recognized him as well. She curved herself upward from the bedticking to press herself closer.

He moaned deep in his throat.

"I love you, Gussie," he whispered. "I love you so very much."

He kissed her mouth, her eyelids, her forehead, her cheeks. He tenderly feathered his lips along her jawline to her ear.

"Love me, Gussie," he pleaded. "Love me, if you ever can."

"I do love you," she answered. "I love you, Rome Akers."

He muffled a shout of joy against her throat.

She arched her neck to give him more access. He took it eagerly, testing and tasting her from the edge of her collarbone to the delicate flesh between her breasts. Such a tender touch took her breath away.

His strong, dependable hands, so warm and soothing, moved upon her fevered skin.

The right hand found its way to her bosom, weighing her breast and urging the nipple to rise, turgid and eager, for his touch. He did not leave her wanting, but took the small, hardened bud between his thumb and forefinger and tweaked it in a fashion that was all pleasure and no pain.

The force of the sensation sizzled down her body to her most secret and intimate places. She gasped from the intensity of it and drew up her legs to try to tamp down the fire.

"Yes, my sugar," he said, so close to her ear. "Yes, I know what you're needing. I know what you're wanting. I need it too. I want it too."

As if to emphasize the truth of his statement, he drew her hand down between them. Through his trousers she felt the long, hard length of him.

She stilled abruptly.

He kissed her and allayed her with whispered, soothing words. "You don't have to be afraid," he told her. "I'll be very gentle. We'll take it very slow. If you tell me to stop, I'll stop."

"Stop," she told him.

There was a moment's hesitation on his part and then he pulled away from her. Sitting back on his heels at the end of the bed, his legs straddled on either side of him.

His eyes were focused completely upon hers. He did not for an instant glance away.

"What are you doing?" Gussie asked him.

"You told me to stop," he said. "So I stopped."

That was good, she told herself. Somehow it didn't feel that way.

"I am your partner," he said, "in everything with you, Gussie. I want what you want."

She was still nervous. She was still afraid. But she did love him and she did want him.

Gussie sat up. She was in a very unladylike position, her clothes all bunched and her legs spread before him. Bravely, in one motion, she pulled both her wrapper and her nightdress over her head and discarded them on the floor.

Rome was watching her. His eyes were so intense upon her skin, the look was almost scorching.

She ran a hand along his shoulders and to his collar, first pushing aside his suspenders and then loosening his tie. When her fingers arrived at the first of the line of pearl buttons down the front of his chest, she hesitated.

"It's been my experience that in any severe and unforeseeable downturn," she said, "and perhaps we can call these loosened bedcovers exactly that, both partners lose their shirts simultaneously."

He smiled at her as she undid all the buttons and peeled the impediment to his bare chest from his back.

"What about trousers?" he asked her. "Do partners lose their trousers simultaneously as well?"

Gussie glanced down and couldn't help blushing at the evidence of his arousal.

"I'm not sure I've heard trousers mentioned in terms of economic conditions," she told him.

"I don't believe I have either," he admitted as they each explored the naked flesh of the other. "But I have heard it said, Gussie, not to mix business with pleasure. And what I want to share with you is totally and completely pleasure."

He slid his arms more tightly around her, easing her closer. Warm flesh against warm flesh was enticing, almost overpowering. Gussie shivered, but she was so hot.

Rome began to shower her with kisses on her face, her arms, her breasts, her belly. She trembled, glorying in the way he touched her.

"Do you remember how you felt before?" he asked her.

"Oh, yes," she answered. The words came out more like a moan than a reply.

"I'm going to make you feel like that again," he promised. "Would you like that?"

What a silly question to ask. She didn't bother to answer, but simply sought his mouth with her own in reply.

His hands were not gentle or tentative upon her. He was certain and eager. He wanted to please her and he knew how. He kneaded her bosom and nipped each breast in turn until she could think of nothing else but his mouth there.

When he moved his head lower and the cool air assaulted the raised, damp point, she whined in complaint.

He ignored her as he lay a trail of delicate love bites from her midriff to below her navel. As his face approached the crux of her spread thighs, she demurely attempted to draw her legs together.

Rome would have none of it. He braced a hand on each knee and opened her wide before him. She gave a little cry of astounded shock before he lowered his mouth to the source of her feminine secrets that twitched with immodest eagerness.

Her dismay quickly fled as incoherence took over. She could not think or wonder or even express herself in words. Her head flailed from side to side and the sounds that came from her mouth were indecipherable, except for their origin, which was ecstatic pleasure. As his tongue flourished upon her with rapidity and persistence, she began grinding her hips to get more, to feel more.

When she reached the pinnacle, it was so vivid, so powerful, she tried to pull away from him. But he held to her and helped her through until she cried out his name in ardent passion, shattering her remaining fears and restraints.

He held her tightly in his arms thereafter, soothing her, praising her. He kissed her and she tasted herself upon his lips. He tasted of her and himself and the indescribable fervor they'd shared.

When she could catch her breath enough to speak, she tried to explain herself.

"That was . . . it was . . . I can't believe . . ."

"I know, my sweet sugar," he whispered. "I know. And there is more."

"More?"

He drew her hand down to her own body, which was now hot and wet and so very sated, it seemed.

"Do you feel that?" he asked her.

She nodded, surprised, intrigued. It was as if the lips of her entrance had opened wide, a puckered, seeking edge raised high.

"You've bloomed for me like a flower," he told her. "I will promise not to hurt you."

Gussie believed him. With no trepidation at all, she unbuttoned the front of his trousers. She had never seen a naked man before and was a little taken aback by both the difference from herself and the sheer dimensions of his body parts.

"How do you keep something that big in your trousers?" she asked him.

Rome gave her a teasing bite and settled himself between her thighs. "I'm hoping, once we're married, I won't have to."

It was as he had promised. Slow and gentle. He eased himself inside with only the mildest of resistance. There was stretching, accommodating, but somehow it was not uncomfortable. In fact, once he was buried completely inside her, Gussie felt a wholeness, a perfection, that brought tears to her eyes.

"Am I hurting you?" he asked, worried.

"Oh, no," she assured him.

"Are you . . . are you sorry to give yourself to me?"

She opened her eyes wide then, hurriedly disabusing him of that notion.

"I love you," she told him. "I have loved you for some time. But at this moment, I love you more than I thought it was possible to love. And I feel more a part of you than I thought it possible for one person to feel for another."

The tears slid from her eyes back toward her temples.

"I'm crying with joy," she said. "With immeasurable happiness. I don't want you to ever stop doing this."

Rome's grin was warm and understanding, his eyes bright with the same emotions that she was feeling. But when he spoke, his words were teasing.

"Stop? Miss Gussie, I haven't even started yet."

20

PANSY WAS MORE NERVOUS THAN SHE COULD EVER recall feeling. It was hard for her to understand what she was so fearful about. If these people did not accept her offering, did not accept her penance, she would simply go back to being the woman she had always been. Even as she comforted herself with this notion, she knew it was impossible. One of the most disturbing aspects of learning the truth about yourself was that you could never go back to believing the lie again.

She was seated upon the dais with a select group of local leaders. Though the stage had been hurriedly made with rough-hewn pine, someone had carried chairs all the way from City Hall, and the stately, overstuffed mahogany looked a little out of place in the natural surroundings.

There was one seat too few. But that didn't matter; the mayor was far too flighty and nervous to sit down. He seemed slightly overwhelmed with the responsibilities that had fallen to him. He consulted in turn with Huntley Boston, the sheriff, Mr. Potts from the newspaper and Reverend Holiday. He glanced in Pansy's direction several times, acting as if he expected at any moment that she might grow horns.

The platform area was brightly lit with lanterns and torches, The approaching darkness in the western sky, painted with bright pinks and purples, would not be sufficient for the crowd to see one another clearly. But the pool of light surrounding the stage showed its occupants more clearly than the noonday sun.

Finally it seemed as if Mayor Honey might start the program.

He hurried to the podium and ineffectively tried to quiet the crowd. After several moments of his not being able to capture attention, Joe Simpson jumped up on the side of the stage, stuck two fingers in his mouth and let loose a loud, blasting whistle.

The din was immediately brought to silence.

"Thank you, thank you," the mayor said, apparently grateful to both Simpson and the crowd. "We are so glad to see all of you here today," he continued. "I am not going to personally address the citizens of this great town. I'm only going to be introducing the other people who are here to address you."

A little spattering of applause ensued.

"Oh, thank you, thank you," the mayor said effusively.

Pansy wondered quite mischievously to herself if the people had been applauding because they were so grateful that the mayor was not going to speak.

Reverend Holiday came forward to offer prayer. He was sufficiently loud, as he always was, and as verbose and lyrical as ever as he asked for continued guidance and protection for the town and the families that resided there. There was one thinly veiled reference to *the benefit to the people as opposed to the enrichment of any single person.*

Pansy didn't allow the words to affect or concern her in any way whatsoever. She was no longer a praying woman. She and God had yet to truly settle their differences about her husband's death. But in that quiet, reverent moment she did offer a silent plea.

Give me the strength to try to make things right, she said.

With a hearty, "amen!" Reverend Holiday left the podium. The mayor jumped up from the pastor's chair like a jack-in-the-box.

"First up to speak to us is Mr. Huntley Boston," the mayor announced. "For any of you who might not know him, he's our local banker and president of the Monday Morning Merchants Association."

Huntley rose to his feet and walked to the podium. The mayor took his chair. His speech was a simple welcome to the people of the community and recognition of specific members of the association for their exceptional efforts for the picnic.

Pansy noted that it was Amos who was thanked as chairman of the fireworks committee. Rome's part in the display was not even mentioned.

Harry Potts, editor of the *Beacon*, was presented for the second address of the evening.

The mayor announced, "He'll be speaking to us about the fifty-year history of Cottonwood and the Founding Fathers who made it great."

The enthusiasm for the newspaperman was not a good deal better than it had been for the mayor. And as Potts unfolded what looked like a very lengthy speech, Pansy knew why.

She sat politely as he went through the past fifty years of history. Describing, as if he knew for certain, how Able Richardson had traveled out from Tennessee seeking fertile farmland. He'd settled on the Trinity

River near a strand of cottonwood trees. When he'd gotten a solid roof over his head, the first house in town, now the Jacks Building on Landingside, he'd sent for his wife and children.

Once they were here, a few neighbors settled nearby. Richardson installed a ferry to connect both sides of the river and facilitate travel in the area. Within the first decade of its existence, Cottonwood was already a prime river crossing and a growing commercial center.

Pansy knew all these facts. She knew the role the Richardsons had played and how their fortunes rose with that of the town. Not that Grover had ever bragged about his family's importance. He considered it what it was, an opportune twist of fate that made his father the founder and himself the legacy. He could just as easily have come from a family history less widely celebrated.

Pansy's own parents had settled in Cottonwood after the war, when her father, a former inmate in a Union prison camp, came west seeking a climate more healthy for his consumptive lungs. Everyone in this town had ties of history to people who had pulled up stakes where they were settled and bravely started over. They'd started out in this new place, maybe not with a completely clean slate, but they'd given it a chance. And the sons and daughters, grandchildren and great-grandchildren, in the audience before her were both the result of that formidable risk and the reward for it.

The newspaperman finished his treatise with a hopeful glance into the future. He foresaw a bright little community facing the twentieth century with fine public schools, adequate business growth and modern amenities.

The last, Pansy thought, was a veiled reference to the sewer system. As if they were still trying to win her over at the last possible moment.

"Our final speaker of the evening," the mayor announced, his voice actually tremulous with nervous jitters. "Our speaker is Mrs. Pansy Richardson, widow of Cottonwood benefactor, Grover Richardson. She is here today to talk to us about . . . I . . . ah . . . I'm sure she can tell you herself. Mrs. Richardson."

Pansy rose from her seat. She was not accustomed to any sort of public speaking, nor did she enjoy having every eye focused upon her. But she had sought this moment, for good or bad; she'd maneuvered and coerced for it. She was not about to shy away from it now.

Pansy stepped up to the podium. She glanced around her, recognizing faces in the crowd. Old Penderghast perched upon a crate near the front, his cane before him, between his knees. His wife, Eliza, sat with him, and her sister, Mrs. Boston, was by her side.

Kate Holiday was trying to both listen and corral a group of noisy children, not all of whom were her own.

Clive Benson, in his much-braided and festooned band uniform, stood with Perry Wilhelm and Matt Purdy.

She saw Amos Dewey. The man these people unknowingly had to thank for her appearance today. She had awakened him from his sleep of sorrow and offered to him herself, her love. His abhorrent rejection of her illustrated how tarnished and disgraced he found her to be. Their eyes met for an instant. She felt the pain so sharply she hastened to look away.

Pansy caught sight of her neighbors, Wade and Vera Pearsall. Wade carried a picnic basket, still covered by a clean dishtowel. His jaw was tight and his eyes narrowed in disapproval. His wife, Vera, was watching Pansy intently and gossiping behind her hand with Loralene Davies and Lulabell Timmons. Both women were nodding over and over, obviously in agreement of every unkind word Vera said.

Lulabell's daughter Lucy and her new husband stood nearby, both sufficiently serious.

A group of younger people centered around Betty Ditham were less long-faced, their interest in the fun of the festivities rather than in the lasting importance of them.

Pansy spotted Helga Shultz and Dr. Wise. The quiet and retiring Mr. Everhard and the fresh-mouthed and intractable Pete Davies. They were all there. All the people she had known all her life. They had helped her grow up, celebrated with her when she married, mourned with her at her husband's funeral and turned from her when she flouted their conventions and affronted their moral sensibilities.

"Ladies and gentlemen of Cottonwood," Pansy began, sternly keeping the quiver out of her voice. "I come to you today both upon my own behalf and upon that of the Richardson family."

She swallowed nervously.

"For myself, I offer apology to you and your families. My life, since the death of my husband, has been far from exemplary. I have outraged your morals and offended your sense of decency."

"Harlot!" The word was a woman's scream and was followed immediately by a piece of soft, smelly, overripe fruit that landed beside her on the stage, splattering the hem of Pansy's gown. The second piece was more on target, landing with an audible splat upon her sleeve.

"Stop it! Stop it!"

The words came from several different voices.

Huntley Boston came forward to shield her and was pelted with a rotten tomato upon his fancy dress coat for his trouble.

"NO!"

The booming voice of Reverend Holiday was heard over the noise of the crowd. The area quieted immediately.

"The Bible says, 'Let he who has no sin cast the first stone,'" the pastor quoted. "Wade Pearsall, if you are thinking that you and your wife are sinless, I'd beg to differ."

Pansy hadn't realized it was her neighbors who had chosen to express their opinion of her in this way. She looked out now and saw Joe Simpson wresting the picnic basket from Wade's hands.

"Please, please, Mrs. Richardson," Huntley Boston begged her. "Do not allow the unconscionable acts of two foolish people to determine your decision about the future of an entire town."

Pansy couldn't ignore his tomato-stained coat or worried expression.

"My decision was made several weeks ago, Mr. Boston," she told him. "It is unshakable. I am not overly concerned about foolish people. I have been a foolish person for a long time myself."

As the gentlemen took their seats, the crowd quieted, more attentive than before. Even the children were silent, observing.

"As I was saying," Pansy continued, "I have outraged your morals and offended your sense of decency. Which, as we have seen, instills in some of you the need to retaliate. I understand your anger. But I ask you instead for forgiveness.

"There can be no excuses for the things that I have

done. I therefore offer none. What I can offer is a sincere apology and repentance. And a promise to attempt, from here on out, to live a life in this community that is upright, worthy and above reproach."

They were all looking at her. All wondering at her. Pansy didn't know if they believed her, if they would give her another chance. But she had vowed to do her part, and she would live up to that.

"As I said, I wanted to speak today both for myself and for the Richardson family. What I have just said to you, about my shame at my past behavior and my vow to live a more circumspect life, that is what I have to say for myself. As the last vestige of the Richardson family in this town, I have different concerns. Please do not confuse what am to say to you now with anything I've said about myself. The one has nothing to do with the other."

She spotted Amos Dewey in the crowd once more. His brow was furrowed. His eyes were watching.

"Before his death, my husband, Grover Richardson, announced his intention to donate land south of the city for a modern lagoon sewer system that would serve the needs of the Cottonwood community, protect the drinking water and end the fouling of the river. Unfortunately, because of his untimely death, Mr. Richardson never signed over the land to the people of Cottonwood. But it was clearly, beyond all question, his intention to do so."

From her sleeve, the one splattered with rotten fruit, Pansy drew out the paper that she had carried there all day.

"I have signed and notarized the transfer of that property from my personal holdings to the community of Cottonwood."

There was a flurry of murmurs through the crowd.

Pansy didn't know if they were pleased at having won or disappointed that it was all over.

Pansy turned, handing the deed transfer to Huntley Boston. Then she opened a second piece of paper and read the carefully thought out words she had written there.

"In honor of the Richardson family, and on this very special anniversary of the fiftieth year of the town that they founded, I would also like to gift the Monday Morning Merchants Association's Sanitary Sewer Project with the sum of eight thousand seven hundred and fifty dollars, the total estimated amount necessary for the construction of the four-pool lagoon system. This should free up funds for the faster laying of lines throughout town and guarantee the success of the city-wide sanitary sewer system."

She looked up into faces of silence. They were all staring at her. Startled, stunned, uncertain.

Her eyes locked with those of Amos Dewey. His brow was no longer lined with worry. He looked proud. He looked pleased and proud. Pansy watched as he raised his hands and brought them together in appreciation. One pair of hands was clapping in the quiet crowd. But it was the right pair and Pansy was moved nearly to tears.

Suddenly Amos was joined in his applause by the gentlemen near the podium and then by old man Penderghast and those beside him and then everyone was clapping, cheering, shouting.

"Thank you. Thank you," Pansy said.

She turned to find the gentlemen behind her had all risen to their feet. In turn they each shook hands with her. Offering words of praise and congratulation, as if she had actually done something more than what she should have, which, in truth, she had not.

When she reached the steps of the stage, people were lined up to greet her. They were warm, welcoming, kind and grateful. She shook hand after hand after hand. Until she reached one that looked very familiar.

She looked up to see tall, handsome Amos Dewy smiling at her from behind wire-rimmed spectacles. He reached past her offered palm to wrap a protective arm around her shoulders.

"Let's get you away from here," he suggested.

Surprisingly, the citizens of Cottonwood allowed him to direct her through the crowd, away from the lantern light and into the privacy of the darkness. Once they were alone, Pansy felt almost shy with him. They had known each other for most of their lives. They had, on one unforgettable afternoon, been lovers, but in many ways they were strangers, utter and complete strangers.

He took out his handkerchief and began to wipe at the disgusting mess upon her sleeve.

"Don't worry about it," she told him. "It's likely stained and will never come clean again."

Amos nodded. "It is perhaps the kind of stain that could be turned into a badge of honor," he said.

"Does that happen?" she asked him.

"I hope it does," he answered.

They smiled at each other.

"Pansy, I'm in love with you," he stated.

She stared up at him and swallowed. It was almost painful hearing the words.

"I loved my Bess and I always will," he said. "But somehow I've come to love you as well. I love your wit, your courage, your honesty. I even love your outrageousness. Bess was none of those things and I never wanted her to be. But you are exactly those things and more and I cannot help but love you for them."

Pansy's eyes welled with tears. She didn't want to cry in front of him, she feared she might not be able to stop.

"I know you love me, Amos," she said. "I knew it that day in the barbershop. And I've known it every day since. But as you knew then and I know now, love itself may not always be enough. You've seen me publicly repent my sin and you've seen the beginning of my new life. I am a heroine this evening to the townsfolk and it seems as if all is forgiven. If because of that you now feel like I'm appropriate enough for you to align yourself with, then I simply have to refuse you. I have vowed to try and live a better life, but I cannot promise that you will always approve of me or that I will be the kind of woman you can forevermore admire."

He heard her out completely before he made comment.

"It was a very good thing you did tonight," Amos told her. "It was good for you. It was good for this community. It was good for your late husband and his family. I am very proud of you for doing it. But, like you, I approached the stage tonight with my decision already made. I realized that I loved you," he said. "And a dear and good friend told me recently that when you love somebody, whatever they have been, whatever they have done, doesn't matter more than your love. I came to hear you speak tonight, knowing that I was going to ask you to be my wife. If you had thrown your own rotten tomatoes or tightened down the screws on that land sale until everyone in town went bankrupt, I would have been sad for all of us, but I would have asked you to be my wife anyway. I love you. And that is what matters most."

Pansy looked into his eyes, seeing the truth there. Seeing the honesty and fallibility and faithfulness. She knew she was seeing her future.

With a bang and a long, loud whistle, a rocket shot high into the air. When it reached its zenith, it burst into a bouquet of colorful stars that fell down from the sky in a shower of light.

"Ooooooh," the crowd called out in awe.

Pansy and Amos smiled at each other.

"Mrs. Richardson, Mrs. Richardson."

Kate Holiday hurried to her side.

"Come watch the fireworks with the reverend and me," she suggested. Casting a glance toward Amos, she leaned closer and added, "It's not the best thing for your reputation to be standing alone in the darkness with a man."

Pansy nodded. "You are undoubtedly right," she said. "But I've heard that the best cure for a bad reputation is a hasty wedding and a boring, ordinary marriage. I believe Mr. Dewey has just offered me both."

Everyone arrived at the church exactly on schedule. But all were completely at sixes and sevens about what they'd discovered. The most fashionable and eagerly awaited social event of the year, Gussie Mudd's wedding to Amos Dewey, had been canceled.

Gossip had rained on Cottonwood last night like Noah's flood. Folks had hardly gotten used to the good fortune that had been visited upon them by Pansy Richardson, before Amos Dewy announced he was going to marry her.

But Amos was supposed to wed Gussie Mudd that next day. No, that wedding was off, Amos had replied, a little ill at ease at apparently having *forgotten* his former commitment. They had broken it off and he was to marry Mrs. Richardson instead.

The community, especially the ladies of the Circle

of Benevolent Service, was immediately called into action to comfort and console one of its own on the loss of her fiancé practically on the steps of the church.

Miss Gussie had no interest in anyone's sympathy as she blithely announced to her friends that she too was getting married as soon as possible.

The Greek-temple wedding cake with the marzipan bride and groom was at the ready. So was the French champagne. The church was adorned with flowers and Miss Ima had gotten the dress altered just in time.

"There *will* be a wedding here this afternoon," Reverend Holiday declared. "And you are all invited to attend. It just won't be the couple that any of you expected."

Speculation was rampant. Which couple would it be?

Some thought it would be Pansy Richardson and Amos Dewey.

Of course, it was already common knowledge that the two had taken their vows in this very church just a little before midnight the previous evening, unwilling to be parted even one more night. But that had been a hurried, hasty occasion. In the clear light of day, many were certain that the two would be taking a more formal approach to marital bliss and would choose to go through with the ceremony once again this afternoon.

Just as many folks were insisting the contrary. Gussie Mudd would never hand over her carefully planned wedding, the perfect wedding she had always dreamed of, to the woman who'd run off with her fiancé.

That Gussie herself would be the bride, marrying this afternoon to her business partner and Amos's rival for her affections, Rome Akers, was the only scenario that made reasonable sense.

Those in the know, however, insisted that was not

possible. Gussie and Rome had left on the morning train to San Antonio to be wed on Marriage Island, a fortuitous spot on the San Antonio River that supposedly guaranteed a long and happy wedlock.

As the whole congregation waited in the summer heat in their best clothes, the debate raged.

Finally the door to the vestry opened and Reverend Holiday, with Huntley Boston at his side, walked in. Huntley, adorned in a handsome, neatly tailored cutaway coat, went to stand in front of the altar.

Everyone assumed the president of the Monday Morning Merchants Association was about to make some kind of an announcement. Perhaps there was, after all, to be no wedding today.

When instead the organ began playing the bridal processional, the entire crowd gave a startled gasp that was followed by stunned silence.

The church door opened and Viceroy Ditham escorted his lovely young daughter, Betty, gowned in Miss Gussie's frothy lace-and-white-silk gown, down the narrow aisle to meet her future husband.

Too much news, no matter how good, can be stunning for a small community. Gossip becomes irrelevant when the world becomes nothing but.

"Do you, Huntley Boston, take Miss Elizabeth Ditham to be your lawful wedded wife?" Reverend Holiday asked.

In truth, somebody should have guessed. Gussie Mudd would never let such an expensive occasion as the perfect wedding go to waste. She had sold it to one of the few single gentlemen in town who was in a position to afford it. That was just good business.

Welcome to the world
of the Avon Romance Superleader
Where anything is possible . . .
and dreams really do come true

We all know there are unspoken rules that govern the acts of courtship. There are the rules of today (if he doesn't call by Wednesday he won't, even if he says he will!) and the rules of days gone by (a lady should never dance more than three times with a gentleman).

But often, what is expected is at odds with what is longed for . . . and how you're allowed to act is different from the way you feel. Heaven help you if you take a wrong step . . . but sometimes it's better to toss the rules away, take matters into your own hands—just as the heroines of these upcoming Avon Romance Superleaders are about to do.

❦

HERE COMES THE BRIDE
Pamela Morsi

JULY AVON ROMANCE SUPERLEADER

Gussie Mudd, the proprietor of a small ice business in Cottonwood, Texas, has determined that at some point in a woman's life she must get herself a man, or give up on the idea entirely. To get her man she decides to play by the rules . . . the rules of business. And she makes a business proposition to her employee, Mr. Rome Akers.

"PEOPLE, MR. AKERS, ARE JUST LIKE BUSINESSES. THEY act and think and evolve in the same way as commercial enterprise. People want and need things. But when they are vastly available, they prize them differently."

"Well, yes, I guess so," Rome agreed.

"So when we consider Mr. Dewey's hesitancy to marry me," she continued, "we must avoid emotionalism and try to consider the situation logically."

"Logically?"

Rome was not sure that logic was a big consideration when it came to love.

"Mr. Dewey has been on his own for some time now," she said. "He has a nice home, a hired woman to cook and clean, a satisfying business venture, good friends and myself, a pleasant companion to escort to community events. Basically all his needs as a man are met. He has a virtual monopoly on the things that he requires."

Rome was not certain that *all* of a man's *needs* had been stated, but after his embarrassing foray in that direction, he chose not to comment.

"He is quite comfortable with his life as it is," Miss Gussie continued. "Whyever should he change?"

"Why indeed?" Rome agreed.

She smiled then. That smile that he'd seen often before. That smile that meant a new idea, a clever innovation, an expansion of the company. He had long admired Miss Gussie's good business sense and the very best of her money-making notions came with this smile.

"I can do nothing about Mr. Dewey's nice home, the woman hired to cook and clean, his business, or his friends," Miss Gussie said. "But I can see that he no longer has a monopoly upon my pleasant companionship."

"I'm not sure I understand you," Rome said.

"In our business if Purdy Ice began delivering smaller blocks twice a week, we would be forced to do the same."

Rome nodded. "Yes, I suppose you are right about that."

"We would be forced to change, compelled to provide more service for the same money," she said.

"Yes, I suppose that's right."

"That's exactly what we're going to do to Amos Dewey," she declared.

Rome was listening, but still skeptical.

"You are going to pretend to be in love with me," she said as if that were going to be the simplest thing in the world. "You will escort me about town. Sit evenings on this porch with me. Accompany me to civic events."

That seemed not too difficult, Rome thought. He did not normally attend a lot of public functions, but, of course, he could.

"I don't see how that will change Dewey's mind," he told her honestly.

"You will also let it be known that you are madly in love with me," she said, "and that you are determined to get me to the altar as soon as possible."

Rome got a queasy feeling in his stomach.

"Amos Dewey will no longer have a monopoly. *You* will be the competition that will force him to provide the service he is not so willing to provide—marrying me."

Gussie raised her hands in a gesture that said that the outcome was virtually assured.

Rome had his doubts.

"I'm not sure this will work, Miss Gussie," he told her. "Men . . . men don't always behave like businesses. They are not all that susceptible to the law of supply and demand."

"Don't be silly," she said. "Of course they are."

"I'm not sure I'm the right man to be doing this. Perhaps you should think of someone who would seem more . . . well more suited to the task."

Her response was crisp and cool.

"I was hoping for a late-spring wedding," she told

him. "When the flowers are at their peak. But I suppose, in this instance midsummer would be fine. Let's say the Fourth of July; that sounds like an auspicious day for a wedding. It is going to be absolutely perfect. The most perfect wedding this town has ever seen. I do hope you will be there, Mr. Akers."

Here Comes the Bride

HEAVEN ON EARTH
Constance O'Day-Flannery

August Avon Romance Superleader

For Casey O'Reilly the world was supposed to be an orderly place where you met, married, and had children with the man you love. But nothing had gone according to plan. Mr. Right never made an appearance, and now, at "thirtysomething," Casey figured she had a better chance at being struck by lightning than struck by love . . . but then the unthinkable happened . . .

SHE WAS MAKING THIS UP. WHATEVER WAS HAPPENING was all in her mind. *It had to be!*

Desperately, Casey rubbed at her eyes and then cupped her hands around them to shelter her face as more lightning, familiar narrow streaks, flashed around her and thunder rumbled.

There was no time for questions as a man slowly, deliberately, walked closer, as though he had no fear of the lightning or the sandstorm. Casey's voice was stuck in her throat. She wanted to ask him who he was, but only garbled noises emerged from her mouth as she watched him unbutton his dark coat above her. His face was hidden by a wide turned-up collar and the cowboy hat pulled low over his brow, but somehow the closer he came, the less she feared him.

He knelt before her and, without a word, wrapped the edges of the raincoat around her, pulling her to his chest and sheltering her from the sandstorm. She could feel the strength of his arms around her back, and immediately sensed peace as she was gathered into the sanctuary of his body. She felt the strong beat of his heart reverberating against her face. She smelled something citrusy, very earthy, about him, and lifted her hand to cling to his soft shirt.

"You are all right, Casey O'Reilly."

She almost jumped at the close proximity of his voice resonating from his chest and into her ear. The low soothing tone sent shivers throughout her body and she found herself clinging even more tightly to his shirt.

"Who . . . Who are you?" she managed to mutter.

"I've come to help," he answered, holding her tighter as another crash of thunder made the ground shake violently beneath them.

"Thank heavens," she sobbed.

Somehow she felt incredibly safe, more so than she had ever felt in her life. Her body was tingling with some strange and powerful energy that was unfamiliar and yet . . . so perfectly wonderful. She felt a renewed strength welling up in her muscles, spreading through her body down to her burning foot. Her chest stopped aching and her headache eased as she held this man who had just walked out of a bolt of lightning and into her life . . .

HIS WICKED PROMISE
Samantha James

SEPTEMBER AVON ROMANCE SUPERLEADER

Glenda knew what was expected of a Highland lass—she must wed a man bold and strong enough to protect her. Love could come later . . . if it came at all. But although she was now without a husband, she had once known the joy of the marriage bed . . . and the pleasure that Laird Egan was willing to reacquaint her with . . .

"WELL, YOU ARE EVER AT THE READY, ARE YOU NOT?"

He cocked a brow. "What do you mean?"

"I think you know quite well what I mean!"

He was completely unfazed by the fire of her glare. A slow smile rimmed his lips. "Glenda, do you speak of my manly appetites?"

"Your words, sir, not mine," she snapped. Her resentment blazed higher with his amusement. "Though I must say, your appetite seems quite hearty!"

"And what of yours, Glenda?"

"Whatever do you mean?"

"You are a woman without a husband. A woman

without a man. I am not a fool. Women . . . well, women have appetites, too. Especially those who know the pleasure that can be found in another's body."

And well she knew. She had lost her maidenhead on the marriage bed, but she had never found lovemaking a chore or a duty, as she'd heard some women were wont to do. Instead, she had found it a vastly pleasurable experience . . . All at once she was appalled. She couldn't believe what they were discussing! To speak of her lying with a man . . . of his lying with a woman . . . and to each other yet!

He persisted. "Come, Glenda, what of you? I asked you once and you would not answer. Do you not find yourself lonely? Do you not miss the closeness of a man's body, the heat of lips warm upon yours?"

Suddenly she was the one who was on the defensive. "Nay," she gasped.

"Nay?" he feigned astonishment. "What, Glenda! Did you not love Niall then?"

Glenda's breath grew short; it seemed there was not enough air to breathe, for he was so close. *Too* close. So close that she could see the tiny droplets of water which glistened in the dense forest of hair on his chest. Niall's chest had been smooth and nearly void of hair, and it was all she could do not to stare in mingled shock and fascination.

She was certain her face flamed scarlet. "Of course I did! You know I did! But I"—she made a valiant stab at reasoning—"I have put aside such longings."

He did not take his eyes from her mouth. "Have you?" he said softly. "Have you indeed?"

A strong hand settled on her waist. In but a half breath, it was joined by the other. His touch seemed to burn through the layers of clothing to the flesh beneath.

"Egan," she floundered. "Egan, please!"

"What, Glenda? What is it?"

She shook her head. Her eyes were wide and dark. Her head had lifted. Her lips hovered but a breath beneath his. The temptation to give in, to kiss her, to trap her lips beneath his and taste the fruit of her mouth was all-consuming. Almost more than he could stand.

She wanted it, too. He sensed it with every fiber of his being, but she was fighting it, damn her! Yet still he wanted to hear her say it. He *needed* it.

"Tell me, Glenda. What is it you want?"

She shook her head. Her hands came up between them. Her fingers opened and closed on his chest . . . his *naked* chest. Dark, bristly hairs tickled her palm; to her the sensation was shockingly intimate. Yet she did not snatch back her hands—she did not push him away—as she should have.

As she could have.

"Egan? Are you here, lad?"

It was Bernard. They jerked apart. Egan moved first, stepping back from her. Did he curse beneath his breath? Glenda did not wait to find out.

She fled. Her heart was pounding and her lungs labored as if the devil himself nipped at her heels. Her feet did not stop until she was safe in her own chamber and the door was shut.

'Twas then that her strength deserted her. She pressed her back against it and slumped, landing in a heap on the floor.

Thrice now, Egan had almost kissed her. *Thrice*.

What madness possessed him? Sweet heaven, what madness possessed *her*?

For Glenda could not deny the yearning that still burned deep in her heart. Just once she longed to feel the touch of his mouth on hers. Just once . . .

RULES OF ENGAGEMENT
Christina Dodd

OCTOBER AVON ROMANCE SUPERLEADER

Miss Pamela Lockhart knew that proper behavior could guide a governess through any trying situation. The rules were straight-forward: never become too familiar with your employer, always take your meals upstairs on a tray, and remember your station at all times. But what happens when your employer is devastatingly handsome . . . and his behavior is anything but proper?

"YOU CONSIDER MARRIAGE THE SURE ROUTE TO MISERY."

"Not really." He stroked his chin, a gesture he had adopted from his grandfather. "The trick to marriage is not letting expectations get in the way. A man needs to understand why women get married, that's all."

Her mouth drew down in typical Miss Lockhart censure. "Why, pray tell, do women get married?"

"For money, usually." He could tell she was offended again, but with Miss Lockhart he didn't have to worry overly much about offense. After all, she didn't. Besides, he thought his assessment quite fair. "I don't blame them. The world is not fair to a spinster. She has no recourse but to work or starve. So if she's asked, she marries."

Obviously, *Miss Lockhart* did not consider his assessment fair. She slapped her mug on the table so hard the crockery rattled. "Do you have any idea how insulting you are? To think a woman is single because she has never been asked, or if she is married she has done so for monetary security?"

He found himself entertained and very, very interested. "Ah, I've touched a nerve. Are you telling me there is a man alive who dared to propose to you?"

"I am not telling you anything." But swept along by her passion, she did. "A man can convey financial security, but whither thou goest, I shall go, and all that rot. A woman has to live where her husband wishes, let him waste her money, watch as he humiliates her with other women, and never say a word."

"Men are not the only ones who break their vows."

"So fidelity is a vow *you* intend to keep?"

Of course he had no intention of keeping that vow when he was forced to make it, and falling into that trap which had so neatly snared his father. "I've supported more women than Madame Beauchard's best corset maker. If I let marriage stop me, think of the poor actresses who would be without a patron."

She wasn't amused. "So nothing about your wife would be sacrosanct, not even her body. Your wife will cherish dreams that you never know about, and even if you did they would be less than a puff of wind to you."

Women had dreams? About *what*? A new pair of shoes? Seeing a rival fail? Dancing with a foreign prince? But Miss Lockhart wasn't speaking of the trivial, and he found himself asking, "What are your dreams?"

"You don't care. Until I spoke, it never occurred to you that a woman could have her dreams."

"That's true, but you are a teacher, and already you

have taught me otherwise." Leaning back in his chair, he gazed at her and with absolute sincerity, and then said the most powerful words in the universe. "Tell me what you want. I want to know about you."

She had no defense to withstand him. She leaned back, too, and closed her eyes as if she could see her fantasy before her. "I want a house in the country. Just a cottage, with a fence and cat to sit in my lap and a dog to sleep at my feet. A spot of earth for a garden with flowers as well as vegetables, food on the table, and a little leisure time in which to read the books I've not had time to read or just sit . . . in the sunshine."

The candles softened the stark contrast between her white complexion and that hideous rouge. Light and shadow delineated her pale lips, showing them in their fullness. Her thick lashes formed a ruffled half-circle on her skin. When she was talking like this, imagining her perfect life, she looked almost . . . pretty. "That's all?"

"Oh, yes."

"That's simple enough."

"Yes, very simple. And mine."

Careful not to break into her reverie, he quietly placed his mug next to hers. "Why do you want that?"

"That's what I had before—"

She stopped speaking so suddenly he knew what she had been about to say. Moving to the side of her chair, he knelt on the carpet. "Before your father left?"

At the sound of his voice, her eyes flew open and she stared at him in dismay. She *had* been dreaming, he realized, seeing that cottage, those pets, that garden, and imagining a time when she could sit in the sunshine. Her countenance was open and vulnerable, and his instincts were strong. As gently as a whisper he placed his fingertips on her cheek. "There's one dream you didn't mention, and I can make it come true." Slowly, giving her time to turn if she wished, he leaned forward . . . and kissed her.

[faint show-through text at top of page, partially legible]

≈

JUST THE WAY YOU ARE
Barbara Freethy

NOVEMBER AVON ROMANCE SUPERLEADER

Allison Tucker knew that today's women were supposed to face their ex-husbands in a modern way—cordially, friendly, and with the attitude that you didn't have a care in the world. But every time she looked into Sam's eyes, she still felt a longing for what might have been if they stayed together—and what could still be . . .

"DID YOU EVER LOVE MOMMY?"

Allison Tucker caught her breath at the simple, heartfelt question that had come from her seven-year-old daughter's lips. She took a step back from the doorway and leaned against the wall, her heart racing in anticipation of the answer. She'd thought she'd explained the separation to her daughter, the reasons why Mommy and Daddy couldn't live together anymore, but apparently Kelly still had some questions, and this time it was up to Sam to answer.

Alli held her breath as she heard Sam clear his throat, obviously stalling for time. In that second she wished herself a million miles away. She hadn't meant to eavesdrop, but when she'd arrived to pick Kelly up after her weekend with her father, she had been caught by the cozy scene in the family room. Even now she could see Sam sprawled in the brown leather reclining chair looking endearingly handsome in his faded blue jeans and navy blue rugby shirt. Kelly was on his lap, her blond hair a mess in mismatched braids, her clothes exactly the same as Sam's, faded blue jeans and a navy blue T-shirt. Kelly adored dressing like her father.

"Did I show you the picture of Mommy when she dressed up like a giant pumpkin for the Halloween dance?" Sam asked.

They were looking at a yearbook, Alli realized with dismay. She'd hidden them away years ago because there weren't just pictures of Sam and Alli in the yearbook, there were other people in there, too, people she didn't want Kelly to know anything about. Why on earth had Sam dragged out the yearbook now?

"Did you, Daddy? Did you ever love Mommy?" Kelly persisted.

Answer the question, Sam. Tell her you never really loved me, that you only married me because I was pregnant.

Alli held her breath, waiting for Sam's answer, knowing the bitter truth, but wondering, hopelessly, impossibly wondering . . .

"I love your mother very much—for giving me you," Sam replied.

Alli closed her eyes against a rush of emotion. It wasn't an answer, but an evasion. She didn't know why she felt even the tiniest bit of surprise. Sam would never admit to loving her. She couldn't remember ever hearing those three simple words cross his lips, not even after Kelly's birth, after the long hours of labor and frantic minutes of delivery.

He hadn't said the words then. Or later in the days and weeks and years that followed, not even when they made love, when they shared a passion that was perhaps the only honest part of their relationship.

Alli clenched her fists, wanting to feel anger, not pain. She'd spent more than half of her entire twenty-six years of life in love with Sam Tucker, but he didn't love her.

THE VISCOUNT WHO LOVED ME
Julia Quinn
DECEMBER AVON ROMANCE SUPERLEADER

If there's one place a proper young lady should not be, it's in an unmarried gentleman's private study . . . crouched under his desk, desperate to escape discovery. Yet that's exactly where (and in what position) Kate Sheffield finds herself. Even worse, Anthony Bridgerton has brought a potential paramour back with him, and Kate is forced to wait out the entire encounter . . .

ANTHONY KNEW HE HAD TO BE A FOOL. HERE HE WAS, pouring a glass of whiskey for Maria Rosso, one of the few women of his acquaintance who knew how to appreciate both a fine whiskey and the devilish intoxication that followed, and all he could smell was the damned lilies-and-soap scent of Kate Sheffield. He knew she was in the house—he was half ready to kill his mother for inviting her to the musicale—but this was ridiculous.

And then he saw Kate.

Under his desk.

It was impossible.

Surely this was a nightmare. Surely if he closed his eyes and opened them again, she'd be gone.

He blinked. She was still there.

Kate Sheffield, the most maddening, irritating, diabolical woman in all England, was crouching like a frog under his desk.

"Maria," he said smoothly, moving forward toward the desk until he was stepping on Kate's hand. He didn't step hard, but he heard her wince.

This gave him immense satisfaction.

"Maria," he repeated, "I have suddenly remembered an urgent matter of business that must be dealt with immediately."

"This very night?" she asked, sounding dubious.

"I'm afraid so. *Euf!*"

Maria blinked. "Did you just grunt?"

"No," Anthony lied, trying not to choke on the word. Kate had removed her glove and wrapped her hand around his knee, digging her nails straight through his breeches and into his skin. Hard.

At least he hoped it was her nails. It could have been her teeth.

Maria's eyes were curious. "Anthony, is there an animal under your desk?"

Anthony let out a bark of laughter. "You could say that."

Kate let go of his leg, and her fist came down on his foot.

Anthony took advantage of his release to step quickly out from behind the desk. "Would I be unforgivably rude," he asked, striding to Maria's side and taking her arm, "if I merely walked you to the door and not back to the music room?"

She laughed, a low, sultry sound that should have seduced him. "I am a grown woman, my lord. I believe I can manage the short distance."

She floated out, and Anthony shut the door with a decisive click. "You," he boomed, eliminating the distance to the desk in four long strides. "Show yourself."

When Kate didn't scramble out quickly enough, he reached down, clamped his hand around her upper arm, and hauled her to her feet.

"It was an accident," she said, grabbing onto the edge of the desk for support.

"Funny how those words seem to emerge from your mouth with startling frequency."

"It's true!" she gulped. He had stepped forward and was now very, very close. "I was sitting in the hall," she said, her voice sounding crackly and hoarse, "and I heard you coming. I was just trying to avoid you."

"And so you invaded my private office?"

"I didn't know it was your office. I—" Kate sucked in her breath. He'd moved even closer, his crisp, wide lapels now only inches from the bodice of her dress. She knew his proximity was deliberate, that he sought to intimidate rather than seduce, but that didn't do anything to quell the frantic beating of her heart.

"I think perhaps you did know that this was my office," he murmured, letting his forefinger trail down the side of her cheek. "Perhaps you did not seek to avoid me at all."

Kate's lips parted, but she couldn't have uttered a word if her life had depended on it. She breathed when he paused, stopped when he moved. She had no doubt that her heart was beating in time to his pulse.

"Maybe," he whispered, so close now that his breath kissed her lips, "you desired something else altogether."

Nationally Bestselling Author

Pamela Morsi

"Her stories are gently humorous, wise and wonderful."
Susan Elizabeth Phillips

HERE COMES THE BRIDE   01366-8/$6.99 US/$7.99 Can
"There comes a time in every woman's life when she must get herself a man or give up on the idea entirely. Augusta Mudd had reached that moment."

SWEETWOOD BRIDE   01365-X/$6.99 US/$9.99 Can

SEALED WITH A KISS   79638-4/$5.99 US/$7.99 Can
Having forsaken her girlish dreams of romance years ago after being abandoned by the man she loved, Prudence Belmont is startled to learn the reckless cad has returned and moved in next door.

THE LOVE CHARM   78641-9/$5.99 US/$7.99 Can
"Pamela Morsi writes about love and life with laughter, tenderness, and most of all, joy." *Romantic Times*